Chelsea Fin... her
time writin... ding
housework at all costs. Her ... offee,
sleeping-in and crazy socks. She lives with her husband and two
children, who graciously tolerate her inability to resist teenage
drama on TV and her complete lack of skill in the kitchen.

Visit Chelsea Fine online:

www.ChelseaFineBooks.com
www.twitter.com/ChelseaFine
www.facebook.com/ChelseaFineBooks

Praise for Chelsea Fine's Finding Fate *series*:

'You'll fall for Pixie and Levi, just like I did'
New York Times bestselling author Jennifer Armentrout
on *Best Kind of Broken*

'By turns humorous and heart-breaking ... has become one
of my favorites!'
New York Times bestselling author Cora Carmack

'Chelsea Fine's style is witty, visceral and fresh. All I
wanted to do was crawl inside this book and live with the
characters. And now all I want is MORE'
New York Times bestselling author Chelsea Cameron

'Eloquently written, Fine's story has a way of making even
the most minor characters leap off the page'
RT Book Reviews

ALSO BY CHELSEA FINE

Best Kind of Broken

Perfect Kind of Trouble

Right Kind of Wrong

Library Learning Information

To renew this item call:

0115 929 3388

or visit

www.ideastore.co.uk

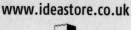

TOWER HAMLETS

Created and managed by Tower Hamlets Council

PERFECT *Kind of*
TROUBLE
CHELSEA FINE

piatkus

PIATKUS

First published in Great Britain in 2014 by Piatkus
This paperback edition published in 2015 by Piatkus

1 3 5 7 9 10 8 6 4 2

A CIP catalogue record for this book
is available from the British Library.

ISBN 978-0-349-40437-0

Printed and bound by CPI Group (UK) Ltd, Croydon, CR0 4YY

Papers used by Piatkus are from well-managed forests
and other responsible sources.

MIX
Paper from
responsible sources
FSC® C104740

Piatkus
An imprint of
Little, Brown Book Group
100 Victoria Embankment
London EC4Y 0DY

An Hachette UK Company
www.hachette.co.uk

www.piatkus.co.uk

To my amazing husband, Brett, who I would totally
handcuff myself to forever.

Acknowledgments

First and foremost, I would like to thank my readers. Thank you for believing in my stories and making this thing I call work a dream come true! I'd also like to thank my incredible editor, Megha Parekh, for her never-ending brilliance in making this story what it is, and my incredible agent, Suzie Townsend, for believing in me from the very beginning. Thank you to my mama, for giving me laughter and love while I write, and to my kiddos, for being so understanding when I pick them up from school in my pajamas. And last, but never least, my amazing husband, Brett. You are my whole world and I love your guts.

PERFECT *Kind of*
TROUBLE

I

KAYLA

*O*n the other side of the casket, a middle-aged woman wearing a navy blue dress glares at me.

The man in the wooden box has only been dead for three days and this woman already has me pegged as the slutty mistress he kept on the side. I'm probably an ex-stripper with a coke problem as well, based on the way she's sizing me up. But this isn't my first rodeo—or my first funeral—and deadly looks like the one Navy Nancy is angling at me are nothing new, unfortunately.

Now feeling a little self-conscious, I slowly slide my black sunglasses on and tip my head down, concentrating on the casket in front of me as the preacher/priest/certified-online minister drones on about peace and eternity.

It's a nice casket, made of polished cherrywood with decorative iron handles and rounded edges. I should care more than I do about the deceased man within, but all I can think about is how that casket probably cost more than any car I've ever been in, and how the man inside is probably tucked against velvet walls lined with Egyptian cotton.

And now I'm angry. Great.

I promised myself I wouldn't be angry today. Bitter? Sure. That was a given. But not angry.

Taking a deep breath, I raise my head and try to avert my attention. Behind my dark shades, I glance around the cemetery. More people showed up than I had expected, most of them looking like they're sweet and respectable. I wonder how well they knew James Turner. Were they friends of his? Coworkers? Lovers? Folks around here probably show up at funerals regardless of their relationship with the deceased. That's the thing about small towns; everyone cares about everyone else—or at least acts like they do.

"James was a good man," the minister says, "who lived a solid life and has now gone on to a better place..."

A roll of thunder sounds in the distance and I turn my eyes to the heavy gray clouds above. The weatherman said it's supposed to rain tonight. They'll bury James, cover his casket with dirt, and rain will fall and seal him into the earth. What an ideal passing.

Screw him.

A woman beside the minister begins to sing "Amazing Grace" as the pallbearers lower him into the grave. Across the way, a teenage boy openly gawks at me, his eyes gliding up and down my body like I'm standing here naked instead of fully clothed. I'm wearing a knee-length, long-sleeved, turtlenecked gray dress, in *July* no less. I'm ridiculously covered, not that Navy Nancy and Gawking Gary care.

When the boy catches me watching him, he quickly looks away and his face burns bright red. I turn away as well and play with the bracelet on my wrist as I focus my attention on the back of the crowd.

A huddle of women dab at their eyes with handkerchiefs. Beside them, a young family stands quietly with their hands clasped together. Nearby, an older couple mouths the words to "Amazing Grace" as the singer starts on the third verse. Looking around, I realize everyone else is singing along as well. *Of course* the people of Copper Springs would know the third verse of "Amazing Grace."

I really need to get out of here. I don't belong in this tiny town. I never have. One last obligation tomorrow then I'm gone.

In the far back of the congregation, a guy moves out from under a large oak tree and I tilt my head. He looks vaguely familiar but I can't quite place him.

He's average height, with dark brown hair, and a dark purple button-down shirt covers his broad shoulders. The long sleeves of his shirt are rolled up to his elbows and he's got on a pair of dark jeans to match the dark sunglasses that cover his eyes. Dark, dark, dark.

He's attractive. Dangerously attractive. The kind of attractive that can suck you into a sweet haze and undo you completely before you even know you've surrendered. I know I've seen him before but for the life of me I can't remember where, which is probably a good thing.

The singer wraps up the fourth verse of "Amazingly Depressing Grace," and a long silence follows before the minister clears his throat. He glances at me and I subtly nod. With a few last words about what a *wonderful* man James Turner was, he concludes the funeral and I let out a quiet breath of relief.

The end.

People disperse, most of them heading to their cars while the rest pass by the lowered casket and throw a handful of dirt or a flower onto the shiny cherrywood top. I step to the side, sunglasses strictly in place, and watch the mourners. Navy Nancy glares at me again and I look away. Wow. She really must think I'm some sort of James Turner hussy.

As offended as I am, I know she's probably just hurting. She was the first person to arrive at the funeral today and she teared up several times during the ceremony so I'm assuming she and James were pretty close. And if judging me makes her feel better on this sad day, then I'll let her hate me all she wants. I watch her leave the cemetery with a small group of other mourners. It's not like I'll ever see her again, anyway.

The guy in the purple shirt steps up to the grave and drops a handful of red dirt on the casket. The red stands out against the brown dirt beneath it and I wonder what its significance is. Then I wonder about the guy in purple. He doesn't seem to be here with anyone else, which is only strange because of how good-looking he is. Hot guys don't usually travel places without an equally hot girl on their arm. But this guy is definitely alone.

He strides to the parking lot and climbs into a black sports car, and all my wondering comes to an abrupt halt. I no longer care about who he is, or how he knew James, or why he looks familiar. Spoiled rich boys are the last thing I care about.

When everyone has left the area except the funeral home people, I carefully walk up to the casket. The heels of my black pumps slowly sink into the soft grass as I stare down at the last I'll ever see of James Turner. I try to muster up some sort of sadness, but all I come up with is more anger.

With a long inhale, I toss a soft white rose petal onto the brown and red dirt, and quietly say, "Rest in peace, Daddy."

2

DAREN

*S*ome people don't name their vehicles. Most people, probably. But there's something about a black Porsche that just makes you want to call it . . . Monique.

I climb inside my sports car, close the door, and look through the windshield at the dark clouds. Looks like Monique might need a bath tomorrow. My eyes fall back to the cemetery and my chest tightens. I still can't believe Old Man Turner is gone.

When I was thirteen, my life took a sharp turn to the shitty side of the street and Turner offered me a job mowing his lawn for fifteen dollars a week. A year went by before he asked me to start taking care of his garden as well, then gave me a raise. Shortly after, I was taking care of his entire yard and did so until last year when he requested that I focus my energy on my "real" jobs.

I didn't know he had cancer at the time. Hell, I didn't even know he was sick until he passed away. We lost touch for only a few months, but apparently, during that time Turner fought a short and intense battle with cancer and lost.

And I didn't even have a clue until last week.

My gut coils as I think about the day I found out—and all the days after—and I let out a heavy exhale. This past week has not been my finest. And now I'm at the funeral of the only man

I ever really considered a father. I didn't even get a chance to tell him good-bye.

I inhale, slow and steady, and I crack my knuckles. It's just been a shitty few years, all around.

Through the windshield, my eyes catch on a gray dress walking away from the casket with hips swinging and blonde hair swishing. I almost didn't recognize Kayla Turner behind those black sunglasses and that cold look she had on. But looking at her now, there's no mistaking.

She used to visit her dad in the summer, so every once in a while I'd catch glimpses of her inside the house while I was out mowing the lawn. And there are some faces you just don't forget.

Back then, she was all elbows and knees and freckles. But damn if Kayla Turner didn't grow up to be a total knockout. There wasn't a breathing soul in the cemetery today that didn't openly gape at her. I thought the kid in the front row was going to choke on his own drool, the way he was drinking her in.

I'm surprised she bothered to show up. She stopped coming around a few years ago and I saw how it tore Old Man Turner up. He missed her fiercely, but that didn't bring her back.

It's nice of her to finally visit again. Too bad she waited until her father's funeral to grace him with her presence.

With a clenched jaw, I start the engine, back out of my spot, and pull out of the parking lot. Monique purrs as I drive away from the cemetery and I want to purr right along with her. Cruising down the road eases the pressure in my chest and I feel like I can breathe again. I put the convertible top down and suck in a lungful of fresh air. Much better.

A distant roll of thunder echoes around. I pass a large gated community and a sour taste slips down my throat. Westlake Estates. The place I lived when life was good.

Well, not good exactly. But easier.

Turning onto the road that leads out of town, I head for work. I have two part-time jobs: one at the cell phone store in Copper Springs and one as a stock boy at the Willow Inn Bed & Breakfast outside of town. My job at Willow Inn is the only one I actually like, though.

Willow Inn is fifty miles south of town, in the middle of nowhere off the freeway, but I make the drive every week because of my awesome boss. Ellen owns and operates the quaint little inn and, in her spare time, she's a guardian angel.

Glancing at the time, I realize I have to be at Willow Inn in an hour and it takes at least that long to get there. Shit. And Monique is low on gas. Double shit.

With a muttered curse, I pull into the nearest gas station—a run-down fill-up place that looks closed except for the blinking neon sign that reads O_EN—and pull up next to a grime-coated gas pump before turning off the engine.

Getting out, I count the money in my pocket with a groan before shoving it back inside. As I start to fill Monique up, my phone beeps and I glance down to see another missed call from Eddie.

Eddie Perkins is the closest thing Copper Springs has to a professional lawyer, and lately he's been the bane of my existence. He's left me eight voice mails in the past week, none of which I've bothered listening to because I'm sure they're all about my dad. But ignoring him doesn't seem to be working.

Stepping away from the car, I listen to the most recent voice mail.

"Hello, Daren. It's Eddie again. I'm not sure if you've received my previous messages but I've been trying to reach you regarding James Turner. As I'm sure you know, he's passed away. A reading of his will is scheduled for tomorrow at 11:00 a.m. at my office, and Mr. Turner's last wishes specifically request that you be present. Hopefully, I'll see you there. If not, still give me a call so we can discuss... the other thing."

The message ends and I stare at my phone. Why in the world would Turner want me at the reading of his will?

Unless...

A thought hits me and it's almost too ridiculous to grasp.

Could this be about the baseball cards? Would Turner have remembered something from so long ago?

A small smile tugs at my lips.

Yes. He absolutely would have. That's just the kind of guy he was.

When I was thirteen, my dad gave me a set of collectable baseball cards for Christmas. I remember that Christmas clearly. It was the same Christmas that our housekeeper, Marcella, gave me a copy of the book *Holes*. It's about a boy who digs seemingly pointless holes as a punishment for something he didn't even do wrong. I was obsessed with the book; I must have read it ten times, and talked about it every day.

My mother and father barely paid attention to my interests. I doubt they ever even knew I'd read a single book, let alone one in particular over and over. But Marcella knew. She always made a point to care about the things I cared about. "You are my favorite boy, *mijo*," she would say.

She always called me *mijo*.

Son.

That Christmas, she'd wrapped the book in a green box with a red ribbon. I remember because that was the same box I decided to keep my collectable baseball cards in.

I brought the box to Turner's house one day to show off my new cards and proudly informed him that I had looked up the value of each one and knew I could sell the lot for at least a hundred dollars. Money was important to me back then. Money was all that mattered. My dad taught me that.

But later that day while I was mowing his lawn, Turner took my box of cards because, according to him, I was "too spoiled to appreciate them."

He was right, of course, but at the time I didn't care. I was furious, convinced he was going to sell the cards himself so he could have the money. But because I was just as spoiled as he'd claimed, I only stayed mad until my father bought me more baseball cards a few days later.

That's how things worked in my family: My parents bought me whatever I wanted, whenever I wanted, as long as I stayed out of their hair. I was an only child and I'm pretty sure I was a mistake. If my parents had *planned* to have me I'm sure they would have put a little more effort into...well, me. But I was an accident and, therefore, an inconvenience. An inconvenience easily soothed with a few new toys.

When I announced to Turner that I no longer cared about my stolen box of baseball cards, he laughed and said, "Someday you might." Then he promised that, someday, he'd return them to me.

I stare at my cell phone where the voice mail screen blinks back at me. Maybe this is Turner's way of coming through on that promise, after death.

The pressure starts to wind its way around my chest again,

thick and tight, and I feel the air seep from my lungs. I can't believe he's gone. Really gone.

A clanging noise startles my thoughts and I whip around to see a tow truck backed up to Monique and hauling her onto its bed. My eyes widen in horror.

"Hey!" I shout at the overweight truck driver, who's got a toothpick in his mouth and a handlebar mustache. "What are you doing?"

He barely glances at me. "Taking her in. Repo."

"Repo?" I start to panic. "No, no. There must be some mistake. A year's worth of payments were made on that car. I still have until next month."

He hands me a crumpled statement stained with greasy finger-prints and an unidentifiable smudge of brown. "Not according to the bank."

I quickly scan the paper. "Shit." I was sure those payments were good through August. I rub a hand over my mouth and try to clear my head. "Listen," I say, trying to stay calm as I appeal to the driver. "We can work this out. What do I need to do to get you to unhook my innocent car?"

He looks bored. "You got four months of payments on you?"

"Uh, no. But I have..." I pull out the contents of my pocket. "Forty-two dollars, a broken watch, and some red dirt."

A few grains of the dirt slip through my fingers and I think about all the weekends I spent taking care of Turner's yard. The lawn was healthy and the garden was abundant, but Turner's favorite part of the yard was the rose garden. I could tell that he was especially fond of his white roses, so I cared for those thorny flowers like they were helpless babies, and Turner wasn't shy about praising me for it. Every Saturday, I'd rake through the rare red topsoil Turner planted around his precious roses, making sure the bushes could breathe and grow. I pricked my fingers more times than I can count, but those roses never withered, and for that I was always proud. I think Old Man Turner was proud of my work too.

The tow truck guy shrugs. "No cash, no car. Sorry." He starts to lift Monique off the ground and I swear it's like watching someone kidnap a loved one.

"Wait—wait!" I hold up a hand. "I can get it. I can get you the money. I just—I just need a little time."

"Talk to the bank."

I quickly shake my head. "No, you see. I can't talk to the bank because the bank hates me—"

"Gee, I wonder why." He doesn't look at me.

"But I can get the money!" I gesture to Monique. "Just put my baby back down and you and I can go get a beer and talk this whole thing out." I flash a smile. "What do you say?"

He scoffs. "You pretty boys are all the same. Used to getting whatever you want with Daddy's money and pitching fits when someone takes your toys away." He shakes his head and climbs back into the tow truck. "See ya."

"But that's my ride!" I yell, throwing my arms up. "How am I supposed to get home?"

He starts the engine and flicks the toothpick to the other side of his mouth. "You should've thought of all that before you stopped making payments." Then he pulls out of the gas station with sweet Monique as his captive and I watch the last piece of my *other* life slowly disappear.

Motherfu—

"Sir?"

I spin around to see a scrawny gas attendant wiping his hands on a rag.

"What," I snap, frustrated at everything that's gone wrong in my existence.

"You gotta pay for that," he says.

I make a face. "For what?"

He nods at the pump. "For the gas."

"The ga—" I see the gas nozzle dangling from where poor Monique was ripped away and I want to scream. "Oh, come on, man! My car was basically just hijacked! I wasn't paying attention to how much *gas* I was using."

He shrugs. "Don't matter. Gas is gas. That'll be eighty-seven dollars."

"Eighty-se—" I clench my jaw. "I don't have eighty-seven dollars."

He scratches the back of his head. "Well I can't let you leave until you pay."

I scrub a hand down my face, trying to contain the many curse words that want to vault from my mouth. With a very calm and controlled voice I say, "Then do you have a manager I can speak to about settling this issue?"

He tips his head toward the small gas station store. "My sister."

Through the store's front window, I see a young woman with curly red hair at the register and a smile stretches across my face.

"Perfect," I say.

As I head for the entrance, a few drops of rain fall to the ground, plopping on the dirty concrete by my shoes. I look up at the dark clouds, fat with the oncoming storm and frown. I really don't want to walk home in the rain.

A string of gaudy bells slaps against the station door and chimes as I enter the store, and the sister looks up from a crossword puzzle. Her name tag reads WENDY. I file that information away.

Roving her eyes over me, her face immediately softens. "Why, hello there," she says in a voice I know is lower than her natural one. "Can I help you?"

I give her my very best helpless-boy grin and sigh dramatically. "I certainly hope so, Wendy."

Her eyes brighten at the sound of her name on my lips. Girls love it when you say their name. They melt over it. It's like a secret password that instantly grants you their trust.

She leans forward with a smitten grin and I know I've already charmed my way out of an eighty-seven-dollar gas bill. And maybe even found a ride home.

"Me too," she says eagerly.

I smile.

Sometimes it pays to be me.

3

KAYLA

I knew today was going to suck the moment I woke up with a spider on my face.

A spider.

ON MY FACE.

This is what happens when the only motel you can afford is a lopsided building called the Quickie Stop.

But the spider wasn't the only thing that kicked this day off to a stellar start.

First there were the mysterious body hairs on the nightstand that I accidentally touched when I tripped over the 1970s porn rug that coats the floor. A *shaggy* porn rug—because a flat porn rug just wouldn't have been gross enough. Followed by the trickle of ice-cold water from the mold-caked shower, which turned out to be the home of my friendly face spider from earlier. And lastly, there was the lovely smell of cat urine that wafted in through the rusted ceiling vent all morning.

So I'm not exactly in a good mood by the time I'm dressed and ready to leave. But I've handled worse. Much worse. This might be a crappy motel room, but it's a luxury establishment compared to the roach-infested place I left back in Chicago.

I catch sight of my reflection in the bathroom mirror and scowl.

I suppose I'm dressed the way one is supposed to be for the reading of a will. A royal blue blouse with a black pencil skirt and black heels. The top is too fitted for my comfort, molding around my breasts and making me feel like I'm on display. And the neckline is relatively respectable but if I were to lean over my cleavage would hang out. Note to self: No leaning. The skirt is worn and a little too short to be considered professional, but it's the only one I have so it will have to do. And the shoes are scuffed up and old, but from far away they look decent enough. Overall, it's not my favorite outfit. I don't like tight clothes that emphasize my hourglass figure. But since my only other options are jeans, pajamas, or the thick gray dress I sweat through in the summer sun yesterday, this is what I'm wearing.

I throw my purse over my shoulder and grab my car keys. All I have to do is get through one stupid meeting with Dad's lawyer— the same lawyer who called last week to shockingly inform me that my father had passed away—then I can pack my things and head home. Although "home" doesn't really mean much when every-thing you own fits in one small brown bag.

My eyes drop to the suitcase on the bed and a ball of stress forms in the pit of my stomach. I have no idea what my next move is. Not just in Copper Springs, but in life. Riffling through my purse, I find my wallet and count the bills within.

Thirty-six dollars. Crap.

I shove a hand into my bra, where I always keep emergency money.

Twenty-one dollars.

I pull off my right high heel, carefully pull up the black leather sole, and lift a precious few bills from the hiding place below— where I keep my emergency *emergency* money.

Eighteen dollars.

So altogether I have... seventy-five dollars. To my name.

Every other penny I had was spent on my trip out here and I couldn't qualify for a credit card if my life depended on it—which it might, if things keep going the way they have—so I'm officially broke. And unemployed. And homeless.

The ball of stress tightens.

I had a job at a diner back in Chicago, but when I asked my boss, Big Joe, for time off for my father's funeral, he refused. So I quit—which didn't go over well.

Unbeknownst to me, my mother, Gia, had borrowed $20,000 from Big Joe to pay off some old debts. I knew nothing about this until I tried to leave and Big Joe started demanding his money. Since my mom was no longer able to pay him back, he *insisted* that I work for free in order to pay off her debt. It was a threat, not a negotiation, and I was scared out of my mind.

My lease was up at the roachy apartment so I packed up my stuff, cashed my last paycheck, and drove out to Arizona. And now, even if I had the gas money to drive back to Chicago, there's no way I'd be able to afford a place to live and I'd be forced to work for Big Joe until my mom's debt was settled. And knowing Big Joe, he'd probably demand reimbursement in other ways too, like by smacking my ass or squeezing my boob. Or worse.

I shudder.

I'm broke, but I'm not a prostitute. I'd rather sleep on a park bench than let myself be groped for favors.

Ugh. I might actually have to sleep on a park bench.

I shake myself from the thought. *One day at a time, Kayla. Just get through one day at a time.* God. Life isn't going the way I'd hoped at all.

I'm supposed to be in nursing school right now with a bright future ahead of me. Instead, I'm on the run from a debt collector, attending unforeseen funerals, and waking up with arachnids on my face.

Stuffing all my emergency dollars back into their designated hiding places, I exit the motel room. It rained all night but the storm passed quickly, leaving the air clean and crisp, and a lungful of fresh air lightens my mood a bit as I head through the parking lot and climb inside my mom's car. Although, I guess it's mine now.

It's the color of dying grass, a few decades past its prime, and beat-up at every corner, but I'm not complaining. It has four wheels and doesn't smell like pee. In my book, it may as well be a limousine.

I drive through the small-town streets of Copper Springs and a hint of nostalgia wafts over me. The best years of my life were spent here; first living as a family when my parents were still married, and then visiting my dad every summer after they divorced and my mom and I moved away.

The cute storefronts and well-manicured streets look every bit as pleasant as they actually are—or were. I haven't been back here in over five years. My plan was to never return at all, but it just seemed wrong not to come to my father's funeral. And if I'm being honest with myself, I needed the closure. Especially after the way my mom passed away...

Don't think about it. Don't think about it.

I swallow and concentrate on the road, forcing my mind to stray somewhere else—anywhere else. I easily find the lawyer's office and park. Then silently give myself a little pep talk.

I know my dad didn't leave me anything in his will, which is no shock. He didn't share his money with me when he was alive so why would I expect his death to change anything? But I can't help but feel a little disappointed.

Being a descendant of the original town founders, Dad owned quite a bit of land in Copper Springs—including most of the town square, which made him relatively wealthy. The most valuable thing he owned was Milly Manor, his stately home on the outskirts of town. Since it was a historic building, my father always let people take tours and pictures of the place. He was always more than happy to share his home with the people of Copper Springs.

So when the lawyer called me last week and explained that my father had donated his estate and all of his belongings to the town, I wasn't that surprised. But when he said he needed my signature to finalize some of Dad's will papers, then I *was* surprised—and not in a good way.

I went through a myriad of emotions: shock, curiosity, bitterness, annoyance. It seemed needlessly cruel for my father to ignore me for five years and then have the balls to ask me to come out to Arizona to sign off on all the expensive crap he wanted to give to other people. Especially when my mother and I lived like paupers and he barely offered us a smile, let alone a handout.

Nevertheless, I'm here, so I will sign his precious papers. Surely, I can do that gracefully. Or at least without cursing or spitting.

Turning off the car, I stare at the lawyer's office door and fidget with my keys, then pull down the visor and fuss with my long hair in the mirror. I already feel out of place and I'm still in my own car. Maybe this was a bad idea. Maybe I should have stayed back in Chicago and suffered through the debt payment. Though, even in Chicago I felt out of place . . . even more since Mom died.

I immediately shift my thoughts, flick the visor up, and exit the car. There is a time to mourn and that time has passed. Straightening my shoulders, I stride inside the lawyer's office.

The first thing I notice is that Mr. Perkins is quite possibly the most unorganized lawyer of all time. Papers and files are everywhere, with no rhyme or reason to their placement, and random articles and pictures are taped up on the walls like this is his seventh-grade bedroom and not the place he practices law.

The second thing I notice is the guy sitting on the black pleather couch against the far wall. Purple shirt. Dark jeans. Devilish good looks...

Ah, hell.

I knew he looked familiar at the funeral yesterday but now, without sunglasses covering his dark brown eyes, there's no doubt.

"Daren Ackwood," I say.

He grins up at me and a dimple appears. "Kayla Turner."

You know how some people are so good-looking you just want to stare at them with your mouth open? Daren is that kind of handsome.

No. Handsome isn't the right word.

He's *beautiful*.

And he has been since he was a kid.

His dark brown hair is short and styled in a messy way that looks like he just rolled out of bed and into a Hot Guy catalogue, and matches the thick eyebrows arching over a pair of chocolate-colored eyes. A golden tan dusts the skin of his corded neck and the sinewy muscles of his forearms, stretching out from rolled-up sleeves and down to long, sturdy fingers. And his mouth is a distraction in itself, all full lips and white teeth, as the edge of his smile dips into that one naughty dimple on his left cheek. He looks like pure trouble.

His devastating good looks, in combination with his family's ridiculous wealth, drew every girl in Copper Springs to him like a magnet—or so I heard.

After age five, I only visited this town once a year so I didn't have a lot of time to make friends. I really only had one close friend in town, Lana, who moved away after high school. But when I was thirteen and Daren started doing yard work for my dad, Lana was beside herself, always making up excuses to come over to my house so she could drool over him. It was ridiculous how smitten she was. And she wasn't the only one.

Soon everyone in town knew Daren worked for my dad, so anytime I'd meet a local girl she would always ask the same giggly thing: "Do you know Daren Ackwood?"

The answer was *no*. I didn't know Daren Ackwood. I saw him through the kitchen window sometimes, and I was always aware of him when he was working in the yard—especially when he didn't have a shirt on—but I didn't know Daren Ackwood, and he didn't know me. We never spoke. We never interacted. Frankly, I'm surprised he knows my name.

For a moment we just stare at each other, him seated leisurely with his legs spread apart and me standing in my last pair of high heels with a bored expression.

"It's good to see you." His eyes slip over me with another dirty smile lifting up his clean-shaven face.

Oh, he's trouble all right. The kind of trouble I can't afford to get into.

I've heard more stories than I care to admit about Daren's sexual prowess. All through high school, Lana kept me up to date on all things Copper Springs, including Daren the Woman Whisperer—that's what she called him.

According to Lana, and every other girl at Copper Springs High, Daren was some kind of god in bed. I doubt any of the things she told me were true, but they certainly gave Daren quite the reputation.

Regardless of the rumors, I know his type. They charm and seduce and leave a trail of broken hearts in their wake. I have no intention of being a left-behind heart. Not for Daren or anyone else. So I'm careful to keep my expression neutral as I glance over his wrinkled clothes.

"Nice outfit," I say. "Did you forget to go home last night?" I raise a judgmental eyebrow, just to drive home my disapproval.

His dirty smile grows. "Something like that."

Whore.

"Oh, hello! You must be Kayla." An older gentleman with thick white eyebrows, a balding head, and a cheerful expression emerges from a door at the back of the office. His short, round frame wades through the minefield of papers and over to me. "I'm Eddie Perkins." He holds out his hand.

I shake it firmly. "Nice to meet you, Mr. Perkins."

"It's very nice to meet you, Ms. Turner," he says. "Though I wish it were under different circumstances." His cheery face sobers. "I'm so sorry for your loss."

Yes, yes. My dad is dead. We're all sad.

I smile politely. "Thank you."

"I'm pleased that you showed up," he says. "Your father didn't think you'd come, you know, but I'm glad you proved him wrong." He smiles warmly then looks around. "Now where...are my... glasses...?" He pats down his suit coat and turns around in a circle as he searches the pockets of his pants.

"On your head, Eddie," Daren says.

He taps his head until his hand smacks against the reading glasses propped in his sparse white hair. "Oh! There they are." He smiles as he pulls the glasses down and sets them on his face. "I'm always forgetting where I put them. Now"—he clasps his hands together—"since everyone is here should we get right down to it?"

I look around and pause. "Everyone?"

The lawyer pulls off the glasses he just put on. "Yes. You and Mr. Ackwood were the only two requested." He shoves a hand into his inner coat pocket and comes up empty, muttering, "Now... where is my handkerchief?"

Wrinkling my brow, I say, "My dad asked that Daren be here?"

"Yes. Oh, here it is." The lawyer pulls a yellow handkerchief from his back pocket and starts cleaning his glasses.

I blink a few times. "Why?"

Daren answers, "Your dad owes me some baseball cards."

I stare at him. "Huh?"

"You are both here to sign papers, Ms. Turner." Mr. Perkins tucks the handkerchief into his coat pocket and props the eyeglasses back on his face. "But first we need to go over your father's will." He scratches his head. "Where did I put the will?" He looks at his messy desk. "It was just here a moment ago." He shuffles a few papers around then starts digging through a tall filing cabinet.

"By the coffee pot," Daren says.

"Oh, that's right." Eddie smiles as he retrieves my father's paperwork from a small kitchenette in the corner.

I love that my father's will was carefully filed between a set of ceramic mugs and a bottle of powdered coffee creamer.

"I still don't understand," I say.

Mr. Perkins looks at me and shrugs. "Perhaps your father's baseball card collection is why Mr. Ackwood's presence was requested."

"It's actually *my* collection," Daren corrects. "Turner was just holding on to the cards for me. Kind of."

I look at Daren first then the lawyer. "I thought my father didn't have any belongings to bestow to anyone. I thought he gave everything away before he died."

"Most everything." Mr. Perkins gestures to the couch. "Please. Have a seat."

I look at my only seating option and inwardly groan. Daren is sitting on the fake leather couch with one tan arm stretched over the backrest while the other casually hangs off the armrest, stretching out his broad chest, and his right leg expands out with his opposite ankle propped on the knee. God. Could he take up any more space?

His brown eyes dance with amusement like he knows just how obnoxious his splayed-out limbs are and is waiting to see how I react. I pointedly avert my gaze and situate myself on the far end of the sofa, squeezing my hips as close to the other armrest as possible to avoid touching him. He looks at me with a hint of a smile. I ignore him and cross my legs with a deep inhale.

Daren smells good. Really good. Like oranges or lemons or something. Clean and fresh.

How in the *hell* does he smell good when he's wearing a walk-of-shame outfit and yesterday's deodorant?

Mr. Perkins leans his round frame against his cluttered desk as he silently reads through the will then looks up. "What it comes down to is this: Mr. Turner donated Milly Manor to the town of Copper Springs and designated a few personal items to some of his close friends."

I tilt my head. "He left personal items to friends?"

He nods. "There were a few things he wanted to give to his loved ones." He refers to the papers. "He donated all of his books to the local library. He left his golfing equipment to Gus Ferguson— you might know him as Golf Cart Gus. And his antique furniture and record collection he gave to Valerie Oswald."

I bite my tongue to keep from cursing. My father donated everything but a handful of possessions, and of course he left those things to a guy named Golf Cart Gus and some woman I've never heard of before. Typical James Turner. Slighting his daughter, even in death.

"Of course, Gus and Valerie weren't requested for the reading today because Mr. Turner settled his affairs with them before his passing." Eddie pushes his glasses up with a plump finger and looks at us. "Which brings us to his unfinished business with the two of you." He leafs through the folder and distractedly says, "Although I don't believe . . . it concerns Mr. Turner's . . . baseball card collection."

"It's actually *my* collection," Daren repeats.

I snap my eyes to him. "Why are you even here?"

"Uh . . . because your father and I had an arrangement concerning my baseball cards. Have I not made that clear?"

"Oh, you've made it clear. You've made it crystal clear," I say, feeling my pulse rise. "I just don't understand why my father is leaving a bunch of crap to people I don't even know."

Daren mocks an offended look. "You know me."

"Do I?" I say, mimicking his sarcasm. "No. I know *of* you, but I don't *know* you. So forgive me if I don't understand what you're doing at the reading of *my father's* will."

His charming good looks ice over and a muscle works in his jaw. "I spent more time with *your father* than you ever did. If anyone's presence here is unmerited it's yours."

Our eyes lock in a gaze of mutual contempt. Daren's attendance at this very personal, and somewhat heartbreaking, will reading makes me want to howl. He knows nothing about my father and me. *Nothing.*

Mr. Perkins clears his throat and we break our gaze to look back at him.

"James Turner's last wishes were to leave something to you both. Something he entrusted to me." He sets the folder down and scratches his head again before scurrying about the messy room. "I know I had it here somewhere…"

I have no idea what the bumbling man is looking for now, but after spending two minutes with him, I'm impressed he managed to leave his house today without forgetting to put on pants.

Daren leans forward, resting his elbows on his knees as he watches Mr. Perkins fret about the room. I watch as he laces his long fingers and casually taps the pads of his thumbs together.

"Ah, yes. Here it is." The lawyer holds up a DVD then slips it into a large TV across the room and cues it up. "James put together this will himself just a few months ago. I only opened the initial package last week. Inside, he requested that the two of you be present for this video message."

He presses Play and my father appears on the screen. His brown hair is grayer than I remember, his green eyes a bit faded, and he's thinner than ever before, but everything else about his youthful face is the same. He was in his fifties when the cancer took him, but he looked like he was thirty and probably acted like he was twenty. Mom always said that's what she loved most about him—his child-like silliness. That's what I liked most about him too.

My heart twists and I drop my eyes to concentrate on a small tear in the couch. That was a long time ago. I look back up.

James Turner is dressed in a tweed jacket and tie, and has his thin-rimmed glasses on. He looks like a college professor from the

'50s. All he's missing is a pipe and a mustache. And he really did smoke a pipe when he was alive.

He was an eccentric man, always goofing around and doing odd things. But he was good to our family when I was young. My parents divorced when I was six, but before they broke up we used to go on a family picnic every Sunday. My dad would send my mom and I on little scavenger hunts for things like white roses and four-leaf clovers and then we'd lay our blue-and-white-checkered quilt on the grass and eat fried chicken until the sun set.

That was before my mom decided she'd rather be single and swept me off to Chicago. And before my dad decided he didn't want a family anymore.

I stare down at the couch rip until I hear my father clear his throat. "Hello, Kayla and Daren." I look up. "If you're watching this, then I assume I'm dead. Which is unfortunate, because I really liked being alive."

I already hate this.

"Nevertheless, now that I'm gone I have a letter I want to leave to you—to *both* of you. The only catch is that you two must agree to wear handcuffs while retrieving it."

I blink, not sure I heard him correctly.

He smiles. "It's really the only way to ensure that you stay together and cooperate with each other. You're both only children with circumstances that have taught you not to rely on others, and being such, I'm sure your first instincts will be to separate and go at it alone. So you'll understand why I feel the handcuffs are necessary."

My jaw drops. It actually falls open in shock.

Handcuffs?

Handcuffs? What the hell?

He continues, "I'm sure this sounds preposterous and I have no doubt you both hate this idea but you might someday thank me for it anyway." He winks at the camera. "Happy hunting."

And the screen goes black.

Is he—what in the—why would—

WHAT. THE. HELL.

I shift my eyes from the lawyer to the TV and back to the lawyer. I don't even know where to start.

"That's it?" I say, stunned. "That five-second message is the entire video from my deceased father?"

Mr. Perkins nervously nods.

I let out a sharp exhale in disbelief. My father has a chance to say his final words to me and he chooses "Wear handcuffs" and "Happy hunting"?

If he weren't already dead I'd go kill him myself.

Daren puckers his lips and furrows his brow. "I don't get it."

Mr. Perkins inhales slowly. "It seems Mr. Turner wants you and Kayla to be handcuffed together while you go find a letter."

My jaw is still hanging open like a broken nutcracker soldier. What the hell is happening right now?

"Yeah, I got that. But go 'find' a letter?" Daren squints. "What does that mean? Is the letter lost?"

I drop my face into my hands, trying to get a grip on the emotion swelling behind my eyes. James Turner couldn't be a normal father, oh no. He couldn't just leave me a message saying he loved me or that he was sorry for being a deadbeat dad these last few years, no way. He had to be his usual pompous self and leave me some cryptic video note.

I pull my head up and blink a few times. I will not cry. I will not cry.

Mr. Perkins refers to his papers again before reading out loud, "'If Kayla and Daren work together while handcuffed, they should be able to complete their task in a single day.'"

All words fail me. I want to cry and scream and laugh hysterically. I might do all three. Right here on this squeaky black couch. In front of God, and Mr. Perkins, and Daren effing Ackwood.

"It's going to take a whole day to pick up this letter?" Daren looks just as baffled as I feel. "Where did Turner leave it, in another state?"

The letter. Right. Because *that's* the crazy piece in this crackpot puzzle.

"'But if they fail to cooperate with each other,'" Mr. Perkins continues, "'their mission may take longer.'"

"Mission?" Daren says. "What are we, spies?"

"So let me get this straight." Shifting in my seat, I press my lips together and try to control the anger bubbling up inside me. "The only thing my father left me, his only child, in his will was a stupid letter? And the only way I can *get* this stupid letter is by handcuffing—*handcuffing*—myself to a total stranger?"

"Wha—" Daren turns to me and makes a face. "I'm *not* a stranger. And I'll have you know, lots of girls would be happy to be handcuffed to me." He pulls a crooked smile. "Some actually have been."

Something in his expression wavers, making me question the cockiness in his eyes—not the fact that girls have played sexy handcuff games with him, just the arrogance with which he announced it, and I stare at him incredulously.

"Yeah, well, lots of girls are morons." I turn back to the lawyer and plead, "Please tell me I'm misunderstanding and that this is all just some horrid nightmare."

"Nightmare." Daren lifts an eyebrow. "That's a bit dramatic, don't you think?"

"You are not misunderstanding, Ms. Turner." Mr. Perkins pulls his handkerchief back out and dabs his lip again. "Your father does, in fact, want you to handcuff yourself to Daren while you retrieve the letter he left you."

I laugh darkly and lean back on the couch with my already broken heart breaking into more pieces than I even knew were left. "Fantastic," I mutter.

It was sad when my father missed by sixteenth birthday. It was hurtful when he stopped returning my phone calls every year after that. But failing to leave me anything in his will other than a ridiculous hide-and-seek game for what is probably a disappointing handwritten message scrawled out on his monogrammed stationery is just. Plain. Insulting.

And I thought the face spider was bad.

4

DAREN

Clearly, Old Man Turner went a little nutty at the end. I knew the guy had some quirks—I mean come on, he stole a kid's baseball card collection—but I never thought he was crazy. Until now.

Don't get me wrong. I wouldn't mind being handcuffed to a hot blonde all day. That's like handing me sex on a platter. But being handcuffed to Kayla Turner all day? That would just piss me off. I don't care how sexy she is in her tight little skirt and skinny high heels. She was a rotten daughter to a man who was nothing but a wonderful father, and I don't think I'd be able to put my judgment of her aside long enough to make it out of this office, let alone go track down some letter. I'd probably end up telling her off and she'd probably end up crying, and then I'd have a blubbering mess attached to my arm. No thanks.

"Eddie, my man." I smile and clasp my hands. "I'm sure there's another way around all this nonsense. Why don't we skip the handcuffing and go straight to the letter part? I'm sure you know where it is. All you have to do is tell us and we'll be on our way."

Kayla nods. "Exactly. Because we're obviously not going to chain ourselves together."

"Yeah. That would be insane." I lean back and stretch my body out again, trying to assume a casual air. "And unless there's a bed and lingerie involved, I'd really rather not spend my day locked up to a feisty blonde."

She scans my face with her big blue eyes. "Really?"

I wait for her cheeks to tint ever so slightly, like most girls' do when I allude to sex in their presence, but she just stares at me like I'm a douche bag. No blushing. No nervous blinking. No shifting in her seat.

I was only trying to get a rise out of her, but shit. Now I kind of feel like a douche bag.

Eddie wrings his hands. "I'm sorry, but I made a promise to James and he was pretty clear about his wishes. It's the handcuffs or no letter."

"Well I'm not doing it," Kayla says, pulling her eyes off mine and crossing her arms in true tantrum fashion.

God. She couldn't look snobbier if she tried.

"If my father had something to say to me," she says, "he could have said it when he was alive and not written it down in some far-away note."

I look at my phone. "Yeah, and I have to be at work in an hour."

"I understand." Eddie nods. "Mr. Turner's will is definitely... unorthodox." He shakes his head with a sigh. "Well then, I guess all you need to do is sign this document that says I presented the will to you both, and we can all be on our way."

I sit up. "What about my baseball cards?"

Kayla rolls her eyes.

Eddie skims the pages again. "I'm afraid there's nothing in here about baseball cards."

"Nothing?" I squawk. "No cards? No green box?"

"Wow." Kayla stares at me. "I've never heard a grown man whine so much about a collection of cards before."

"It's not about the cards," I snap, shooting her a dark look. She couldn't possibly understand how much getting that box back would mean to me. I turn to Eddie. "There must be some mistake. Turner promised I'd get them back."

He tucks the handkerchief away. "I'm sorry, Daren. There's no mention of any cards in the will. At least not that I remember..."

As Eddie fidgets through the papers again I curse under my breath.

"Don't act so surprised," Kayla says. "My father never cared about anyone but himself."

I halt my inner turmoil and scowl at her. "Your father was a good guy. One of the best," I bite out. "So ease up."

She ignores me and stands up. "Where do I sign so I can be on my way?"

I make a sound of disgust. "You're sure in a hurry to leave daddy dearest in the dust."

"And you're sure in a hurry to snatch up his baseball memorabilia," she barks back.

"They were *my* cards," I say. "Cards that your father stole from me when I was a kid, by the way, but you don't see me spitting on his grave."

Her expression grows cold. "The man barely acknowledged me when he was alive and now he's handing out his house and furniture to random people, while his *daughter* gets sent on a letter hunt. So yeah." She straightens her shoulders. "I want to get out of here and never think about James Turner again."

Pain flashes in her eyes, brief but palpable, and I pull back. This seems heavier than your average run-of-the-mill daddy issues.

She's obviously filled with anger. But more than that, Kayla looks almost...heartbroken.

After searching his mess for a few minutes, Eddie hands us two pens then points to a few lines on his paperwork where we need to sign. I stand up and scratch out my signature, disappointment rolling over me.

It's funny. I hadn't thought about that box of cards for years, but yesterday when the idea that I might get it back entered my mind, something inside me burst with hope. And not because selling those baseball cards could buy me a better life, but because inside that box are memories. Good ones. And I could use a few good memories.

Once we're done signing, Eddie stacks his paperwork and sighs. "Well, I thank you both for your time. Sorry things didn't work out the way you were hoping."

Kayla lifts her chin, clearly pissed her father didn't leave her a giant pile of cash. Serves her right, though. The girl didn't even visit when he was dying. She was too busy living it up with her gold-digging mom in Chicago.

I've heard the stories. I know all about how her mom, Gia, was a bombshell who wanted to be single so she divorced James Turner and took all his money. If the rumors are true, Turner shelled out a good chunk of his net worth to Gia in the form of alimony payments and even more to Kayla in a giant trust fund he set up for her. He showered his ex-wife and daughter with money, yet neither of them spent a penny to come visit him on his deathbed.

I don't blame him one bit for cutting Kayla out of his will.

As we leave, Eddie smiles at Kayla. "It was a pleasure meeting you, Ms. Turner." He nods at me. "And good to see you again, Daren."

I smile tightly. "Always a blast, Eddie."

Not.

His expression sobers. "You and I really need to get together soon to discuss your father—"

"I know." I shift uncomfortably. Kayla glances at me and I look away and say to Eddie, "We will."

He nods, but doesn't look convinced. I've been brushing him off for the past eight months so his skepticism is understandable.

I open the door for Kayla and wait. She eyes me cautiously like I'm a vampire inviting her into my den of bloodlust and savagery instead of a nice guy holding a door open for her. She may not be my favorite person in the room, but I still have manners. I lift a brow and gesture for her to go first.

She hesitantly moves past me, careful not to touch me or my fangs, and murmurs, "Thank you."

I follow her outside where we make eye contact for a quick moment. A part of me wishes I knew her better or liked her more than I do. Turner being gone makes me feel like I've lost a father, and it wouldn't suck to have someone to share that loss with. But it doesn't seem like Kayla wants to share anything with anyone. She scans my face again, all torn blue eyes and quivering lips, and my defenses drop to the ground for a split second. But just as quickly she turns and heads down the sidewalk, tapping away in her high heels. No good-bye. No *nice seeing you*. No pleasantries whatsoever.

I guess I didn't say farewell either, but still. She doesn't have to be such a brat.

As she passes the storefront for the Laundromat, a woman with her arms full of clothes and a baby approaches. Kayla smiles and opens the Laundromat door for them, bending to retrieve a fallen shirt that slips from the woman's large pile then cooing at the chubby baby in the woman's arms when he starts to cry until his tears dry right up.

Okay, so maybe that wasn't bratty. But that doesn't mean I have to like her.

Her blonde hair hangs to the center of her back and swishes against her blue top, the golden strands glinting in the sun as she moves along. She has a graceful walk, each step light and flowing in perfect harmony with the swing of her hips. She's curvy in all the right places and perfectly proportioned, and as she turns her face to the side, looking up and down the street, I trail my eyes down her profile. Long eyelashes, flushed cheeks, and full pink lips stand out against her pale skin like the cherry on top of a delicious dessert.

I let out a low whistle. Like it or not, Kayla Turner is the hottest almost-brat I've ever seen.

———

I've only been car-less for a matter of hours and I'm already going crazy. Copper Springs isn't like the big cities with their subways and taxis. The bus stop at the edge of town is the only public transit service here—unless you count Golf Cart Gus, who's really just a retired mechanic who sometimes gives people rides in a golf cart he won two decades ago on *The Price Is Right*—so after walking from Eddie's office to my job at the cell phone store and then to the hospital to make another payment, I'm exhausted.

I miss Monique.

Pulling out what's left of my cash, I count the bills and grimace. Minus the thirty dollars I just put toward Connor Allen's medical bills, I'm now down to twelve dollars. Every credit card I ever had access to is now either maxed out or closed and I don't get paid again until next week.

I know my boss at Willow Inn, Ellen, would front me the money if I asked. But I also know that if I ask her for a favor, she'll try to jump into my life and save me, which is more than I can handle right now. Twelve dollars will just have to last until next Friday. And then the money shit cycle will start all over again.

Last year, two horrible car accidents occurred in my life, and only a few months apart. The first accident severely injured a decent man named Connor Allen, leaving behind a hefty hospital bill. The second took the life of my high school girlfriend, Charity, and I was so beside myself with guilt that I didn't care to be alive anymore.

My stomach churns, slowly twisting into turmoil, and I have to take a few deep breaths to keep my hands steady and my feet moving until I come up to Latecomers Bar & Grill and let myself inside.

The smell of sautéed vegetables meets my nose and the churning in my stomach turns to a fierce growl.

I miss food too.

It's still pretty early so most of the seats are empty. There's a table of guys by the window, a couple in a corner booth, and a burly guy posted at the bar, but otherwise the place is dead. Which is how I prefer it.

"Hey," Jake Sanders says from behind the bar, tossing his dark hair out of his eyes as he sets a tray of clean glasses down.

At forty years old, Jake is doing pretty well for himself. Not only is he the head chef of Latecomers but he's also the owner. His uncle left him the flailing establishment after he passed away and Jake didn't hesitate to hone his cooking skills and turn the place into a rather fine restaurant, bringing the family business back from the brink, while reviving the nightlife in Copper Springs at the same time.

Most people don't expect a bar to have amazing food, but Jake is a culinary genius and every plate that comes out of Latecomers's kitchen is mouthwatering. He also brews his own beer, which makes me hate the guy a little, just for being so damn talented. I don't envy the hours he works, though. Jake practically lives here.

I tip my chin and half-smile back. "What's happening?"

"Oh, you know." He starts unloading the glasses. "Just beer and business and the business of beer."

I grin. "So you still don't have a life, huh?"

He barks out a sardonic laugh. "This place *is* my life." He gestures to the end of the bar. "Your seat's open."

I nod my thanks to him and head that way. My "seat" is the barstool on the far right where it's almost too dark to see anything. Jake deemed it "mine" last year after the back-to-back car accidents hit me like a ton of bricks and I fell into a serious bout of depression. At the time, I thought it was a little ridiculous to have a designated spot at the bar because, you know, I'm not a fifty-two-year-old alcoholic, but now ... well, now I'm grateful.

I slide onto my barstool, prop my elbows on the bar top, and drop my face into my hands. This day, this week—hell, this whole last *year*—has been shitty. And it doesn't look like it'll be getting easier anytime soon.

"Hey, good lookin'."

I glance up to see a pair of dark blue eyes shining at me and I smile warmly. "Hey, Amber."

Her wavy red hair is pulled back into a ponytail, showing off the many earrings she wears in both ears and the small tattoo just behind her jaw.

Amber Keeton is the closest thing I have to real family anymore. And for three months, back in middle school, when my mom left my dad to marry Amber's dad—who happened to be the town's beloved preacher—we actually *were* family. It was a broken, disgraceful family, but still. She was there and that made things bearable.

God, that whole mess was a nightmare. One day, I was just a rich kid from a decent home with two seemingly happily married parents, and the next day my mom was moving me into Brad Keeton's house and introducing me to my new "sister." Just like that, my world upended.

Anytime a preacher leaves his wife for another woman, it's big news. But in a small town like this, it's a downright scandal.

My dad lost his shit and started guzzling back Jack Daniel's like it was water in the Sahara, drinking himself into raging blackouts at Latecomers every other night. While Amber's mom, in the true fashion of a scorned preacher's wife, wailed all over town about the devil in her husband. She then started a prayer chain for his wretched soul, in a desperate attempt to save him from his sins—and no doubt heal her wounded pride at the same time.

Prayer chains are gossip trains at their finest. Lord have mercy on the reverend and his harlot—or at least let their sins entertain us for a while.

And that they did.

Mom and Brad were quickly shunned from all the social circles for "living in sin" and Amber and I couldn't go anywhere without people staring or whispering. We were the offspring of a cheating reverend, a rich home-wrecker, a God-fearing housewife, and a raging lush—and no one let us forget it.

My mom and Brad eloped shortly after, but being married didn't make things better. It did the opposite, in fact. Amber was just as horrified and shell-shocked as I was by their union so we instantly teamed up to get our parents to split. Just like in the movie

The Parent Trap, we schemed and plotted and tried our best to make their lives miserable. But it turned out my mom and Brad didn't even need their fourteen-year-old children to break them up.

Two months into their marriage, Mom was sleeping with the pool guy and Reverend Keeton was canoodling with a horse veterinarian he met online. Shortly after that, they split. Mom moved to Boston to go "find herself"—without me, of course; I begged her to stay, or at least take me with her, but she said being a mother wasn't her "destiny"—and Brad moved to Kansas to be with his horse doctor. But the whispers and the stares stayed behind, and linger still today.

But one good thing came out of it: Amber. Bonded by the town's disapproval and our parents' outlandish behavior, we became permanent allies. To this day, Amber is one of the only faces that I'm ever happy to see.

She nods at my outfit. "I see you haven't had a chance to change clothes yet."

I glance down at my wrinkled shirt.

Yesterday at the gas station, Wendy the Manager was more than willing to forgive my atrocious gas bill and give me a ride home. She was a little too willing, actually.

I know the difference between a *kinky* crazy look in a woman's eyes and a *nutzo* crazy look. And Wendy was definitely leaning toward the serial killer end of the spectrum when we got in her car and she sank her fingernails into my bicep, licked the *back* of my neck, and aggressively invited me to come back to her place to meet her pet ferret.

I have nothing against ferrets. I do, however, have something against ferrets eating my flesh after I've been hacked to pieces by a neck-licking psycho. So I very politely declined and had her drop me off at Amber's house so she and her pet ferret wouldn't know where I slept.

Wendy the Manager retracted her shockingly sharp claws from my arm and begrudgingly dropped me off at Amber's, where I crashed on the couch after explaining to Amber how Monique had been hauled off by a merciless tow truck. This morning, I didn't have time to run home and change before heading to Eddie's office.

"Not yet," I say, looking at Amber. "Think you could give me a ride back to my place later?"

"Your place?" She lets out a frustrated sigh. "Daren, you can't keep staying there."

"I can and I will. It's a very crucial part of the facade I need to continue pulling off in order to not be categorized as the town outcast."

"You're being ridiculous. No one would treat you differently if they knew."

"*Everyone* would treat me differently," I argue. Then consider. "Except you. Because you're the best person in the world." I smile, hoping my compliment will distract her from pursuing the topic.

She doesn't fall for it.

"I don't like it," she says, her mouth in a tight line. "Why don't you just move in with me and my roommates?"

I scoff. "And be the token male in a house filled with nonstop estrogen? I don't think so. But thank you, anyway."

Amber lives with three other girls in a two-room apartment across town. And while living with four women might sound ideal to some guys, I know the reality of the situation: shoes all over the place, makeup strewn about the bathroom counter, tampons everywhere . . . yeah. I don't think I'm ready for any of that. But it's nice that Amber keeps offering.

"Your call." She shrugs. "But the offer still stands."

I nod. "I appreciate that."

"I'll give you a ride after we close up tonight, as long as you don't mind waiting." She wipes down the counter.

"Of course not." I grin. "I'll help you close."

"Deal." She grabs a frosted glass from a freezer below the counter. "So what's your poison tonight?"

My face falls. The last time I was drunk was a few days ago at the Fourth of July Bash out on Copper Lake. Old Man Turner had just died so I swigged my sadness away until I was inexcusably hammered. And then I scared the crap out of the only *other* face that ever makes me happy, Sarah "Pixie" Marshall, when my stupid ass tried to drive drunk with her as my terrified passenger.

Just thinking about the fear in Sarah's eyes makes my stomach knot. That was a whole new low for me. Pixie was Charity's best friend and, therefore, someone I've always cared a great deal for. I would never intentionally hurt Pixie. Not in a million years. God, I really need to apologize to her.

I shake my head. "I think I've had enough poison for a while. I'll take a lemonade."

"Ooh. Very badass of you." Amber fills the frosted glass with lemonade, and scans my face. "What's wrong?"

I run a hand through my hair. "I just need to straighten some stuff out with Sarah, that's all."

"Sarah 'Pixie' Sarah?" she asks, setting the lemonade down in front of me. I nod and her face lights up. "Aw . . . I miss her. How's she doing?"

I shrug. "She's been working at Willow Inn with me and Levi all summer."

She arches a brow. "Have those two figured out they belong together yet?"

"I don't know," I say. "But God, I hope so. She deserves a win for once, you know?"

She nods silently and carefully eyes me. "I know a few people who deserve a win."

I avoid her eyes and focus on more pertinent matters. Like eating.

"Hey so…" I swallow, hating this part of my current circumstances. "Since I'm staying here until you close anyway, I was thinking I could maybe help out in the kitchen. Again. You know, if Jake needs a hand with the dinner rush. Again."

She frowns. "I can spot you dinner, Daren. I know you love to cook, but you don't have to keep coming in here and doing chores to earn a meal."

"I don't *keep coming in* for that," I say harshly, even though that's a lie. I've helped Jake in the kitchen at Latecomers five times in the past week. "I'm just, you know, tight on cash right now. That's all."

If he had room in the payroll budget, I'm sure Jake would hire me on the spot. But Latecomers is maxed out on employees, all of whom love their jobs and probably have no intention of quitting anytime soon. So for now, Jake lets me cook alongside him every once in a while and, in return, I get a free meal.

Sympathy flashes in Amber's eyes, but only for a split second. She knows I hate being pitied.

"Jake always welcomes an extra set of hands in the kitchen," she says then winks. "Especially if those hands belong to an aspiring chef."

"Right." I smile and start to get up but her hand smacks against mine, pinning me to the bar top.

"Not so fast," she says. "The dinner rush won't start for another hour or so. I think you should have dinner before you head back to the kitchen. Something tells me you haven't had much to eat today."

I gently slide my hand out from under hers. "I'm fine."

"No, you're not. You're hungry."

"No, I'm not."

She flicks the bar towel at me. Hard. "Quit being so prideful and sit your ass down." The determined look in her eyes is anything but playful.

I slowly obey and return to my barstool. She slaps a black bar napkin down in front of me, thwacking the counter so hard that the burly guy seated a few stools down looks over. Then she calmly moves the glass of lemonade on top of the napkin.

"Now," she says pleasantly, all hardness gone from her eyes. "What can I get you for dinner, sir?"

I stare at her, biting back a smile. It never ceases to amaze me how some women can go from sharp-as-steel to sugar-sweet in the blink of an eye.

"Surprise me," I say.

As she spins around and moves to the computer, I watch her type in an order and shake my head.

After high school, Amber started working at Latecomers to save up for college. After our parents divorced, her life didn't fall to pieces like mine.

When my mom left for Boston, my dad was a hopeless wreck and burned through his own wealth faster than a speeding bullet in a cloud. High school ended and I had no choice but to work night and day to help pay bills. I had my job tending to Old Man Turner's yard, and even though he grossly overpaid me for my work, it still wasn't enough so I started working at the local cell phone store so I could make a little extra cash and keep a cheap phone bill. But with the enormous bills we had every month—the mortgage, the expensive cars, the boat—I quickly started sinking.

Amber, however, was able to set herself up with a decent job and a gaggle of roommates to make rent cheap. Now she's moving to Phoenix in the fall to start classes at Arizona State University while I'll probably be selling cell phones in Copper Springs forever, not to mention paying off Connor's fifty-thousand-dollar medical bills for the rest of my life.

I drop my face back into my hands. I'm not sure how much longer I'll be able to pull this off. My two jobs aren't enough to keep me afloat with all the responsibilities I have, and without a car, I'm not sure if I'll even be able to keep my jobs—particularly the one at Willow Inn, since it's so far away. And that's the job that pays the most and I like the best.

I'm screwed. But that's nothing new.

5

KAYLA

*M*y stomach grumbles. I've barely eaten today. And yesterday all I had was an apple and a bag of Cheetos. Dinner is a must. If I can grab a full meal tonight then maybe I won't have to worry about breakfast or lunch tomorrow when I'm on the road.

I hate driving alone, especially at night, so I'm not heading back to Chicago until morning. Though I'm not sure what my rush is. It's not like I have anything to return to—except for Big Joe and his demands.

I've had to work so many shifts these past few months just to stay ahead of my bills that all of my friendships back in Illinois have faded into acquaintanceships. So much so that I doubt anyone even knows where I am. Or that I even left Chicago.

Wow. That's an unsettling thought.

But it's probably for the better. If Big Joe found out that I took off, he'd probably send his goons to come drag me back to the diner. Maybe it's best if I never return at all.

There's nothing and no one waiting for me back in Illinois. No home. No family...My heart drops to the floor as I realize, for the first time, that I'm technically an orphan.

I'm twenty-one and I can take care of myself but there's

something very lonely about not having loved ones waiting for me anywhere in this world. In recent years, my father wasn't much of a parent but he was still *somewhere*, aware that I existed. And deep down, in the back of my mind where I let hope run free, I knew that if I needed him—if I really absolutely desperately needed my daddy—he would come through for me.

I had no reason to believe such a thing, but the little girl inside me refused to think otherwise. Even when I hated him, I still hoped for him. And maybe that's what hurt the most. More than the rejection. More than the abandonment. The deepest cut was the relentless hope I carried, and it bled endlessly. Even now, with him dead and gone, it's still bleeding.

I swallow back the lump in my throat and change out of my outfit.

Aside from the gray dress I wore yesterday, the royal blue blouse and black pencil skirt are the only "nice" clothes I own, so I'm careful not to snag or rip anything as I take them off. I slip out of the skirt, set it on the bed, then gingerly undo the buttons of my top before sliding it off my shoulders and folding everything neatly back into my suitcase.

I notice a new tear in the seam of the suitcase and I sigh. First my family tree, then my job and home, and now my suitcase?

Is there anything in my life that isn't falling to pieces?

I shake my head and silently scold myself for being so dramatic. I will *not* be a whiney baby. Sure, life has thrown a few fastball lemons at me lately, and sure, I'm broke and homeless, but I'm also an intelligent adult who can figure this out. My life. My future. My money. I *will* figure it out. All of it.

I swap the skirt on the bed for an old pair of jeans with holes in

the knees—from years of wear and tear, not for fashion purposes—
and my stomach rumbles again.

But before I figure *anything* out I'm going to eat so I don't faint
on the disgusting motel carpet. God, I'm hungry. All I've had today
is the granola bar I scarfed before heading to the lawyer's office for
the will reading.

Just thinking about my father's ridiculous will brings back all
my irritation from earlier. The man doesn't speak to me for five
years and when he finally does, he wants me to go on some kind
of weird letter hunt with the town's biggest playboy? What was
he thinking? Why couldn't he have just given the letter directly
to me without involving any bondage playtime with Daren Ackwood? And why on *earth* is Daren Ackwood a part of this equation
anyway?

He was my dad's gardener, for crying out loud. He was an
egotistical rich kid who probably only kept the gardening job so he
could afford to buy condoms for all his sexual conquests. And my
father deemed him worthy of his will? It doesn't make sense.

Just how chummy were Daren and my dad? Were they drinking buddies? Were they football friends? I never saw them have a
conversation that lasted longer than two minutes so how close could
they have possibly been?

I tug my old jeans on with a scoff.

Pretty damn close, I guess, if my dad felt comfortable leaving
that stupid letter to us both. Ugh. And what could he possibly have
to say to us in one silly note?

Dear Daren and Kayla. I'm holding your baseball cards hostage
and screwing you over one last time, hee-hee?

The whole thing is ludicrous.

Pulling a gray T-shirt from my tattered suitcase, I yank it over my head and flip my hair from under the collar with a huff. I look in the mirror and relax a little.

The formfitting blouse and skirt served their purpose today but I'm far more comfortable in loose clothes. Or relatively loose clothes. My curves are still noticeable in this outfit but at least I don't feel like my breasts are on display.

I grab my purse, let myself out of the motel room, and walk to the lobby—if you can even call it that. The Quickie Stop's lobby looks less like the registration desk of a motel and more like the drive-thru at a liquor store.

It's no bigger than my motel room, with walls that were probably white at one time but are now more of a grimy yellow color, and gray laminate flooring that's heavily scuffed, stained, and peeling up where the glue has lost its hold. The registration desk is eight feet wide and topped with a matching laminate counter, scarred with scratches and a few sections of penned graffiti. And the wall behind the counter is lined with shelves of cigarettes, small bottles of alcohol, and an obscene amount of condoms.

The man sitting behind the desk looks the way you'd expect the night shift employee of a seedy motel to appear. Mid forties, overweight, mustache, stained polo shirt, and a lump of tobacco chew bulging under his bottom lip.

His face brightens when he sees me walk in and the corners of his mouth curl up to reveal yellowing teeth. I try to ignore the way his eyes peruse my body as I approach, but seriously. Guys are pigs. It's not like I'm dressed like a hooker here. Yet this guy is slowly sinking his eyeballs into the most private places on my body.

"Well, hello there," he says eagerly as he straightens in his chair.

He probably doesn't mean to come across like a creep, but I can't help but be reminded of every scary movie ever when his grin grows bigger.

"Hello," I say politely, taking note that his name tag reads OWEN. You know, just in case I need to dole out details to the police later.

"How can I help you?" He ogles me and spits into a plastic cup. Gross.

"I was wondering if there was a place nearby to grab dinner. Something…affordable?" I hear the pathetic hope in my voice and want to slap myself.

It's not like I'm starving. And it's not like I don't have a penny to my name. I just don't want to blow twenty percent of what little money I do have on a crappy sandwich and a side of droopy fries.

The only reason I'm asking for eating suggestions at all is because the Quickie Stop is on the opposite side of town from where I grew up, so I'm not familiar with the food prices around here, and I don't feel like driving across town just to eat.

Ogling Owen leans in, happy to help. "Your best bet is Latecomers Bar & Grill. It ain't nothing fancy, but they got really good food and lots of booze." He wags his eyebrows, like he's hoping I'll get hammered tonight and beg him to take me to bed.

Seriously. Pigs.

"I can give you directions," he says, reaching for a pen.

"No, that's okay. I can look it up." I wiggle my phone at him so he sees that I don't need help—and that I have a way to call 911 if he decides to get extra creepy on me.

I might be dirt-poor, but I *always* find a way to pay my phone bill.

And besides, I already know where Latecomers is. I've never been inside before but I remember the area well enough to know how to get there.

"But hey, um..." I shift my weight and try to muster up the courage to ask my next question. "Do you have any discounted room rates here? Like, buy two nights get the third night half off or anything?" My voice shakes, actually *shakes*, on the last word. Super pathetic.

He looks intrigued. "You thinking about staying longer?"

I try to keep my face neutral. "Possibly."

His gaze roves over me again as he spits back into his chew cup. "We don't have nothing like that here. Weeknights are fifty-five a pop. Weekends are sixty-five. But"—he leans in and gives me another yellow-toothed smile—"I could probably make an exception for you." His eyes graze over my chest. Again.

"That's okay." I take a step back. "I don't want you to bend any rules."

Men who offer you favors simply because they find you attractive aren't offering you a favor at all. They're offering you a silent contract with a dozen strings attached. I don't do strings.

Desperation crosses his face. "It wouldn't be any trouble at all—"

"No really. It's fine." I smile tightly. "Thanks." I spin around and speed-walk out of the drive-thru lobby without another word.

Ogling Owen and his greedy eyes unsettle me. And the fact that he knows where I sleep is unnerving as hell. A shiver runs down my spine as I get in my car and lock myself inside before pulling out of the parking lot. I cannot wait to get out of this town.

When I reach Latecomers, the bar is packed so I have to drive around the parking lot for five minutes before finding a free space.

The moment I step inside, the aroma of savory dishes greets my nose and my mouth starts to water. But looking around at all the people waiting to be seated, my excitement wanes. I probably won't be getting a table anytime soon.

Four middle-aged men at a table near the door halt their conversation when they see me, but not in a slimy way. In fact, they seem to be trying *not* to look at me as they shift in their seats and take gulps of their drinks. But they're men and my DNA was designed to draw male attention.

I turn away, facing the other side of the restaurant where two women seated by the front window glare at me. I give them a nervous little smile. Their eyes travel over me and they look away with disgust. Like I somehow forced my boobs and butt to curve out the way they do and pranced into this restaurant with the sole purpose of displaying my beauty. In a *baggy T-shirt and ratty jeans.*

I can't win with women. I just can't.

They see me and either hate me immediately for being born the way I look, or don't hate me but also don't bother to get to know me because they assume my looks mean I'm a bitch.

My eyes drift about until they fall on an open seat on the far end of the bar and my hope lights up. I shuffle through the crowd with several mumbled apologies. A guy already seated at the bar eyes me lewdly as I walk by. I look away and quickly make my way to the open seat. It's at the dark end of the bar, which doesn't thrill me but at least I'll be able to sit by myself and not draw attention.

Beside the open barstool sits a couple; a brawny guy with several tattoos and a raven-haired girl with big hoop earrings. They laugh together as they enjoy their beers.

As I slide onto the open barstool, the girl eyes me and I smile. "Hi there."

She gives me a dirty look.

"Oh, I'm sorry," I say quickly, lifting off the barstool. "Is this seat taken?"

"No," she sneers then whips her attention back to her date.

I pause, half on and half off the barstool, slightly confused and a little offended. Why are girls rude like that? It's not like I'm here to steal her boyfriend.

With a shaky breath, I resume my seat and try to relax as I scan a small plastic menu on the bar. All I want to do is enjoy a hot meal and forget about this whole day. And maybe make a plan for my life.

Last year I was in nursing school, barely scraping by, but at least I had a future ahead of me. And now I have no money to go back to college and if Big Joe ever finds me he'll probably beat the twenty-thousand-dollar debt out of me.

I stare at the bar menu and try to contain the panic rising in my chest.

A pretty bartender with long red hair and large blue eyes comes up to me with a warm smile. "How are you doing tonight?"

"I'm good." I smile back, grateful for the distraction from my dreary thoughts and pleased she doesn't seem to hate me like the girl beside me. "How are you?"

"Busy and bustling." She cocks her head. "You look familiar. Have we met?"

She looks familiar to me too, but so do a lot of people in this town.

"I don't think we've met before," I say. "But I used to come to Copper Springs in the summertime and stay with my dad, so maybe we've seen each other before?" I say. "I'm Kayla."

"Kayla... Turner?" She covers her mouth. "Your daddy. Oh, I'm so sorry for your loss."

My smile becomes strained but I force it to stay in place. "That's very kind of you. Thanks."

"Can I get you a drink?" she says, setting a black napkin down in front of me. LATECOMERS is stamped in copper lettering across the top. "It's on the house."

I shake my head. "You don't have to do that."

"I want to. I'm Amber, by the way." She smiles.

My smile becomes easy again. "Nice to meet you."

She grabs a rocks glass. "So what's your poison, sweetheart?"

Before I can reply I hear, "Yeah, sweetheart. What's your poison?"

Turning to my other side, I see that the dark corner of the bar is not as vacant as I thought. There's one more barstool capping off the end, and on that barstool sits a pair of dark brown eyes and a wrinkled purple shirt.

So much for forgetting about today.

6

DAREN

*T*his is the problem with small towns. You can't avoid anyone. Ever.

I don't know why I'm surprised to see her. There are only three places to eat dinner on this side of town, and Latecomers is the only one with decent food. It only makes sense that Kayla would end up here. But sitting right next to me? Come on.

She's traded her skirt and blouse in for a pair of ripped jeans and a gray T-shirt, but she still looks hot—even with her eyebrow arched in irritation like it is now.

"Of course," she says, looking at me in exasperation.

I grin. "It's a small town."

Amber looks back and forth between us. "Do you two know each other?"

I say, "Yes—"

"No."

"Seriously?" I stare at Kayla. Why does she act like we've never met before? And why does it irk me so much that she does? "I'm not Stranger Danger over here, Kayla. *You know me.*"

She looks at Amber. "I'll just have a beer, please."

Amber gives me a questioning look before slowly saying, "You got it." Then she reaches for my empty dinner plate.

I stop her hand. "I'll clean it up."

Kayla looks at me, then around at the patrons, and asks Amber, "Does everyone clean up their own plates here?"

She laughs. "No. Daren is only insisting on cleaning his plate because he's working in the kitchen later."

At the word "working" Kayla glances at me then looks back at Amber. "Oh. Okay." She flushes a bit. "I just didn't want to be rude and not clean up after myself if that was how it worked here." She gives a nervous laugh, which makes her look adorable. Almost.

She's still a brat for taking Old Man Turner's money and shutting him out of her life.

"Nope." Amber smiles. "I'll clean up any dishes you use. So don't you worry about a thing."

She shuffles away, leaving Kayla and me on our own. We're seated at the end of the bar top where it makes an L shape so I have a perfect kitty-corner view of her face. It's a pretty face—a sweet face—but at the same time it's a sexy face. Long eyelashes and a small nose. Plush lips and high cheekbones.

I tap my finger on the counter between us. "I think you and I need to work on our relationship status."

She turns to me and manages to look both amused and pissed off. "Excuse me?"

"We are not strangers," I say. "I've seen the inside of your bedroom, Kayla. I think that qualifies me to be at *least* an acquaintance of yours."

"Wha—" She looks horrified. "When? When have you ever seen my bedroom?"

I shrug. "Sometime in the tenth grade I think? Your dad bought you a new dresser and I helped him move it into your room."

Her eyes bulge. "What?"

"*Love* the puppy posters, by the way," I say with an exaggerated voice. "*Super cute.*"

Her face starts to redden. "I hate you."

"Ditto. The point is," I say leaning forward, "we're not strangers. But since you insist on telling people that we are..." I give her my most charming smile and hold out my hand. "Hi. I'm Daren Ackwood—all-around nice guy and legendary lover. Nice to meet you."

She doesn't even look at my hand. "No."

I blink. "No?"

"No."

Amber returns with Kayla's beer. "Here you go," she says, carefully setting the mug down so it doesn't spill. She looks at my outstretched hand, still hovering in midair between Kayla and myself, and raises a brow.

"Kayla won't shake my hand," I explain, pulling my arm back.

Kayla looks at Amber. "He introduced himself as a 'legendary lover.'"

Amber slants her eyes to me. "You didn't."

I shrug innocently. "It's supposed to be funny." And it's supposed to work, dammit. It always works.

Amber shakes her head with a sigh and says to Kayla, "Don't mind Daren. He's full of himself, but he's harmless. I swear."

My mouth falls open. "Traitor."

Amber shrugs. "You are full of yourself."

"Yeah," I say. "But you're not supposed to tell people that."

"Oh, honey." She smiles. "Kayla already knew. Now if you'll excuse me, I have some thirsty patrons to attend to." With a glint in her eye, she turns and walks away.

"I like her," Kayla says smugly, watching Amber walk away.

"I do too. Usually," I mutter.

A guy seated down the bar looks over at Kayla before nudging his buddy's arm and jutting his chin her way. Both guys eye her appreciatively as one of them says something. They start laughing and Kayla turns her face in the opposite direction.

It's a small movement, so slight it could have been coincidental, but the annoyance on Kayla's face tells me she's more than aware that guys are staring at her. I look around for a moment. Lots of guys.

I lean back in my chair and cross my arms, diverting her attention. "So tell me, Kayla. Why are you still here? I thought you'd be long gone by now."

She takes a sip of her beer. "I don't like driving at night so I'm waiting until morning."

"Where are you staying?"

"Uh…" She starts to play with her paper napkin, fringing the edge with tiny tears. "The Quickie Stop?"

I lift my eyebrows. "The shitty place off the freeway?"

She doesn't make eye contact. "Yep."

"That's the shadiest motel in four counties. Why are you staying there? Why not the Willow Inn outside of town—or Martha's Bed & Breakfast in the town square?"

"Because I'm on a budget." She shoots me a cool look as if that's somehow my fault.

I must really have a talent for pissing this girl off.

"Well fancy meeting you two here." Eddie Perkins wedges himself between Kayla and the black-haired girl beside her with a wide grin. "How are you kids doing tonight?"

See what I mean about not being able to avoid anyone?

"Hi, Mr. Perkins," Kayla says pleasantly.

"Please, call me Eddie." He looks back and forth between us. "Are you two here together?"

We glance at each other.

"No way—"

"Hell no—"

Eddie lets out a chuckle. "Well okay then." He leans over the bar. "Hello, Amber."

She looks up with a smile. "Hey Eddie. I have your to-go order ready in the back. I'll grab it in a second," she says, pouring a martini for another customer.

"Thanks." He turns his attention back to us. "Sorry things didn't work out the way you two were hoping today."

We both nod and shrug.

"Thank you for taking care of everything for my dad's will," Kayla says.

"Certainly," he says. "Anything for James. I'm just glad it's all done with now. And it was a treat meeting you. James wasn't sure if you'd come, because of what happened with your mother and all."

Her eyes flick over his face, hard and wary. "It was... It seemed like the right thing to do."

I focus on my lemonade glass, feeling like an intruder on their conversation. I don't know what happened with her mom but whatever it was must have been unfortunate.

"Well I'm glad you came. Both of you," he says, looking at me. He scratches his chin. "It was an interesting will though, wasn't it?" He shakes his head. "James always had an odd sense of humor, but asking you to handcuff yourselves together for money? Well that's just a bit over-the-top, even for him."

We whip our eyes to him.

"Did you say money?" I jolt up in my seat, my heart pounding as Kayla's gaze zeroes in on him like he's the only thing in the room. She grips the edge of the bar and leans in.

"Well...yes," Eddie says. "The letter James wrote explains how to find the money he left you two." He wrinkles his brow. "Did I forget to mention that earlier?"

"Yes!" we say at the same time, loud enough to turn a few heads at the bar.

"Oh, my. I could have sworn..." Eddie rubs his mouth. "What a mistake. Well, I apologize. But that's what the will said. If the two of you agreed to be handcuffed together, you could pick up James's letter and follow his instructions to the money he left you."

Kayla's eyes grow wide. "Seriously?"

"Seriously." Eddie nods.

"Holy shit," I mutter.

I'm so elated right now I could shout. Old Man Turner left money, for *me*, and all I have to do to get it is lock myself up to his super-hot daughter for a few hours?

Hell To The Yes.

Kayla's mouth hangs open in shock as she whispers, "I can't believe this."

"There are a few caveats, of course," he continues. "You'd have to stay handcuffed until you found the money, and you'd have to share the money—"

"Sure. Yeah. Of course." I nod impatiently. "So how much money are we talking here? Three zeros? Four?" I lower my voice. "Six?"

Eddie shakes his head. "I'm not allowed to disclose that information. James felt that you knowing the amount would negate his purpose in leaving it to you."

Kayla blinks a few times. "That makes no sense."

Eddie shrugs. "But that's the nature of wills. They don't have to make sense."

"What about the papers we signed today?" I say. "Does that mean we forfeited the letter?"

"Because that was *before* we knew that the letter was more than just a letter," Kayla points out.

I scoot my chair around the corner of the bar so I can be closer to the conversation, and pull up right next to Kayla. She smells like coconuts. I glance at her throat. Coconuts are delicious.

Eddie waves us off. "You have twenty-four hours to change your minds. If you decide you do wish to be handcuffed after all, you can swing by my office tomorrow and we'll draw up new papers. Thank you, Amber." He smiles as she hands him a brown paper takeout bag. "Now if you'll excuse me," he says. "I have a pile of paperwork waiting for me at home and those documents aren't going to read themselves."

As he moves to leave, the wheels in my head start turning. I'm not crazy about Kayla. But if being handcuffed to her all day can dig me out of this money pit I'm trapped in, then chain me up! I need that money.

All I need to do now is convince Kayla that she needs it too.

7

KAYLA

I'm speechless. And it's taking everything in my power not to run after Eddie and beg him to draw up new paperwork right here at the bar. My father left me money.

My father.

Left *me* money.

I'm so shocked and relieved I could squeal. I might, actually. No, that wouldn't be cool. I will not squeal in a room filled with people who are already judging me because of my bra size.

I slide my eyes to the raven-haired girl beside me who hasn't stopped throwing dirty looks my way since I sat down, especially since Daren started talking to me. She's probably a casualty of Daren's undoubtedly long trail of broken hearts. Poor thing. I kind of feel bad for her. Broken hearts are the worst.

And speaking of Daren...he sure as hell better be on board with getting cuffed to me because we are *going* to get that letter.

Eddie wriggles his way through the crowd and out the front door with his food. The moment the door closes behind him, Daren and I snap our eyes to each other.

"We're doing this," we say at the same time. Followed by a confused, "You want to do this?"

I nod. "Yes."

He nods back with bright brown eyes. "Me too."

I shrug. "It's not like we'd have to stay handcuffed for very long."

"Of course not," he agrees. "We'll let Eddie cuff us, grab the letter, then uncuff ourselves once we know where the money is."

"Right. And then I'll go get the money."

"Whoa." He holds up a hand. "You mean, *we'll* go get the money."

"No. I mean *I'll* go get the money," I say. "Why would *we* go get the money?"

"Uh, because Turner left half of it to me?"

I scoff. "Yeah, because he didn't think I'd show up. But guess what?" I mock a gasp. "I showed up."

"And we're all honored by your presence, Your Majesty." He smiles sharply. "But that doesn't mean you get to swipe my half of the inheritance."

"Swipe? You're rich," I spit out. "What do you need the money for?"

"*I'm* rich? You're the one who's been living off of Daddy's dime for the past ten years."

"What are you talking about?" I scrunch up my face in confusion. "I'm broke."

He scoffs. "Sure you are."

My eyes widen. "I am."

He shrugs and spins the ice in his glass. "Well, that's too bad because half of that money is mine."

I purse my lips.

Greedy. Selfish. Spoiled. Rich boy. There's no way I'm sharing the only thing my father left to me. *No way.*

I didn't get to have him in my life for five long years, and as insane as it sounds, the fact that my crazy father designed some kind of weird letter hunt for me to go on makes me feel loved—or at least remembered. And I don't feel like sharing my father's last memory of me with some pretty-boy heartthrob who has nothing to do with my family.

And besides, if I want to get into nursing school I'm going to need tuition money. Lots of tuition money. This might be my only opportunity to make something better of my life. There's not a chance in hell I'm going to hand over half of my future to Daren Ackwood.

Not that he needs to know that.

"Fine," I sigh in feigned reluctance, rolling my eyes to really sell it. "We'll split the money."

He nods. "Damn straight we will."

"Hi, Daren," coos a female voice behind me.

I turn to see a blonde Barbie doll standing beside a brunette Victoria's Secret model, both wearing revealing tops and seductive smiles.

"Hey, Lizzy. Tanya." Daren flashes them his dimple. "You two look lovely tonight."

They giggle. They actually giggle. Grown women shouldn't giggle.

But he's right. They do look lovely, tight shirts and all. They're very attractive and from the way they're sizing him up I'm guessing they know Daren intimately.

"This is my friend, Kayla," he says, gesturing to me. "Kayla, meet Lizzy and Tanya."

I nod at them with a tentative smile. "Hello."

They look me up and down. Then flash me fake smiles and even more fraudulent greetings.

"Love the shoes," the Barbie says. I think she's the one named Lizzy. She nods at my old sneakers with an air of satisfaction.

The other one—Tanya—says, "Nice...shirt." She glances at my chest where I'm sure she's doing girl math to see which of us has greater boob mass.

It takes all the self-control I have not to tuck my feet farther under the bar or cross my arms over my chest. There's nothing wrong with my shoes. They're old and ripped up a bit, but it's not like they're clown shoes with neon patches on them. And my shirt is completely normal. But still I feel an itch of insecurity start somewhere deep inside me and I want to slap myself for letting it exist.

They're clearly trying to impress Daren with their false niceness. But from the look of disapproval on his face, he isn't fooled at all.

I don't have a lot. But I'm not ashamed of what I do have. And these two bullies are only picking on me in their passive-aggressive ways because they're threatened by me. If I wasn't so used to girls treating me this way, I might say something snotty in return. But instead, I smile as pleasantly as possible and remind myself that they are human beings with feelings.

I glance down at my ratty shoes and say, "Thanks. I try to dress comfy as often as possible." I look at them and appeal to the one thing I know we have in common: being girls. "High heels might look cute but they're a real bitch, am I right?" I smirk.

They hesitate. Clearly they weren't expecting me to respond with such civility. The Lizzy girl breaks out a real smile.

"Totally." She glances down at the expensive pumps she has on. "Pain. In. The. Ass."

"Tell me about it," Tanya adds, tapping her own fancy shoe.

For a brief moment, we aren't enemies.

Then Tanya turns her attention back to Daren. "So, handsome..." He grins. "We looked for you last night, but couldn't find you."

His smile teeters. "Yeah, well. It was a long day."

Lizzy pouts her lower lip. "We wanted to cheer you up. It must have been such a sad day for you."

His eyes flick to me and, for a split second, I see real loss in them. He clears his throat. "It was a little rough but I'm doing okay."

Tanya places her hand on his knee and a silky smile slides over her face. "You think you might need some cheering up tonight?"

Lizzy slips on her own sexy smile and leans forward.

What are they, a package deal?

To his credit, Daren has the decency to look mildly uncomfortable. "Actually, ladies, I'm all set for tonight. But I appreciate your concern."

They each shoot me a look of contempt, clearly assuming that *I'll* be cheering him up in their place tonight, and just like that, they're back to hating me.

I can't win.

After saying their farewells, the girls saunter away and Daren turns to me with a pointed look.

"Did you notice how I introduced you just now? As my *friend*. And it didn't even hurt." A smile plays at his lips.

I take a sip of my beer and watch Barbie and Victoria slither through the crowd. "If those are the kind of 'friends' you keep then I'm not so sure I want to be part of the group."

He gives me an apologetic look. "Yeah. Sorry they weren't cool. They're not as bad as they seem. I swear. They just have self-esteem issues and jealousy problems. And you're..." He looks me over. "Well, you're probably everything they want to be."

Ha.

"I seriously doubt that," I say.

"You're beautiful, is what I mean," he says casually.

Most guys can't compliment a girl without looking slightly uncomfortable. Not Daren, though. Nope. He's cool as a cucumber.

He adds, "Some girls aren't nice to beautiful girls."

I mimic Tanya. "Tell me about it."

As he takes a sip of his drink, I play with my napkin again, suddenly aware that he's sitting right next to me. He sets his glass down and my eyes follow the movement. His purple sleeves are rolled up to his elbows, exposing his tan forearms and hands. His has nice skin—flawless skin, actually—stretched over lean muscles and long fingers. My gaze travels up to his face and finds him watching as I shred my napkin to pieces. Our eyes meet and I swiftly look elsewhere.

The first time I saw Daren, I was thirteen and drinking a glass of iced tea in my father's kitchen. I remember because upon seeing him I choked a little on my tea and it dribbled down my chin. He was the same age as me but with his broad shoulders and strong jawline he looked older. When I asked my father who the boy in the backyard was, he replied, "A good kid who needs something to be proud of," whatever that meant. Then he told me his name was Daren Ackwood and I immediately registered the identity.

Ackwood.

Wealthy family. Adulterous scandal.

I'd heard the gossip around town and immediately felt sorry for the boy pushing the lawn mower. If *I* knew the dirt on his family, surely everyone else in town knew it too. And that couldn't be easy for him.

After that, I didn't give much thought to Daren Ackwood.

Until two summers later. We were both fifteen and Daren was in the yard, mowing the grass, but this time without a shirt on.

If I had been drinking iced tea at that time, I certainly would have choked on it all over again. He was more attractive than ever before and now had layers of muscle lining his tan chest. Those muscles rippled with his movements and glistened with his sweat, and for the first time in my life, I wanted to touch a boy—*really* touch a boy. Which was strange for me because I was as prudish as they came.

I slant my eyes to Daren on the barstool next to me and bite my lip. If fifteen-year-old Daren looked appetizing without a shirt on, I bet twenty-one-year-old Daren looks downright delicious.

Ugh. No.

No, Kayla.

Boys are bad.

I'm not a prude like I was all those years ago but I'm not free and easy with my sexuality either. I've learned through a series of disappointing boyfriends that boys only care about my body and their own pleasure.

I rarely pay guys any attention anymore, yet here I am, fantasizing about Daren Ackwood just like I did when I was a teenager. Ugh.

"So how much are you thinking?" he says.

I blink and pull my eyes off his chest. "What?"

He shrugs. "How much do you think your dad left us?"

At his question, my new incredible reality comes screaming back at me with bells and whistles.

My head jumps with ideas but doesn't quite land anywhere. My father and I hadn't spoken since before my sixteenth birthday so I didn't know him well enough to guess. I know his family came from old money—enough money that my mom would bitch and moan about what a jackass he was when he stopped sending her child support and alimony—but actual numbers are just speculation.

Unless this is all just a cruel prank and my crazy dad is messing with my hopes, dangling the prospect of inheritance money in front of me like an unreachable carrot.

I shake my head. "I have no idea. A few thousand dollars, maybe?"

He lets out a low whistle. "That would be nice."

I frown at him and his designer shirt. A few thousand dollars is pocket change to a guy like Daren. To me, it's the difference between sleeping on a park bench and having a bed to crawl into.

"Or knowing my father," I say dryly, "it might only be twenty bucks."

"Maybe." He nods with a grin. "But then we'd each be ten dollars richer."

He has a point.

"So it's decided then?" I toss the napkin aside and face him. "We're going to handcuff ourselves together for what may or may not end up being a twenty-dollar bill?"

Amusement flashes in his eyes. "I'm game if you are."

"Oh, I'm game," I say with a slow smile. "I'm very game."

He lifts his glass with a crooked grin. "Then here's to handcuffs."

I lift my drink to his. "Here's to handcuffs."

8

DAREN

After cleaning up my plate, I head back to the kitchen. Jake is at the grill, calling out instructions to the staff when I walk in.

"Daren," he calls out. "You're on prep."

"Sure thing," I say. "Thanks for letting me help out. Again."

"Anytime." He shouts out an order to the guys on the line and flips a burger before giving me a curious look. "What's up with you?"

"What do you mean?" I start washing my hands.

He shrugs. "You look...happy."

I smirk. Hell yes, I'm happy. I just found out that I'm heir to an inheritance.

"Was it the blonde out there?" Jake nods toward the restaurant. "Is she the reason you're in such a good mood?"

"What? No." I scrub my fingers. "Well kind of, yes. But not like that."

He slants his eyes to me. "Riiight."

I scoff. "Come on, Jake. When have you ever known me to get *happy* over a girl?"

He considers. "Good point." He throws a raw steak on the grill and pulls a cooked one off. "So what's up with you then?"

I shrug. "Nothing."

Yet.

After I finish washing up, I head to the chopping block while biting back a smile.

I still can't believe it. James Turner left me an inheritance, that old dog.

Twenty dollars would be fine. But if it was more money...if it was a *lot* more money...my whole world could change. All the shit I've had to deal with these past few years, all the stress, it could all disappear—or some of it, at least—and I could have options.

And I didn't think I'd ever have options. Not as far as my future was concerned.

I spend the next hour and a half slicing and dicing ingredients while bantering with the kitchen guys.

I love being in the kitchen of Latecomers. I love being in kitchens, period. There's nothing quite as invigorating as the hustle and bustle of cooking. The prep, the flavor pairings, the sautéing and grilling. It relaxes me in a way nothing else ever has.

The first time I ever "cooked" was when I was nine. Marcella was making spaghetti sauce and asked me to help stir the simmering tomatoes. While I was stirring, she started to toss in some olives and I made a face. I hated olives in my spaghetti sauce. Laughing, Marcella asked me what I *did* like in spaghetti sauce. I told her I wasn't sure what I liked because I didn't know all of the ingredients. So she pulled out some basil, mushrooms, onions, and spices and had me taste each one. Then she let me make my own spaghetti sauce using the ingredients I liked. I cut up the mushrooms and onions and sprinkled oregano. Then I stirred the simmering sauce, the rich aroma filling my nose, until it was ready. We sat down to eat together, just the two of us in my parents' giant kitchen, and I took my first bite.

It was the most amazing spaghetti sauce I'd ever had.

I asked Marcella why it tasted so much better than the kind she made. She laughed and said, "Because you created it, *mijo*. Food always tastes sweeter when you work hard to make it."

From that day on, I was obsessed with cooking. Marcella obliged me in every way she could. She taught me how to whisk, measure, knead, and dice. And I never grew tired of it. Even after we could no longer afford Marcella and she had to move away to find work, I still spent endless hours in the kitchen.

It wasn't the same, though. The kitchen wasn't as warm or happy without Marcella. There was no one to talk to. No one to call me *mijo*.

Nothing was the same after Marcella left. She was the last piece of warmth I had in an otherwise cold home. And the only comfort I could find in her absence was in the heat of a kitchen. So cooking became my haven and has been ever since.

Halfway through the dinner rush, I realize we're running low on dessert so I exit the kitchen door to get more from the spare freezer out back. The freezer is located in a fenced courtyard on the side of Latecomers, next to the parking lot. Jake has plans to make it a patio with outdoor seating but for the time being it's more of a storage area.

As I reach the freezer, something on the other side of the short fence catches my eye. Kayla stands outside of Latecomers, helping an elderly woman walk down the steep steps of the entrance. She holds the old woman's hand in her own and carefully guides her down the stairs and over to where a taxi waits. Kayla gets the woman settled in the cab before shutting the door and walking away.

I watch her sexy hips swinging through the parking lot until she's just a few yards away.

I open the courtyard gate and smile. "A friend of yours?"

Kayla spins around, clutching her chest. Then sighs in relief when she sees me. "Oh. Daren."

"Sorry," I say. "Didn't mean to freak you out."

She waves me off. "It's fine. I'm just jumpy. Uh…no. I didn't know that woman, but she was having trouble and no one was around to help her." In the soft yellow glow from the courtyard lamps, her hair shines golden and her big blue eyes glimmer. She really is stunning.

"That was nice of you," I say, smiling. "So how was dinner?"

"It was good." She nods and her blue eyes widen. "It was *really* good, actually."

I laugh. "You sound surprised."

"Well I am. I'm not used to bars having gourmet food. But it was really fantastic."

My chest swells with pride. Even though I didn't make her dinner, I'm still proud of the kitchen that did.

"So this is where you work?" She gestures at the closed kitchen door behind me as she approaches.

I step back so she can enter the courtyard then glance over my shoulder. "It's more like the place where I help out in the kitchen, occasionally," I say. "I like to cook so sometimes the owner, Jake, let's me jump on the line."

She tilts her head. "I wouldn't have pegged you as the cooking type."

"No?" I arch a brow. "What type am I?"

"Well the professional lover type, obviously."

I grin. "That too."

The teasing in her eyes along with the lightness of her smile does something soft to my insides. This is a different Kayla than the one I was sitting next to at the bar. That girl was stressed and burdened, but this girl...this girl is hopeful and happy.

The only reason I can think of for the change in her tone is the inheritance. Does the idea of getting money please her so much that she's suddenly this cheerful person? Does it please *me* that much?

I remember Jake's comment earlier, about my being happy, and realize with a sinking feeling that yes, the idea of an inheritance has made me happy. Money would alleviate some of my problems and, therefore, it gives me a security in my future that pleases me.

I'm not sure how I feel about money having so much control over my contentment. It makes me sound an awful lot like my dad.

"So what is this place?" she asks, nodding to the courtyard around us.

I look up at the small twinkle lights strung above the area. "Right now it's just storage space. But Jake wants to make it into a dining patio. You know, so people can rent it out for private parties or whatever."

"It's cute." She walks around, checking out the rosebushes that line the fence and the Tuscany-inspired mural painted against the back wall.

"So where you off to?" I step closer so we're both beside the painted wall. "Back to your humble abode at the Quickie Stop?"

She scoffs. "Humble indeed. But yeah."

I glance at the dark parking lot beyond the fence and the even darker streets that lead to the edge of town, and frown. "By yourself?"

She faces me with a cocked eyebrow. "Yeah. I've got my own driver's license and everything."

I smile at the ground. "Okay, that's fair." I glance at the dark streets again. "I'm just a concerned citizen that wanted to make sure you got home safely. That's all."

She nods. "How very kind of you, citizen. Would you rather I be going back to the Quickie Stop *with* someone?"

The idea of Kayla going home with someone—anyone, other than me—rakes down my spine like nails on a chalkboard. I don't know when I got so possessive of this girl but holy hell. My veins are on fire.

How very unexpected. And somewhat annoying.

I don't get possessive of women. Ever. Sure, I care about Amber and Pixie but that's different. I care about them like sisters. I'm *protective* of them. I couldn't really give a damn who they, or any other female in this town, go to bed with.

But Kayla?

Hot jealousy darts through my veins.

How very annoyingly unexpected.

I set my shoulders back in a casual manner. "Not particularly," I say coolly. "I just wasn't sure if you had a ride or not."

"Oh." She runs a finger over her lips. "And what, you were going to offer me a ride?"

I watch the tip of her finger skim over the pink fullness of her bottom lip and my breath hitches. She can't say things like "give me a ride" and touch her mouth at the same time. That's just not fair.

"Well I *might* have offered you a ride," I say, inwardly cursing as I remember sweet, precious Monique, "except I'm pretty sure you're not supposed to take rides from strangers. And since that's what you and I are..." I sigh dramatically. "It would have just been a waste of time to ask you."

She smiles behind her moving fingers and I start to wonder if she'd let me kiss her. My guess is, yes. Maybe.

I want to kiss Kayla. Badly. But the idea of kissing her, of touching her at all, also makes me a little nervous. And I'm never nervous when it comes to women.

Goddammit. Everything about this girl is unexpected.

"You're so obsessed with us not being strangers," she says, and her eyes shine. "That can't be healthy."

I probably shouldn't kiss her. We have an inheritance to claim tomorrow. We have shit to follow through with. Kissing her is a bad idea. A very bad idea.

"No. Probably not." I step closer so we're only inches apart. "But I can't seem to let it go."

She doesn't move away. She doesn't break eye contact.

Yes. She'd definitely let me kiss her. I'm sure of it.

My heart pounds and it's all I can do to keep my nonchalant demeanor in place.

"Is that what we are, Kayla?" I lower my voice with a crooked grin. "Strangers?"

She meets my crooked grin and raises me a tipped chin. Her eyes are steel and sure, not giving anything away, and I suddenly feel *un*sure.

I lean in.

She doesn't react. But she also doesn't back away.

Kissing her is a bad idea.

Her lips part, ever so slightly, a thin seam of wet flesh forming between the soft skin of her pretty lips, and all my reservations vanish.

9

KAYLA

I jolt in surprise when Daren's mouth meets mine. I was flirting—*shamelessly* flirting—with him, but only because I didn't think he'd act on it.

Clearly, I underestimated his audacity.

I'm not even sure what possessed me to tease him in the first place. I'm never like this. I don't flirt. I don't lure. I'm quiet and careful, and usually shut off from all males unless they go out of their way for my attention. Not because I'm a snob, but because most of the time guys just want to get me naked and I don't have the time—or the patience—to entertain random guys for the sake of getting them off.

So everything I've done tonight leading up to this moment with Daren is completely out of character for me. Yet here I am, with his lips pressed against mine in this little courtyard and all I can think about is how *good* his mouth feels up against me.

His hands skim up my arms and cradle my face, drawing a shiver out of me as his lips softly swipe over mine. My eyes flutter closed and I gasp, unsure.

Sensing my hesitation, he pulls back slightly. His lips set before my mouth, a featherlight touch as he loosens the cradle of his hands. The pad of one thumb brushes my jaw as he waits.

I know I should pull back and walk away. But the careful stroke of his thumb moving up my cheek and to my ear, the hot breath of his exhales warming the tender skin beneath my jaw...

It's all so good, so fulfilling, sending pleasures of warmth through my body and awakening a hunger in the depths of my being. A hunger that only grows when he runs his thumb over my lower lip and gently pulls it down so my lips are partly opened.

"Tell me to stop and I will," he whispers. His words drift between my lips and tickle my waiting tongue.

Fighting between my better judgment and the lust sprawling through my lower belly, I sink against him and whisper, "Don't stop."

Instantly, he crushes his lips against mine, more fully than before, and I eagerly kiss him back. He grips my jaw, not roughly but not gently either, as he runs his tongue down the seam of my lips and I open for him, softly moaning as his tongue slips inside my mouth and rolls over my own.

Our mouths meet in a hungry collision, kissing and pulling and licking at each other. My breaths come out in shallow pants as my body becomes alight with need. He tips my chin up, exposing the sensitive skin of my throat, and moves his mouth to my windpipe where he lightly suckles.

I exhale into the night, my eyes fluttering once again in the hazy glow of the twinkle lights above us, as I arch my back and push my chest into him. My nipples tighten with need, brushing against the hard muscles of his chest as his hot mouth moves against my throat, up to my jaw, and then to my ear.

Letting out a little whimper, I grab at his shoulders as he trails his hands down my spine and to my hips. Our kissing becomes rough and heavy, hot tongues gliding over each other and licking furiously at lips and teeth and skin as I roll my hips into his. I feel his hard erection against my belly and wetness pools between my legs.

He nips my bottom lip and I sink my nails into the back of his shirt with another quiet moan. Grabbing my hips, he yanks me against his body and I rub against his hardness feverishly, wanting him with an unfamiliar desperation. He groans and pulls back for air. My pupils widen at the sight of his swollen lips, wet from our kissing, and the heaviness in his eyes.

Seeing him want me just as badly as I want him has me licking my own swollen lips, and his eyes follow the slow movement of my tongue. Then suddenly, I'm no longer standing. He lifts me into his arms and presses my back against the painted wall behind us. Opening my thighs to wrap around his waist, I shiver again as the new closeness brings friction to my most needy area.

As the softness between my legs grows hot and wet, I let out a succession of whimpers, jerking my hips a little when he rubs against me just right, and my eyes roll back into my head.

Sliding my hands down to his pants, I rub my open palm over the bulge in his pants. He feels so long and thick, and so very hard. The aching tightness in my core melts with need as I rub against him more fervently.

Groaning, he grabs my ass and squeezes firmly. He grabs my chin and takes my mouth captive again. He runs his hand under my shirt and up my bare belly, taking my breast in his large palm and roving his thumb over my painfully tight nipple through my bra.

God, this feels good. Good in a way I've never experienced before. Good because I *want* it. I want Daren and his mouth. I want Daren and his hands. I want Daren and his...

Then reality hits me.

What am I doing? Making out with Daren Ackwood against the back wall of a bar? No. I'm not this person. I'm careful. Cautious. I don't get swept away like a horny teenager and give in to my every whim—even if that whim is telling me that I like Daren's fingers inching my bra cup down to reach my naked nipple. This is the opposite of what I do.

"Wait," I say, panting as Daren's soft lips brush against my throat. Again.

I instinctually tip my head back and groan. Why does this have to feel so good?

He pulls back slightly, just as out of breath as I am, and slowly slips his hand out of my bra. My nipple aches in protest, wanting to be plucked and prodded again, as my core continues to pulse and ache.

Clutching me against the wall in his strong arms, he searches my face with his deep brown eyes. "What's wrong? Are you okay?"

"Yeah...I'm good." I swallow, tasting him on my tongue. "I'm really good. I just...I have to stop."

I wait for him to argue like most guys would do. Or nuzzle my neck and say something sweet to try and get me to reconsider. But instead, he nods and gently sets me back on my feet.

"Yeah. Sorry," he says. His chest rises and falls with heavy breaths as he rubs a hand over his mouth. "I sort of got carried away there."

I blink, surprised by his conceding response. "No, you're fine. Sorry. It's—it's just..." I reach for the right words. "I...I just can't..."

He waves me off with a small smile. "No, I get it. We're good."

"Are we?" I squint at him, still out of breath and quivering between my thighs. "Because we agreed to be handcuffed together tomorrow and I don't want things between us to be weird."

He raises a brow. "Weirder than being handcuffed while we track down a letter?"

I can't help but smile.

"It'll be fine," he says. He must see the uncertainty in my eyes because he adds, "Really. This never happened." His smile falters a bit, but his pleasant expression is genuine, which makes me wonder if maybe I was too hasty putting the brakes on our tongue tango.

I'm grateful that he's being so cool but at the same time slightly disappointed that he isn't fighting harder to keep me in his arms.

God, Kayla. What is your problem tonight? You do not *hump guys you barely know in parking lots. Pull it together!*

"Right." I nod once. "This never happened."

He takes a few steps back and takes a deep breath. "Want me to walk you to your car?"

"No," I say quickly, shaking my head. "No. I'm fine. But thank you."

I don't trust myself at all right now. Nothing about the last ten minutes was normal behavior for me. Who knows what I'd do if Daren walked me to my car? Probably invite him back to my motel room for some shaggy-rug shagging. God.

"Okay. Well." He nods. It's awkward.

I lift a shoulder. "I guess I'll see you in the morning?"

"Yep." He grins. "Bright and early."

We step farther away from each other and do a weird almost-wave as we say good-bye. Then I turn and slip out the courtyard gate before darting away. If it weren't so dark and eerie in the parking lot, I would hang my head.

Instead, I keep my chin up and my eyes alert until I'm safely shut inside my car, then start the engine as I remind myself that this never happened. It never happened.

Except it absolutely did.

———

The next morning, I slip back into my royal blue blouse and pencil skirt before driving to Mr. Perkins's office.

Sleep was a lost cause last night. My mind was too busy racing with possibilities of an inheritance from my father, and scolding myself for getting hot and heavy with Daren.

I still don't know why I gave in to him so easily. Sure, he's attractive and charming but so are a lot of guys, and you don't see me wrapping my legs around every hot man who passes me on the sidewalk, and then rolling my hips up against their hard bodies.

A warm shiver runs through me, turning me on at every nerve ending as the memories of last night swim around my head. The whole thing was complete madness.

One minute, we're talking about being strangers, and the next minute, Daren's kissing and touching me like a bandit. Like a super stealth bandit.

Never in my life have I been so turned on—and we were only kissing. I can only imagine the levels of arousal I'd reach had his hands wandered to truly naughty areas. Maybe all the stories Lana told me about Daren were true. Maybe he is some kind of woman whisperer.

But it doesn't matter. Stopping before things got naughty was the right thing. I wanted so badly to just let go and get swept up in the desire of it all, but when sanity peeked through my lust and reminded me that I couldn't get caught up in a guy right now I knew I had to listen.

I've spent the past few years taking care of my mother instead of myself, and the past few months just trying to scrape by. The last thing I need is another complication.

I don't have anything in my life figured out. But I have a clean slate. It's a dirt-poor slate, wandering aimlessly through the Arizona desert, but it's mine to start over with and throwing a guy into the mix won't do me any good.

I need to get my life in order and figure out what my future holds before I even *think* about getting involved with someone. And while meaningless sex might work for some people—probably people like Daren—it's not my style. But oh how I wish it were because damn. It felt good to be touched.

I reach Mr. Perkins's office and quickly park before climbing out of the car in my high heels.

The inheritance really could be only twenty dollars—or less—and spending an afternoon chained to Daren Ackwood to find it could be a complete waste of time, not to mention horribly awkward given our romantic encounter last night, but it's worth a shot. Because if it turns out to be a substantial amount of money, everything could change.

Not only could I go back to nursing school, but I could afford a decent apartment and buy myself some time to find a new job—one where my boss isn't demanding I work for free or flash him in order to pay off my mother's debt.

Ugh. My life can really only go uphill from where I'm at.

I know money can't buy happiness, and I believe that. But it would be nice to be out from under Big Joe's threatening thumb. And sleeping in a cockroach-free apartment while eating regular hot meals wouldn't be bad either.

I hurry down the sidewalk toward Mr. Perkins's office, tripping a little in my shoes. Maybe wearing the skirt and heels again wasn't such a great idea. But I wanted to look professional and responsible, and the gray dress is too hot and the only other pair of shoes I own are my beat-up sneakers from last night. I didn't think a pencil skirt and a pair of dirty sneakers really said *I can be trusted with my deceased father's money.* So I went with the pumps.

I wobble as my shoe catches on a small pebble and curse under my breath.

High heels really are a bitch.

Up ahead, I see Daren round a corner and hurry toward the office, now just a few yards down the sidewalk. I relax a little, knowing he's not there yet. As we near each other, my stomach fills with butterflies. I don't know what I'm more anxious about—the inheritance or seeing Daren.

We reach Eddie's door at the same time.

"Good morning." He smiles broadly.

"Morning," I respond with a cheerful smile of my own.

Our smiles are exaggerated, like we're trying to prove just how "okay" we are with the thing that never happened last night. Then our eyes meet in brief a clash of lust, and tension fills the air.

Daren is the first to break it. "So. You ready to do this?"

"I am," I say.

The tension returns, but this time it's laced with nervousness. We're about to lock ourselves together. For money. The morning after we dry humped each other against a bar. It's nothing less than weird and desperate. Which begs the question, why is Daren doing this?

I know why I'm subjecting myself to this craziness but I'm still not sure why Daren has agreed—especially without knowing how much money is at stake. Is he in it for the thrill? Is he just bored?

Whatever his reasons are, I'm grateful.

We enter the office and Eddie looks up from his messy desk, his glasses perched on his shiny head. Today he's wearing a yellow button-up shirt with a plaid bow tie to match his plaid pants. The look suits him.

"You've returned," he says brightly, standing to greet us. "I guess this means you've come to a decision about Mr. Turner's letter?"

"We have," I say.

Daren nods. "Yes."

"Excellent." Eddie clasps his hands together. "What have you decided?"

Daren and I exchange an anxious look. My stomach does a flip-flop, afraid he's going to change his mind, but then he gives me a subtle nod and I nod back.

We turn to face Eddie, hold out our wrists, and at the same time say, "Cuff us."

10

DAREN

*W*hen I fantasize about being handcuffed to a hot blonde, there's usually not a balding lawyer and a last will and testament involved. But standing in Eddie's cluttered office with Kayla at my side, I realize that perhaps I haven't been dreaming big enough. Because unlike my other fantasies this one might end with a few dollars in my pocket—if I can handle being handcuffed to Kayla all day without touching her.

I shouldn't have kissed her last night. I don't regret it—not in the slightest—but I still shouldn't have done it. I knew the moment she pulled away what a mistake it was. Because I *cared*.

I cared that she changed her mind and no longer wanted my hands on her. I cared that she politely rejected me. I took it personally, and I never take anything girl-related personally.

My first instinct was to *do better*, for Christ's sake. To do better and earn her approval; win her affections.

I've made a point in life not to seek out the admiration of any one woman. Women in general, sure. I want females as a whole to like me and enjoy my company—and I strive to achieve just that. But I don't work for the approval of any one specific girl. Not ever.

I've learned the hard way that wanting, or working, for such a thing is useless, and will leave me burned.

I really hope my gut reaction to Kayla pulling out of my arms last night was a momentary weakness and nothing more.

Looking at her now, as we stand in Eddie's office, I can't help but think back to how she felt in my arms, all supple and needy. God, she was hot. And she was honestly into it too, like a hungry wolf with a slab of meat as she moaned and wriggled against me.

There's a difference between the whimper of a woman who's just having fun and the sound of a woman starving for pleasure. And Kayla Turner needs to be pleased. Badly.

But not by me, apparently. She probably thinks she's too good for me. And in reality, she is. But the truth still stings.

Eddie looks down at our outstretched wrists and chuckles. "Well I'm pleased to hear that." He waves our hands down. "You can relax, though. First I need you to sign some documents." Slipping on his glasses, he moves around his desk and starts fumbling through papers. "Now where ... did I put ... those documents from yesterday ... ?"

I eye the familiar pile of papers stacked behind his desk. "On the filing cabinet."

Eddie shuffles over to the cabinet and scoops up the folder. "Aha."

As he silently reads through it, I slide my eyes to Kayla. Her blonde hair is pulled back into a sleek knot at the base of her neck, with little wisps falling around her face. She nervously bites her lip as she watches Eddie, and the sting of rejection returns to my veins.

Oh, she's good. Playing up the neglected-daughter act for Eddie just like she tried to play me last night. I still can't believe she wanted to take the entire inheritance for herself. *I'm broke*, she said with those pouty blue eyes of hers. Yeah right. "Broke" probably means she can't afford to summer in Europe or buy herself a new yacht. That trust fund of hers must be running low.

Well that's just too bad. I don't care how attractive—or how hot a kisser—Kayla is. She's not keeping half of the inheritance Turner left to me. She didn't even try to be a part of his life while he was alive, for Christ's sake. Why the hell should she get to benefit from his wealth now?

From what I hear, she and her mother are used to living the high life with all of Turner's money so Kayla would probably just blow the inheritance on something stupid, like a bedazzled Jet Ski or a pony. I, on the other hand, actually *need* the money. So when we find it, I'm keeping every last penny.

I look at her and try to solidify my resolve. I deserve that money. I do.

"There are a few stipulations in Mr. Turner's will," Eddie says when he's done scanning the page. "The biggest being that I cannot unlock the handcuffs until you find the inheritance." He clears his throat and reads, "'Arrangements have been made with a handful of local townspeople to help Kayla and Daren complete their quest. If any of these helpers catch Kayla and Daren without the handcuffs on, they have been instructed to report to Eddie immediately.'"

"Seriously?" Kayla says.

"Seriously," he says.

"Local townie spies." I purse my lips. "Fantastic."

"'If Daren and Kayla are caught without the handcuffs on and reported, they automatically forfeit their inheritance and the money will then be donated to the charities listed on page seven of this form...'" Eddie skims the remainder of the page then pushes his glasses farther up his nose as he eyes us. "Are you two sure about this?"

I look at Kayla. She'd *better* be sure. I try to flash her one of my killer smiles—the kind that says *you can trust me with your hopes and dreams and body*—but I'm too anxious to pull it off. Partly because I'm still not over the fact that she *doesn't* trust me with her body, but mostly because the possibility of having money in my pocket by the end of the day is just too important. My future, or lack thereof, is riding on Kayla's cooperation.

Fortunately, her gold-digging roots have bred her to be just greedy enough to agree to this plan because she nods at Eddie without glancing at me.

"Absolutely," she says with complete confidence.

"Well all right then." Eddie rummages through the papers on his desk and comes up with a large, flat manila envelope. Opening the envelope, he pulls out a set of handcuffs. Not the fuzzy kind used in the bedroom, but honest-to-God police-grade handcuffs made of steel. I don't know what I was expecting, but it certainly wasn't hard-core manacles.

Kayla's eyes widen. "Those look...real."

Eddie nods. "They are."

She shakes her head. "Of course my father couldn't pick out a set of cushiony handcuffs. He had to choose the same kind of hand-cuffs that felons get marched to prison in."

Eddie wrinkles his nose at the cuffs. "It does seem a bit harsh, doesn't it?"

I sigh. "Well at least we won't have to wear them for very long."

Kayla nods. "Yeah. Thank God it will only be a few hours." She glances at me and adds, "Tops."

"Right." I nod, though I can't imagine it taking us even an hour.

Eddie hands us each a pen. "I just need you both to sign here." He points to a paper that looks identical to the one we signed yesterday. "But this time sign saying you agree to the terms of the will and accept the offer."

We take turns. For a moment, I feel like I'm signing my life away, but my nervousness is short-lived as I think about the overwhelming medical bills waiting for me at the county hospital and the fate of my living situation come the near future. I quickly scrawl out my name.

Kayla signs her name beside mine with the penmanship of an artist, making my signature look like a manic toddler got hold of a ballpoint pen. I watch her curl the end of the *r* in her last name. Handwriting shouldn't be that pretty.

"All right." Eddie puts the pens away and looks at us. "Are you ready?"

I hold out my left wrist while Kayla holds out her right, and we watch in silence as Eddie slides the handcuffs over our hands and locks them closed with a few *click-click-clicks*. He's careful to leave enough room for us to move our wrists, but the cuffs are still pretty tight.

"Wow. These things are heavy." Kayla lifts our chained hands up and down a few times and I move my wrist to accommodate the movement.

They really are surprisingly heavy.

I turn the steel manacle around my wrist. "And uncomfortable."

Kayla mutters, "I guess handcuffs aren't supposed to be cozy."

We drop our wrists and let them hang heavily at our sides. The back of my hand brushes the back of Kayla's hand and her soft skin instantly warms against mine.

We glance at each other and jerk away like the touch is searing hot. I bite back a smile. If touching me for a split second has her this agitated, then I'd hate to think how she's going to feel after being handcuffed to me for an hour—or longer. I might be hauling a blonde mess of irritation back to Eddie's office later.

Taking a step back, Eddie looks us over with a raised brow. "You two look like downright criminals."

I say, "Gee, thanks."

"So now what?" Kayla asks.

"Now," Eddie says, "I give you directions to the letter."

He hands her a small white envelope. She reaches for it with her cuffed hand, aggressively yanking my wrist up.

"Easy," I say as the handcuffs whack against my wrist.

She crinkles her nose in apology. "Sorry." Then she carefully moves her bound wrist as she pulls a piece of paper from the white envelope. She reads aloud, "'The blue suitcase in the hall closet,'" then looks at Eddie. "What does that mean?"

He shrugs. "I just hand out the papers."

"The suitcase in the hall closet?" I frown. "That's not directions. That's like…a clue. Does he mean the hall closet in his house?"

"Oh! The one with all the umbrellas?" Kayla looks at Eddie expectantly.

He shrugs. "I wish I could help you folks but I honestly have no idea."

"Okay. That's okay," Kayla says. "I'm sure he meant the hall closet at Milly Manor."

"Yeah. And I know for a fact Turner used to have a blue suitcase," I say. "There was one in his garage for like ten years."

Kayla turns to stare at me. "Why were you snooping through my father's garage?"

"I wasn't snooping." I jut my chin. "I was squeezing through all his old junk so I could put the lawn mower away every other Saturday, remember?"

"Oh yeah." She turns back to Eddie. "So what are we supposed to do, then? Just go grab the letter, then the money, and then come back to your office so you can unlock these things?" She jiggles the cuffs.

"Yep." Eddie holds up a set of small handcuff keys. "I'll be here until five p.m."

"Oh we'll be back long before then," I say.

"Definitely," Kayla adds and we hurriedly exit the good law-yer's office.

It's not until we're standing on the sidewalk, in the bright light of day, that the true oddness of our situation sets in.

Everyone walking past us, or seated across the street at the café, or peering out through store windows, turns to stare at the hand-cuffed couple standing outside the lawyer's office.

We really do look like criminals. And with Kayla wearing that tight skirt and those high heels, we look like sexy criminals, which only draws more eyes.

Looking her over more closely, I notice she's wearing the exact same clothes and shoes she had on yesterday. There's a small stitch on her shirt where it's been mended and her heels are dirty and scuffed.

Huh. Not the designer outfit I'd expect a spoiled princess to sport, especially not two days in a row. It doesn't really fall in line with my idea of a trust fund baby.

"Everyone is staring at us," Kayla murmurs as a faint blush spreads over her cheeks. She turns away from the onlookers and faces me, but steps so close to my chest she's nearly buried in it.

I look down at her and cock my head. Hmm. Not the reaction of a diva beauty queen. Not at all. Her modest behavior is almost... endearing. And very confusing.

"Yeah..." I say slowly. "Well you *are* wearing high heels and handcuffs. You look downright sinful."

She looks up and her mouth falls open. "Me? What about *you?*"

"Trust me." I watch a group of construction workers stop what they're doing as they eye Kayla's ass. "No one is looking at me." A trio of women seated at the café across the street see me and immediately start to whisper. Some scandals just don't die. "Okay. Maybe a few people are looking at me."

She sees the construction guys and makes an annoyed noise before stepping even closer to me. The scent of coconut fills my nostrils and a vision of rubbing coconut oil all over her body suddenly pops into my head. I try to push it away, but then she leans in, pressing her shoulder and hip against me, and the vision becomes much more explicit.

I start to grow hard against her soft body—until I see her nervously bite her lip and furrow her brow at the construction workers, and my thoughts return to reality.

She's clearly uncomfortable with those guys checking her out, and the insecurity in her eyes tugs at something strong and unfamiliar inside me.

"Good heavens!" I hear.

An elderly couple walks past us, looking horrified when they see the glinting metal binding us together, and the old woman's mouth drops open.

I smile at them reassuringly and explain. "We're not felons," I say, shaking my head. "We handcuffed ourselves together on purpose." They look even more horrified. "Not for a kinky reason," I quickly add. "For money."

Kayla mutters, "Please stop talking."

The couple hurries past us, *tsk*ing and shaking their heads as they move down the sidewalk, and I turn to Kayla. "Can you believe that? They didn't even try to hide their judgment."

"Gee, I wonder why." She glowers at me. "Let's just go so we're no longer standing on display for the whole town." She looks around. "Where's that pretentious car of yours?"

"My car is not pretentious."

She lifts a brow.

"Okay. My car is a little pretentious," I concede. "But it's a good car." I think about poor Monique being towed away from me. "A sweet car. A beautiful, loyal, loving vehicle that deserves to be treated nicely."

She grimaces. "You're being kind of weird about your car."

"I know." I nod with a sigh. "I have attachment issues."

"Clearly," she says. "So where is it?"

"My car? Uh…" Good question. "My car is far away. Far, *far* away." Poor thing. "It would take a very long time to walk to it." Wherever it is. "Let's use your car," I suggest with a grin.

She hesitates and for a second I think she's going to argue, but then she says, "Fine," and digs around in her purse.

Pulling out her keys, she leads me by the wrist down the side-walk and to the nearest parking lot, pulling me behind her like I'm a dog on a leash. She walks me to the back of the parking lot and over to a small green car covered in scratches, dents, and rust.

Not the vehicle I pictured Kayla Turner driving.

I expected a Cadillac. Or at least something with nice rims and tinted windows. Nothing about Kayla's appearance or possessions or behavior makes sense anymore.

"Don't judge," she says as she unlocks the doors.

"I wasn't judging."

"You're worse than that couple back there. I can feel the judgment rolling off of you," she says bitterly. "Not everyone can afford to speed around in a Porsche."

"Trust me," I say. "I know."

All too well.

She heads for the driver's side as I head for the passenger's side and we grunt as the handcuffs pull tight against our wrists as we move in opposite directions.

She sighs in frustration. "Okay. Let's not be dumb about this. Why don't you get in on the driver's side and climb over to the passenger seat. Then I can get in behind you and drive."

Heading to the driver's door, I duck inside the car and awkwardly crawl over the center console, my elbows and knees knocking into the dashboard.

"Ow."

"Watch it."

"I can't fit—"

"Ugh. Quit yanking my wrist."

"Quit yanking *my* wrist."

Her car is a disaster. Books. Socks. Bottles of hair care products. There's crap everywhere. I carefully wade through the minefield of girl mess until I reach the other side. Then, folding my body up like an accordion, I finally manage to squeeze down into the passenger seat.

Kayla climbs in after me and says, "Real smooth."

I flex my jaw. "I'm six feet tall and your car is the size of a marshmallow. The fact that I fit inside it at all is a miracle, let alone defeating the center console obstacle course you have set up here. What is this, a water bottle?" I hold up a giant plastic thermos. "It's the size of a sink." I point to the many other items she has crammed into the console cup holders draped over the seats. Sunglasses. A nursing uniform. A pair of sandals. A diner name tag. "What's happening here?" I say. "Are you undercover? Suffering from multiple identities?"

She points at me. "Lay off my mess. I just drove eighteen hundred miles cross-country and didn't plan to have any passengers. If you have a problem with the contents of my 'marshmallow' car then we can always crawl into your pretentious little Porsche." She arches an eyebrow. "What's it going to be, cowboy?"

"Cowboy?" I pull back. "Well that just makes no sense at all. It's not like I was yee-hawing or tipping my hat at you."

She moves to exit the car. "Pretentious Porsche it is."

"Okay, okay." I hold up my hands, yanking her attached wrist up with mine. "I'm sorry. Your messy car is perfectly fine. I happen to be a big fan of..." I look around at the clutter. "Granola bar wrappers and packing tape." Her eyes narrow and I flash her a broad smile. "I'm kidding. Now would you please just drive?" She doesn't move so I lift our cuffs and merrily say, "The sooner we get the inheritance the sooner you'll be rid of me."

She starts the car.

I hold my wrist by the steering wheel as Kayla uses both hands to back out of the parking spot. She shifts into gear and pulls out onto the main road before lowering her cuffed wrist to the center console and driving with one hand. I place my attached wrist beside hers as we drive in silence. Her hand looks small and delicate next to mine.

"So..." I say, feeling the need to make conversation and break the tension from the tangible annoyance she feels toward me. "It was a beautiful funeral."

She inhales. "I guess."

"I was kind of surprised to see you there."

She keeps her eyes on the road. "Why? He was my father."

I shrug. "Yeah, but you didn't bother to visit him when he was sick, as far as I know, so I just figured you wouldn't bother with the funeral either."

She cuts her eyes to mine and something flashes in their blue depths. Something vulnerable and hurt. "I didn't *bother to visit* because my father didn't bother to tell me he was sick." Just as quickly as it appeared, the spark of emotion melts into bitterness and she glares back at the road.

I furrow my brow. "Really?"

"Really," she says sharply. A beat passes. "My own father didn't care enough about me to let me know that he was dying. And as far as the funeral is concerned, I came because I needed closure." Her voice wavers with emotion and she clears her throat. "I was surprised to see you at the funeral—alone. From the stories I heard growing up, I assumed Daren Ackwood always traveled with a flock of large-breasted groupies."

I grin at the superiority in her tone. "Are you jealous you were never in my flock?"

She gives me a sugar-sweet smile. "I pity all the brainless hens who were."

I let out a small laugh. "Sure you do." My smile fades. "But with the funeral...I didn't exactly feel like company. So no hens for me."

She glances at me and I look away, my chest tightening as I stare out the window. Turner and I didn't grow close until after he and Kayla were estranged, so there's no way she'd understand how important he was to me. Not that I'd try to explain it to her. I doubt any explanation I gave would do justice to my relationship with him anyway.

I wouldn't know where to begin. His importance in my life grew so slowly, so quietly, that pinpointing the exact moment he became a crucial part of who I am is impossible. My first memory with James Turner was when I was eleven and I tagged along when he and my dad were golfing together. Turner accidentally hit a ball into a tree and asked me to go get it because, and I quote, he was "an old man." I teased him for that and addressed him as Old Man Turner for the rest of the day. The name sort of stuck and I continued to call him Old Man Turner as I got older, even though he was always very youthful and energetic. I think he liked the nickname because it made him feel special. And he was.

He was like a father to me—a good one, which is why I hold so much resentment for Kayla turning her back on him.

"Can I ask you something?" I scratch my jaw as we drive along. "What happened with you and your dad? Why did you stop talking to him?"

She furrows her brow. "I didn't stop talking to him. He stopped participating in my life."

I let the silence hang between us and wait.

Marcella once told me that the best place to have a conversation with someone is in a car or in the dark. Because when no one is required to make eye contact, people feel safer and are, therefore, more honest.

I never gave much thought to Marcella's claim. Until now.

"He was supposed to come out to Chicago for my sixteenth birthday," Kayla continues, spilling her story. "I was ecstatic and couldn't wait to see him. But he didn't come," she says simply. "He didn't call or write to tell me he wasn't coming. He just didn't show up. There I was, waiting by the door in my yellow birthday dress, and he was back here in Arizona not giving a damn about me. I cried for days."

I open my mouth to speak but can't find anything to say. It's hard to believe James Turner would miss his only daughter's sixteenth birthday. Especially since he remembered mine and gave me a present—and not just any present; an old pocket watch that had belonged to his grandfather. A family heirloom.

This is valuable to me, Turner had said, handing it to me. *Be careful with it.*

It looked expensive with a bronze chain and a turquoise centerpiece, and the face smoothed over with age.

I shook my head at him. *I can't take that. I don't deserve such a gift. And besides, it belongs to your family.*

He locked eyes with me and waited until he had my full attention. Then he smiled. *Gifts are not things that you earn or deserve. They are a way for the giver to show their appreciation for you. And Daren*—his eyes glimmered—*you are a part of my family.*

His words held more weight than any others I'd ever heard but I was too young and foolish to come up with any reply other than *Thanks.*

I took the watch and carried it in my pocket all the time, showing it off to my friends at every opportunity. I had a lot of things that money could buy but Turner's watch was more important than anything I owned. It was a gift from the only man in my life who gave a damn about me, which made it priceless.

But a few months into my junior year of high school, I accidentally dropped it. I watched with horror as the antique watch plummeted to the ground and shattered into pieces. It was the only thing of value I was ever entrusted with and I had been careless with it. The pocket watch never worked again and I felt so ashamed.

I had broken something that was precious to James Turner.

I never had the balls to tell him about the watch, though, fearing the disapproval I'd surely find waiting in his eyes. But I kept it, broken pieces and all, because it was the greatest birthday gift I'd ever received. I still carry it in my pocket to this day.

I glance across the car at Kayla. I can't believe that the same man who entrusted me with his family heirloom would abandon his daughter on her birthday.

"There must have been some kind of misunderstanding," I say. "I'm sure your dad wanted to be there for your birthday."

She sets her jaw. "Oh yeah? Then maybe you can explain why, after my birthday, it just got worse. He never called—or returned my calls. He never answered my e-mails," she continues, no longer talking to me but sort of ranting at the windshield as she drives. "I mean, he stopped sending me birthday cards, for God's sake. The smallest of gestures and he couldn't be bothered. Then he cut my mom and I off, so we had no money. But the worst part was that he no longer wanted me to come stay with him over the summer. He didn't want me around." Her voice cracks. "It was like he was trying to erase me. And in a way, I guess he did."

I watch the pain in her eyes and shake my head. "That... doesn't sound like him."

The pain morphs into icy contempt. "Well neither does stealing a little boy's baseball cards, but hey. Sometimes people suck."

I want to ease the hurt in her voice and assure her that her father wasn't the jerk she thinks he was, but the sharpness of her tone warns me off. She doesn't want comfort. She wants to be angry. So I stay silent.

Turner never really spoke about Kayla. And the few times her name came up, a look of sadness would cross his face before he'd hurriedly change the subject. Back then, I figured it was because Kayla was some kind of tyrant teenager. But now, seeing the heartbreak on Kayla's face, I wonder if maybe there was more to it.

But how could a good man like Turner call me family and neglect his own blood? It doesn't make any sense.

Kayla and I don't speak for the rest of the trip. When we finally turn onto Milly Manor Drive, I sit up and look out the window. I haven't been here for almost a year, but everything looks the same. The same cracks in the sidewalk. The same trees.

Kayla slows down and parks in front of the large estate.

Staring up at the impressive home made of red bricks and trimmed with white, I can understand why the town of Copper Springs takes such great pride in the place. Rich ivy coats the outside of the house, sprawling up to the pitched roof and around the brick chimney. And bright green grass blankets the front yard, crawling up to the wooden white steps of the wraparound porch. The grounds are unkempt and heavily overgrown, an obvious sign that Turner never hired a replacement when I stopped caring for his yard, but even with all the unruly vegetation it's a nice place. And with its location being so close to the town square, I'm sure it will make a great museum—or whatever else Copper Springs might make of it.

"Home sweet home," Kayla mutters dryly.

I glare at her. "God, you're bitter."

Her hardened gaze drops to the steering wheel and becomes soft as snow in an instant. "Not usually," she says quietly. Then she looks back at me with raw honesty in her eyes. "I'm sorry. This whole thing is just . . . hard for me."

"Right. No. I get it," I say, nodding as, once again, my defenses drop to the floor at the vulnerable look in her eyes.

Why the hell does this girl affect me like she does? One minute, I'm pissed at her for hating her father, and the next I want to comfort her and feed her cookies and shit. I'm a nutcase around her.

She turns the car off and we exit the vehicle the same way we got in, but this time I follow her out of the driver's door. I can't help but grin as I watch her butt wag in front of me as she tries to clamber out of the car with a grown man attached to her. She really does have a perfect ass. And the way it's bobbing up and down in front of me is enough to make a man beg.

She catches me eyeing her and glowers. "Pervert."

"You're taking up my whole line of vision." I grin. "What am I supposed to do, close my eyes?"

"Yes," she snaps.

I snort. "Right."

With a huff, she turns and drags us up the front steps of the porch. At the front door, she stops. Her gaze bounces around the doorknob, the mail slot, and the potted plant beside the welcome mat with sentiment and anger warring in her eyes, but she swiftly masks the battle with a look of indifference.

"Do you have a key?" I ask.

"Crap. No." She puts a hand to her forehead. "I didn't even think about the key. I should have asked Eddie back at the office." She curses. "Now we have to drive all the way back."

"No we don't." I walk back down the steps, pulling her along through the side gate. She fumbles after me, trying to keep up with my long strides, and more blonde hair falls loose around her face.

She swats a bug away from her face with a scowl. "Where are we going?"

I lead her to the garden against the back wall, where dozens of white roses grow. "Here."

The red dirt at the base of the plants sticks to my shoes and I smile. When I first started taking care of the rosebushes, I hated the rare red topsoil because it got everywhere. My clothes, my shoes, my skin. But Turner insisted on using it, year after year. I inhale through my nose. Damn, I'm going to miss him.

I crouch—forcing Kayla to bend down a little—and pick up a small boulder at the base of the plants. Then I start digging through the red soil beneath.

Kayla's cuffed hand flops around beside mine as she stares at me like I'm crazy. "Why are you clawing through the dirt?"

"Because..." I pull out a shiny silver key and grin. "I know where the spare key is."

11

KAYLA

*D*aren knows where the spare key is? Come on!

"How did you know that was there?" I say as we stand up.

He dusts off his hands and shrugs. "Your dad told me."

I go to cross my arms, realize I can't with our attached wrists, and settle for propping my free hand on my hip instead. "He just *told* you where the key to his million-dollar estate was buried?"

"Actually, he asked me to find a good place to hide it. So technically, I told *him* where it was buried." He tilts his head with a smile. "Why do you look so angry?"

"I'm not angry." I drop my hip hand and swallow back my jealousy. "I just find it hard to believe that he trusted you so much."

His lips form a tight line. "That's because you don't know him as well as you thought."

"Obviously."

He shakes his head and mutters, "Whatever," as he starts pulling us back through the yard and toward the front door. "Let's just finish this."

I stumble up the porch steps behind him—damn these high heels—and wait at his side as he sticks the silver key into the lock, then swings the door open.

Dust flurries float through the air, lit up by the sunlight spilling in from the doorway as we step inside.

The house smells the same as I remember. Like vanilla pipe tobacco and cherries. It's a smell I associate solely with my father and for some reason my heart squeezes and my eyes begin to burn as I breathe it in. I close my eyes to keep the stinging at bay.

I can picture my father seated in his leather chair in the study, puffing on his old-fashioned Sherlock Holmes pipe while he leans back and reads one of his favorite books. Thin white swirls of smoke would lift out from the pipe and float up in the air until they disappeared into the tall ceiling. When I was seven, I remember giggling as he tried to blow out a perfect smoke ring for me. Being only a part-time pipe smoker, he was impossibly bad at smoke formations, but he tried anyway. The two of us ended up laughing as I sat in his lap on his leather chair with the scent of vanilla smoke teasing my nose.

"So." Daren's voice interrupts the memory and I open my eyes. "Where's this suitcase closet?"

I shake off the nostalgia trying to cling to my skin and straighten my shoulders. "Over here." I walk him through the living room and down the hall to a skinny door on the left. Then I open the closet.

Inside, several trench coats hang below a shelf of hats, and three old umbrellas stand propped up against the wall. And in the back, on the floor beneath the coats, is a blue suitcase.

"Jackpot!" Daren says with a smile.

I give him a disparaging look. "Jackpot? Really?"

His smile grows. "Oh, come on." He rolls his eyes. "Don't act like me saying 'jackpot' is tacky. You know you wanted to say something just as clever. Like 'Eureka!' or 'Tallyho!'" He raises his fist in exaggerated glee with each exclamation.

I try to look annoyed, but a small smile tugs at my lips when he adds "Bingo!" with an especially exuberant expression. What a goofball.

"I knew it." He points at my smile. "You like me." He shows off his dimple and nods. "You think I'm obnoxious but you still like me. Do you want to kiss again?" He leans in and wiggles his eyebrows.

"Oh my God. You're ridiculous." I drop my smile but can't help the warmth that spreads over my cheeks and down my body. Because a tiny part of me does want to kiss him again. It's such a foreign feeling for me, wanting to kiss a guy. Yearning to touch him. And I'm not sure if I like it. It makes me feel out of control, like I can't trust myself.

My eyes sweep over his mouth where his lips, so soft and warm against mine last night, curl into another playful grin, and my heart skips a beat.

Maybe I can't.

"Can we just do this already?" I say.

"What, kiss? Or have sex?" He looks around. "The floor is kind of dirty but if you insist…" He reaches for the button of his pants.

"Ugh. I'm done talking to you." I kneel on the floor.

His smile widens. "Oh so now you want to give me a blow job? Make up your mind, woman."

"Shut up." I aggressively yank his wrist down so he's forced to kneel beside me, where we're within reaching distance of the suitcase. "I'm down here for the suitcase, you idiot." I can't help but glance at his jeans, remembering how large he felt in my hand last night.

"Here, I'll get it." He drops the teasing attitude and reaches for the suitcase. As he stretches out his arms, his biceps flex and I trail my gaze up his shoulders and over his profile.

He's built like a model. Lean and cut, with a chiseled jaw and long eyelashes. His mouth is large and masculine but his lips look soft and he smells good. Again. Like citrus.

He slides the suitcase from the closet and positions it by our knees. It's an old piece of luggage, with a hard outer casing and a thick plastic handle. Tipping the suitcase up at an angle, he pops open the latches. The lid sticks a little at first, but after working at the seam for a moment, he's able to coax it open with his long fingers.

Inside are three sealed envelopes. One with Daren's name on it, one with my name on it, and one that reads TO YOU BOTH.

Daren and I lift out the envelopes labeled with our names and take turns opening them. We find a note from my father inside each one.

Daren reads his note privately while I silently read my own.

My sweet Kayla,

As you read this, you are most likely handcuffed to Daren Ackwood. Despite what you may think or assume, Daren is a good soul. If he were anything less, I would not have asked you to lock yourself to his side. Which brings me to why you are here at all. My death.

I love you more than you will ever know, and more than I could ever explain. These last few years being apart from you have been torturous for me. There is so much I've wanted to explain. So much I've wanted to make up for. I realize my apparent absence from your life has made you skeptical of me, and probably of love as well, but please know that it is not what it seems. My love for you is and will forever be very real. The last five years without you have been pure heartache for me, and I hope you will choose to remember me as the father from the years before, not the one who's been away from you recently.

Since I didn't have a chance to say good-bye to you before passing, I've written my thoughts on these notes. But more than anything else, I want you to know that you have always been the greatest part of my life—always—and I am amazed and proud of who you are and who you will become.

I encourage you to share this note with Daren. He is one of my favorite people and I trust him beyond measure, as I hope you will, someday, as well.

I love you.

I blink at the note. Then blink again. Nothing in it makes sense. The last few years were pure heartache for *him*? Ha. And Daren is a good soul that he trusts beyond measure? Double ha.

There's no way in hell I'm showing Daren this note. The last thing that guy needs is more air to fill his big head.

At the bottom right-hand corner of the paper is the word "Through" written in black marker and the number fourteen written below that. Just that one word and number. Nothing else. I turn the paper over but it's blank on the other side. Through fourteen? Weird.

Folding up the note, I quickly tuck it into my purse and glance at Daren. He's staring at his own letter, looking perplexed.

I nod at his note. "What does it say?"

He blinks up at me then swiftly shoves the note into his pocket. "Nothing. Let's see what's in this last envelope." Reaching into the suitcase, he grabs the remaining envelope, opens it, and pulls out yet another note from within.

As we lean in to read it, our shoulders brush. His body heat wraps around me in the small hallway, tucking me into his citrus scent and I'm momentarily distracted.

No.

I shake myself.

I *will not* like him—or his awesome-smelling soap, or shampoo, or whatever that heavenly orange scent is coming from.

Getting a grip, I focus on the words scrawled out in my father's handwriting.

Daren and Kayla,

You've agreed to be handcuffed together! I can't tell you how pleased I am by this. I realize handcuffs are uncomfortable and quite distasteful, but I wanted you to take this inheritance seriously. More importantly, I wanted you to work as a team. Because life is a series of working with others to achieve mutual goals. And that is lesson number one. The money I've left you is elsewhere. Use the enclosed key to open #23 at the train station.

Daren shakes the envelope, and an oddly shaped golden key falls into his palm. It's large and heavy, with a square top and thick teeth. I've never seen anything like it.

He holds it up with a small smile. "Well now we know where the money is."

"I guess we do." I inhale deeply, my spirits lifting to crazy levels of giddiness as I stare at the key. This is really happening. My life is really going to change.

"You okay?" Daren cocks his head.

"Yeah." A slow smile stretches across my face. "I'm good. Just excited, that's all."

"Then what are we waiting for? Let's go find us an inheritance!" He tucks the key in his pocket and moves to stand.

I follow suit but as I try to pull myself up, my heels wobble and I lose my balance and fall back. My chained wrist pulls Daren down with me but where he kind of slides to the floor on his knees, I end up landing square on my butt with my legs sprawled beneath me and my skirt hiked up to the palest skin of my thighs.

Daren looks at me with a suppressed laugh and throws my words from earlier back at me. "Real smooth."

"Hey," I snap. "It's really hard to get off the floor when you're handcuffed and wearing heels and a skirt."

He stands. "Oh I have no doubt. That's why I opted for my casual shoes today." He mocks, "They don't do much for my calves but they're quite comfortable, and they go with *everything*."

"I hate you."

"No, you don't." His eyes skim my naked thighs and his smile shifts from amusement to appreciation.

I yank the tight material of my skirt down as far as possible and he clears his throat and moves his eyes back to mine.

"Here." He has his genuine smile back on. "Give me your hand." He reaches for my left hand as he threads his fingers through my cuffed right one. Then he starts to pull me up.

It's a practical gesture but it feels intimate. His fingers, laced between mine, are big and warm as they fold over the back of my hand and lift me up.

I manage to stand without flashing him or toppling over. "Thanks."

Once we're on our feet, we quickly untangle our hands. As his fingers slide out of mine and his skin rubs against my skin, something low in my belly twitches. My eyes drift up the sinewy muscles of his forearm and bicep, across the thick muscles of his chest, and down his lean stomach to his hips where he's brushing dust off his jeans. For a brief second, I wonder what those hips would look like without jeans on. Then I mentally slap myself.

This is Daren Ackwood, for God's sake. Mr. Sleeps-With-The-Whole-Town. I will *not* get sucked into his funnel of good looks and sexy hips.

I glance him over again and frown. Goddamn Daren and his bandit kissing, getting my body all worked up and bringing on unsolicited belly twitches. I really need to get away from his fingers and hips, STAT.

"Let's hurry up and finish this." I start tugging him back toward the front door.

"Yes, ma'am. But first?" He stops walking and the handcuffs snap me back. "I'm going to find my baseball cards."

"What?"

"You heard me." He moves in front of me and marches down the hallway, whipping me behind him.

"No way," I say as I'm reluctantly towed behind him by our steel restraints. "We don't have time for you to play card detective."

He doesn't look back. "Sure we do."

"What is *with* you and these baseball cards?" I say. "You'd think you were twelve by the way you're so emotionally attached to these things."

He looks over his shoulder and grins. "I have attachment issues, remember?"

I roll my eyes.

"Seriously, though. They were a Christmas present I got when I was thirteen. All valuable collector's cards." He takes us back into the living room where he opens the cabinet in the corner and starts going through the shelves. "I barely had a chance to enjoy them before your dad jacked them."

I nod. "Uh-huh. And why, exactly, did he 'jack' them?" I make air quotes and Daren frowns at my fingers.

"He *jacked* them," he says, "because he thought I was too spoiled to appreciate them."

I snort. "You probably were."

"I was." He nods. "At the time."

I raise a brow. "You admit you were spoiled?"

"Oh yeah. I was totally spoiled." He shrugs. "Growing up, my parents bought me anything I wanted whenever I wanted, as long as it kept me out of their way. I had all the money and freedom in the world. And I took it all for granted."

He looks back at the shelf. "I thought having money was the most important thing in life. Money got me video games, popularity, friends…girls. But as I got older, my home life started to crumble, and I realized that there was a huge difference between the kind of rich that my father was and the kind of rich that, uh…that your father was." He glances at me. "Your dad had an appreciation and humility—for life, for money, for *people*—that my father never had. And when I was young I was just like my father. Selfish. Ungrateful…So yeah." He looks back at the shelf and resumes his search. "I was a spoiled brat and your dad knew it."

I watch him for a moment, wondering what he meant by his home life starting to crumble. I know about his mom running off with the reverend, Brad Keeton, and how his dad started drinking after that, but the way he said *as I got older* makes me think there's something more to the story.

I muse, "Sounds like you deserved a lesson in appreciation."

He tosses me a crooked smile. "I may have been a spoiled brat but that's still no excuse for a grown man to steal a kid's baseball cards. And frankly, I think Turner's lesson on gratitude would have been better spent on you."

I blanch. "Excuse me?" His insult stings, but the casual tone with which he said it hurts more. "I'm not spoiled. I—I'm the *opposite* of spoiled."

"Sure you are." He moves from the cabinet to the entertainment center, dragging me along as he looks inside, under, and behind every nook and cranny. "Didn't your father set up a trust fund for you?"

"What? *No.*" I blink. "No. Why would you think that?"

He lifts a shoulder. "That's what I heard."

I scowl. "From who?"

"It's a small town. From everyone."

"Well I don't know what people told you, but I do not have, nor have I *ever* had, a trust fund. That's ridiculous."

He eyes me skeptically before moving to the sofa. "Maybe I'm wrong then."

Everywhere he goes, I have to go but all I want to do is storm off. Damn these handcuffs!

"Yes. You are wrong. You know nothing about me," I say as he crouches down to look under the couch. "And I *seriously* doubt my father hid your baseball cards under the couch." I look down at him with an exasperated breath.

He frowns at the nothingness beneath the sofa. "Where would he have put them?"

I pinch my lips together. "He probably has a secret vault where he stashes all the toys he takes from little kids and the candy he steals from babies."

"Laugh all you want," he says, "but if he stole something from you when *you* were thirteen, you'd be just as mad as me—" He sits up and his words catch in his throat when he comes face-to-face with my skirt.

With him still crouched on the floor, and me standing beside him, my bare lower thighs are right at his eye level. An exhale leaves his mouth and his hot breath grazes the inside of my legs, floating up my skirt and between the bare skin of my thighs. I suddenly forget about his insult and my anger as my head clouds with desire.

He looks up at me from under those long dark eyelashes of his and my entire body flushes. My throat goes dry. My nipples harden. I want to swallow but my brain doesn't seem to be working as I stare down at his large pupils boring into me.

He rocks back on his heels and my leashed wrist swings back with his, our arms moving in sync. I watch his Adam's apple bob with a thick swallow as his eyelids grow heavy and his gaze returns to my legs. I grasp for something to do or say, anything to distract me from the fact that there is a hot beautiful mouth breathing against my thighs. And not just any mouth. Daren's mouth.

I've got nothing.

Nothing but white-hot arousal and naughty, naughty thoughts.

Jolting me out of my stupor, Daren clears his throat and leans away. I'm finally able to swallow as I watch him slowly stand, and time crawls along in the silence.

He swallows as well. "Will you please just help me find my baseball cards?"

Baseball cards...baseball cards...Oh, right. That's what we were talking about.

"Why don't we just forget about your search and go to the train station and get the money instead?" I suggest, my voice somewhat raspy. "Then you can buy all the baseball cards in the world."

He stands and brushes off his hands. "No way. Those cards aren't replaceable. They...they're important to me. Please?" His eyes turn pleading. "Will you please help me look?"

I don't know why he's so obsessed with something he's managed to live without for ten years, but I don't have the heart to continue arguing with him. And honestly, if he keeps pouting with those puppy dog eyes of his there's no telling what I'll do to please him.

"Fine," I say, totally caving.

God. What *is* it with this guy?

"Awesome." He smiles. "The baseball cards are in a green box about this big"—he holds his hands out in a shape of a square—"with a red ribbon around the lid."

I nod and we begin our search. Though it's not a very efficient search, since we're, you know, in *handcuffs* and can't split up to cover more ground. And our movements are awkward as hell as we move from room to room, each of us trying to go in different directions. We're not smooth at all, especially once we reach the kitchen.

As we walk past the cabinets, the handcuffs snag on a drawer and cause Daren to lose his balance. He knocks into me, I knock into the table, the table knocks into the wall, and then a picture falls off the wall as I topple toward the floor. Daren quickly grabs my waist and pulls me upright but the framed photo crashes to the tile and shards of glass skid everywhere.

Not. Smooth. At all.

"Wow," I say slowly. "That was like something out of a cartoon." I jingle our handcuffs. "We're not very coordinated with these things, are we?"

"Not in the slightest," he says with a quiet chuckle. "Are you okay?"

"Yeah, I'm fine." I realize he's still holding me and the tips of his fingers suddenly feel hot on my hips.

I casually slip out of his grasp and try not to make eye contact with him. Instead I look at the kitchen floor. Shattered glass splinters out from the busted picture frame, leaving a photograph bent and buried beneath the rubble. I carefully retrieve the fallen picture from the glass.

It's a photo of me with my parents at one of our family picnics. My mom is dressed in all white with an orange scarf in her hair and pink lipstick, and I'm in a polka-dot dress with a pair of Mary Janes, holding up a white rose.

White roses were a common item my dad would ask us to find on our mother-daughter scavenger hunts because they grow wild all over Copper Springs. Mom would always pick them so I wouldn't prick my finger on the thorns. Then we'd bring them back to my dad and he would cut off every thorn before handing them back to me to keep. I inwardly smile. I loved those scavenger hunts. They always started the same way: with the first clue written on a small piece of paper tucked into an envelope, just like the ones in the blue suitcase...

My heart skips a beat.

No. No way.

My father wouldn't stage a scavenger hunt to collect the inheritance money...would he?

No. That would be preposterous.

Shaking my head with a sigh of relief, I gaze down at the photograph and run a finger over my parents' happy faces. I've seen this picture a thousand times, but now that the happy people in the photograph are gone, it means so much more to me. I glance at the wall where a square of paint, slightly darker than the rest of the wall, shows where the frame used to be. I'm surprised my dad kept this picture hanging up all these years.

When my mom left, she broke my dad's heart. He was careful never to bad-mouth her when I'd come stay with him during the summer, but I wasn't blind. I could see the hurt on his face whenever he'd mention her.

My mom was no angel. She was smart and friendly, but she was terribly selfish. She said my dad was too good for her and that's why she left him. That he treated her like a queen and it put too much pressure on her. While that was probably all true, I think the real reason my mom left is because she didn't want to be tied down to a nice guy in a small town. She wanted drama in a big city.

She got it.

"Polka dots," Daren says, leaning over my shoulder as he looks at the picture. "Nice."

I hurriedly tuck the photo into my purse. "I don't think your baseball cards are in the kitchen. Let's move along."

We spend the next hour riffling through my dad's house and all his things. It's a weird feeling, being back in the place I grew up. Nothing much has changed. The furniture is still in the same place. The mail is still piled by the back door. And pictures of my mother and me still hang on the walls. Like we still live here. Like he never cut us out of his life.

I'm not sure if this breaks my heart or infuriates me. Either way, it's an enormous contradiction to his behavior these last few years.

After we've ransacked all the bedrooms, Daren and I move down the hallway and into the study. The study was my father's special place to work and think. It was his favorite room in the house and mine too.

It looks exactly the way I remember. The walls are still lined with books and the large globe I used to spin around and around as a child still stands in the corner, now coated with dust.

And of course the study still smells like smoky vanilla.

I try to ignore the burning behind my eyes as I sift through my father's personal belongings, but it's almost too much. The pictures. The vanilla. The lingering presence of all my happy memories.

Daren opens the top drawer of my dad's old desk and freezes. Then he looks at me. "Liar, liar, pants on fire."

I wrinkle my brow. "What?"

He pulls a stack of papers from the drawer and drops them on the desk with a *thwack*. Dust flurries go flying from beneath what looks like a collection of bank statements.

He clucks his tongue admonishingly. "Kayla Turner, you little fibber."

"What are you talking about?"

He points to the top of the page where it reads KAYLA TURNER TRUST FUND in bold letters and my jaw drops.

"What?" I say in a near whisper as I scan the first few pages in disbelief. It does indeed look like I have a trust fund set up in my name. Or *had* a trust fund.

The statements show a series of withdrawals over the past few years, some large, some small, with the last one being two years ago. The trust fund now has a balance of zero.

Beside me, Daren lets out a quiet whistle. "Wow. You burned through that pretty fast."

I blink rapidly, staring at the statements in complete and utter confusion. "I didn't...I can't..."

"In the future," he says, scratching his cheek, "if someone asks you if you have a trust fund, the correct answer is yes. Even though yours has no more money in it. Fibber."

I look at him. "This isn't right."

"Don't get me wrong. You're a *hot* fibber." He grins. "But you're a fibber nonetheless. Not that I blame you. My entire identity is built on fibs—"

"No. You don't understand. I've never seen this before in my life." I hold up the papers. "I never had a trust fund. Hell, I barely had a bank account. My dad must have set this up and used it himself."

He squints at one of the pages in my hand. "Then why were all the withdrawals made in Chicago?"

He points and I follow his finger to the location details for each withdrawal. Every single one reads CHICAGO, ILLINOIS.

"What? This makes no sense." I shake my head.

He studies me. "You really didn't know about this trust fund?"

"No! My father never mentioned it to me. Not once."

He frowns. "Then who made all the withdrawals? Your mom?"

"I guess..."

It's the only logical answer, but even as I stand here staring at the proof I can't believe it. I don't *want* to believe it. My dad set up a trust fund for me, and my mother not only knew about it, but cleaned it out?

My blood begins to boil. No. There has to be a better explanation.

I gather up all the papers, even the ones left in the drawer, and wrap them in an empty file folder I find on the desk.

"I'll sort through all this later," I say more to myself than to Daren as I stick the folder in my purse.

He eyes me. "Are you sure?"

I nod and take a deep breath. "Let's get back to looking for your baseball cards."

Daren runs a hand through his hair. "I don't think they're here. We've looked pretty much everywhere." He closes the empty desk drawer. "Let's just go to the train station."

Suddenly eager to leave Milly Manor and all my unnerving questions behind, I heartily agree. "Yeah. Okay."

As we start to leave, Daren's phone rings. He wriggles it out of his pocket, glances at the screen, and answers, "Hey, Ellen." He listens. "Sure. I can probably run some supplies out to the inn tomorrow. What do you need?"

As he continues his conversation I run my eyes over the desk again, looking for any papers I might have missed regarding the trust fund. My eyes stop on a framed photo at the edge of the desk and I gingerly pick it up.

There are pictures all over Milly Manor, but there is only one in the study. And it's a picture of Dad and me at the lake when I was nine years old.

We're each holding a fishing pole and I have on the biggest grin. We didn't actually fish that day because I thought it was mean to hurt the fishes but he went along with my tender heart and we "pretend fished" all afternoon and ate my favorite sandwiches: peanut butter and jelly with bananas.

In the picture, I'm wearing the heart-shaped locket he gave me for my birthday that year. I lost the necklace years ago, but it was always one of my favorites. My dad used to write me notes on tiny scraps of paper that said things like "I love you," or "Have a good day," or "I love being your daddy!" and I'd store them in that locket for safekeeping.

Then when I returned to Chicago, I wore that necklace every day knowing my father's teeny notes were hidden in the locket. It was like having him with me everywhere I went, tucked inside the heart around my neck.

My eyes start to burn again. He wasn't always a bad father. In fact, he was the best. Which is probably why it hurt so much when he stopped wanting to see me. And why it still hurts now.

"It seems like your dad really loved you." Daren's voice startles me and I blink away the emotion in my eyes. I didn't realize he was off the phone. "He kept all your pictures up," he continues, nodding at the photo in my hands. "You two look happy there."

We do look happy—like a real family. A sinking feeling overwhelms me. I don't have a family anymore. I barely had one to begin with, but now...

"That was a long time ago." I put the picture back on the desk. "Let's go." Without a word, I lead Daren by the wrist out of the house I grew up in.

12

DAREN

*W*ell that didn't go at all like I'd expected—and not just because I didn't recover my box of baseball cards. Watching Kayla's face filter through all those emotions as we moved through the house was rough.

She acts bitter and angry toward her father, but her facial expressions as we walked from room to room were anything but. She's hurt, obviously, but she also seems sad. And lonely. Two sentiments I'm far too familiar with.

And the fact that she didn't know about her own trust fund threw another wrench into my pile of Kayla Turner preconceptions. James wasn't lying about setting up a trust fund for his daughter. But Kayla wasn't lying about not having one either. Which most likely means Gia was the fibber in the family. Yikes.

I follow Kayla to the car and we climb inside, awkwardly fumbling before finally plopping in our seats.

As she puts her seat belt on and drives away, the wisps of blonde escaping her hair tie drift away from her face revealing her flushed cheeks and blue eyes, lost in thought.

Her lips are coated with some kind of clear gloss, shining against the pale skin of her chin and throat as she bites down on the bottom one. I stare at her bitten lip, now slightly swollen, and the sight of her thighs, right next to my mouth when I sat up from searching under the couch, flashes in my mind.

It was all I could do to not flick my tongue out and run it up the soft skin of her legs. And from the way her eyelids had grown heavy as she stared down at me, she probably would have let me. Hell, she probably would have grabbed my head and directed my tongue where to go.

Growing hard, I shift in my seat and try to get myself under control.

Dammit. I shouldn't have kissed her last night. If I hadn't pressed my mouth to hers and felt her tongue roll over mine, then I'd surely have more control over myself today. But I couldn't help myself. Something about Kayla drew me in like a siren song, enchanting and impossible to resist. And much like the Sirens' prey, I'm now surely doomed. Because now I've tasted Kayla and all I want is more.

Things would have been fine if she hadn't sunk into the kiss with such craving. If she had kissed me back with your typical strangers-kissing-in-a-parking-lot desire—you know, part curiosity, part greed—I could have been satisfied with just one kiss.

But Kayla kissed me back with the passion of a long-lost lover. Desperation on her lips. Sounds of desire escaping her throat. She kissed me back like I was something she needed. I've never felt needed like that before.

We come to a stoplight and the engine idles loudly. The light turns green and the engine groans before we're on the move again. Looking out the windshield, I stare at the rusted hood of her little green car and frown.

Just another unexpected piece of the Kayla Turner puzzle.

Stitched up clothes, empty trust fund, a run-down vehicle . . .

Is it possible I was wrong about Kayla? Was she telling the truth about being broke?

"So," Kayla says into the silence. "Instead of leaving our inheritance in a bank account, my father stashed it in a train station locker. Super safe, Dad."

I quietly laugh. "Yeah, it's not the most secure place in the world. But I guess it makes sense. He really liked the train station."

"That's right," she says slowly, nodding. A hint of a smile tugs at her lips. "He used to talk about how the train brought Copper Springs to life. He'd say"—she lowers her voice—"*Before the train got here, this town was just a plot of land. But the train brought people—*"

"*And the people brought heart,*" I finish.

She smiles with a nod then glances at me curiously. "So what's the deal with you and my dad? You guys were close?"

I inhale deeply and shrug. "My dad wasn't the greatest. He was a decent businessman but he wasn't a great father. Your dad, though, he was all right." I look at her. "Did you know they used to be good friends, our dads?"

She furrows her brow and shakes her head.

"They were golf buddies," I say. "I used to caddie for my dad sometimes. Not because I cared about the game but because I liked being around my dad. It made me feel like I was important to him, you know? So Turner—your dad—got to know me when I was a kid on the golf course. My relationship with Pop was strained and Turner saw that.

"Your dad offered me a job taking care of his lawn when I was young and at first I was like *hell no*. I was a rich kid. I didn't need to work. But my dad would constantly say, 'People without money or power are useless to me,' and being a jobless, powerless kid, I was one of those people. So I thought if I could make my own money then maybe my dad wouldn't think of me as useless anymore—"

"What?" she squawks, holding up a hand. "No offense, but your dad sounds like a dick."

I nod. "Oh, he is. Trust me."

She waves me on. "Please continue."

I swallow. "I didn't want my dad to think I was useless so I took Turner up on his offer and started mowing the lawn. Over the years, my relationship with Pop just got worse. He and my mom went through some shit that you might not have heard—"

"You mean the Reverend Keeton thing?"

I cock my head. "How do you know about that?"

She shrugs. "I was good friends with Lana Morris growing up and she always filled me in on the latest Copper Springs gossip."

"How nice of her to keep you in the loop," I say dryly. "But yeah. My mom left my dad and married Amber's dad, and the town brought out their pitchforks for both our families. All hell broke loose and my mom and Brad got divorced. Then my mom moved to Boston and my dad sort of spiraled down a dark path of booze. So while my own parents were pretty self-involved and caught up in all their crazy drama, your dad was there for me." I laugh softly. "Sometimes I hated it because he was always giving me advice and trying to keep me in line. But most of the time, it just felt good to be noticed, you know?" I gaze out at the road. "Then last year, someone I really cared about—a girl named Charity—died in a car accident. For a while, I blamed myself for her death. I became self-destructive and didn't really want to live anymore. I was on the edge. But two people helped pull me back; made me believe there was something important inside of me. One of them was my boss, Ellen." I pause. "And the other was your dad."

Charity's death—among other unfortunate events last year—really ripped me up. Afterward, Turner could see it in my eyes: the recklessness; the blatant disregard I had for myself. So he gave me more work. He wanted more things planted in the garden and more trees pruned around the yard. And while I was busy tending to all that, he was at my side, planting new vegetables and trimming the hedges right along with me. Most days, we worked in comfortable silence. But every now and then, Turner would ask about my life then comment on how well I was "handling" everything. I started to live for those moments—the brief exchanges between us where he would praise me and I wouldn't feel like a total failure. And then one day, I was better. Not healed completely, but better. Because of Turner.

"So yeah," I say, clearing my throat. "He and I used to be pretty close."

As I watch the road fly by, my chest starts to hurt. I should have kept in contact with Turner instead of wallowing in my own problems this past year. I should have tried harder to show him how important he was to me.

Kayla eyes me in silence, her free hand wrapping around the steering wheel tightly. Then she quietly and sincerely says, "Well I'm glad he was there for someone," and returns her gaze to the road.

I stare out the window. Me too.

13

KAYLA

*A*re you sure this place is still open?" I shade my eyes and squint up at the rusted sign that reads COPPER SPRINGS TRAIN STATION hanging above the old building. Cobwebs litter the corners of the sign and dust covers the windows of the station. "It looks deserted."

Daren exhales. "It shut down a few years ago. But the people who have lockers here still use them sometimes. I guess your dad was one of those people." He looks at me with a gleam in his eye. "You ready to claim an inheritance?"

A spark of glee shoots through me as I grin back. "Oh I'm ready."

I am ready and excited, but I'm also nervous and filled with adrenaline. Today might be the beginning of a new life for me. Daren's chest rises with a full breath as if he's anxious as well and I wonder if this could be a new beginning for him too. Studying him for a moment, I realize I don't know much about him. Nothing, really. I know about his parents' taboo behavior and his sexual reputation, but I don't know anything real. Anything that matters. And a part of me wishes I did.

The double doors at the front of the train station screech as we open them and step inside. Dim light filters in through the clouded windows and gives the large, musty lobby a weird yellow glow.

"The lockers are over here," Daren says, heading right.

"I'm guessing you've been here before?"

He nods. "Growing up, we had a housekeeper named Marcella who was like a second mother to me. Before the station closed, Marcella would come here to pick up her family members when they'd visit, and sometimes she'd bring me along. I loved Marcella's family." He smiles. "They were all loud and loving and always excited to see one another. They were even excited to see me, which rocked my world. Marcella treated me like a son and her family did the same."

"Do you still talk to her?" I ask.

His eyes shadow over. "No. She passed away a few years ago."

I quietly say, "I'm sorry."

I do the math in my head, tallying up the lost loved ones in Daren's life. My father. The Charity girl. And Marcella. Empathy swims through my veins as I scan his face. He knows I'm watching him, but he continues to stare straight ahead.

"Here they are," he says, pointing ahead.

On the side of the station stands a set of lockers. All of them old. All of them looking as if they haven't been touched in a decade. They probably haven't.

Our footsteps echo as we walk to the lockers.

"Twenty-three…" Daren says, perusing the numbers.

My eyes drift back and forth across the rusty lockers. "There." I point to one on the left side. We step up to it and I pull the golden key from my purse and hold it up. It looks too large to fit in the small keyhole.

Daren frowns. "That's weird."

I try to insert the heavy key anyway, but it's much too big. "Did we get the wrong locker number?" I pull the suitcase note from my purse and reread it.

"Nope," Daren says, reading it over my shoulder. "It says twenty-three."

I look around. "Is there another set of lockers in the station?"

"Maybe." He glances around. "But that key looks too large to fit in any locker."

I examine the key. "You're right." I blow out my cheeks and look up. "Let's walk around and see if there are any other cabinets or storage areas."

Our cuffs clank together as we set off to search the station. It's completely deserted, but not in a spooky way. The high ceilings are framed with beautiful wood molding and dramatic floor-to-ceiling windows cover nearly every wall. Long wooden pews stripe the floor and a row of private phone booths line the side wall. I bet this was a vibrant place when the train was running. I can imagine dozens of people bustling about, reading the newspaper or calling a loved one while they wait for their train.

"I've never been on an old-fashioned train before," I muse out loud as we walk past an old ticket counter.

"Neither have I," he says, looking around. "I've never even been on an airplane."

"Never?"

"Nope. The farthest I've been from Copper Springs is fifty miles outside of town at Willow Inn, where I work."

"No way. Surely you've been farther away on vacations or something."

He shakes his head. "My parents used to travel a lot but they never took me with them. 'It's not a vacation if your kid is there,' my mom would say."

I gape at him. "That's horrible."

He shrugs. "She was just being honest. My mom was never

crazy about being a parent—neither was my dad. Honestly, I probably wouldn't have liked vacationing with them, anyway." He says this with a smile but hurt flashes in his eyes.

I stare at him, half-confused and half-sad. His parents sound awful. In fact, his entire childhood sounds somewhat depressing and a little lonely.

He acts so cool and confident but a few times now I've noticed a ding in the armor of arrogance and playfulness he wears so easily. He's cocky but wounded, charming but lonely, with the sureness of a wealthy man and the desperation of a pauper. I can't figure him out, but one thing is certain.

Daren is not as tough or undamaged as he lets on.

"What?" He smiles at me crookedly. "You're making a weird face."

I shake my head. "I'm just surprised, that's all. I pictured you jetting around the world every summer in a private plane with an entourage of other rich people."

His eyes harden. "I told you. I'm not rich. My family used to be wealthy but we—*I*—don't have money anymore." He looks away, dismissing the topic. "Let's check by the baggage area."

I follow him in silence, wondering how he can claim to be "not rich" when two days ago I saw him driving a Porsche and right at this moment he's wearing an outfit that probably cost more than my car is worth. But I drop the subject, not wanting to argue with him right before finding the inheritance.

It's not an overwhelmingly big station, so we're able to walk through the entire place rather quickly, without success.

"Nothing," Daren says after we make two rounds of the building. "No other lockers or storage units of any kind with the number twenty-three."

I tuck a wayward strand of hair behind my ear. "There has to be something we've overlooked. This is the only train station for miles. Let's check outside on the platform."

We pass through the waiting area to the outside where more dust and cobwebs fill the corners. The platform has no storage areas, and the old railroad tracks are rusty and covered in dead leaves. On the other side of the tracks are several empty crates and a string of out-of-service train cars covered in dirt and frozen in time on the maintenance tracks beyond.

Aside from that, there is nothing.

I rove my eyes over the area. "Maybe we should go back to Milly Manor and check the suitcase again. Maybe we missed some instructions or better directions or something." I bite my lip. Or maybe my father didn't actually leave us any money and this is all just a waste of time.

"Kayla, look." Daren points ahead as his gaze zeroes in on something past the empty crates.

"What?" I follow his eyes to the old abandoned train in the distance. Five boxcars sit side-by-side on the maintenance track, and the very last car is red and stamped with two giant white numbers: a two and a three.

He gives me a wide grin. "Eureka!"

"No," I say, shaking my head. "You don't think..."

"Oh, I think." He nods with bright eyes. "I very much think."

My jaw falls open. "My dad hid money in an old *train* car? What did he do, pack a bunch of bills in a duffle bag and toss it onto a pile of hay? Geez. Did no one ever tell him about safety deposit boxes?"

He laughs. "I don't care where he hid it. I'm just glad we found it."

Hurrying down the platform steps, we cross over the railroad tracks, pass the empty crates, and walk over to the red boxcar on the old maintenance tracks.

The door of the train car reminds me of a garage door, where the lock is at the bottom beneath a wide industrial handle. I pull the big golden key from my purse again and hold it up to the lock.

"Perfect match," Daren says.

I wedge the key inside the hole and, with a few jiggles, the wide door unlocks with a loud *click*. Standing beside each other, we wrap our hands around the large horizontal handle and, using all our strength, pull up the heavy door. The hinges squeak and moan as it rolls up and locks into place. We peer inside and...

Nothing.

Well, not nothing, exactly. But certainly not money.

The boxcar is completely empty except for a single, folded piece of paper.

"What the...?" Daren sighs.

My face falls, speechless.

"What do you suppose it is?" He tips his chin at the piece of paper.

"A check for a million dollars?" I say hopefully.

The paper is in the very back of the train car so the only way to reach it is to climb inside. Which won't be easy since my chest barely reaches the bottom of the car and we can't climb in one at a time because of the handcuffs.

I lift up on my tiptoes. "How do you want to do this?"

Daren scratches his jaw. "Why don't I hoist you inside first then I'll jump in. Come here." He turns me around to face him and I step into the circle of his arms.

The summer sun is now high in the sky, burning down on us.

I stare at his chest where his T-shirt pulls tight against the hard muscles of his pecs, and a trickle of sweat slowly slides down the back of my neck.

The corded muscles of his neck ripple as he turns his head. "Hold on to my wrists. Then I'll lift you up." He places his big hands on my waist.

His thumbs slide under my shirt, grazing the bare skin of my stomach, and a warm zing shoots down my belly.

I look up at him. "Did you do that on purpose?"

"Do what?" His expression is neutral but there's a glimmer in his eye.

"Whatever," I say, eyeing him shrewdly as I wrap my hands around his wrists.

He glides the pads of his thumbs over my tummy again and another, more powerful, zing darts straight down my belly and between my legs as I suck in a breath.

I narrow my gaze at him and his eyes dance with amusement.

"Cut it out," I say.

"Cut what out?" he says.

"You know what." I try to look stern.

"I certainly have no idea what you're talking about." A mischievous grin spreads across his face and I can't stop the smile that starts to play at my own lips.

"Daren…"

His eyes lock on mine and the twitching low in my belly starts up again. Then his gaze drops to my mouth and I absently part my lips.

Hunger lights his eyes as he leans in and whispers, "*Now* do you want to kiss again?" His words flutter over my ear like soft, warm butterflies beating their wings against my sensitive skin and a shiver runs through me.

The answer is *yes*. I do want to kiss him again. It felt so good to have his mouth on mine last night. To feel him up against me. To give in to the wild passion inside me.

When I don't answer, he brushes his thumbs over the naked skin of my stomach again, but this time dips them inside the waistband of my skirt and skims the lacey top of my panties.

I inhale sharply, tightening my fingers around his wrists as my nipples harden and heat builds in my core. I rub my thighs together, trying to alleviate the ache slowly building between my legs, but it's no use. I'm already a tight bundle of need.

How come this beautiful man, who smells like clean citrus, can make me melt with just a simple touch? And how come it's always so difficult for me to snap out of his sexy gaze?

I blink away from Daren's pretty brown eyes and playfully whisper, "No," before shifting back a few inches.

His eyelids, which were heavy with desire just moments ago, open fully as he scans my face and throat.

"Liar," he says with a smile.

I smile back, grateful he doesn't try to convince me otherwise. I'd surely give in if he did. Because Daren *affects* me.

Every other guy on the planet is just that: a guy. But Daren is a force. And I am a feather.

"Ready?" he asks, getting back to business as he moves slightly away from me.

My body protests and disappointment washes over me, but I pull it together and try to look unfazed as I nod and brace my hands against his wrists. "Ready."

Bending his knees, he easily lifts me up and sits me on the box-car's open frame. Then he steps back and hoists himself into the car beside me. He carefully stands up, and offers me a hand to help me to my feet.

My high heels waver on the uneven metal floor of the train car but Daren keeps me upright until I'm standing on my own.

Good God. I'm never wearing high heels again.

We walk to the back of the boxcar to retrieve the paper. I'm still hoping it's a check. Or a savings bond. Or a money order. Daren swiftly picks it up, unfolds it, and both our faces fall. Another note.

Daren mutters a curse and I groan.

"Why couldn't I have had a normal father?" I say.

Daren reads the letter out loud. "'Congratulations on finding this clue. Lesson number two: Always bring the heart. Wherever you go, however you get there, bring a loving air with you and leave kindness in your wake. Life is too short to keep your heart to yourself. Now I'm sure you're frustrated and wondering where the money is, but not to worry! The money is very real and will soon be yours. The next place you'll need to go is the thing Kayla liked more than stickers and the thing Daren looked forward to every February. Ask for the Turner key.'"

"Another clue?" My mouth hangs open. Oh my God. This really *is* another one of my dad's quirky scavenger hunts. I can't *believe* he thought a scavenger hunt would be a good way to share his money with me. Ugh!

I throw my arms up in exasperation, accidentally whipping Daren's wrist against the wall of the boxcar with a loud bang.

"Hey now," he grunts. "There's no need for violence."

"This is all just a big game, you know."

He blinks at me. "What is?"

"This!" I gesture around wildly, accidentally thwacking his hand against the train car. *Again.*

He rubs his banged-up hand with a scowl. "Okay first of all, cool it with the hand gestures. Second, what do you mean this is a game?"

"This thing that we're doing?" I hold up the note. "It's all a big scavenger hunt that my dad must have orchestrated before he died."

"A scavenger hunt?" He screws his face into a befuddled look.

I nod. "He used to make scavenger hunts for me all the time when I was little. And now he's sending me on another one and giving us clues to find the inheritance."

He bobs his head. "Cool."

"No. Not cool," I say, pointing at him. "Annoying."

He scoffs. "So we follow some clues, so what? Why is that annoying?"

I let out a sigh. "Because scavenger hunts were something my father used to do for me back when he still cared and was all involved in my life. Being sent on one now just feels...insulting. Like I'm a puppet in his little game—a game he didn't bother playing with me for *years*, mind you—and now he thinks he can just handcuff me to strangers and send me out on wild-goose chases whenever he pleases. Don't get me wrong, I'm beyond grateful that he left me money in his will. But by wrapping this inheritance in a scavenger hunt and asking me to play along, he's destroying one of my favorite childhood memories." I rub a hand down my face, my heart twisting. "It just hurts, that's all. I don't want to be his puppet. I want to be his daughter."

14

DAREN

*K*ayla looks positively forlorn. Her rosy cheeks have lost their color, her bright eyes are clouded with sadness, and her pouty lips are... well, they're still sexy as ever. But the point is that she's obviously unhappy and I don't know how to change that. So I try to distract her.

"Well frankly, I'm disappointed," I say in a righteous manner. "For the last time, Kayla Turner, *we are not strangers.*" I let out a dramatic breath. "Good God, woman. What does a guy have to do to achieve 'friendship' status with you? I thought tonguing each other would do the trick but clearly we didn't do it right. So come on. Let's try it again." I sigh in mock weariness, waving her in. "I'm willing to rub tongues all day if that's what it takes. Hell, I'll tongue you all night if it'll get me off your Stranger Shit List."

She shakes her head and snorts through her downtrodden expression. "You are shameless."

I place a hand against my chest. "I prefer to think of myself as an opportunist."

"That too."

"So what do you say?" I flash my dimple. "Are we friends yet?"

Amusement plays in her eyes. "Why do you care so much about being friends with me?"

I scratch my cheek, feeling more unsettled than I care to admit by her question. "No idea. I'll get back to you."

She straightens her shoulders. "Okay. Well while you're pondering that, I'll be over here trying to figure out this clue." She pulls the note from my hand and examines it with a frown.

"What does 'something you liked more than stickers' mean?" I glance at her.

She shakes her head. "I don't know. What about your thing? Something you looked forward to in February? What, like Valentine's Day?"

I choke on a laugh. "Yeah, no. Valentine's Day is my least favorite holiday. Too much pressure."

"Oh-kay. Good to know where you stand on that," she says, raising her eyebrows. "So it's probably safe to assume this clue doesn't have anything to do with Cupid's holiday." She mutters, "One possibility down. A trillion more to go."

"Let's head back to the car and do our sleuthing on the road. I'm starving."

"Yeah. Me too."

I tuck the paper clue in my pocket as we walk to the edge of the boxcar and stare down. "Do you want to climb down first or should I?"

Below, the ground declines into a steep hill just a few feet from the boxcar, but the drop to the flat area before the descent isn't too bad.

Kayla says, "Let's just jump."

"All right."

She takes off her shoes and grips them in her free hand while I wrap my cuffed hand around hers.

"On the count of three," I say. "One...two..."

"Wait. Wait," she says. "Are we jumping *on* three or *after* three? If we jump at different times and go flying in different directions, we could snap our arms off at the cuffs."

Girls. So dramatic.

"Yeeeah, no." I shake my head and press my lips together. "We might bruise a wrist—or two—but I'm pretty sure our arms won't *snap off.*"

"Still." She juts her chin. "On three or after three?"

"After three," I say.

She nods.

"One...two...three!" I tighten my hand around hers as we jump out of the boxcar. But we overshoot it and jump too far out. We miss the flat area and land in the dirt with heavy thuds at the top of the hill. Then we promptly tumble over each other down the steep decline.

Our bodies flail in opposite directions as we roll, but the handcuffs force us to smack back together as we topple over each other, skidding through the gravel and dust in a tangle of limbs until we finally reach the bottom of the hill and come to a dusty stop.

Kayla lands sprawled across my chest with her long hair no longer tied back but now completely loose and splayed over my face. My right knee is wedged between her legs, where her skirt has ridden up and is now barely covering her ass. And our shackled hands are trapped between us, with my open palm pressing against her large, soft breast.

There are worse ways to fall out of a train.

Kayla raises her head and glances over our bodies before removing her breast from my hand and lifting her gaze to mine. Her blonde hair is tossed all around her face, tangled with tiny pebbles and twigs while smudges of dirt mark up her face and her clothes are covered in dust. Her blue eyes stand out against her flushed cheeks and throat, and there's a dead leaf stuck to the shiny gloss on her pink lips as she tries to catch her breath.

I let out a low chuckle. "You're a hot mess."

Her eyes rove over my ripped clothes, dirty skin, and dusty hair with a sparkle. "So are you."

We sit upright and stare up the hill at boxcar #23.

She sighs. "Well at least we can say we've been on an old-fashioned train now."

I smile. "We sure can."

15

KAYLA

I'm hungry. I'm handcuffed. And I'm covered in dirt and dust.

Today isn't going as smoothly—or as quickly—as I imagined.

I glance at the afternoon sun as we drive through Copper Springs. The day is almost over and we've hit a dead end. My father's scavenger hunts never lasted this long. There would sometimes be lots of clues and, therefore, the game took longer, but never an entire day.

"Where should we eat?" I say as I turn down Main Street.

He shrugs. "Someplace that's not too fancy."

"And somewhere affordable," I add.

"Yes." He nods. "Affordable is good."

We cruise past the grassy park in the center of the town square and find it bustling with people who are milling around a large Ferris wheel. Happy music plays from speakers perched on the tall park lampposts while street vendors and performers show off their goods and talents under colorful tents and canopies.

A large banner strung across the grassy town square reads COPPER SPRINGS 32ND ANNUAL CONFETTI CARNIVAL.

A smile curls up my mouth. I almost forgot about the Confetti Carnival. Once a year, the local vendors put on this merry festivity as an excuse to show off their latest merchandise and promote their businesses. They put on carnival games, petting zoos, and concerts. They also give away free things. Like food.

"You know what's better than affordable?" I say, finding a parking spot at the end of the street.

"What's that?"

I grin at him. "Free."

He looks back at the carnival—where vendors are handing out free bags of popcorn, complimentary soft pretzels, and unlimited candy samples—and brandishes his dimple. "Brilliant idea."

The first place we head is the pretzel cart followed by the popcorn machine. Daren scarfs two bags of popcorn down before I even finish one. I'm not really one to judge, though, with my mouth stuffed with pretzel and both my fists filled with junk food. Daren washes down his two bags of popcorn with a giant pretzel, which he eats in three big bites. I freeze with a Red Vine halfway to my mouth and stare at him.

Damn. Looks like Daren was just as starving as me.

Next, we head to the cotton candy cart and wait in line. Above hang two confetti cannons, which will go off at midnight to mark the end of the Confetti Carnival. It's like colorful snow, falling on the town in the midst of summer. I always loved the confetti snow.

Across the park, two girls with ample cleavage on display catch Daren's eye and smile. They can't tell he's handcuffed to me because the cart is blocking our wrists but, based on the *come hither* looks on both their faces, I doubt a handcuffed third party would be any kind of deterrence.

I glance at Daren and watch as he gives them a little smile and a chin nod. Their faces brighten and one of them licks her lips while the other wiggles her eyebrows.

Wow.

I tilt my head. "More friends of yours?"

Daren looks at me and the cocky smile is quickly replaced with a look of indifference. "It's a small town. Everybody knows everybody."

I nod. "Right."

I bet not everybody "knows" those girls the way Daren Ackwood does.

"Next!" calls the cotton candy man with a smile.

As we step up to the cart, I recognize him as Charles Abernathy, one of my father's old buddies.

He smiles at us. "Hello, Daren. Good to see you."

"You too, Mr. Abernathy." Daren nods.

"It's a shame about your dad. How's he doing?" he asks in a serious tone. "Is he still up at county—"

"I haven't spoken to my dad so I have no idea how he's doing," Daren says. The sharpness in his expression is a stark contrast to the smooth cockiness he was wearing just a moment ago. He was like this with the lawyer yesterday too. Tense and closed off about his dad.

I slide my eyes to him, wondering what the deal is with his father.

Daren slips on another casual grin. "We'll take two cotton candies, please."

Mr. Abernathy nods sympathetically. As he reaches for a paper cone, his eyes bounce off me and he looks back.

"Kayla Turner?" His face instantly lights up. "Is that you?"

I smile broadly. "Hi, Mr. Abernathy. How are you?"

"Well I'm doing wonderful now that I've seen you. It's been, what…five years? And now you're all grown up and just as pretty as your mother." He sighs and shakes his head sadly. "I'm so sorry about your father. He was a great man and will be deeply missed."

His words are genuine and laced in mourning. I try not to let that upset me as I nod. But the bitterness seeps through like an oozing wound nonetheless.

Mr. Abernathy twirls two paper cones around inside the cotton candy machine until he's formed identical balls of fluff.

He hands them to us merrily. "You two take care."

We walk away with two pink clouds of happy spun around paper cones. Finding a shady spot beneath the tall oak tree in the center of the square, we try not to draw attention to our handcuffed wrists as we eat.

"This is the best lunch I've ever had," he says, shoving the last of his pretzel into his mouth.

"I know," I say over a mouthful of popcorn.

Two middle-aged women walk past us with looks of confusion. I glance over our appearance and try to see us through their eyes.

We have dirt on our faces, candy in our mouths, and metal restraints around our wrists as we stand in a corner of the park.

We look like two jacked-up toddlers in time-out.

"Okay. Ick. I'm done." I hand Daren the rest of my cotton candy, my stomach now feeling grossly full. My nutritious lunch consisted of salted butter fluff and colored sugar fluff. I totally wouldn't blame my heart if it just decided to quit its job.

Daren finishes off the rest of my cotton candy and nods to a nearby bench. "Want to sit?"

We sit down and watch Mr. Abernathy hand out more cotton candy for a moment before I turn to Daren. "So what's the deal with your dad?"

He lifts an eyebrow. "What?"

I take a Red Vine from his hand and bite into it. "Your dad. Why do you get weird when people bring him up?"

He gives me a crooked smile. "Did Lana not fill you in on all things Luke Ackwood?"

"Apparently not." I swallow my bite.

He scratches his cheek. "Did she tell you about my dad's tendency to drink like a fish?"

I hesitate, feeling guilty for listening to gossip about Daren's family. I never really gave it much thought before, but listening to gossip is an ugly thing to do. "She might have mentioned something about that."

"She's a reliable source, that one."

I shake my head. "You don't have to tell me. I shouldn't have asked in the first place. That was nosey of me. God. I'm sorry."

"No. It actually might be nice to get to *tell* someone the truth. Everyone in town has just always known what was going on, so I rarely have a chance to tell the story." He looks away and even though his lopsided smile stays in place, his inhale is strained. "My dad is in jail for an aggravated DUI. He got hammered, went driving, and nearly killed a guy named Connor Allen last year. So he's been doing time at county for the past eight months."

I sit frozen with the Red Vine in my hand. "Whoa."

He laughs quietly. "Whoa is a good response."

"That's heavy, Daren," I say. "I'm sorry."

He shrugs and looks up at the Ferris wheel. "No one died so it wasn't as bad as it could have been."

"Yeah, but still." I chew off another bite of the Red Vine and stare out at the townspeople in the park. A couple across the way eye

Daren and mumble to each other, which reminds me of the ladies at the café this morning. "Is that why people sometimes look at you and whisper?"

He sighs. "That and the fact that my harlot mom lured the good preacher into her bed of sin seven years ago."

I make a face. "People still whisper about that?"

"You'd be surprised how eternal some gossip can be. What about you?" He turns to me. "Last night, Eddie mentioned that something happened with your mom. Any scandalous gossip there?"

"Oh." My heart starts to pound as I deliberate on what to say. "My mom, uh…" I shift my weight. "She passed away. A few months ago."

His lips part. "Oh God. I'm sorry. I—I didn't know."

I swallow. "It's okay. No one did. She was—she was sick for a long time." I quickly add, "Not sick like my dad, but just…she wasn't well."

He inhales deeply and slowly shakes his head. "Wow. You lost both your parents in the span of only a few months." He leans back and lifts our adjoined wrists. The handcuffs clink together. "Kind of makes all this seem petty."

I consider. "Not really. Believe it or not *this*"—I jangle our restraints—"is the most exciting thing I've done in a long time."

He laughs under his breath. "Then you need a life."

"God, tell me about it." I smile. "It's on my To Do list, trust me. I've just been so busy these past few years with my mom that I've hardly had time for myself." I flash back to the bank statements from earlier, and anger simmers in my chest. Those Chicago withdrawals had to have been my mother. No one aside from my parents would have had access to an account opened in my name.

I mutter a curse and shake my head. "I still can't believe my mom knew about the trust fund and didn't tell me. And then she drained it completely? Ugh." The simmer becomes a low boil as I think about the money. I know what she did with it and the idea makes me sick to my stomach. Especially since that money could have bought us—bought *me*—a better life.

Daren frowns. "She probably didn't tell you about it *because* she spent all the money."

"No doubt. But God." I exhale through my nostrils. "Steal someone's money and keep it for yourself? What a shitty thing to do to your own daughter."

"Very shitty and very low." He flexes his jaw. "You really didn't know?"

I shake my head again. "We were dirt poor, Daren. I mean, we had a little money when my dad was still sending alimony and child support, but once those payments stopped we were nearly destitute. Meanwhile, he was back here swimming in money."

He studies me for a long moment then looks away. "Hmm."

I stare at him. "What?"

He shrugs. "Obviously, your dad knew your mom was dipping into the trust fund, right? So he probably assumed you and Gia were living comfortably. Which means..." He leans in. "He didn't purposely leave you and your mom broke. He thought he was taking care of his family—or at least taking care of you. So maybe you should cut him some slack on the money front."

I start to argue but stop when I realize Daren's right. Mom was making large, consistent withdrawals from the trust fund, so my dad had every reason to believe we were financially secure.

"You're right," I say as guilt weighs down on me. "I guess I got so used to blaming my dad for everything tough in my life that I just directed all my financial bitterness toward him. Wow." I bite my lip. "I'm a brat."

"No. Your *mom* is a brat," he says, shaking his head.

I slowly nod. "Yeah."

We sit in easy silence for a few moments as I think about my mom and all the trouble her selfishness has caused me. I loved her. Dearly. But she made it hard sometimes. And now this? I wish I could say her stealing from me is a shocking revelation, but it's not. It pretty much falls in line with her behavior these last few years.

I look up at the statue of the town founder, Lewis Copper, just a few yards in front of us and wonder if he ever had a crazy mom—or a nutty dad, for that matter. Probably not like mine.

I shift on the bench and glance down at our locked wrists. It's nice sitting beside Daren. Easy. I can't remember the last time I was so relaxed around a guy. Then again, it's been a while since I've been around a guy at all. But Daren feels different. He's too pretty for his own good, probably, but he's not a bad guy. I'd even go as far as to say he might be one of the good ones.

He looks over and smiles at me with a piece of cotton candy stuck to his lip. He's handcuffed to me on a park bench in public, while we feast on all things unhealthy, and he seems perfectly content. Yeah. He's definitely one of the good ones.

"Right here." I brush a finger over my lip to show him where the cotton candy is stuck on his mouth.

"Are you asking for a kiss? Again?" He sighs and leans over. "Okay, fine…"

I laugh and push away his face. "No, you arrogant weirdo. You have cotton candy on your lip."

He darts his tongue out and swipes the sugary goodness from his mouth. I stare at his lips.

"Did I not get it all?" He licks his lips again.

"What? No. Yes. It's gone." I cut my eyes away and stare at anything other than his lips. Or tongue. My eyes settle on the statue. "Why do you think they do that?"

He follows my gaze. "Erect giant stone replicas of old white men who demanded things be named after them? No idea."

I toss some popcorn in my mouth. "I bet Lewis Copper wasn't even a cool guy. I bet he was a grumpy old man with a drinking problem."

"And a wife who hated him," he says.

"And an irritable bowel."

"And really bad body odor."

I shake my head. "But yet he got a friggin' statue made of himself."

"With a plaque." Daren tips his chin at the foot of the statue.

On the plaque is an engraved picture of a steam engine, which brings my thoughts back to the clue at the train station.

"Bust out that clue again," I say. "Let's see if we're any better at deciphering it when we're hopped up on sugar and carbohydrates."

He pulls the note from his pocket and we stare at it.

"Are you sure you don't remember what you liked more than stickers?" he says.

"I don't even remember liking *stickers*," I say. "My dad once bought me a sticker book when I was like six, but instead of decorating the pages with the flower stickers inside, I stole a roll of stamps from his office, licked every last one of them, and stuck them to the pages." I laugh thinking back to how his eyes bulged when he saw what I'd done. "He was so mad."

Daren scratches his jaw. "Maybe that's the clue." He looks at me. "Stamps."

I consider for a moment. "Maybe...but what would that mean for your part of the clue? Are there special February stamps that you looked forward to getting in the mail each year?"

He shakes his head. "The only thing I ever looked forward to getting in the mail was the swimsuit issue of *Sports Illustrated*."

I roll my eyes. "Of course."

He pauses. "But it *did* come out every February."

"Really?" I say. "Huh. Do you think that's the clue then? A magazine?"

He shrugs. "I can't think of anything else it would be. And if the clues are stamps and a magazine then we need to go..."

My mind races. "To a magazine store."

"A magaz—in Copper Springs? You're not in the big city anymore, Blondie." He shakes his head. "Maybe we need to go to a stamp museum or something."

"Oh sure." I sneer. "A *stamp museum* in this tiny town makes total sense, but a magazine store? Preposterous."

He squints at me. "God, you're sassy. I'm just trying to draw a connection between stamps and magazines here."

I gather all our junk food trash and toss it in the garbage can beside the bench as I shrug. "Well, they both come in the mail."

We whip our heads to face each other and say, "The post office."

He says, "Turner probably left the money in a postal box for us."

"Yes!"

Quick as lightning, we dart up from the bench and take off in opposite directions—only to be whipped back into each other by our linked wrists. My chest slams into his rib cage as his knee pushes into my thigh.

"Seriously?" I pull back from him and huff. "Where are you going?"

He points behind him. "The post office is that way."

"Since when?" I make a face.

He juts his jaw. "Since the old one burned down and got moved from Main Street to Langley Drive."

"Oh." I straighten my skirt, which has once again ridden up my thighs. I don't know why I even bother.

He looks up at the sun hanging low in the sky. "It's almost closing time. We need to hurry."

As we speed walk through the park toward my car, people everywhere turn and stare.

Don't mind us, folks. We're just a couple of kids bound together with metal on the hunt for what may or may not be a twenty-dollar bill. We're not desperate or anything.

We reach the car and quickly climb in. The drive to the Copper Springs post office takes less time than it takes for us to get our linked bodies out of the car as Daren climbs over the console with the grace of a one-legged chicken, cursing and thwacking his elbows and knees against the dashboard.

"You're like a bull in a china shop," I say.

He tries to fold his long legs into the driver's seat one at a time but ends up kicking the steering wheel and honking the car horn.

"A very noisy bull." I shake my head.

He climbs out of the car with a scowl. "Well maybe my bull-horns wouldn't make so much noise if they weren't being crammed into an Oompa-Loompa-sized car."

"If you complain about my car one more time," I say, "I will track down your precious Porsche and draw all over it in lipstick."

"Easy, tiger," he says. "There's no need for violence."

We walk toward the post office's entrance, but stop in our tracks when we see the CLOSED sign on the door.

"Shit," Daren mutters.

"We're too late?" I say, wanting to scream. This day has been a complete waste. "What now?"

A muscle flexes in his jaw as he shakes his head. "I don't know. Come back in the morning?"

"And what are we supposed to do until then?" I say, lifting our joined wrists. "Stay locked together all night? I don't think so. We need to find Eddie."

"Okay." Daren pulls out his phone and calls the lawyer. "Hey, Eddie. It's Daren... Yeah, so Kayla and I haven't been able to find Turner's money yet... Oh yeah, it's been super fun, but we need to get into the post office and the post office is closed. So it looks like we're going to have to delay this scavenger hunt until morning. Do you mind if Kayla and I swing by your place in a few minutes so you can unlock the handcuffs? Just until tomorrow of course. We'll put these babies back on first thing..."

Daren listens to Eddie on the other end of the line for a moment. "Uh-huh... uh-huh... I see... Right, well of course... True, but... uh-huh... uh-huh... okay, then." He smiles at the floor. "Thank you so much. You have a good night too." He hangs up and purses his lips.

"So...?" I prod, waiting.

Daren rocks back on his heels. "So Eddie says he can't unlock the cuffs until we've found the money. No exceptions."

My mouth drops open. "You have GOT to be kidding me. Doesn't he know that being handcuffed together means we can't leave each other's side?"

"I'm pretty sure, yes."

"Then how does he expect us to *sleep* tonight?"

Daren holds up our chained wrists with a grin. "Side by side?"

Un. Believable.

16

DAREN

*I*f I weren't so exhausted, I'd be offended by the horrified look on Kayla's face.

"That's not happening," she says, shaking her head adamantly. "No way. We're going to pick the lock on these things. Now." She yanks up our wrists and jiggles the handcuffs.

A family of four walks by with confusion in their eyes as they stare at our criminal restraints.

Kayla casually lowers our wrists and half-smiles at the family. "We're not dangerous. Promise."

The parents gather their children close and shuffle past us without looking back.

I slant my eyes to Kayla. "People don't think we're dangerous. They think we're crazy," I say. "And we are. But if we want to pick the lock, we probably need to do it somewhere other than outside the post office. I don't want someone to see and report us to Eddie."

She nods at her car. "Let's just get back in the front seat and do it in there."

I shrug. "Or we could just do it in the backseat."

We glance at each other.

The back of my neck grows warm and a tinge of pink stains her cheeks as we stand locked in a hot gaze. I would love nothing more than to *do it in the backseat* with Kayla. But she's made it clear that doing anything with me, in the backseat of her car or elsewhere, isn't on her agenda and I need to respect that.

"You know," I clarify, "just so I don't have to climb over the center console again."

"Right." She nods. "Of course."

Walking back to the car, we pass three different guys who stop to gawk at Kayla. They crane their necks to follow her. They eye her lewdly. They adjust themselves.

God. It must suck to be a girl.

Kayla doesn't pay the guys any attention, but I can't help but want to pop them in their drool-covered jaws. She's not a walking centerfold for them to openly ogle. She's a human being.

The hot protectiveness slipping through my veins is new to me. It's not the same as when I want to protect Amber or keep Pixie safe. It's thicker than that. Meaner. And it's rooted so deep inside me I can't pinpoint when it came to life. But it's very much alive and thrashing wildly in defense of Kayla.

I trail my eyes over her face, down her body, and to our joined wrists, oddly satisfied by the fact that she's literally locked to my side. Twisted, I know. But everything about this girl tangles me up.

Kayla opens the back door on the driver's side and motions for me to get in. I awkwardly scoot over to the other side, knocking cups and shoes and other miscellaneous items out of my way as I go. She follows after me, slipping into the car gracefully and crossing her legs like we're sitting down for tea and not about to break into a set of steel handcuffs.

The setting sun warms the car and all the noise from the street—the birds, the pedestrians, the traffic—disappears the moment she closes the car door. The only sound now is our staggered breaths.

She uncrosses and recrosses her legs. Her black skirt rides up, showing more of her legs, and I inhale through my nose. If I have to see her thighs one more time today I might just explode.

Which is weird for me because I don't explode. I am a cool cat. I do not get worked up and feverish over girls. Until now. Until Kayla.

Twisted. Tangled. I'm a total mess.

"So." She lets out a breath and lifts our adjoined hands. "Do you know how to pick locks?"

"Nope. But Google probably does." I pull my phone from my back pocket and search for *how to pick handcuff locks*. Then sort through the results.

She leans over my shoulder. "Do the wikiHow page."

I scroll down. "Nah. I'm going to do the How Things Work page."

She clucks her tongue. "I'm telling you, wikiHow is better."

I look at her with a cocked eyebrow. "How would you know? Do you find yourself handcuffed often?"

I immediately picture Kayla handcuffed in other, more sexy situations and all the blood in my body darts for my pants. Dammit.

She lifts her chin. "Do *you*?"

"Yeah, I'm not answering that." I pull up the How Things Work page and scan the directions. "Okay, we need a paper clip or something that's small, flexible, and strong."

Uncrossing her legs, she pulls her purse onto her lap and rummages through it with both hands, forcing my attached wrist to hang above her bag.

"Your purse is as messy as your car," I say.

"I know. And you're welcome."

"For what?"

"For this." She pulls out a bobby pin and holds it up. "A less messy purse might not have had a lock-picking device inside."

I nod. "Point well made."

Readjusting our wrists so I can see better, I read through the how-to process and I bring our hands to my lap. Her wrist falls dangerously close to my love tool, so I have to slyly reposition our hands so those delicate fingers of hers aren't near any stroking zones. I can't help but wonder if she's ever given a guy a hand job.

And *has* she ever been handcuffed before? Maybe to a bed? I picture her lying in a tangle of sheets with her pink lips parted as she moans, and her blonde hair tossed around her flushed cheeks, and her throat exposed as she arches her back...

Dammit. Now I'm hard.

What the fuck? I am not a teenager. I have more self-control than this. Usually. I do not like this whole Kayla-Turner-getting-under-my-skin thing. I do not like it one bit.

I glance at Kayla. She's focused on her phone, looking up lock-picking strategies on wikiHow and completely oblivious to my current state of arousal. I carefully adjust myself and think about grandmas and baseball until I get my body under control.

Looking back down, I insert the bobby pin into the lock hole on my cuff and slowly bend and turn its small tip inside. Nothing. I try a different angle.

"I think you're turning it wrong," Kayla says, leaning over my shoulder again. The smell of coconut wafts all around me and I purse my lips. "Let me do it."

She pulls our wrists back to her lap and slips the pin into the lock on her cuff.

I shake my head. "That's the same way I was just turning it. And now you're wrecking the pin. Let me try again."

I bring our hands back to my lap and fidget with the lock, more aggressively than before, determined to get us out of these things before I get hard again.

"That's the wrong way," she says.

I dig deeper into the keyhole. "No, it's not."

"You have to twist it *up*, not to the side. I'll show you." She reaches for the pin.

"Back off, Blondie." I swat her hand away and twist the pin.

"You're doing it wrong," she sneers. "Turn it the other way."

"Shh."

"The *other* wa—"

The bobby pin snaps in half and the top breaks off inside the lock. I hold up the broken pin as we stare at the clogged keyhole.

"Great," she mutters.

I twitch my lips. "I don't suppose you have another bobby pin in that glorious bag of yours?"

"Nope."

"Okay. Uh..." I say. "We could go buy a lock-picking kit."

Not that I have money to buy a lock-picking kit. My palms start to sweat and I wipe them on my jeans.

"Where would we buy a lock-picking kit?" she says.

"The hardware store?" I think for a second. "Actually, I'm not sure. The store owner is pretty stingy about what he stocks. I doubt breaking-and-entering tools are something he splurges on. But maybe the drugstore?"

She leans against the seat and sighs. "Maybe instead of parading around a store in search of a lock-picking kit we could just go buy a pair of bolt cutters and cut the handcuffs off."

I raise my eyebrows. "Right. Because that won't look suspicious. 'Hi Eddie. I know you said we had to keep the handcuffs on all night, but would you believe these babies just sawed themselves in half?' Yeah, no. I'm not forfeiting the money because your wrist was being a wuss."

She rubs her temples and inhales through her nose. "You're right. The money is worth it. We'll just have to figure out sleeping arrangements for one night and then get back here, bright and early."

I nod, not sure where Kayla and I are going to sleep tonight. I'd offer up my place, but ...

I give her my best grin. "So I guess we're off to the Quickie Stop for the evening?"

She scoffs. "If you think I'm going to stay the night with you in a porn motel with handcuffs on, then you're crazier than my hunt-making dad."

I shrug. "All right. Let's go back to my place, then. You have everything you need, right? Because I don't feel like driving across town just to pick up your pajamas. You can wear one of my T-shirts to bed. Or nothing at all, if you wish." I wink at her. "And I'm sure you'll sleep like a baby in my bed. Women rave about how comfortable it is." I plaster on a smile and wait.

Please, dear God, let the idea of sleeping on an oversexed mattress freak her out or piss her off enough to bow out. There is no way—*no way*—I'm letting Kayla see where I live.

She eyes me skeptically like she knows I'm full of shit and purses her lips in hesitation. She doesn't want to sleep in a motel room with me, but she also doesn't want to sleep in a manwhore's bed. Decisions, decisions.

Her shoulders fall just a smidge, and I know I've won.

"Fine," she says between her teeth. "We'll stay in my hotel room." She opens the back door and starts sliding out.

I follow after her and groan as we then climb into the front seat. It's really quite ridiculous, all the crawling and climbing.

She starts the engine and pulls away from the post office. The sun has fallen behind the horizon now, so the sky is a light purple color and dotted with a handful of stars.

We drive to the edge of town and out of the city limits, following the stretch of freeway I take when I drive to my job at Willow Inn.

Crap.

Ellen.

I really need to call and let her know there's a small chance I might not be coming into work tomorrow.

I glance down at the handcuffs.

A medium chance.

Pulling out my phone, I dial Ellen and get her voice mail. I leave a brief message about my possible absence tomorrow before shoving the phone back in my pocket.

The engine revs as Kayla picks up speed.

"Slow down, Danica," I say. "We don't want your Oompa-Loompa-mobile to peter out and die a slow, green death in the middle of the road."

She glances in the rearview mirror once, twice, three times and looks increasingly more worried with each view.

"What?" I look behind us. "What's wrong?"

She bites her lip. "Do you see that black sedan three cars back?"

"Uh...yeah?"

Her eyes dart from the mirror to the windshield. "Do you think it's following us?"

"To the Quickie Stop? Not likely."

"No, I mean in general. Like following me." If it weren't for the slight tremor in her voice, I'd be scoffing at the idea. But Kayla seems genuinely concerned, so I keep my body language relaxed and my voice casual.

"I don't think so," I say. "There aren't very many streets in this town, so that black car is probably just going the same general direction as us. And besides, I seriously doubt anyone in town wants to be seen with us, let alone follow us around. We're the dirty couple in handcuffs, remember?" I grin at her but her eyes stay locked on the mirror.

Okay, well this isn't normal.

"Kayla?" I draw out the word.

She clutches the steering wheel even tighter. "Huh?"

"Why are you so freaked out?"

I watch her swallow. "Okay, well. It's going to sound crazy, and I'm sure I'm just being jumpy and overdramatic, but…" She chews on her lip. "My mom sort of owes my ex-boss twenty thousand dollars. And Big Joe wanted to collect from me right before I left Chicago by making me work at his diner for free, or something like that. And when I quit he sort of threatened me so I fled town."

My eyes widen. "And you didn't think to mention this sooner? Like say, *before* we agreed to chain our wrists together and make ourselves one incredibly awkward and slow-moving target?"

"I didn't think Big Joe would come after me!" Her voice squeaks.

"Listen. There's no need to stress." I say. "That black car is probably just some little old lady on her way to get groceries." I inhale softly. "No one is coming after you."

I look calm, but oh. My. God. Kayla has some Chicago diner

villain coming after her for twenty grand? Holy shit. That's like movie-quality drama. And I'm handcuffed to it!

"You're right." She nods and takes a steadying breath. "I'm probably just being paranoid."

I give her a reassuring smile. "Exactly. Everything's fine." I tap my fingers on the center console then furrow my brow. "Wait. If your mom passed away, how does she owe someone money?"

She shrugs. "She must have borrowed it before she died. I knew nothing about the debt until after she was gone."

I stop tapping my fingers. "So…your mom siphoned all the money out of your trust fund in addition to borrowing twenty thousand dollars from a restaurant thug?"

"Yeah," she says slowly, her eyes flicking to the side.

I look out the window. "That's a lot of money. Do you have any guesses on where it all went?"

"I have my theories," she mutters.

But she doesn't say anything else on the matter so neither do I.

Several minutes later, the black sedan disappears and Kayla visibly relaxes. The seriousness with which she's taking the whole Big Joe debt thing alarms me. I don't know what we're in for. Mobsters with guns. Street thugs with baseball bats. A lawyer with a strongly worded letter. It could be anything, really.

But fortunately, Kayla no longer has to face "anything" alone. She has me, bound to her side at all times. For a fleeting moment I'm ridiculously grateful for James Turner and his handcuffs idea.

Soon, we pull into the Quickie Stop. I look over the old motel and let out a low whistle.

It really is a shady dump and looks like the setting of a low-budget porno flick. I glance at Kayla as she parks and grabs her purse from the backseat.

Why in the hell is she staying at a shithole like this? Especially with someone who may or may not be coming after her for money. She's way too pretty and sweet to even step foot onto the premises, let alone lay her pretty head on one of the nasty room pillows.

I wrinkle my brow as she rummages through her purse. Is she really as broke as she claims? Is she so low on cash that she chose the frugality of this place over the safety of Willow Inn or Martha's Bed & Breakfast?

Well I don't like that idea at all.

Not just because I hate the fact that she's sleeping at this dank motel, but because her being poor puts a serious dent in my plans to keep the entire inheritance for myself. I was okay with ripping her off when I thought she was a selfish brat who could afford to sail around the world in a yacht. But now that I know just how *not* selfish or spoiled she is and how difficult things are for her financially right now, taking money from her is no longer an option. Especially after how Gia robbed the trust fund.

I run my eyes over Kayla's small hands, still digging around in her purse, and my chest tightens. There's no way I could ever steal from this girl.

She pulls out her room key—which is an actual metal key hanging from a tacky green plastic keychain—from the depths of her bag and starts to get out of the car.

I get out of the car as well and follow her to door #3. The motel only has sixteen doors. Two look busted and unused, while the others are scraped up and covered in questionable stains and dents.

Bars are in front of every room window, laced with cobwebs and dirt. And the small lights that hang outside each door give off a dull orange glow, which makes the place look like something from a horror movie.

What. In. The. Hell?

As Kayla inserts the key and opens door #3, visions of the world's creepiest game show pop into my head.

What's behind door number three? A dead guy! And what's behind door number two? A murderous clown with a butcher knife!

Flicking the switch inside, Kayla lights up the tiny motel room and I can't help but make a face.

Shaggy orange carpet sticks up from the floor, matted in some places and clumped together in others. The full-size mattress on the bed is lopsided and covered in a stiff bedspread from the 1970s. It's orange with brown and green stripes, and has several cigarette burns in it. The smell of stale smoke and urine fills the air, while mysterious stains coat the walls and ceiling—yes, *ceiling*—complementing the various cracks and dents in the drywall. And the small bathroom in the back has a toilet that looks clean enough, but is probably disgusting inside, and a yellowing sink beneath an old mirror marbled with gold.

A cockroach skitters across the bathroom floor before disappearing into a small hole behind the toilet.

"Yeah, no. We're not staying here," I say, shaking my head as Kayla tries to walk us into the room.

She swings her head to me. "Why not? Is my hotel room not good enough for you, Pretty Boy?"

"Your *mo*tel room isn't good enough for the cockroach I just saw dance across the bathroom tile."

"Well I'm sorry I can't afford five-star accommodations everywhere I go like your family, but this is how normal people live."

I want to correct her about my family's lifestyle, but there's no point. "This is not how normal people live," I say. "This is how lowlifes with drug addictions and sex appointments live."

She juts her chin. "Well too bad. This is where we're sleeping tonight. It's been good enough for me for the past two nights, and it will be good enough for you tonight. So suck it up." She shuts the door behind us and secures the three locks on the back.

It's a bad sign when the motel installs three fucking locks on their guest room doors.

I open my mouth to protest once again, but think better of it. Our only other option isn't much better than this, if I'm being honest with myself. And if Kayla's going to be sleeping in a shithole like this, at least I'll be with her, which makes me feel a little bit better about tonight. It makes me feel downright pissed about the last two nights, though.

Looking around, I notice the only personal item in the room is a suitcase on the bed. Inside the suitcase are a few clothes and some personal items: a framed picture, a few books, some papers. When Kayla said she "fled" Chicago I assumed she meant temporarily. But why would she bother packing such things if she planned on returning to Chicago?

17

KAYLA

After washing the dirt off our skin and out of our hair as best we could, we turn to stare at the motel bed. Sleeping handcuffed to another person—at least when there's no kinky stuff involved—is just plain awkward.

"So I guess I'm taking the left side of the bed?" Daren says, nodding at his cuffed left wrist as we stand facing the bed.

I tuck a strand of hair behind my ear and curse this whole day under my breath. "Well you *could* ... but I'm a belly sleeper."

He blinks. "A what?"

"A belly sleeper," I say. "I sleep on my stomach, not my back."

"Well I guess tonight, you're going to have to sleep on your back."

I merrily suggest, "Or you can just sleep on your stomach."

He shakes his head. "That's not something I do."

"Ah, but it's something you *could* do." I smile sweetly.

"Hmm." He rubs his chin. "I'm not used to having this kind of problem when I'm sleeping with a girl. Usually the only thing up for debate is who gets to be on top first—"

"Ew."

He shrugs. "I'm just saying. These are uncharted waters for me."

I turn to him. "You mean to tell me no other girl has ever asked you to take a certain side of the bed or sleep a certain way?"

"Nope."

"Not even a girlfriend?"

"Meh," he says. "I don't really do the 'girlfriend' thing."

"Another guy afraid of commitment. Shocking," I mutter. "Listen. I'm a girl, handcuffed to a guy, in a dirty motel room. Can you please just be cool about this and sleep on the right side of the bed on your stomach?"

He groans. "Fine."

"Thanks." I smile. "Now turn around so I can change into my pajamas."

With a loud sigh, he turns around while I yank a pair of sleep shorts from my suitcase and kick off my dirty heels. I'm definitely wearing my sneakers tomorrow.

There's no way to take my shirt off completely, given that we're cuffed together, so I just pull my skirt off and slip my shorts on. Our handcuffs clang with my movements and, as I pull my shorts up over my hips, the side of Daren's hand grazes my leg. Hot desire darts between my thighs and the muscles low in my belly tighten. I see his lips curl up in a smile.

"Try not to be so happy about all this," I say.

His smile grows. "Too late."

I roll my eyes and straighten the shorts. "Okay, I'm done. You can turn around now."

He turns and looks me over. "Cute." Then he starts unbuttoning his jeans.

"What are you doing?"

He says, "Oh. Well I didn't have time to run home and pack my jammies so tonight I'm sleeping in my undies."

The thought of Daren lying next to me in his underwear all night just makes my belly tighten even more.

I trap his hands at the waist of his jeans. "Uh-uh." I bore my eyes into his. "Your pants are staying on tonight."

A tiny voice inside my head protests, *No! Take his pants off. Take everything off*, and my throat goes dry. Why am I so lust-driven around Daren?

Maybe it's not him. Maybe I just really need to get laid. When's the last time I had sex? Or rather, when's the last time I had *good* sex?

I frown. It's been a long time, if ever, really.

My eyes fall to Daren's lips, tracing the shape, and I wish I could be his tongue and play in his mouth.

A long, *long* time.

Snap out of it, Kayla. You will not be a horndog while chained to this arrogant—yet astoundingly pretty—boy.

Daren's mouth falls open. "But I hate sleeping in jeans."

"And I hate changing in front of strangers. I guess neither of us gets to have their way."

"For the love of God." His eyes grow wide. "We. Are. Not. Strangers."

"Aw…" I smile mockingly. "It's so sweet how you want to be my friend."

"That's it. We're kissing again. Come here." He reaches for me.

I lean away with a smirk. "Fat chance. Now button up your pants and let's go to bed."

He flashes his dimple. "Now there's a sentence I never thought I'd hear a girl say to me."

"God. You're so freaking proud of your sex life, aren't you?" I turn off the lamp, throwing us into darkness save for the orange light glowing in through the window, and follow him to the bed.

"Actually, I am," he says, sounding sincere. "I'm kind of a stud in the sack."

He pulls back the gross comforter and climbs onto the sheets, sliding over to the right side. If he weren't acting so conceited, I would probably thank him.

"Yeah, yeah. You're a 'legendary lover,'" I say, sounding bored as I crawl in after him. "Every guy says that."

We lie down as far away from each other as possible, him on his back, me on my tummy, with our cuffed arms stretched between us.

"Yeah," he says. "But I'm actually telling the truth."

"Right."

"It's one of the few things I'm actually good at." He pauses. "The only thing, actually."

There's something almost sad in his voice and it confuses me. Most guys sound like proud pricks when they talk about their sexual skills. But Daren sort of sounds...wistful.

I scowl into the darkness. "What is this? Some kind of weird pity party?" I snort. "If you're fishing for compliments, you've come to the wrong place. I know nothing about your sex life, and even if I did, I wouldn't be stroking your ego while lying beside you in the dark, in *handcuffs*."

The moment the words leave my mouth I feel the atmosphere change. As if bringing attention to our overtly sexual predicament woke our libidos up—not that mine was ever asleep.

I feel the mattress move as Daren shifts. "I wasn't asking you to stroke my ego," he says. "I was just explaining why I take pride in my sexual prowess. Some guys are good at sports, or playing guitar, or making money...and I'm good at sex." He says this like it's a fact and not his ego on parade.

"Well good for you," I say, and just to piss him off I add, "I'm sure you're a solid six in bed."

"A si—" He mocks a gasp. "That's just mean."

"A six is generous," I say. "Most guys are a two."

"Obviously you've been sleeping with the wrong guys."

Tell me about it.

My sexual history isn't exciting. I've slept with three guys. The first was my high school boyfriend. He was an okay guy and sex with him wasn't horrible, but it also wasn't amazing. I'm pretty sure the only reason he dated me was because of sex. He didn't seem too interested in me otherwise. But I didn't know better at the time.

My second sexual partner was a wannabe musician I worked with at the diner. He was five years older than me, covered in tattoos, and decent in bed. But that was all he ever wanted to do. Day in and day out. Sex, sex, sex. I eventually got sick of being his on-call orgasm and broke up with him. He cried. Actually shed tears. But the next night he went home with another waitress. I guess his broken heart mended quickly.

The last guy I slept with was my ex-boyfriend Jeremy. He was a meathead who loved parading me around town like I was his show pony. He always wanted me to get dressed up so he could take me out and "be seen." And sex with him was a minimal-kissing lights-always-on event that made me feel kind of used. Three months into our relationship, I realized he knew nothing about me other than what I looked like, and when I brought that to his attention, he didn't seem too bothered by my concern and instead turned all the lights on and asked me to get naked. I dumped his ass on the spot.

It seemed like I was nothing more than an ass and a pair of boobs when it came to guys. So after dumping Jeremy, I decided I didn't need to share my body with anyone else unless they were going to see the person inside. The me that existed beneath my lips and breasts.

I have yet to come across such a guy.

"How's your wrist feeling?" Daren says, lightly moving our cuffs.

I turn my hand over. "It's okay, I guess. It's a little sore, but not bad."

"Mine too," he says. "I'll try to take it easy tomorrow so you don't end up with any bruises."

"Thanks," I say.

He shifts. "These things really are uncomfortable."

"Yeah. I definitely understand why people use the fuzzy kind for sex play."

He laughs. "Tell me, Kayla. Have you ever used the fuzzy kind—or any other kind of restraints—for 'sex play'? I bet you have. I bet you're into all sorts of kinky things."

I roll my eyes. "Not everyone is a whore like you."

"Ooh. Ouch." The bed squeaks as he turns to face me. "Why do you think I'm a whore? Because I have sex with a lot of girls?"

"No. I think you're a whore because you're not picky about the girls you have sex with."

"How would you know?"

"Because all I heard about growing up is how you'd slept with half the town—and that was just when we were in high school."

"Wow. Your Lana friend sure was a blabbermouth," he says, sounding slightly offended.

"So you admit the rumors were true."

"In my defense, the town is pretty small." He scoffs. "And excuse me if we can't all get our validation from people merely looking at us."

I scowl into the dark, feeling my playful energy fade away with the insult. "What's that supposed to mean?"

"It means that of course you can be picky about who you sleep with," he says. "You feel good about yourself every single day. All you have to do is step out into public and everyone within a five-mile radius starts to drool over your beauty. I don't get that kind of validation just by waking up. I have to work for my self-worth. And I happen to be really good at sex. So forgive me if I like to feel good about myself."

My blood boils. What he just said is everything I fight against being seen as. It's the reason people don't give me a chance and why I try so hard to change their minds. And Daren just used it against me.

I turn the light on and whip my face to him. "First of all, my good looks don't give me my self-worth. There's more to me than just my boobs or my butt or my face. But people can't *see* me—the real me—because they're too busy staring at me. My heart and mind are invisible. I'm a person, and people forget that. They forget that I can hurt and be insecure, just like anyone else. Second, you having sex to feel good about yourself is complete and total bullshit. I don't care how good you are in bed, Daren. You're valuable simply because you're you. We all are."

I snap the light off and flop back on the pillow. My blood is no longer boiling but my heart is pounding ferociously. Maybe it was mean to call him out like that, but I've been watching him struggle all day to maintain that casual confidence and playboy attitude of his, all the while thinking he was just trying to piss me off.

But now that I know his false arrogance comes from a place of insecurity and not a need to annoy the crap out of me, I can't just let him get away with believing that's who he is and all he's worth. That would be as bad as me believing my importance is derived from the way I look. And no one deserves to feel that way. Especially Daren.

18

DAREN

I stare at the dark ceiling as a torrent of contradicting emotions invades my chest. I'm angry that Kayla thinks I'm a whore. I feel guilty for implying that her self-worth is directly related to her appearance. But more than anything else, I'm stunned that she called me valuable, and said it with conviction, even though she was upset with me.

I'm just some guy she's been stuck with all day. I'm not one of her family members or her boyfriend—hell, I can't even get the girl to call me her *friend*—but still, she thinks I'm valuable.

I sit up and turn the light back on. "Kayla."

She turns to face me with a huff, her blue eyes lit with defensiveness. "What."

I press my lips together. "You're a really good person."

The defensiveness slides into confusion. "What?"

"Sorry that I made you feel like your looks were all that mattered. I don't think that, not at all. It was a shitty thing for me to say." I pause. "I mean, you *are* extremely hot"—I grin and her expression softens—"but that has nothing to do with your significance as a person. And what you said, about me being valuable… it's probably the nicest thing anyone's ever said to me. So thanks." I turn the light back off and lie down.

A beat passes.

"Sorry I called you a whore," Kayla says.

I quietly chuckle. "Don't be. I am a whore. But you were wrong about me being afraid of commitment."

"Oh really?"

"Yep," I say. "Girls always think it's a commitment thing. Like there's something wrong with a guy if he doesn't drink the relationship Kool-Aid you females are always trying to shove down our throats. When in reality, the reason I don't want to lock myself up to someone"—I rattle our handcuffs—"metaphorically speaking, of course—is because girls are just as bad as guys when it comes to commitment. If not worse."

I can almost hear her eyes roll. "Oh please."

"See? This is what I'm talking about." I shake my head in the dark. "You think girls can do no wrong. That guys are just big bad wolves who walk around breaking hearts at their every whim." I scoff. "Girls are every bit as ruthless. They leave. They break hearts. They use guys." I exhale. "So I don't buy into the bullshit anymore. I just have fun. If a girl comes along and happens to want a relationship with me, I step away. I don't sleep with her or lead her on. But if a girl is only in it for fun or just needs to feel desired for a few hours—*and also understands* that I'm not going to do the relationship thing with her—well, then . . . I do sleep with her. And we both leave feeling better about ourselves. If that makes me a whore then I'm okay with being a whore."

She laughs. "So sex is like a public service you provide?"

"No." I smile. "Well, maybe a little."

"Oh my God. You're unbelievable."

"Hey, you'd be surprised how many girls out there just want to be touched and feel wanted. It's an epidemic, really."

"I'm sure it is." I hear the smile in her voice. "Well whore or not, I still think it's sad that sex makes you feel good about yourself. Or whatever."

I cluck my tongue. "You only think it's sad because you've never had the pleasure of experiencing Daren the Legendary Lover first-hand. But we can fix that, you know. Right now, even." I bounce on the mattress so the springs creak and groan. "We have a cheap motel porn bed at our disposal and everything."

She playfully scoffs. "As flattered as I am that you'd extend your public-servicing penis to me, I think I'm going to pass."

I sigh dramatically. "Your call. But if you change your mind, I'll be here all night." I playfully tug on the handcuffs. "Right beside you."

"Good night, Daren," she says, giving the handcuffs a little tug back.

I smile at the ceiling. "Night."

———

From behind the post office counter, Jonah Maxwell lifts one of his shaggy white eyebrows as he eyes our handcuffs. It started pouring this morning, so not only are we chained to each other, but we're also dripping wet.

"Are you two running from the law?" the postman asks.

A fair question.

"Uh, no sir." I shake my head. "We're actually here on official legal business."

"Like running from the law?" he says, his eyebrow creeping higher.

Kayla steps forward. "Actually, we were hoping you could help us. My father recently passed away. Maybe you knew him, James Turner?"

Jonah's face brightens. "You're James's daughter? We loved James." His features soften sympathetically. "The wife and I were so sad to hear he'd passed. He was a good man, your father. I'm sorry for your loss."

Her expression tightens but her voice remains pleasant. "Thank you." She clears her throat. "That's actually why we're here. In his will, my father asked me to come to the post office and ask for the Turner key?" She gives him a killer smile and I wonder if anyone, ever, in the history of the world, has been able to say no to that smile. Probably not.

Jonah smiles back. "Well let me see here." He pulls something up on his computer screen and reads, "James Turner. Box number twelve. Keys can only be given out to James Turner himself, or to the joint custody of Kayla Turner and Daren Ackwood." He looks from the computer to us. "I suppose that's why you're both here?"

I nod and hold up our cuffed wrists. "We're joint."

"Well okay then." Jonah disappears in the back and returns shortly with a postal key. Handing it to Kayla he says, "Here you go, dear. It's nice to finally meet James's daughter. We heard so many great things about you over the years."

She pauses with the key in her hand. "You did?"

"Oh yes." He smiles. "Your father was always talking about his little girl and showing us pictures. He was very proud of you and bragged nonstop about you going to nursing school."

Looking at Kayla, I tilt my head. She's compassionate but tough. Kind but careful. Yes. Nursing definitely suits her.

"James always said you'd be an amazing nurse," Jonah continues. "Said that caring heart of yours was designed to help others."

She swallows, looking taken aback. "Oh. That's...wow." Her expression is torn. Half-curious. Half-sad. "Well thank you. For the key." She smiles at Jonah and the storm in her eyes momentarily lifts.

"Sure thing, darlin'."

She says, "Have a good day," then turns and pulls us around the corner to where the PO boxes are.

Two guys standing in the corner instantly perk up the moment she comes into their view. Even with her leashed to my arm, they gape at her shamelessly, grunting and nodding their appreciation for her body.

After hearing Kayla talk last night about how people don't "see" her, I feel differently about these guys, and men in general, who stare at her. I still feel protective like I did yesterday, but now I also feel irritated. And defensive.

I want to protect her from the shallow eyes and snap judgments of onlookers because she deserves to be seen. Like a pretty vase filled with priceless gems, she's valued more for her surface beauty than the riches inside. I get it now, and I feel like a shallow dickhead for every girl I've ever judged on appearance.

Kayla ignores the guys in the corner, keeping her focus ahead as rain beats against the post office windows and blurs the world outside.

We scan the boxes in silence until I find number twelve, point to the keyhole, and grin. "Yahtzee!"

19

KAYLA

*M*y heart starts to pound as I insert the key into box number twelve, turn it over, and pull open the small metal door. Inside is another sheet of paper and we both groan.

Daren puckers his lips. "And...the scavenger hunt continues."

"That it does," I mutter, pulling out the note and closing the box. I read it out loud. "'Life Lesson number three: Money is a journey. It comes and it goes and sometimes you have to work hard to find it. Your next clue is at the place where you can see the whole world.'"

I stare at the note, speechless. I can't believe he remembered.

"What?" Daren cocks his head at me. "Do you know what that means? The place where you can see the whole world?"

Thunder rolls in the distance as I nod. "It's in the forest by the Ridge Burn. My dad and I used to go pretend fishing out there sometimes and there was this tree we went to..." The memory is so raw I can almost taste the forest air. I shake myself. "I'm pretty sure that tree is where we need to go."

We exit the post office and hurry through the summer rain to my car. Soon my eyes are on the road that leads out of town but my head is somewhere else entirely. Somewhere seven years ago, when I was fourteen and Josh Blackhill had just broken my heart.

I remember my father had taken me pretend fishing and told

me the world was so much bigger than Josh and that my broken heart had so much more to look forward to. He walked me to a giant tree beside the river and we climbed it together.

I remember thinking how silly it was for a teenage girl to be climbing a tree with her father, but inside I was having a really great time. It had wonderful climbing limbs, and the trunk was sturdy and smooth, so we were able to climb higher than I'd ever climbed before.

When we reached one of the upper limbs, we settled into a seat-like branch and my dad pointed out at the forest. From where we sat, we could see above all the other trees for miles and miles.

From way up here, you can see the whole world, he said. *And when you can see the whole world, your troubles don't look so big.*

I looked out to the mountains in the east and up into the big blue sky with a smile, wondering if I'd ever seen anything so pretty in my whole life. While I was in that tree, I forgot about Josh Blackhill and my broken heart. Because Daddy was right. From way up there, I could see the whole world.

"...should have come with a warning label." Daren's voice pulls me back to the road as the wipers slide across the windshield in rhythmic beats.

"What?"

He says, "I was just saying that your father's will should have come with a warning label. Who knows how long this scavenger hunt is going to go on for?"

I nod absently. "Yeah. Who knows."

"And now he has us driving all the way out to the Ridge Burn?" He whistles. "What could possibly be so significant about an old tree?"

I look through the gray weather at the mountains in the east and exhale slowly.

Plenty.

20

DAREN

*T*he Ridge Burn.

I used to come out here during the summers and play Capture the Flag with my high school buddies. I was never really good at the game. In fact, I was never really good at any sports. Running and catching and competing were never really my strong suit. Now, sexing and charming and making girls melt? *Those* were activities I could win a gold medal in.

I rub at my wrist where the skin is slightly raw and shiny. "Your father could have at least picked handcuffs that weren't so wickedly uncomfortable."

"I guess it's better than wearing fuzzy cuffs where people would think we're on some kind of kinky sexcapade," she says.

"Oh right. Because looking like chained-up fugitives on the run is so much better."

Eleven miles down Canary Road, we pull into a muddy clearing and park by the Ridge Burn.

"So how far away is this magic tree of yours?" I stare out at the wet forest.

The rain is more of a light drizzle now and less like a downpour so at least we can see relatively clearly.

"A hundred yards or so." She shuts the engine off.

"Wonderful."

We climb out of the car and I stretch my stiff limbs. She leads me by the wrist through the woods for fifteen minutes until we come to a large tree beside the river that looks exactly the same as every other tree we've passed.

"How do you know this is the one?" I gaze up at the thick trunk reaching into the low gray clouds.

She sighs quietly. "I just do." She marches around the trunk. "Look for another clue."

I search high and low for anything that might be a clue. My eyes catch on a small green pole sticking up out of the muddy ground at the base of the tree and I stop.

"Could that be it?" I point to the pole.

"Maybe." She hurries to dig it up and, once the dirt is cleared away, there is a box. It's no bigger than a shoebox, but it's large enough to hold a few stacks of hundred-dollar bills.

"Bingo!" I smile.

She grins at me then opens the box.

Another piece of paper.

She pulls out the paper inside and reads, "'I'm pleased you remember this tree, Kayla. It holds a special place in my heart, just like you. Lesson number four: The world is bigger than what you know. There is more to life than what you see and what you think. And if you ever reach a place where you think you know it all, then you are most definitely lost. Now go home to the place where winning is relative.'" She frowns. "What does that mean?"

"It means your dad had a fantastic memory." I smile and shake my head, shocked that Turner remembered a conversation we had years ago. "It also means we've got a long drive back up and through Copper Springs."

"What?" she says, dragging behind me as I start heading back to the car. "Why?"

"Because I'm pretty sure your dad wants us to go to Copper Field."

"The baseball stadium?"

"Yep."

As we drive back in the direction we just came from, I think back to when I was thirteen and had my baseball championship game out at Copper Field.

I was no good at sports. But I was a guy, and guys in small towns are expected not just to play sports, but to excel at them. So my father put me in baseball and forced me to stay in it for ten years. Ten long years of misery.

The championship game came and, unfortunately, I was up to bat right when we had two outs and the game was tied. If it had been a movie, that would have been the moment where I finally hit my first home run and scored the winning point, and we'd win the game and the crowd would go wild.

It wasn't a movie.

I struck out and the other team came up to bat and hit a home run on their first swing. So essentially, I was blamed for our team losing. My father was sorely disappointed and my teammates were giving me shit about how lousy I was, but Marcella still believed in me.

She came to every one of my baseball games, rain or shine, and sat in the stands with a beaming smile like she wanted the whole world to know she was proud of me.

That was my favorite part of playing baseball—Marcella's proud smile watching me from the stands. God, I miss her.

But at that particular game, even Marcella's confidence in me wasn't helping. I started thinking about how I really was lousy, and how I was always going to be a loser. I wasn't a good student, I wasn't good at sports, and I had no real talents…I was just lousy, in general. And maybe I always would be.

But Marcella wasn't the only spectator rooting me on that day. Old Man Turner came to every single one of my baseball games too. We didn't usually talk or say hi, but I always saw him in the stands, watching me and cheering for me.

After the game, while everyone else got into in their cars to go celebrate their win, I cut across the field to where my bike was stashed and Turner's voice surprised me.

Not your best game tonight, he said.

I turned to him and glared. *Thanks for noticing.*

He shrugged. *Winning a baseball game isn't everything.*

Tell that to them. I nodded over at my disgruntled teammates and their fans.

He shook his head. *You've got it all wrong.* He walked up beside me. *Winning is relative. Winning in baseball isn't the same as winning in life. And winning in life, well…that's the only game that counts.*

I had no idea what he was talking about, but I nodded anyway. *Sure.*

He slapped me on the back and started to walk away. *Life is the only game that counts, Daren,* he called over his shoulder. *Remember that.* Then he disappeared into his car.

I didn't understand why my boss at the time, and a man I barely knew, would bother to show up at all my games, let alone give me a pep talk after I bombed one terribly, but I was grateful nonetheless. It was nice that he cared enough to give me some advice—even if that advice was odd and cryptic.

Winning in baseball was the only kind of winning I was interested in at the time. Because my father saw me as such a huge disappointment in sports, my teenage ego was convinced that if I could win a baseball game—or at least not lose it completely—then I would earn his approval.

It wasn't until years later that "winning in life" became something I understood, and then something I wanted. But here I am, almost a decade later, still striking out on that one.

The rain picks up once we reach Copper Field. We get out of the car and climb up a muddy slope to the plateau where the field is situated. Our shoes make sucking noises as we step through the thick, wet dirt and finally reach the top.

It's a junior league field, but it still has stadium lights, three stories of bleachers, and an electric scoreboard.

Kayla looks around at the deserted field. "So why is this place where winning is relative?"

I hesitate for a moment. "Your dad saw me bomb one of my baseball games once and told me winning was relative. I think he was trying to encourage me or something." I shrug.

"He came to your baseball games?" she says in surprise. "Wow. He must have really cared about you."

I nod. "I think he did. I should have appreciated him more before he was gone." I look at her. "I didn't know he was sick either, you know. I guess he didn't want anyone to know about his failing health."

She inhales deeply. "So you didn't get to say good-bye to him either?"

I shake my head. "That was probably the worst part of finding out he was gone. Not getting any real closure."

She stares at the ground and slowly nods before bringing her blue eyes up to mine. "I'm sorry you lost him."

I swallow. "We both lost him."

Heartache fills the space between us, drifting up and around our linked arms and floating over the damp field. But locking eyes with Kayla eases the sadness and lets something else seep in. Something quiet and hopeful. Something that stretches out my lungs and pulls at my gut.

I suddenly want to pull Kayla close and wrap my arms around her. I want to kiss her and touch her, but the desire isn't the same as it was at Latecomers the other night. That desire was heady and filled with lust. This is a wanting born from the same deep roots as the hot protectiveness I felt yesterday and the need to comfort I've felt every time Kayla's let her guard down.

It's steady and powerful and it leaves my throat dry as I stare into her eyes.

"Yes," she says quietly. "We both lost him." She blinks a few times then clears her throat. "We should keep looking."

With our moment of heartbreak over, we walk around the field for a few minutes searching for anything that could be a clue. We check the field first then the bases. It's silent, except for the patter of rain on the dirt and the light tingling sound of our handcuffs.

But there is absolutely nothing on the field. No notes. No keys. No green poles. Nothing.

I pull the clue out of my pocket and reread it.

"What?" Kayla leans over.

I point to where to clue reads *go home to the place where winning is relative.* "I think 'go home' means go to home plate."

We walk over to the mud-covered home plate. Scraping the wet dirt aside with my shoe, I stare down to where it reads DONATED BY THE MYERS FAMILY and say, "Tallyho!"

She scrunches her face. "You think that's the clue?"

"What else would 'go home' mean?"

Her eyes light up. "Don't the Myerses own the bakery in Town Square? Maybe they know something about my dad's will."

I shrug. "It's worth a shot."

A crack of thunder booms around us, followed by a flash of lightning in the distance. The rain starts coming down in buckets so we begin to jog. With our wrists locked together, it's hard for either of us to run with any kind of grace. We awkwardly maneuver back to the edge of the plateau.

We start down the muddy slope, both of us thrusting our free arms out to help keep our balance, but the soft dirt is too wet and pliable for us to find any traction. I start to slip and Kayla grabs my arm and pulls me back. I'm too heavy for her to hold, though, so we tumble backward into the mud and starting sliding down the hill.

I dig my feet into the mud, but it's no use. It's too slick and we're too heavy to be stopped. We slide through the mud, Kayla still clutching my arm, until we reach the bottom and roll over each other. We land on our sides, facing each other through the muck as rain beats down on us.

Kayla looks pissed. "I hate these handcuffs."

I share her frustration. "Me too."

We carefully stand. I try to flick off as much mud as possible from my clothes and arms while Kayla tries to comb the mud from her hair with her fingers. The rain helps a little, washing away the dirt as it soaks us, but we're still filthy as we climb back into her little green car.

We don't speak during the drive. The scavenger hunt is kicking our ass and we know it. So the silence between us is more weary than anything else. I look down at our adjoined wrists and inhale.

Once we find the inheritance, Kayla and I won't have hand-cuffs, or any other reason to spend time together. She'll go back to Chicago and I might not see her again.

My stomach falls at the thought of Kayla leaving. I've kind of started to enjoy spending time with her. She's different than I first thought. She's... refreshing. The idea of her leaving, of me never seeing her again, brings a tightness to my chest similar to what I felt at Turner's funeral and it's all I can do not to cough it away.

Driving out to the Ridge Burn and Copper Field sucked up the entire day, so we arrive at the bakery shortly before closing. Now, here we are, standing on the sidewalk as the sun starts to set on this rainy day, and we still don't have the inheritance.

We stop outside the glass double doors of the bakery and stare at our reflection. Kayla's blonde hair is wet and matted with mud. My clothes are soaked and covered in mud. And smudges of dirt streak both our faces and arms, right down to our linked wrists. We look like we've been through war.

I open the bakery door and we walk inside, careful not to track in mud as we keep our feet on the entry mat. Mrs. Myers is by the counter, sweeping up some spilled sprinkles with her gray hair pulled into a bun and her round body covered in a chocolate-stained apron.

She looks up. "Daren? Oh my. You're a mess." Her eyes fall to our cuffed hands. "What happened?"

I lift our wrists. "Turner thought it would be hilarious to tie us up and send us on a scavenger hunt around town."

Hearty laughter bubbles out from her. "Of course he did. That James. He was a hoot." She comes over and leans up on her toes to gives me a kiss on the cheek. "I'd hug you, but you two look like you got in a fight with a swamp." She turns her full attention to

Kayla and gapes. "Good heavens. Is this little Kayla Turner, all grown up?"

Kayla smiles. "Hi, Mrs. Myers."

"My goodness, child. I haven't seen you since you were just a little girl." She clucks her tongue. "And now look at you. Every bit as pretty as your mama was. You know, I fed Gia every day when she was pregnant with you."

"Really?" Kayla says.

"Yes. Blueberry tarts were her favorite." Mrs. Myers looks us over with a happy sigh. "I'm glad you're here. James told me you'd be coming, you know."

My eyebrows shoot up. "He did?"

She nods. "Before he passed, he asked me to hold on to an envelope. He said he had a special treat in store for you and Kayla. He failed to mention anything about handcuffs, though." She smiles. "James always had a creative imagination, and now look at him, chaining the two of you up and sending you all over town." She laughs. "It sounds like a complete ball. You must be having so much fun."

We raise our eyebrows and look down at our muddy wet clothes.

Fun. Right.

She bustles behind the bakery counter and throws a look at Kayla. "Give me just a moment and I'll be back with your daddy's note." She disappears into the back.

I take a cookie from a nearby display tray and bring it to my mouth.

"What are you doing?" Kayla slaps my hand and the cookie goes flying, joining the sprinkles on the floor.

I glower. "I was trying to eat a cookie. What are *you* doing?"

"That's stealing," she says, looking aghast.

I make a noncommittal noise. "They're more like samples than anything else."

She shakes her head. "I can't believe you."

"I'm starving," I say defensively. "We haven't eaten all day. Aren't you hungry?"

We didn't stop for lunch today, which was fine with me since I'm broke, but I was surprised Kayla didn't suggest we stop for food.

"No, I'm fine," Kayla says. Right on cue, her stomach growls.

"Ha!" I point at her stomach. "Liar."

I reach for the cookie dish and she smacks my hand. Again.

"Cut it out," she snaps.

The front door opens and I turn to see Valerie Oswald enter the bakery with a large box.

"Navy Nancy," Kayla whispers, looking the woman over.

I turn to Kayla. "Navy who?"

"That woman." She juts her chin in Valerie's direction. "I saw her at the funeral."

I nod. "That's Valerie Oswald. She's the property manager for all of your dad's business developments in the town square."

"Oh." Kayla nods.

Valerie looks at us and upon seeing Kayla narrows her eyes. Then she sees me, and then the handcuffs, and her eyes widen. "What on earth...?"

She frowns at Kayla and I wonder why. Kayla clearly doesn't know Valerie yet Valerie seems to dislike her.

"It's a long story," I say, smiling. "But basically, James asked us to do this in his will. Have you two met?" I gesture to Kayla. "This is James's daughter, Kayla. Kayla, this is Valerie."

Kayla still looks uncomfortable but manages to smile nicely. "Hello there. Nice to meet you."

"Your James's *daughter*?" The iciness in Valerie's gaze instantly melts into warmth as she sets down the box and holds out her hand. "Oh, how very nice to meet you. Your father was a terrific man."

Kayla shakes her hand. "Thank you. It's nice to meet you too."

"Found it!" Mrs. Myers returns, waving an envelope in her hand. "Oh, hello Valerie." She smiles. "What brings you in so late?"

Valerie picks the box back up and hands it to Mrs. Myers with a smile. "I just wanted to return your chocolate fountain. Thank you for letting the town use it for the Confetti Carnival. It was a hit, as usual."

"There was a chocolate fountain?" I say under my breath. "Dammit. I can't believe we missed that."

"I know," Kayla adds. "I love chocolate fountains."

"Of course." Mrs. Myers smiles at Valerie. "You know I always love contributing to the Confetti Carnival."

"Well we appreciate it." She turns to leave. "Well I need to get going. Thanks again." She smiles at us. "It was a pleasure meeting you, Kayla."

She leaves the bakery and Kayla bends to pick up the cookie she knocked out of my hand earlier. "I'm sorry about the cookie on the floor," she says to Mrs. Myers as she throws it away. "Daren thought they were samples. We can pay for it."

I turn to her and mouth, *Traitor.*

Mrs. Myers waves her off. "Nonsense dear. Anything that doesn't get eaten tonight gets tossed, anyway. In fact, if you two wouldn't mind taking some of these goodies home with you, that would save me a trip to the trash." She gestures to an array of baked treats behind a glass display.

"Oh no, no," Kayla argues. "We couldn't take your food."

"Hush, child." She hands the envelope to Kayla and shuffles behind the counter, grabbing a paper bag. She starts piling left-over cookies and brownies into a bag and my mouth starts to water. "Here you are." She shoves a bag overflowing with treats into my arms and winks at Kayla. "I put a few blueberry tarts in there too, just in case you have the same taste as your mama."

Kayla smiles. "Oh wow. Thank you for all these desserts."

She and I both pull out a cookie and stuff our faces. Well, I stuff *my* face, but Kayla takes dainty bites and spends time chewing like a person with manners.

"Of course. I'd do anything for James and his family." Her eyes sparkle. "Did you know I introduced your parents?"

Kayla's eyes sparkle right back as she grins. "I did *not* know that."

Mrs. Myers nods. "Your mother was in here one day, buying up all my blueberry tarts when James walked in. I introduced him to her and a few short months later they were married." She chuckles and happily sighs. "They were quite the pair."

Kayla smiles. "Yes. That's what I've heard."

She clucks her tongue. "James never did recover from your mama leaving. Poor thing. Valerie Oswald never had a chance. Did you know she was in love with your father?"

Kayla frowns. "The woman with the chocolate fountain had a thing for my dad?"

"Oh, yes. She wanted James's heart something fierce. But he loved you and your mama, and no other woman could compete."

Kayla lifts a brow. "Well that explains why Valerie didn't like me when she first saw me. She must have thought I was his girl-friend or something."

Mrs. Myers laughs. "Valerie is just protective of James, that's all. And I can't imagine anyone not just loving you to pieces the moment they meet you."

Kayla laughs. "Well that's sweet of you to say—especially since you don't really know me."

She grins. "Oh, baby. I know all about you. James talked my ear off about his little girl. And then you come in here covered in dirt and handcuffed to my sweet Daren? Well, I knew the moment I saw you that you were every bit as wonderful as James described."

I watch Kayla's face soften and her eyes fill with emotion. It's obvious she's not used to people showing her the kind of warm acceptance and compassion that Mrs. Myers is well-known for.

Kayla blinks a few times and I intervene so she doesn't have to respond or try to hide the emotion creeping up her face.

"Well we should get going to let you finish closing up," I say. "Thank you so much for your generosity, Mrs. Myers." I tip my chin at the bag in my hand and smile.

"I hope you enjoy the blueberry tarts." She moves her eyes from Kayla and smiles broadly at me. "And good luck on your treasure hunt." She waves good-bye as we exit the bakery armed with more sugar and chocolate than a Wonka factory.

Back outside, the rain has let up, leaving only the heavy clouds and damp air behind. We climb into her car and Kayla tears open the new clue and reads out loud.

"'Daren. I hope the game of life has been good to you. Even if you don't feel like you're succeeding, remember you're still in the early innings. Lesson number five: The only game that matters is the game of life. And a few lost innings aren't a lost game. By now, I'm sure you're both frustrated with me, and probably ready to get your handcuffs off. Go to the lavender ranch at the end of Canary Road for your final clue. Then you're done!'"

Her face lights up. "The last clue! We're almost finished."

"Awesome," I say, munching on a cookie as I frown at the setting sun. "All we have to do now is go to an abandoned lavender field ... in the middle of the desert ... at night ... without flashlights ..."

"Yeah," she says, biting her lip. "Not ideal."

"Maybe we should wait until morning."

She nods. "You're probably right. But I don't have my motel room still booked. That's why my suitcase is in the car. I thought we'd be done by now and I'd be headed back to Chicago. And as much as I love being your sugar mama, I don't have any money to book another room. So let's stay at your place tonight."

"At *my* place? Uh ..."

"What? Do you live with eight frat boys who eat with their feet and fart a lot, or what?"

"No. Not exactly." But that would be better than the truth. Anything would be better.

"Then what?" She juts her chin.

"My place is just a bit of a mess and not really ready for company. You wouldn't like it."

She sneers. "Then why don't *you* shell out the cash to get us a hotel room? It's about time you and your designer shirt start contributing to this little adventure. I mean, I've paid for *everything*. Like our room last night—"

"You would have paid for that room even if we'd found the inheritance," I point out.

"Okay, then what about my car? Who paid for all the gas that's been toting you around all day? *Me*." She pauses. "Where the hell is your Porsche anyway?"

"Uh ... in the shop."

She furrows her brow. "I thought it was parked *far, far away*."

I scratch my cheek. "It is."

She looks at me, skeptical. "It's parked far, far away in a shop?"

"Yep." I nod. "Far, far away in a shop of all the other repossessed cars in the county." I force a smile.

She pulls back. "Your car got repossessed?"

"Yes," I say, shifting in my seat. "And it's not my car. It's my dad's. Technically."

She looks confused. "Why?"

"Because I had to sell my own car to pay some bills and I needed a way to get to and from work. Ergo, I drive my dad's car."

"No." She blinks impatiently. "Why was the Porsche repossessed?"

"Oh." I inhale. "Because I don't have the money to make any more payments on it. My dad made a year's worth of payments on the Porsche before he went to jail, which is the only reason I was able to drive it for so long. I couldn't sell it because my dad owed more on the loan than it was worth, but I also couldn't afford to keep it because the payments were ridiculous and I have no money," I say. "Ergo, the Porsche was repossessed."

She scans my face. "So you don't have *any* money?"

"Nope." I shake my head. "I already told you that."

"I thought you were being dramatic." She sighs. "Well I don't have any money either. So unless you feel like sleeping in my car, we need to stay the night at your place."

For a moment, I seriously consider sleeping in her car.

"Fine," I say, sucking up my housing insecurities with a groan. "We'll go back to my place. But just for the record"—I point at her—"I warned you that you wouldn't like it."

She smirks. "I'm sure it's fine."

I shake my head as we pull out of the parking lot.

Famous last words.

21

KAYLA

*D*aren's been acting weird ever since we left the bakery. Weird in a fidgety, shifting-in-his-seat, jutting-his-jaw-every-five-minutes kind of way.

Gripping the steering wheel, I follow his directions as the sun disappears and the rainy day transforms into a cloudy night. I glance in the rearview mirror for the hundredth time and bite my lip. The same black car has been behind us since we left the town square. It could be nothing. Or it could be Big Joe.

"What?" Daren says, watching me bite down on my lip. "What's wrong?" He turns to look behind us.

"I think someone is following us again," I say.

He watches the headlights in the distance for a moment. "It's probably just someone headed the same direction as us. If it *was* this boss guy of yours—what's his name again?"

"Big Joe."

"Really? That's what he goes by? *Big Joe?*" Daren scoffs. "What is he, a mobster?"

I don't answer and his eyes widen.

"Are you *shitting* me? Your mom owed money to a mobster?" he says then runs his free hand through his hair and mutters, "Oh fuck, fuck, fuck."

"I'm not *sure* that he's a mobster," I say defensively. "I just know he's a bad guy."

Just then, the car following us takes a turn and is no longer behind us. I sigh in relief as I stare at the empty road in the rearview mirror.

"See?" Daren smiles at me. "No one is following you."

I nod and let out a little laugh. "Wow. I feel dumb. I keep thinking we're being followed and we're clearly not. I'm so jumpy. Sorry."

"No, it's fine. I'd be freaked out too if I thought someone who may or may not be a mobster was after me." He playfully grins, which helps ease my anxiety. "But you're safe." His eyes stay on mine. "And besides, you have me." He wiggles our cuffed hands. "I'll protect you. You know, with my free hand."

I chuckle, my fear slowly draining from my veins as he winks. I'm oddly comforted by the fact that Daren is physically attached to me. I've gotten so used to being on my own that I've forgotten how nice it is to have someone to share things with. Excitement. Adventure. *Fear.* Having someone at my side makes everything better. And it certainly makes this whole thing with Big Joe less scary.

"Oh my!" I smile at Daren. "You're my knight in shining... steel manacles."

He bows his head. "At your service, milady."

My smile stays in place for the next few miles as we joke about sword fighting with handcuffs on, and soon all my fear has completely melted away. Daren has that effect on me, I'm learning. He has a way of distracting me from things that might otherwise get me down. It's kind of... sweet. He's sweet.

We drive to the ritzy side of town where the neighborhoods are all gated with grand entrances and Daren directs me to a gated community called Westlake Estates. I turn in and pull up to the security booth at the front of the community. No one is manning the booth at this late hour, leaving the security completely at the mercy of a keypad.

I lean back in my seat so Daren can easily reach the keypad. "Do you want to—"

"Five six four five," he says.

I stare at him. "Did you just give me the code to your gated community?"

"I did."

I grin. "Oh my. I might just have to start calling you my friend now."

He scoffs. "It's about time."

With a laugh, I punch in the numbers. A buzzing noise sounds from the box before the nine-foot-tall grand gates slowly start to open.

I marvel at the rolling hills and water-featured entrance of Daren's community and I swear I can almost hear angels singing as we drive through. This is easily the most expensive neighborhood I've ever been in.

"Just follow this road all the way to the stop sign," Daren says. "Then take a right until you come to a driveway at the end of a cul-de-sac."

I do as he says and he points ahead of us. "That's it, right there."

My lips part. Of course he lives on the top of a hill in a cul-de-sac—a cul-de-sac that no other houses are on. He owns his own freaking cul-de-sac! I'm so collecting gas money from him. I cruise up the steep driveway at the base of a mansion. And it is a *mansion*.

He points to the side. "Drive around back and park beside the pool house."

"You have a pool house?" I shake my head. "Why am I not surprised?"

He lets out a strained sigh. "Just park."

The neighborhood is well lit, with fancy lampposts every few yards, but the mansion and pool house are completely dark. No lights turned on, inside or out.

I bite the inside of my cheek. "Does anybody else live here?"

He shakes his head. "My mom lives in Boston and my dad's in jail, so now it's just me."

"You have this huge house all to yourself?"

"Something like that." He points to a nearly hidden area beside the pool house. "Just pull under that tree and park."

It seems weird to park in the most isolated area of the yard, but I don't question his logic as I pull forward and turn off the car. Once the headlights go out, the only light in the car is from the dim moon filtering through the clouds.

With dried mud still caked to my skin and clothes, I grab the bag of goodies and open the car door, scooting over as Daren and I repeat our getting-out-of-the-car-while-handcuffed routine. He seems to have more difficulty in the dark, grunting and cursing as he bangs his knees on the dashboard and knocks his head against the roof. I almost pity him.

I glance at his dark mansion.

Almost.

When we're both out of the car, I grab my suitcase from the trunk before following him to the back of the house. Instead of heading to the back door, however, Daren moves to a window *beside* the door. Jiggling the frame, he pops the window out of place and slides it to the side. My wrist flops around next to his. Then he starts climbing in.

"What in the—what are you doing?" I say, completely confused.

He picks up my suitcase and tosses it inside along with the bag from the bakery. "I don't have a key."

"How do you not have a key to your own house?"

"It's a long story," he says half in and half out of the window.

"This *is* your house, right?" He doesn't answer and I gasp. "Are we breaking into some rich guy's place?" My voice grows louder. "Because I am NOT going to be an accomplice in your shady criminal behavior. We already have handcuffs on! If you think—"

He yanks me up against his body and closes his hand over my mouth as I warm against the hard muscles of his chest. "Would you keep it down?"

Teetering, I have to lean against his leg so I don't fall over, which forces me to press even more of myself up against his broad frame. All I can think about as he stares at me in the moonlight is how pretty his long eyelashes are and how I'm really starting to like the smell of oranges—even though he's breaking us into some rich guy's house.

"I'm trying not to draw attention to us," he says. "And you yelling isn't helping." He swallows and looks away. "And this *is* my home. Kinda. So you can calm down." His fingers lightly brush against my throat as he lowers his hand from my mouth.

I can't tell if the gentle touch was an accident or not, but my hungry body doesn't care. It just wants him to do it again.

"This is 'kinda' your house?" I say, frustrated and turned on. "What the hell does that mean—oompf!"

He pulls me inside and I topple over the windowsill and into the house. He catches me before I fall to the floor but I'm already in a rage as I straighten in his arms.

"Are you crazy?" I glare at him, the tips of my breasts brushing against his chest as we stand face-to-face.

"No. I'm just in a hurry to get your loud mouth out of earshot from the neighbors." He shuts the window behind us.

Looking around, I take in the inside of the mansion. It's large and dark and...

Completely abandoned.

I turn and stare at him. "You have a lot of explaining to do."

22

DAREN

I hold up a hand. "Before you freak out, just remember you're the one who insisted we stay at my place."

She shakes her head as she looks around. "Did someone rob you or something?"

I scoff. "I wish it were that simple."

"So what's the story then?"

"You want the story?" I nod. "Once upon a time, my mom left and my dad became a raging alcoholic. Then three years ago, he lost his job and, instead of looking for a new one, he decided to drink and gamble away all his money. He managed to burn through his life savings, lose the house, and rack up three DUIs all in a matter of nineteen months. I got two jobs and tried to keep all the bills afloat, but last year, when his drunk driving nearly killed Connor and the poor guy had to have two major surgeries just to walk again, the hospital bills started piling up. So now most of the money I make goes toward Connor's medical debt, the house I grew up in is in foreclosure, and my reckless father is serving two years in county jail."

She rubs the back of her neck. "So you live here?"

I inhale through my nose. "Technically, no one lives here. The bank repossessed the house two months ago and put it into foreclosure. But since the market for large homes moves so slowly, it hasn't been listed for sale yet so it's just been sitting here abandoned. And because I can't afford to take care of both myself and the medical bills, I've been sleeping here."

She furrows her brow. "I don't get it. Why are you paying medical bills for the guy your dad hit? Isn't insurance supposed to do that?"

"Yeah, but neither my dad nor Connor had insurance. But Connor has a family and a good job and a mortgage..." I shake my head. "I just didn't think it was fair to make a good sober man pay for my dad's irresponsible behavior."

Anger boils inside me as I think about my father's response when he first found out he'd nearly killed Connor. He was still hammered as he waved it off: *Well too bad. Connor will just have to find a way to pay his own damn bills.*

I wanted to disown him, right then and there.

Kayla looks around again and breathes out a laugh. "Well at least this place is nicer than the Quickie Stop."

I snort. "Everything is nicer than the Quickie Stop."

She nods. "Good point. So...where do we sleep?"

"Upstairs. Come on." Grabbing her suitcase, I lead her through the dark kitchen into the equally dark living room.

"Did the bank turn the electricity off?" she asks as we stop at the bottom of the staircase.

"No. But I try not to turn on the lights at nighttime. I don't want to draw attention to the fact that a homeless guy is living in an abandoned house." The moment they leave my mouth, I immediately regret my words.

I just told her that I'm homeless. *Homeless.*

I don't *need* Kayla's approval, but I certainly don't want her disdain. And telling her I'm homeless isn't going to help.

Who am I kidding? I do *want* her approval. I shake my head. Story of my life. Always chasing after the approval of women. First my mom. Then Marcella. And finally Charity.

And I lost each one. My mom didn't want me, and Marcella was forced to leave me. And Charity...well, Charity was my first love and I blame myself for the events leading up to her death. I'm no good at hanging on to women, as desperate as I am to do just that, so the fact that I care about the look in Kayla's eyes right now scares the shit out of me.

I let out a nervous laugh. "God, sorry. I won't blame you if you completely freak out right now."

She slowly shakes her head. "I'm not going to freak out."

I eye her skeptically. "Why not?"

She cocks her head and quietly says, "Because I'm homeless too."

23

KAYLA

Things have definitely changed since yesterday. Yesterday, I was the bitter daughter of a crazy man who was handcuffed to the arrogant son of a wealthy one. Tonight, I'm the poor daughter of a much beloved man who is handcuffed to the desperate son of an alcoholic.

"You're homeless?" Daren repeats with a baffled expression.

It's the first time I've said "I'm homeless" out loud, and I thought it would feel different coming out of my mouth. Shameful, maybe? Sad? But instead I feel…fine. Maybe even a little brave.

There's something about sharing the same destitute state with Daren that makes me feel courageous. I'm not alone so I'm not afraid.

I nod. "My lease was up before I left Chicago, and I couldn't pay next month's rent, so I gave up my apartment and came out to Copper Springs without any money. Or a plan. The only thing I really have is my mom's old car, which, fortunately, is paid off."

"So we're both homeless and broke, and neither of us have a plan for our life?" he says. "Whoa."

"Whoa, indeed."

"I guess we have more in common than we knew," he says.

"And I guess we both have a lot riding on this inheritance."

He nods. "It's kind of the only thing I have to hope for right now."

The desperation in his voice has me suddenly rethinking my plan to take all the money for myself. I didn't have an issue scamming a spoiled rich kid who introduced himself to me as a "legendary lover," but this guy—this penniless guy who sleeps in a vacant house and pays off a stranger's medical bills simply because it's the right thing to do—I can't take money from. And honestly, he deserves it more than I do.

"Well." Daren pulls a cookie from the bakery bag, breaks it in half, and hands a piece to me. Then holds up his own piece. "Here's to having no plan."

I hold up my own cookie half. "Here's to poverty."

"And homelessness."

"And scavenger hunts for money," I say.

We tap our cookies then each take a bite. Our eyes hold for a beat and I'm suddenly acutely aware that we're alone in the dark, and a ping of desire races through me.

His eyes drop to my mouth and I absently lick my lips. It wouldn't be completely crazy for me to give in to what I want, would it? I'm an adult, after all, and just because I don't *usually* want to be with a guy doesn't mean I *shouldn't* be with one. Sure we're in handcuffs and covered in filth, but just because the setting isn't ideal doesn't mean the instinct is wrong...right?

Right?

My gaze falls to his lips and we lean toward each other. His hot breath feathers across my jaw as our mouths meet, ever so slightly. I want to taste him again and shove my hands in his hair. I want to—

A flash of bright light bursts into the house and we jump back, temporarily blinded. At first I think it's the police. They've discovered us breaking and entering into this giant mansion that belongs to the bank, and now we're going to be poor homeless people in jail.

But then I realize it's only a pair of headlights from a car turning down the street and I let out a sigh of relief. We look at each other with nervous little laughs.

"One of the pitfalls of living here," Daren says. "You never know when you might get busted."

"You are a true daredevil."

"I try." He smiles, but the sizzle in the air has vanished and now it's just awkward between us. He looks down at our muddy clothes. "We should probably wash up. This place might not have any furniture, but it *does* have hot running water."

"Oh man. A shower would be *great*," I say, rolling my head back. After suffering the Quickie Stop's icy dribbles and pet spiders all week, anything warm and critter-free would be just heavenly.

"Come on," he says, carrying my suitcase.

We walk up the grand staircase, down a wide hallway on the second floor, and into a large bedroom on the right. He flicks on a light switch.

In the corner is a queen-size mattress lying directly on the floor, no bed frame, and covered in bedding that probably cost more than a month's worth of rent on my old apartment. Beside the mattress is a small table stacked with books, a half-empty box of crackers, and a few papers.

Through the open double doors of the closet hangs a small collection of very expensive clothes and off to the side is a private bathroom, with an elaborate walk-in shower and separate garden tub.

Daren definitely lives in style—or used to, at least.

"Nice room," I say. Then stare in confusion at the only window in the room. It's above his bed and completely covered with cardboard.

He follows my gaze. "That's so no one can tell someone's inside the house when I have a light on in here."

"Gotcha." I nod then point to the books on the table. "You're a reader?"

He nods. "Sometimes."

"Huh." I run a finger down the book spines. "What's your favorite book?"

He smiles sheepishly. "All those are pretty good. But my favorite book of all time is actually a children's book called *Holes*."

"Really? Why is that?"

He lifts a shoulder. "I don't know. It's about this kid who has a bunch of bad things happen to him even though he didn't do anything wrong. I guess I sympathize with that or something."

I study him for a moment, surprised by his confession, and then look around. "You don't own a copy of *Holes*?"

His expression looks strained for a brief second. "Uh . . . I used to, but not anymore."

I want to ask why, but the shadows in his eyes make me hesitate. My breath catches as my eyes drift to a velvet-lined box on the small table. Inside is a tremendously ornate diamond necklace. It sparkles so brilliantly it almost looks like its own source of light. "What is that?"

Daren follows my gaze and picks up the shiny necklace. "This was my mother's. My dad gave it to her for their anniversary when I was little."

"It's stunning," I say in awe. "Is it real?"

"Oh yes. It's real and worth a sick amount of money." He looks at the diamonds. "Over the past few years, I've had to sell or pawn pretty much all of my family's possessions. But I couldn't let go of this."

"Because it's too valuable?" I nod.

"It's more than that." He swallows. "My parents weren't really involved with me, you know, so most of my memories of them are really stoic. But the day my dad gave this necklace to my mom, she was elated. I'd never seen her in such a good mood. She pranced around the house all giddy. My dad turned on some music and the two of them started dancing in the living room, laughing and singing along with the song. I was seven at the time and had never seen them goof around like that so I couldn't help but watch. My mom saw me spying on them and waved me over. I ran to their arms and the three of us danced together in the living room like a happy family. It's the best memory I have of my parents. And it was all because of this necklace." He chuckles and shakes his head. "I know it seems crazy because I could probably sell this thing and pay off most of Connor's medical bills. But I don't know." He looks at the sparkling stones. "I can't bring myself to sacrifice my only souvenir of that day for money."

Watching him, I feel a piece of my heart break off and deliver itself into Daren's hands, permanently. He somehow got a hold on me and now it's too late for me to wriggle free, even if I wanted to. Which I don't.

"I like that you kept it," I say.

He scans my face. "And I like that you like that."

A beat passes.

"So why do you choose to stay here?" I ask, changing topics as I glide my eyes over his room. "Why not crash with one of your buddies?"

He shrugs and places the necklace back into the velvet casing. "Because even if they said I could stay for free, I'd still feel obligated to pay rent. Besides, most of my friends are snobs so I don't really talk about my, uh, circumstances. I doubt they'd be very understanding if they knew how broke I was."

"Then they're not real friends," I say, growing defensive on Daren's behalf. He shouldn't need to hide his circumstances in order to be accepted. "What about your many adoring lady friends? I'm sure they're very understanding."

He scoffs. "Like I would tell women."

"What do you mean?"

He smiles bitterly. "My 'lady friends' think I'm still living the good life, surviving off of some hidden bank account my father gave to me before he went to jail. I have the Porsche to thank for that assumption. They have no idea all my family's money is gone. If they did, they'd probably forget I existed. Women are shallow like that."

I open my mouth to protest, but realize he has a point. "Huh. I guess it's kind of the same the other way around too. If I looked different than I do, or if I grew warts all over my face and shaved my head, guys would probably stop paying attention to me too," I say. "But not all women are shallow."

He shrugs. "Most of the women I know."

I prop a hand on my hip, my defensiveness growing into anger. "Then you need to meet different women."

"I'm not saying *you're* shallow," he says, leaning in. "I'm just saying that if the women in this town knew just how poor and homeless Daren Ackwood was, they wouldn't be waving to me at the bar. That's just the way it is."

"So you lie to them instead?"

"No, I let them believe their assumptions about me."

"Because otherwise you'd be shunned."

"Not shunned, exactly. Just...undesired. Women don't want to take a homeless guy home with them."

I sadly nod. "And if you aren't wanted for sex then you have nothing else to offer."

"Exactly—what? No." The smug smile he just had on quickly vanishes. "That's not what I'm saying."

"Yes, it is. God. Would you listen to yourself?" I search his face. "You shouldn't have to lie to get people to like you. And if you do, then those people aren't worth your time. Where you live doesn't matter, Daren. *Money* doesn't matter—"

"I know that," he snaps. "But other people don't. And this town—this whole world—is filled with *other people.* Is it so bad that I want them to wave to me at the bar?"

I stare at him, rolling his words over in my head. "I didn't wave at you."

"What?"

"At the bar the other night." I shrug. "I didn't wave at you."

"Right. You refused to even shake my hand. You were a little judgmental when you first saw me at Eddie's office so you put me on your shit list and wrote me off because you assumed I was rich and arrogant."

"Exactly." I point at him. "I didn't like the Daren Ackwood who had money and fast cars and a mansion in the hills. But the real you—the dirt-poor Daren who always took care of my dad's garden and pays off some poor guy's medical bills and smiles all the time, even when shit goes wrong—I like that guy. And I've never even had sex with you." I pull back, wishing I could slap some sense into this ridiculously beautiful and dreadfully insecure guy. "So what does *that* do to your whole theory about women liking you for money and sex, huh?" I lower my voice. "It blows a hole right through it, that's what."

He stares at me in silence, dozens of emotions flicking across his eyes. My heart pounds as I meet his gaze and the room feels thick, like time has frozen us in place. Perhaps that passionate little rant of mine was too much. I do this sometimes. I want to encourage people so badly that I overstep my boundaries.

And let's be honest here, I pretty much just told the guy that I like him. Which is all very third grade and awkward as hell, but I don't give a damn. Daren needs to know that he's wrong about his self-worth, that he's important regardless of what he does or doesn't have. And it sure as hell doesn't sound like anyone else in his life is going to tell him that.

He keeps staring at me until it starts to feel uncomfortable. Why doesn't he say something? I realize I didn't really set him up for a great comeback or response, but come on. At least nod or something.

Taking a step forward, he moves to stand before me. The short chain between our handcuffs softly jingles as I tip my chin to look up at him.

He leans in a bit so our faces are just an inch apart and sinks his eyes deep into mine. Then quietly he says, "I see you."

For a moment, I'm too stunned to speak and incredibly moved by the fact that he listened last night when I spoke about my appearance. His words are more than just a response, they're a gesture, and aside from throwing myself into his arms, I don't know what to do with them.

So I just nod and clear my throat. "I'm sorry I was judgmental of you. I made assumptions about your wealth and character, and that was unfair of me. I'm sorry."

"I wasn't any better," he says. "I thought you were some spoiled princess, living off your daddy's trust fund money all these years. That was lame." He hangs his head a little. "I'm sorry. I really am."

I smile. "We're cool."

He smiles back and echoes, "We're cool."

"So about that shower..." I say, gesturing to our muddy state.

"Ah, yes. Follow me." He leads me into the bathroom and turns on the shower. Water sprays down, steaming up the bathroom as he lifts our connected wrists and frowns.

"So I guess we're showering together, then?"

I nod. "I guess so."

"Excellent." He gives me a devilish grin. "Group showers are my favorite." He starts taking his pants off and I hold up a hand.

"We're not showering together naked."

"Why not?" He stops unbuttoning his jeans.

"Because."

He smiles. "Because...?"

"Daren."

"Okay, fine," he says. "But I'm not showering in my dirty jeans. These babies are coming off." He yanks his pants off and I can't help but stare at his body, wanting to run my hands up his legs and sink my teeth into his ass.

But I won't do that. Probably.

I look down at my own dirty jeans and frown. Showering with them on would be pointless. I quickly take them off, already feeling myself start to blush as I avert my eyes from Daren's and kick my jeans over to my suitcase, feeling a tiny bit nervous about being half-dressed around him. Which is ridiculous.

When I finally look up, Daren's eyes are carefully fixed on my face and obviously struggling to stay there.

"What are you doing?" I ask.

He licks his lips. "I'm trying my very hardest not to look at your amazing body."

I tilt my head. "Why?"

"Because I don't want you to think I'm some disgusting pig who just wants to drool all over you," he says. "Although, side note, I do want to drool all over you. I just don't want to be piggish about it."

I roll my eyes. "If we're going to take a shower together, you might as well look at me now."

He drops his eyes and his gaze darkens with desire, which in turn makes me aroused. I really like that *he* really likes what he sees—and that's never happened to me before.

I'm usually nothing but embarrassed or uncomfortable when I let a guy see me naked, or almost naked. The moment my clothes come off is usually the very same moment the guy's eyes become vacant and he stops viewing me as a human being and starts treating me like his personal sex vessel.

But Daren's eyes aren't vacant at all as they stroke the outline of my panties and the curve of my hips. In fact, they're full and swimming with more emotions than I can count. White-hot desire blazes in their depths, but so do awe, happiness, nervousness, and hope.

He pulls them up to my face. The same emotions continue to flicker in their brown depths as he scans my eyes, which only makes me want to show him more of my body.

"Do you have a pair of scissors?" I ask.

He blinks, clearly not expecting that question. "Uh...maybe." He shuffles through a few bathroom drawers and finds a small pair of hair scissors. "Will these work?"

"Perfect." I take them from his hand and start to cut along the seam of my royal blue shirt.

"What are you doing?"

"Since we can't take our shirts off and I don't feel like wearing the same shirt another day in a row, I'm cutting mine off." I finish and the shirt falls away from my body, drifting to the floor in a dirty blue heap and leaving me standing in just my black bra and panties.

Daren rubs a hand over his mouth. Then over his head. Then his mouth again.

"Now what are you doing?" I ask.

He bites down on his fist. "I'm trying not to comment about how beautiful you are because I don't want you to think I only see your body," he says. "But it's really hard because I've never seen anything so perfectly lovely in my life."

I bite back a smile but can't contain the heat that spreads over my cheeks and neck. But I'm not embarrassed. I'm flattered. "Quit being so afraid of me. You can look at me, Daren. I'm not going to hold it against you. I swear."

"Oh thank God," he says in one fluid breath, shamelessly looking me over.

I smile and snip the scissor blades, feeling strangely powerful under his hot gaze. "Want me to cut off your shirt?"

He looks down in horror. "But I like this shirt."

"You really need to work on your attachment issues," I say. "What are you going to do, wear it in the shower and then to bed and then all day tomorrow?"

"Ew. No. Definitely not."

"Then let me cut it off and sew a new one on you after the shower."

He lifts a puzzled brow.

"I sew. Trust me. Now, come on. Snip, snip." I step up to him and he turns to the side and lifts his arm so I can cut up the seam.

With every slice of the shears, a small bit of his tan skin is revealed. The sides of his toned ab muscles. The ripples of his lean rib cage. The thick muscle of his pec and shoulder.

I realize I'm breathing heavy and shake myself as I cut off the remainder of his muddy shirt and strip it from his body.

Then the two of us stand in the bathroom, both in just our undies, as steam begins to fill the room from the hot shower spray behind us. Steam begins to build low in my belly as well and I'm suddenly nervous.

I want Daren but it's hard to trust my desires when I'm not used to them being so powerful and overwhelming. Instead, I hastily turn away and slip into the shower, pulling Daren in with me by the cuffs.

The hot water feels amazing as it drenches my hair and runs over my shoulders and back. We shower without speaking, taking turns in the spray and with the soap as we scrub the dirt from our skin. The silence isn't awkward but rather tense and filled with unspoken yearning. Every once in a while, my eyes get lost on Daren's body, trailing up and over his muscles and masculine lines. And just like when I was fifteen, I want to touch him.

His eyes are better behaved than mine, staying primarily on my face or the shower walls. The new passion-ridden part of my soul doesn't like this and wishes he'd stare at me like he was before. Wanting me. *Seeing* me. He glances at my breasts or panties every few minutes, but the desire in his eyes is brief and well controlled.

This just makes more pieces of my heart float over to his hands.

We go to trade places again and our eyes lock. In the running water, his eyelashes have clung together making tiny black triangles above his brown eyes. And up close like this, his brown eyes look deeper than usual. They aren't just brown. They're tan and golden, with a ring of green just around the pupil, and small flecks of yellow within the ring. They're beautiful and...deep.

He smiles at me playfully. "You want to kiss me again, don't you?"

YES, I DO.

"You're relentless." I smile. "Stop trying to get into my pants."

"What pants?" He grins at my panties and I splash water at him. "I'll have you know," he says, "that I'm not trying to get into anything at this particular moment. In the shower."

"Are you not a fan of shower sex?"

"Listen to you, talking about sex all casually in your wet black panties," he says. "Are you trying to kill me? And to answer your question, no. I'm not crazy about shower sex."

"Interesting," I say, drawing out the word.

He shrugs. "Showering with a girl is hot, don't get me wrong." He gives me an overexaggerated wink and I flick water at him again. "But it's not ideal. You're standing up and there's usually not enough space to maneuver in, and then you have to keep the girl wet in spite of all the wetness of the shower, but warm even when the hot water isn't on her...it's tricky. There are a lot of factors involved. It's convenient for cleaning up afterward, but it's not my favorite place to have sex."

"I see," I say. "So what *is* your favorite place to have sex?"

"A bed," he says simply.

I laugh. "A bed?"

"Yeah. Why is that so funny?"

I shrug. "I don't know. I guess I just thought a Legendary Lover like yourself would choose someplace more exotic than a bed."

"No way. A bed is the most ideal. It's comfortable, so nobody's knees or elbows or backs get scratched up. It's warm, so the girl can relax and I don't have to work twice as hard to keep my body heat around her. And it's large, so there's plenty of room to switch positions and move around."

It sounds like he actually cares about and has put a lot of thought into making sure his sex partners are comfortable, and not just how easy it is for him to get off.

He runs a hand through his wet hair and looks at me. "What's your favorite place to have sex?"

"My favorite place?" The question throws me for a moment and I scramble for an answer. "Well, it's probably... I don't know, maybe..."

He waits.

I frown at the shower wall.

"You don't have a favorite place, do you?" He smiles, but more out of curiosity than amusement.

"Sure I do. I just need to think—"

His smile fades. "Do you not like sex?"

"What? Of course I do." I move my eyes away and reach for the soap. "Everyone likes sex."

At least everyone is supposed to like sex.

He's quiet for a minute glancing over my face and body in a way that's more clinical than sexual.

"What?" I snap.

He spies a stroke of mud still on my forearm, and gently takes my arm in his hand.

"I'm just trying to figure out why a girl like you wouldn't like having sex. Trade places with me again." He places his hands on my shoulders and we switch places so I'm now standing under the warmth of the shower and he's in the decidedly colder side.

I huff in offense. "Just because I didn't have a particular sexing spot at the tip of my tongue when you asked doesn't mean I don't enjoy sex." I pause. "And what do you mean A GIRL LIKE ME?"

He slips the bar of soap out of my hand and slowly lathers it up against my arm. "A girl who clearly has a lot of passion in her soul and loves with her whole heart. A girl who has a lot to give but gives it with discretion. A girl who knows herself better than most and trusts herself even more." He slips the soap back into my hand and proceeds to gently caress my arm, and then my shoulder, with both of his hands gliding the foamy soap over my skin. "A girl who cares for others deeply and finds value in the most rejected things." He flicks his eyes to mine, stroking my skin as the hot spray runs the soap off my arm and shoulder. "A girl like you."

The sound of the falling water fills the space between us as my head goes hazy with the gentle touches of his hands, washing me. I want to say something, respond in some way, but just like earlier in his room, I'm lost for words. All I feel and see is Daren and his deep brown eyes, caring.

"I like sex," I say lamely.

He nods and takes the soap from my hands where my fingers have started to wrinkle from clutching so long. "You know what I think? I think sex is difficult for you to enjoy because you're so pretty. I think having sex makes you feel used by guys—even the good ones—because they can't see the real you."

I say nothing, my eyes trapped in his words.

"Kayla," he says, running his hands up my arms and to my neck where he cradles my face. "I'm not like those other guys." The water continues to fall around us. "I do see you. The real you."

He leans forward and for a second I think he's going to kiss me, but instead, he reaches behind me and turns the shower knob off. The spray stops falling, leaving the bathroom silent but for the dripping faucet at my back and my pounding heart.

24

DAREN

After our shower, we towel off and I yank on a pair of shorts to sleep in as Kayla turns away. She dresses in a pair of tiny gym shorts and a strapless shirt before cutting her bra off her shoulders. Then she rubs coconut-scented lotion on her arms and legs and the movement puts me in a trance until she catches my eyes and I look elsewhere.

I've been trying so. Damn. Hard not to ogle her gorgeous, perfect body and it's killing me. But I know she has issues with guys caring too much about her appearance and I want to be different. I want her to trust me. Even if that means depriving myself to the point of pain, which is exactly what I've been doing.

We don't speak for several long minutes. When I looked in Kayla's eyes and saw all those fears and walls she had up between herself and not just sex, but guys in general, I was desperate to assure her in some way.

And I didn't want her to think of me as just another guy. I wanted to be more. And when I told her I was nothing like the guys she's known in the past, I was telling the truth. I don't know those other guys, but I know me. And I care about Kayla Turner with a fierceness I didn't know I was capable of.

I just need to figure out what to do with it.

"Wow. I know celebrities who would envy a wardrobe like yours," she says, walking over to my closet.

I follow her and pick out a clean shirt. "Yeah. It's ridiculous, but aside from my mom's necklace it's the only piece of my old life that I still have."

"And you have attachment issues."

"Precisely."

She takes the shirt and looks at the rest of my closet. "What's with the shirts hanging off to the side? Are they for special occasions or something?"

"Uh, no." I smile. "They have tears in them." I pull a sleeve out from one of the shirts and show her a small rip in it. "I don't have the money to take them to a tailor, but I can't bring myself to throw them away because I know how much they cost."

She shrugs. "I can fix them after I sew this shirt on you."

"Really?"

"Yep. Sewing is, like, my thing. I always carry around a little sewing kit." She points to her suitcase beside the wall.

"That's awesome."

She takes my ripped clothes out of the closet and sits cross-legged on the floor beside the suitcase. I sit across from her. Rummaging through her bag, she finds her sewing kit and carefully cuts along the sleeve before tucking the shirt around my body and stitching it up. I watch her hands as they move over my body, small and precise with each pull of the needle, until she's finished.

"Wow. It looks perfect," I say, staring at the seam. "Thanks."

"Sure." She pulls the first of my torn shirts onto her lap. "Because my mom and I were always low on cash, buying clothes was a rare occasion. So when I did buy clothes, I tried to buy items that would last a long time. But even nice clothes don't last forever." She carefully rethreads the needle and goes to work on the first torn shirt. "So I've gotten used to sewing up my clothes so they'll last longer."

"Smart," I say, watching her work. "You seem to be really good at it too."

She shrugs. "I'm okay. My mom was better, though. She taught me everything I know about sewing before she died." Her eyes storm over.

I quietly ask, "How did she pass away?"

She inhales deeply. "My mom had a drug problem for a long time, but I didn't find out about it until a few years ago. I should have known earlier that she had a drug problem. In a way, I think I did. The day she pawned her wedding ring and didn't even get emotional made me suspicious, but I shrugged it off because she was my mother. And when I found out she sold my My Little Pony collection online and claimed that it had been stolen, I was heartbroken, but I let it go because she was my mom, you know?" She shakes her head. "But a real mother, a sober mother, wouldn't be so heartless or deceitful. The signs were there all along, but I ignored them all—because she was my mother.

"We always lived paycheck to paycheck, but last year she told me we were completely broke. I had just started nursing school at college, but had to quit and get a job to help out with the bills. I worked full-time at Big Joe's diner and made pitiful wages, while my mother worked as a maid at a hotel. But then she got caught stealing money from the hotel and was fired from her job. After that, she didn't bother looking for more work. She'd just lie on the couch all day, popping pills. A few times I found her unconscious and had to call 911 to get her stomach pumped. It was terrifying. But worse, it was like she didn't want to be alive anymore.

"I tried to get her help. I tried to cut her off and take care of her, but she always found a way to get more drugs. She'd steal from her friends or sell our things until a few years ago. Which, now that I know about the trust fund, makes total sense because the trust fund became accessible three years ago when I turned eighteen. So of course she stole from that. No wonder she was able to use for so long. Her habit—and her personality—spiraled, until she wasn't the woman who raised me anymore. She was just a selfish, vacant look-alike. And so sick. Then one day I came home and she…" Kayla pauses with the needle in the air and swallows. "I was too late that time."

The air leaves my lungs as I think about the terror she must have felt, losing her mother that way. "Kayla, I'm so sorry."

She lifts and lowers a shoulder. "I saw it coming. Anyone who knew her could have seen it coming. It was hard, especially because I'd been in nursing school and kept thinking that maybe if I'd been more stern, or seen the signs sooner, I could have saved her. But I eventually came to terms with her death and I'm okay now."

She goes back to sewing and my throat goes dry. I can't imagine the horror of that experience for her.

I say, "Is that what you want to do? Be a nurse?"

She smiles at the shirt. "Yeah. I want to finish nursing school but I can't afford it right now. What about you?" She holds the needle in her mouth while she readjusts the material in her hands.

"I don't have money for college either," I say. "I'm just sort of bouncing around from job to job. Two of them, actually."

She nods. "That's right. What do you do again?"

"I work at the cell phone store in town so I can afford my phone bill."

"Brilliant."

"And at Willow Inn out by the lavender ranch, where I run supplies to and from town. And sometimes as a dishwasher at Latecomers when I'm low on cash and want a hot meal."

She shakes her head. "Wow. I had no idea you worked so much." Finishing with the first shirt, she moves on to the second.

I watch her set the needle between her lips and wish I was that needle. She pulls it from her mouth and goes back to hemming the shirt. Her blonde hair falls across her face, stroking her pink cheeks as she tucks it back. And her blue eyes narrow in concentration as her delicate fingers carefully weave the thread through the shirt.

I watch her in amazement.

"What about you?" she asks, her voice bringing me back to reality. "If money wasn't an issue, what would you do?"

"Honestly?" I hesitate. "I would go to culinary school and learn to cook."

She looks up. "You like cooking?"

"I love it," I say, pointing to the stack of cookbooks on the table across the room. "Remember I told you about our housekeeper, Marcella? Well growing up, she let me help her out in the kitchen, and she taught me all sorts of things about food and cooking. That's when my love for all things culinary began, with Marcella."

Kayla smiles. "It sounds like you really loved Marcella."

I nod. "I did. She was great. My mother wasn't really good with words or showing love and I think Marcella tried to make up for that, you know? She once told me that real love isn't something you plan or earn, it's something that just hits you—like a bolt of lightning—and changes you forever." I smile to myself. "Marcella changed me forever, that's for sure. She was never too busy or too impatient for me. Even when I made a mess in her kitchen, which I did a lot when I would experiment on different recipes, she would just sigh and shake her head and say, *Mijo, you're lucky I love you.*" I pause because Kayla's face keeps getting happier. "What?"

"That's just…" She grins. "That's really cute. And it's great that you're so passionate about cooking. I want to eat something you make."

Happiness fills my chest and I suddenly want nothing more than to feed this girl. "Okay." I grin. "Maybe if we find the money tomorrow I can whip up a hot meal for us in celebration."

She smiles. "I'd like that." Finishing with the last shirt, she puts her sewing supplies away and slowly yawns.

"I guess we should probably get to bed," I say. "We have a long drive in the morning." I look at my frameless bed and shame pricks under my skin. "Sorry we're pretty much sleeping on the floor."

"Are you kidding me? I'll take crashing on the floor of a mansion over sleeping on a dirty motel bed any day." She winks. "Even though your mattress has probably seen just as much action as the Quickie Stop one."

I watch her carefully, wondering if the idea of me having sex with lots of women on my mattress—or just having lots of sex, in general—bothers her at all. But the teasing in her eyes looks genuine and unaffected.

Disappointment leaks through me and I try not to overthink why.

"Actually," I say as we stand and I put my shirts away. "This particular mattress hasn't seen any action at all."

She scoffs. "Bullshit."

I shake my head. "Swear to God. What I said yesterday, about women thinking my mattress was comfortable? *That* was bullshit. Although it is rather comfy. But since I'm not in the business of broadcasting my homelessness, I never bring women back here. So my mattress is a virgin."

"Huh." She looks at said mattress. "Well consider me honored."

I smile.

We crawl onto my mattress and I turn the lights out, throwing us into darkness so complete I can't even see my hand in front of my face as we try to get comfortable.

"Shit," I mutter. "I forgot you like to sleep on your belly. Here, switch sides with me."

I start to crawl over her just as she tries to sit up and we smash into each other, causing Kayla to tumble back. I lose my balance and fall on top of her, with our chests and hips locked together.

The smell of coconut wafts over me, sweet and hazy. As I sink against her soft, supple body, my dick starts to grow hard. I know I should get off of her, but the fit is so perfect I can't seem to move.

She exhales and her hot breath feathers against my throat in the dark. Carefully balanced on my elbows, I silently command myself to climb off of her, but before I can move, she arches her back.

It's a slight movement, barely palpable, but it tells me what she wants. I slowly brush my fingertips up her stomach, feeling her belly dip in as she sucks in a sharp breath, then trail them up to her face and cup her cheeks.

I've never been with a girl in complete darkness before and something about it is oddly intimate. I can't see her. I can only feel her, which should make it less personal. But I can hear her breathing, and feel her heartbeat against my chest, and everything about it makes me want to be careful with her.

I lower my face until I can feel the heat of her exhales against my lips. She rolls her hips up so her body meets mine and I push against her even more, touching my lips to hers.

She kisses me back, softly. Just our lips brushing each other in the black. I pull back to breathe, surprised that my heart is beating so fast, and hear the faintest of protests. A tiny whimper sounds from the depths of her throat telling me she wants more, and that's all the invitation I need.

25

KAYLA

*A*s Daren hungrily brings his mouth back to mine, I part my lips and moan as his tongue slides inside my mouth. I slip my hands under his shirt and press my fingertips into his back, pulling him closer to me as I open my legs, desperate to give in to the wild passion I've been denying these last few days. I kiss him back, exhaling heavily as our tongues meet and slip around each other. I move my hips against his, thrilled by the hard length of his erection rubbing against my center.

My heart beats wildly. I want to kiss him and feel him and please him all at once, moaning into his mouth as he trails his free hand along my rib cage while keeping our cuffed hands pinned beside my head. I slide my hand up his bare back, gripping the corded strength beneath my fingers as he shifts above me.

Tugging on his shirt, I lift it up and he helps me pull it off him and down to our connected wrists. Wishing I could see his naked chest just a breath away, I blindly reach my free hand out, roving it over his shoulders and down to his rippled stomach once I find him in the dark.

I love the way he breathes against me, warm and alive and filled with wanting. Where our bound wrists lie, he laces his fingers through mine and holds our hands there, a steady place where we connect.

He lightly sweeps his tongue up my throat, gently tipping my head back so he can kiss my collarbone and then lower. I run my hand into his hair and hold his head against my throat where his tongue is now licking a hot trail up to my ear.

Pulling back, he lifts my shirt off and pulls it down to where his is tangled in the handcuffs. The cool air of his room drifts over my already hard nipples, tightening them even more as Daren's palm glides over my naked breasts and lights a current inside of me.

I exhale in pleasure as he lightly squeezes my breast with his big hand and rubs his thumb over my nipple. He squeezes my other breast, harder than the first and I moan.

"I like it when you moan," he says and I can hear the smile in his voice.

Arching my back so my breast fills his palm again, I say, "I like it when you make me moan."

He softly plucks at my left nipple then my right. I feel his mouth come down to my chest and he licks a hot, wet trail between my breasts as he takes them both in his hands and massages them under his palms before lightly pulling at their hardened tips.

I whimper and his hot, wet tongue is suddenly wrapped around my left nipple, tugging it into his mouth with a groan. With every hot suck, my core tightens and pulses, growing wetter as my thighs flex.

With my hand still in his hair, I hold him to my breast. He pulls his mouth back and my nipple tightens under the cool air breezing over the wetness left behind.

He pulls my other nipple into his mouth and I moan a little

louder, loving the darkness and the freedom it gives me to enjoy this without reservation.

It's pitch-black. Completely blinding. Without the light, all I have is Daren. The warmth of his body above mine, the feel of his heartbeat against my chest, the sound of our tangled breaths coming out in pants and searching for a place to land.

In the darkness, in this place where nothing is visible, I feel beautiful. The way I look does not exist. But who I am is very much real, coming out in soft gasps and unfamiliar emotions. Desperation. Eagerness. Desire. Affection.

I run my hand down his back and to the waistband of his shorts, slipping my hand inside to the hot length of his erection. I run my fingertips along the soft wet tip of his hardness then softly grasp him in my hand. He's so thick and hot it makes my core ache in need. I slip my hand out with every intention of pulling his shorts off but the moment my hand is free he presses himself between my thighs. The rock-hard length of him rubs against my soft center again and I wiggle to add more friction, wanting more.

I softly whimper. "Daren."

"I know," he whispers beside my ear. "I'll give you everything you want."

A shiver runs over my body and his fingertips lightly brush over the tiny shiver bumps on my stomach as his hand moves down to my shorts. He pulls them off in a few short movements, leaving me in only my panties. Then, finding my knees, he runs his hands up the inside of my legs and trails his fingers over the sensitive skin at the top.

Then he spreads my thighs, opening me up all the way. I let my legs fall open, reflectively arching my back as the cool air in between our bodies wisps over my wet panties.

With my body fully opened, he skims his fingers up and down the inside of my thighs and I exhale and let my head fall back. The barely-there touch, causing a needy ache inside me, is soft and careful—and only for me.

He can't see me or my reactions, so I know the light brushing of his fingers over my tummy and the underside of my breasts and the inside of my arm aren't for his benefit, but for mine. They're so I know he's there. Connecting us softly.

He rubs a thumb over the wettest part of my panties and I jerk. He does it again and my thighs quiver as I let out a gasp.

He gently suckles on my earlobe as his thumb finds my clit through the thin material of my panties and strokes tiny circles around it.

I pant as my thighs jerk. "Ye—yes."

Slipping his fingers inside my panties, he gently strokes me between my legs and I whimper. I'm already wet and hot, but his long fingers, slipping in and around my slick folds, make me even more aroused.

His mouth finds mine and he traps my moans and my gasps as he works me closer... closer...

I'm panting and shaking. I let my thighs fall open even more and squirm beneath him eagerly.

Closer...

He teases my entrance with one thick finger and slides it inside. My tiny inner muscles squeeze him with need. He adds another finger and starts to move them in and out of me, drawing out more wetness from my center. Then withdraws both fingers, shoves my panties to the side completely, and uses his thumb and forefinger to softly pluck at my clit.

I cry out at the touch, feeling my core tighten and ache as he rolls over my clit again and again.

Closer...

He pushes his big fingers back inside while his thumb continues to tickle against my most pivotal place. My body tenses as I reach the peak, and my thighs begin to quiver as pure ecstasy courses through me, pulling a cry from my throat. Daren bends to kiss me as my climax washes over me in waves, and I bend my back in a tall arch to meet his mouth and his skillful fingers. And then—

The phone rings.

26

DAREN

*N*o.

It rings again.

No, no, no. Dammit.

I slowly withdraw my fingers from Kayla's tightness, gently cupping her between her legs as her thighs shake around me and her arousal spills onto the bed. I kiss her deeply, sucking in her quiet moans and whimpers and loving every desperate cry. Pleasing this woman is pleasure in itself.

I shift above her, willing the phone call to disappear and leave me to this plush, naked body I have beneath me in the dark.

But it rings again, and this time Kayla pulls away from my mouth and breaths out, "Do—do you need to get that?" Small spasms continue to run through her and she lets out a wanton sigh.

"No," I say, my fingers still playing inside her panties where she's wet and warm and ready for me. And I am most definitely ready for her. Fuck, I'm hard.

Not a chance in hell.

Kayla seems distracted now, shifting as the phone rings again. "Sh—shouldn't you at least see who's calling?" she pants.

I hang my head. Only one person would be calling me at this hour.

"Probably," I say, out of breath. My dick aches in mean protest as I slip my hand out of her panties. "Is that okay? I'm so sorry."

"Yes. Of course," she says, scooting out from under me with quivering legs. I curse all the phone gods in all the land as I lift away from her hot naked body and reach for my phone. I adjust myself but it doesn't help. I'm already so hard it hurts.

"Hello?" I say, bracing myself.

"Hi, Daren. Sorry to bother you at this hour, but it's important," says Eddie Perkins. I knew it.

"What?" I say, pissed off and irritated.

"Your father's arraignment for the accident charges is tomorrow, and he's refusing to plead guilty."

"Shocking."

"I need you to come down to the courthouse and talk some sense into him—"

"No." I start shaking my head even though he can't see me. "No way. I'm done speaking to him."

"You're the only one he will listen to and if he doesn't plead guilty and this goes to trial he could end up in prison, Daren. Prison."

"He deserves prison."

Eddie sighs. "You and I both know you don't mean that. Will you please come?"

I clench my jaw, hating that my father has spiraled so far down that I feel like *I'm* at the bottom of a deep, dark pit. "Fine. I'll try to talk to him."

"Thank you," he says. "I really appreciate it. I'll see you at eight a.m. tomorrow."

I hang up and throw my phone back on the nightstand with a curse.

Beside me in the dark, Kayla quietly says, "What's wrong?"

"Nothing." I shake my head. "Just some stuff I have to do in the morning for Eddie."

"Oh." She shifts on the bed and I feel a tug against the handcuffs.

"Fuck," I mutter, running my free hand through my hair and pulling at the ends. I hate my father. Then I turn back to Kayla and quietly say, "Sorry."

The darkness makes it impossible to read her face, but the passion that filled the room just minutes ago has all but evaporated, and I'm sure her sexual desire probably went with it.

"No problem." Her voice is soft.

I run my fingers up her arm and to her jaw, wishing I could see what she wanted right now. She covers my fingers with her free hand, holding them to her face.

"You seem upset. Maybe we should just get some sleep," she says. "And we have to get up early, anyway."

I inhale slowly, frustrated and irritated with Eddie for calling so late and my father for being such a dick that his decisions now affect my sex life. "Yeah." I nod even though Kayla can't see me. "Maybe you're right." I find her face and gently kiss her on the lips, not wanting her to think I'm pissed at her in any way, and she kisses me back.

It's a sweet kiss. No heat. No wanting. It's a goodnight kiss.

I pull away and she fumbles to put her shirt and shorts back on, the mattress shifting beneath her movements as she yanks it back up her arm and over her head. I do the same. Then we lie back down.

I feel her body heat beside me but we're not touching anymore.

Silence falls over the room as I stare blindly into the black and mentally curse my father for ruining my life and interrupting the feel of Kayla Turner in my arms.

27

KAYLA

*T*his morning, we brushed our teeth side by side at the bathroom mirror. We turned our backs on each other while we got dressed. And then we descended the staircase in the big empty house and got in my car.

Not once did we mention last night. And *so much* happened.

Getting swept up in the heat of the moment in Daren's bed was a game changer in itself. But I also told him about my mom dying—something I haven't told anyone other than the paramedics and cops. It's strange how comfortable I am with Daren. Telling him actually made me feel...lighter, in a way. Like talking about my mom unloaded a burden I didn't know I was carrying. Between working and taking care of my mom, I haven't had much time to maintain my other relationships. So I didn't really have anyone I could talk to about my parents passing away. But Daren makes it easy.

And it doesn't hurt that he knew my dad—and cared a great deal for him. I glance at him as we finish our breakfast cookies and my heart dips a little as I realize that I'm going to miss him when this is all over. When the handcuffs come off, will I ever see him again? Will he ever want to see me again?

Scanning his face, I try to read his eyes but there's nothing familiar in their brown depths. He's been like this all morning. Pensive. Anxious. I know we're going to meet Eddie and his dad, but I don't understand why that has him acting so nervous. The handsome happiness he almost always has on is locked away, somewhere behind the shadows passing his face, making me wish I knew how to take them away.

"So where am I going again?" I ask as we pull out of the driveway.

"The courthouse," he says. "It's on the north side of town. Just take the main road until you reach the turnoff by Wilcox Farm."

We drive in silence. Every few minutes, I catch him staring at me. Sometimes his gives me a small smile and other times he quickly glances away.

Being with Daren last night was amazing. The way he touched me and moved against my body. I didn't feel like a piece of meat in his arms. I felt like myself. I felt important. But now, even chained to his side, I feel a hundred miles away from him.

Daren clears his throat. "So about my dad..." he begins. "He's uh...he's not the most pleasant guy, so don't let him bother you or freak out when we get there, okay?"

Now *I'm* nervous. "Why would I freak out?"

"I don't know. I just...I haven't seen my dad in almost a year. We weren't on speaking terms when he went to jail, so I'm just not sure how he'll react to me today."

I nod. "Okay."

This is obviously a big deal for Daren and the only reason I get to peek into this very personal part of his life is because of these stupid handcuffs. Shame sweeps over me as we drive. My desire for this inheritance has inadvertently made me intrude on his life.

From the corner of my eye, I see him stretch his neck and crack his knuckles. Anxiety rolls off him, filling my tiny car with a thick tension. I glance at our cuffed wrists. If there was no inheritance, I would be fine. I don't need a lump of money to get my life in order. I'm smart and capable. Do I really want to force Daren to show me a part of his life that has him squirming? Am I that financially desperate?

I look at his profile and think about how he likes to cook and is working so hard to pay off a stranger's medical bills. For all the beauty of his face and body, his heart is the most stunning thing about him. And here I am, using him to get money.

"Maybe we should swing by the hardware store and find some bolt cutters to snap these things off," I suggest, lifting our joined wrists. "That way you can have some privacy with your dad."

He looks taken aback. "But then we'd forfeit and you wouldn't get any money."

I shrug. "So what? It's just money. I'll make do."

He stares at me for a long moment before shaking his head. "No. I can't ask you to do that. Besides, it'll be fine today. With my dad." He gives me a lopsided smile that looks more strained than sincere. In fact, everything about him looks strained. His shoulders are rigid, his jaw is flexed, and his eyes are hard and distant. No smile in the world could mask the turmoil in his expression.

Stressed. Angry. Nervous. Afraid. His eyes flip from one emotion to the next, never settling.

My stomach twists in anguish, not for myself, but for him as he stares out the window and murmurs, "It will be fine." A sure sign that it will be anything but.

28

DAREN

*D*o you know how difficult it is to be granted entry into a public courthouse when you're handcuffed to another person but not for legal reasons?

Pretty fucking impossible.

Kayla and I spent a good hour with the security guards, answering questions and giving recorded statements about why we're handcuffed together explaining that, yes, we chose to be chained together and, no, we are not under duress.

Eddie came out at one point and helped smooth over some of the confusion. It took eight security guards, two police officers, and one notary public to get us cleared for entry, but we managed to make it inside.

And that wasn't even the hard part.

The hard part was biting my tongue when I walked into the holding room and saw my dad laughing with the bailiff. He hasn't taken any of this seriously since day one.

I glance at Kayla. She gives me an encouraging little smile and I quickly look away. She offered to cut off our handcuffs and forfeit her inheritance—an inheritance that would give her a better future—for *me*. And she didn't even bat an eye.

No woman has offered to sacrifice something so important for me. I don't know what to say. Or think. Or feel about Kayla right now. So I'm avoiding eye contact until I figure it out.

"Daren, my boy!" My dad waves at me with his cuffed wrists and smiles. "Like father like son, eh?"

I curl my lip. "I'm nothing like you."

"Ouch." He mocks a look of hurt. "Are you still pissed about Connor? Because you don't have to pay his bills, you know. He can get a loan from the hospital or work with his insurance company—"

"No, Dad. Just—" I inhale. "Just no. Someone needs to pay for the medical care he needed because of your horrendous decision making. And it shouldn't be the guy who just recently learned how to walk again."

I purse my lips, thinking about the first time I saw Connor after the accident. It was the first court date and the poor guy was sitting in court in a body cast with two black eyes and a breathing tube sticking out of his neck. And my father wasn't even fazed.

He sighs. "Then I guess you're welcome to be that martyr. Sweet Jesus, is that little Kayla Turner?" Dad's eyes light up as he looks Kayla over. "My goodness, girl. I haven't seen you in ages."

"Hi, Mr. Ackwood." She smiles politely.

"Call me Luke." He smiles back. "Now why in the hell are you handcuffed to my son?"

She bites her lip. "Well, uh…"

"None of your business," I say, taking a seat in one of the metal folding chairs on the other side of the table. I pull one out for Kayla as well and she sits beside me, crossing her legs.

She pulls her phone and a pair of earbuds from her purse and holds them up. "I'm just going to…" She puts the buds in her ears and soon I hear the distant sound of music streaming from her phone. I let out a silent sigh of relief, grateful she won't have to listen to this conversation—however it may go.

I look at my dad. "Eddie tells me you're refusing to plead guilty."

"So that's how it's going to be, then?" he says, spitting the words out like I've greatly offended him. "You're not going to speak to me for ten months, and then when you do come to see me, you come leashed to Kayla Turner without explanation and try to give me legal advice?" He laughs out loud. "Oh, my boy. That's priceless."

Eddie shuffles into the room, looking out of breath and a little bit sweaty. "Sorry. Sorry. I forgot which room number we were in and got a tad bit lost. But I'm here now!" He smiles.

My father says, "Eddie, why is my son handcuffed to Kayla Turner?"

Eddie frowns at me. "You haven't found the money yet, I'm guessing?"

I shake my head. "Turner's letter turned out to be more of a scavenger hunt. We're still looking."

Eddie makes a face of concern. "Oh my."

Dad looks at me. "What in the hell does a scavenger hunt have to do with your handcuffs?"

I flex a muscle in my jaw. "Old Man Turner left us money in his will but we have to be handcuffed together until we find it."

Dad laughs again. "Well isn't that a kick in the pants? Chained to a pretty girl and searching for treasure."

"Can we please get back to why I'm here?" I say, my patience less than thin.

"Yes, yes." Eddie pulls up a chair and sits. "Here's the problem,

Luke. If you don't plead guilty, and this thing goes to trial, you could serve up to eight years if we lose."

"Then we'd better not lose." He grins nonchalantly.

Eddie's phone rings and he glances at the caller ID before standing back up. "I have to take this. I'll be right back." Once again he leaves, and I turn to my father.

"This isn't a game, Dad." I look at him sternly.

He leans forward. "Don't you think I know that? But I don't want to storm into a courtroom and plead guilty to almost killing a man."

"But you did almost kill a man!" I say. "You are guilty."

"Which is exactly why I want to go to trial." He sneers at me. "Why do you want me to plead guilty so bad?"

I lower my voice and lean in. "Because it's the right thing to do."

He eyes me for a moment then shifts his gaze to Kayla and shakes his head. "Doing the right thing doesn't always get you to the right places. I did the right thing with your mom. I was faithful to her. I was loving and honest and all that sappy shit a good man is supposed to be. And what did she do? She fucking left us."

"Dad." I rub a hand down my face. "This isn't about Mom—or any other woman."

He waves me off. "It's always about a woman. And let me tell you something else." He lowers his voice. "Kayla Turner isn't going to stick with you either."

"She's not *with* me, Dad. We're just together to find the money."

"Say whatever you want, but I know that look in a man's eyes. The look that says *I want to be worthy of this girl*. The look that says *I want to do the right thing for this girl*. But at the end of the day it doesn't matter."

I roll my eyes and sigh.

"Because you aren't good enough for her," he continues quietly. "And I know she's handcuffed to you now, and you're probably thinking that you stand a chance, but she's just using you. That's the truth, and the truth hurts.

"Look at her, Daren. She's young and beautiful, and she wants someone who's stable and has money. And as soon as she gets that inheritance and you two unchain yourselves, that's just what she's going to go find. You don't stand a chance, son. All the good looks in the world won't keep a girl like Kayla Turner waiting around for you while you get your shit together." He purses his lips and shakes his head. "She's going to leave you. Women always leave. Hell, your own mother left you." He inhales. "So if you know what's best for you, you'll drop this high-flying fantasy of yours where you and Kayla live happily ever after and get back to reality."

I don't like my father. I despise him, mostly. But I can't argue with his words. He's right. Kayla deserves something more than me. This world we've created, with scavenger hunts and handcuffs and sleeping in the dark, has always been temporary. I've always been temporary.

Eddie bustles back into the room and puts his cell phone away. "Sorry about that." He sits back down. "Have we made any progress yet?"

Dad leans back in his seat. "I still don't want to plead guilty, Eddie. I'd rather take my chances in the courtroom…"

They start discussing their odds in court while I sit back, pretending to listen. My eyes drift to Kayla, who's scrolling through the music on her phone, oblivious to the conversation that just happened. I run my eyes over her soft face and slender arms and my chest tightens as I think about last night.

I had that soft face in my hands and her sweet body tucked

beneath mine. She was kissing me back with passion—I couldn't have imagined that. The way she moaned and exhaled; the way she moved against me and melted around me...those aren't things I imagined. But could she really just be swept up in this hunt and last night was just a part of the game?

I study her for a moment. Is she faking it for the sake of the inheritance? For the fun of it? It doesn't seem likely, especially since she was willing to forfeit the inheritance in the car this morning. But maybe that's all fake too.

I rub a hand over my mouth, totally confused. This is why I don't get attached to girls. They get in my head and make me second-guess everything. Then they get in my heart and scare the shit out of me with the prospect of being left behind.

What happens when we find the inheritance? Will Kayla leave? My heart drops as the answer seeps in. She will. She'll leave me.

She shifts in her chair and gives me a small smile. I smile back, but it's forced and feels wrong on my lips.

"...at least consider what we're asking, Luke," Eddie says to my father.

I tune back in to the conversation.

My dad sighs. "Fine. I'll think about pleading guilty. *Think* about it."

"Excellent." Eddie looks at me. "Isn't that good news?"

I nod. "Yes. Good news." I stare at the table with a heavy feeling in my gut.

That might be good news, but the fact that Kayla Turner is probably going to leave me is not.

Dad was right. The truth hurts.

29

KAYLA

The drive out to the old lavender ranch is tense and uncomfortably silent. Daren hasn't said a word since we left the courthouse and I'm not sure if I should speak.

I carefully say, "So that seemed to go...okay."

"Don't," he says.

I blink, slightly hurt, but say nothing else.

I wonder if maybe he's being cold because of what happened last night. I know he's a womanizer, and I know he's not big on commitment, so maybe he's upset because he woke up this morning and realized he, literally, can't escape me. Then everything with his dad this morning just angered him even more.

"Listen," I begin, hoping to alleviate some of the stress radiating from his side of the car. "What happened last night...it wasn't a big deal."

He nods at the road, working a muscle in his jaw without looking at me, then slowly swings his head to me and sneers. "Oh, I know." He scoffs and glares back out the window. "I know."

I stare at him in confusion.

What the hell is that supposed to mean? He *knows*? Like he had no intention of caring about me or us beyond sex? God. I was just trying to let him off the hook, but wow.

I bite back a curse. Maybe I was wrong about Daren. Maybe he's just like every other piggish guy I know.

A few miles later we pull into the old lavender ranch, and I park just inside the gate. We get out of the car and are immediately assaulted by a miniature tornado of dust, sweeping over the deserted ranchland and funneling dirt into the sky. It blows over us quickly but my skin and clothes are already coated in a thick film of dust. Fantastic.

I wipe my hands over my face and rub out my eyes. Daren does the same. When we open them, we instantly spy a note pinned to a post of the ranch sign.

I look at Daren, waiting. "What, no 'Eureka!' or 'Tallyho!' for this one?"

"Aha!" he says with false exuberance and a lame expression.

"Whatever." Restraining the scowl I want to throw his way, I hastily unpin the note from the post and scan the message inside.

Congratulations, this is your last clue! Your money is in a safe place through the trenches. Good luck!

"Through the trenches...?" I say. "What does that mean?"

Daren turns around a few times. "Maybe there are some trenches dug out around the ranch somewhere?" His attitude seems lighter now that we've read the note, and I breathe a little easier.

We search the grounds, sweating under the hot afternoon sun, but find nothing even remotely close to a trench.

I bite my lip. "Maybe he has some trenches around his garden back at his house?"

Daren shakes his head. "I practically built that garden. No trenches."

We brainstorm a while longer but can't come up with any solid ideas.

Daren kicks at the ground and curses. "This is so fucking annoying." He throws his arms out. "Why couldn't he just tell us where to go? Why did he have to make it so goddamn impossible with our cuffed wrists and these stupid hints?"

"I don't know." I shrug. "Let's keep thinking. Maybe he meant—"

"No." He shakes his head. "This is dumb. We don't even know how much money we're jumping all these hurdles for. For all we know, your dad left us a quarter."

"Maybe, but I really think—"

"And the handcuffs! Why?" he says with dark eyes, pissed. "Why did he ever think this would be a good idea?" He jiggles our handcuffs somewhat aggressively.

I narrow my eyes. "Why are you in such a bad mood?"

He glowers at me. "No reason."

"Then quit bitching and help me figure this clue out," I snap.

His sour attitude doesn't make any sense. If he wants out, I already offered to cut off the cuffs. And if he's scared I'm going to get clingy, he can relax since I told him last night wasn't any big deal. I eye him for a moment. Maybe something else is going on here? Maybe something happened between him and his dad to set him off? I'm so confused.

Forty-five minutes and two mini dust tornados later, we still have no idea what "through the trenches" means. And now we're covered in dirt that clings to our faces and limbs thanks to the sticky sweat glistening on our skin.

Another gust of wind blows more dust into my hair and eyes and I swat it away angrily. Daren swats at the dirty wind, accidentally meets my eyes, and quickly looks away with a scowl as he wipes his brow.

Now I'm convinced his sour attitude is because of what happened between us. The bastard can't even look me in the eye.

"Maybe he meant a different kind of trench. Like a war trench," Daren suggests.

I scoff. "Yeah, I'm sure he wants us to trek through a battlefield and go digging through some war trenches."

He juts his chin. "Do *you* have any better ideas? Because all you've done for the past twenty minutes is complain. *It's hot. I'm tired.*" He scowls. "What is your *deal?*"

"What is *your* deal?" I say. "You're the one who's been in a pissy mood all morning and hasn't spoken to me since we left your dad."

He snaps, "Why do you keep bringing up my personal shit? It's none of your damn business. Can't you just forget about my life for one fucking second?"

I scoff. "Not a problem. Consider yourself forgotten."

He scoffs back. "I already have."

"What's that supposed to mean?" I pull back, struggling to decode his expression. I shift my jaw. "Is this about last night?"

"Nope. Last night was *no big deal* and nothing happened," he says with contempt. "Nothing that mattered, anyway."

His words cut deep—deeper than I'd like to admit—and he doesn't even look remorseful.

My mouth falls open. "What a shitty thing to say."

"Shittier than you using me to get your daddy's money?"

"What?" I shake my head in disbelief. "If *anyone* is being used it's me. You're just using *me* to get the money—and maybe get lucky along the way," I snap.

He looks like I just slapped him. And in a way I guess I did.

His face falls. "Are you for real right now?"

I don't really think he's been using me. If anything, I think he just doesn't know what to do with me. But his words still sting and I'm too hurt to care about his feelings.

I shrug. "Well that's what you do, isn't it? You're an opportunist, trying to get laid at every corner."

He clenches his jaw and angrily nods. "Yep. Yeah. You've got me all figured out. I found out we were going to be handcuffed together and I was like, 'You know what? This would be a *great* opportunity for me to get in frigid little Kayla's pants.'" He scoffs. "I'm not the one who was practically begging for it."

"Ex*cuse* me?"

"Oh please. You spread your legs and practically begged me to do you."

My throat closes in as I feel all the blood rush to my face. I'm embarrassed and furious, but mostly I'm in pain. My heart aches like he's stabbed a butcher knife into its core and is mercilessly twisting. All I want to do is hurt him back.

I glare at him. "Don't flatter yourself." And just because I'm a horrible person, I add, "I felt sorry for you, that's all. You're homeless, for God's sake. You sleep on the floor and can't even afford to eat. You have no future and any women who knew the truth about you would run away screaming. Nobody wants you, so I felt bad. It was going to be a pity lay."

Oh God. I went too far. The look of heartbreak on his face cuts into my lungs, making it hard to breathe as I watch his every fear claw at his self-esteem, stripping him down into the tattered shreds of worthlessness he already thinks he is.

I open my mouth to apologize but he cuts me off before words can form.

"Well good thing it didn't happen then." His face turns to stone. "It was just going to be a victory lay for me. Just another notch on my belt. But now? Meh." He shrugs. "You're not really worth my time. There's really nothing to you except some tits and an ass. And I can get that anywhere."

Pain.

Pure, black pain. That's what this is.

We're piercing each other, one sharp arrow of insecurity after another, puncturing holes in our already ruined facades. I'm pissed and hurt, and on the verge of tears. All I want to do is run away from him. Goddamn these fucking handcuffs!

I swallow and try to keep my tears at bay. "You know what?" I say calmly. "I don't really need the money. We're stuck and can't figure out the clue anyway." I look him over. "I'm done."

He shifts his jaw and looks me over as well. "Me too."

More pain.

"Good. Let's go." We head back to the car and climb inside. I'm proud of my ability to keep the keys from shaking as I jam them into the ignition and turn.

Nothing.

I try again. The car makes a whirring noise but doesn't turn over. Again and again. Still nothing.

Daren grunts in frustration. "Here, let me try." He grabs the keys and tries himself, but the car won't work.

"The battery's probably dead," I say.

Daren mutters, "Fuck."

We sit in silence for a good full minute.

"What now?" I stare at the steering wheel.

He rubs a hand down his face and exhales. "I don't know."

"We're in the middle of nowhere with no food or water." I pull out my phone. "And no freaking service."

"I know."

"We need a plan, Daren."

"I know! I don't know what to do ... Wait. Yes I do. Get out."

"What? Why?"

"Just get out of the damn car," he barks.

I sneer at him but get out anyway.

"Willow Inn is about a mile away," he says. "If we hike through the forest we can be there in half an hour and Angelo, one of my coworkers, will be able to get these damn things off of us so we can figure out what our next move is. So come on." He marches past me, leading us into the trees. "Let's hurry," he says without looking at me. "I want to get these damn things cut off of us as soon as fucking possible."

"Me too," I say, but even as the words leave my mouth a little piece of my heart falls away.

30

DAREN

I've never been in this heavy of a fight with a girl before. I've never had a *reason* to fight like this with a girl before— probably because no girl has ever meant anything to me or mattered in a way that I felt was worth getting hurt over. But this hurts like hell.

Kayla's words about me being a pity screw...I know she didn't mean them. I could tell by her quivering lip that she was just trying to lash out at me, but I've never been more hurt by words in my life. Except maybe when my mom left and told me *her love for me wasn't enough for her to stay in an unhappy life*. That rejection was pretty awful. But Kayla rejecting me is a whole different kind of pain.

I don't know why she matters so much to me, but she does. And now she's marching through the trees beside me and all she wants to do is be done with me. She's even willing to give up the inheritance money to get away from me.

This is what I do. I drive valuable, important women away from me. Women are willing to leave behind great wealth just to flee from me. I could almost laugh out loud.

I'm completely unwanted.

We walk for a little over a half hour—in tense silence—until I see the inn in the distance. At first, I'm relieved. But then I see two figures out back and I bite back a curse.

Levi and Ellen.

Of course Ellen and Levi are out back when I'm trotting up to the inn with a girl chained to my wrist. I swear to God, it's like I'm trying to ruin my questionable reputation. Or at least keep it intact.

They look like they're having a deep conversation. Good. Maybe Kayla and I can sneak past them without being noticed. That would be good. Levi and I aren't exactly pals right now. Or ever.

The last time I saw him, Levi was choking me on Monique's hood because I'd tried to drive drunk—with his girlfriend, Pixie, as my captive. Needless to say, Levi's not one of my biggest fans.

His eyes shoot to mine. Ah, hell. I hate the way he's staring at me, and I hate the way Ellen is now staring at Kayla. And I hate myself for bringing all this on.

"Daren?" Ellen takes a step forward as we near.

"Uh, hi." I smile sheepishly and start to wave with my cuffed hand, causing Kayla's wrist to yank up with mine.

She whips her arm down and hisses, "Use your other hand."

"What the *hell*...?" Levi stares horrified at me and points to Kayla. "Did you *kidnap* this girl?"

"What? No!" I say. "Hell, no. You think I *wanted* to be hand-cuffed to this girl?"

Kayla glares at me. "Oh. Like I wanted to be chained to you?" She rolls her eyes. "Please."

"Will someone please explain what's going on?" Ellen looks around in confusion. "And where you guys came from?"

I sigh. "It's a long story."

"It's a stupid story," Kayla corrects. She sneers and my anger bubbles up.

I glare at her. "Are you incapable of shutting up for even a second?"

"Oh, I'm sorry," she snaps back, raising our cuffed wrists. "You'll have to excuse my bad mood. I've been attached to a *douche bag* for two days."

"And who are you?" Ellen asks.

She holds out her free hand. "I'm Kayla."

"Ellen." Ellen slowly shakes her hand, glancing between the two of us.

Kayla cuts her eyes back to me. "See how I used my *non*-cuffed hand to do that? It's not rocket science."

I narrow my eyes at her before turning back to Ellen. "Is Angelo here?"

Ellen hesitates. "Uh, yeah . . ."

"Excellent. If anyone can get us out of these things, it'll be him. Come on." I pull Kayla by the cuffs to the back door and inside the inn—while she mutters death threats and curse words at me—and walk us through the lobby and into the dining room.

Angelo is behind the bar, right where I thought he'd be, wiping it down with a white rag. His bar is always ridiculously clean, but still the guy insists on polishing its surface day in and day out.

He looks up from his shiny bar top, glances at our cuffed wrists, then goes back to wiping like seeing a guy chained to a girl is an everyday occurrence for him.

"Looks like you two had an interesting day," he says.

"Something like that," I say. "You don't by any chance have a pair of bolt cutters here, do you?"

"At the inn?" Angelo laughs gruffly and shakes his head. "We ain't got no bolt cutters here."

I curse under my breath and see Kayla's shoulders slump from the corner of my eye.

"But if you're trying to get out of those handcuffs, I might be able to help," Angelo says, waving at our metal manacles.

"Really?" I say.

He nods at a nearby dining table. "Sit down and put your wrists on the table."

We do as we're told and Angelo walks up, reaches into his back pocket, and pulls out a leather case. Pulling out a thin tool with a hook on the end, he shoves the case back into his pocket and slips the hook tool into the lock on the cuffs.

I'm not at all surprised that Angelo carries a lock-picking kit in his back pocket. Because why *wouldn't* a guy tote a shady tool kit around in his back pocket?

First he pulls the broken bobby pin from the lock, then ten seconds later our cuffs pop open and we're free. Just like that. Where was Angelo two days ago when I wanted to pull my hair out and pee in private?

"There you go," Angelo says. He smiles at Kayla. "Sorry you were attached to this schmuck."

She half-smiles back. "Me too," she says, but there's no venom in her voice.

Her eyes meet mine in a sad exchange, both of us feeling remorse but neither of us brave enough to apologize.

We nod our thanks to Angelo and leave the dining room and enter the lobby, where Ellen is behind the front desk. When she sees us, she lifts her brows.

"I see you found Angelo and were able to…untangle your-selves," she says, nodding at our unchained wrists.

Kayla shifts away from me, like she's just realized she's no longer bound to my side and can now put space between us. That hurts.

"Yeah." Rubbing my wrist, I clear my throat. "Hey, um…I know this is unprofessional, and probably crossing the line, but I was wondering if maybe you might—"

"Of course you can stay here tonight," she says then looks at her computer.

"Seriously?" Gratitude and relief flood my veins.

"Seriously," she says. "But I only have one room available. Is that going to be a problem?" She looks first at Kayla then me.

"Uh…" I glance at Kayla, who quickly looks away.

"That won't be a problem at all," Kayla says.

I look at Ellen and pinch out a smile. "Right."

No problem at all.

31

KAYLA

*W*hen Daren said he worked at an inn, I pictured something like the Quickie Stop. Something with doors on the outside, peeling wallpaper, and chipping paint.

But the Willow Inn is cute, and even kind of quaint. It sort of reminds me of every inn I've ever read about in a book or seen on TV. It has a very "Sweet Home Alabama" feel to it and there are dozens of purple flowers in the field out back.

Ellen seems nice. She looks nothing at all like what I pictured Daren's boss to be. She's sexy and confident, and she smiles at me like she actually cares. And not once has she looked me up and down, sizing me up like most women do upon meeting me. That alone makes me want to hug her.

She hands us our room key and Daren leads the way. I trail a few steps behind him, my eyes fixed on his broad back. It's weird to be anywhere other than at his side. It's weird to be free of the handcuffs. Nothing about the tension between us feels liberating at all.

By the time we reach the top of the staircase and get into room number seven, I'm exhausted and eager for a shower—one without a guy attached to my wrist.

Thinking about last night makes my heart ache and my throat

close in. I swallow and blink and wring my hands, not sure what to do with myself. I've never felt so torn up by a guy before.

Daren flicks on the light switch. The room is really cute, with pale green walls and honey maple furniture. A king-size bed sits against the far wall, flanked by two nightstands. A chaise lounge is positioned under the large bedroom window and off to the side is a bathroom with vintage faucets, a walk-in shower, and a claw-foot bathtub.

"You can take a shower first," he says, not looking at me.

I shift my weight. "That's okay. You can go—"

"No, really. You go first," he says firmly.

I silently roll my suitcase into the bathroom, closing the door behind me. The moment it latches shut, I let out a long breath and lean against the door. Daren shouldn't matter so much to me. He shouldn't. But here I am in this sweet little bathroom wishing I could go back in time and undo all the damage of the day.

I quickly shower, rinsing the dust off my body and washing my hair methodically. Suds run over my wrist, where there's a small bruise from Daren and me yanking on each other these last few days. He probably has a small bruise too.

I run my thumb over the bruise and my heart twists. Being handcuffed to him was annoying and difficult, but it was also kind of fun. And it meant I was never alone. I don't think I realized how lonely my life had been until I had Daren chained to my side every day. Being locked together wasn't convenient, by any means, but having someone just *be* there was...well, nice. It was more than nice. It felt like I was home.

And now I'm lost.

I turn off the shower and towel myself dry before changing into a clean pair of pajamas. I stare into the mirror. My hair is wet and stringy, sticking to my head in a tousled way. My blue eyes are framed by blonde eyelashes, making them look small and plain without any makeup on. I look as average as possible—and this is the best I've looked the entire time Daren and I have been looking for the inheritance.

I've been a mess around him. Dirty. Wet. Haggard. And he's been a disaster around me. But as I think back over the last three days, I can't recall a single time when he assessed me. I saw attraction in his eyes, but for the most part, he looked at me like I was a person and not just female. I can't remember a guy ever doing that before.

Gathering my things, I exit the bathroom and step into our room. Daren is sitting on the chaise lounge with the phone to his ear. Our eyes meet and longing flashes in his gaze—not just sexual longing, but emotional want. As if we've found something in each other we didn't know we needed. Compassion. Friendship.

Acceptance.

And now, without the handcuffs to physically bind us together, we're afraid we'll lose everything we just found.

Whoever he's speaking with on the phone must say something because he drops his eyes and says, "Yes. I'm glad to hear that."

I step over to the bed and crawl under the soft covers on the left side.

"Yeah, well it was the right thing to do, Eddie," he says. "Let's not give him more credit than he deserves...Okay, yeah. We will. Later." He hangs up and glances at me.

"Was that about your dad?" I ask, pulling the sheets up to my chest.

He nods but doesn't look at me. "He pleaded guilty."

I nod as well. "That's good."

Daren clears his throat. "I'm going to take a shower."

He enters the bathroom and a few seconds later I hear the water turn on. I turn off the lamp on the nightstand beside me, and the room goes dark except for the single lamp on Daren's side of the bed.

I rub my wrist and look at the small bruise. It's barely there and barely hurts but it's a little reminder of my attachment to him.

I frown at the ceiling, thinking about how we decided not to look for the inheritance anymore. My heart falls a little bit as I lie in the bed. I could really use that money to go back to nursing school. It's always been my dream, and with my current circumstances it's simply impossible.

My palms start sweating and my heart starts to race as I think about how I have nothing. No plan. No money. No home. And no Daren.

God, I miss him. He's only a few yards away from me, but I miss him.

There's something about Daren—something vulnerable and honest that I connect with easily. Something I've never found in anyone else and can't quite imagine living without. And when we leave this place and go our separate ways I'll have to do just that.

My heart clenches, and tears threaten once again.

I've never known love before, at least not with a man who wasn't my father, but this deep sadness in my chest is most definitely heartbreak. And heartbreak is an effect of only one thing: love.

Is this what love is? This painful, unhinged thing? This polarizing madness that swings from joyous to suffering in the blink of an eye? And if so, why do we let it consume us the way it does? Why do we so willingly surrender to its violent currents and unpredictable winds?

Daren exits the bathroom, now finished with his shower, and his eyes lock on mine. A handful of heartbeats pass as we gaze across the room in a silent exchange of hope and loss, and I suddenly know the answer.

This is why we give into the storm of love. This *something* that is neither word nor feeling, found in quiet gazes and cookies in the dark. Hidden in cotton candy secrets and gentle shower soapsuds. It creeps up on you and slips inside, and before you know it, love owns you completely. But when it leaves, it rakes your insides, ripping at your soul until you're shredded and undone. Then, and only then, do you realize you were in love.

Daren's brown eyes snap away from mine and all the pieces of my heart that have been drifting into Daren's hands these last few days start to break into even smaller pieces, crumbling in his grasp, and I'll never get them back. Because this is love, and all those pieces of my heart I handed over as my down payment on *us* are no longer my own, but Daren's forever. And right now they're bleeding like crazy.

I roll onto my side so my back is to him as a tear rolls from the corner of my eye. It's the first time I've been in a nice bed in months and I already know I won't be able to sleep.

32

DAREN

I listen to Kayla cry softly into her pillow, and my throat begins to tighten. Every fiber of my being wants to roll over and pull her into my arms, begging her to forgive me. I want to take her face in my hands and kiss away her tears. I want to undo all the damage I've caused.

I can't stand this—not having her smiling eyes on mine, not having her wrist banging into mine every few minutes. It's like I've lost a piece of myself.

And it hurts. God, it hurts.

I fucked up so bad.

I stare at the ceiling and clutch at my aching chest as I listen to Kayla sniffle. I broke her. I broke Turner's daughter.

Just like his priceless pocket watch, Turner entrusted me with Kayla and I damaged her. Crushed her to pieces.

Sleep won't come for me. But I don't deserve it anyway.

———

The next morning, I wait until Kayla has already left the room before padding into the bathroom and washing my face. Even though I work here, I've never been in this room before. Generally, when I stock the supplies I don't go into the guest rooms.

I finish washing my face and dry it with a towel then look in the mirror. I have two days of scruff that looks very out of place on my usually clean-shaven face. There are dark circles under my eyes and a faint bruise on my left wrist and my hair is a matted mess. And even though I smell clean from my shower last night, I feel rotten.

Mostly because of the Kayla thing, and partly because I have no plan. I know I'm getting to a point where I'm just going to run out of money. My jobs aren't enough to continue paying Connor's medical bills, and now that Kayla and I have decided to forfeit the inheritance, I don't even have a backup plan.

A knock sounds on my door. I open it to see Ellen waiting in the hallway.

She smiles. "Breakfast is ready."

I frown. "What are you talking about?"

"Breakfast is included with every night's stay," she says. "You know that."

"Yeah," I say. "But I'm not a guest. I'm a freeloader who crashed your inn and stayed in one of your rooms last night."

"No," she says, drawing out the word, "you're an employee of Willow Inn. And all employees get five guest nights for free each year." She grins. "I'm glad to see you're taking advantage of your employee benefits. Now hurry and come downstairs before Mable throws away your hot food and complains about it all day."

"But I—"

"Do *not* make me tell Mable you don't want her breakfast, you hear me?" She sharpens her eyes.

"Yes, ma'am," I say.

Her smile is back. "Good. See you in ten." Then she disappears from my doorway.

Shaking my head, I finish getting dressed before making my way downstairs. In the dining room, all the tables are set for breakfast and most of them are full.

"Morning, Daren," says Earl Whethers, one of the inn's regulars, seated at the nearest table.

"Morning, Earl," I say. "Where's Vivian?"

He chuckles. "At the bar." He points to where his wife is seated at the bar top, trying to sweet-talk a shot of whiskey out of Angelo.

"Vivian, like I said yesterday and the day before," Angelo says. "The only drinks we serve at breakfast are mimosas."

She curls up her lip. "You're no fun, Angelo."

"Sit down, sit down," Earl says to me, and pulls out a nearby chair. "Ellen says you're off today, so I've decided you should join me for breakfast." I take a seat. "So what brings you to town?" Earl says with a wink.

"The car I was riding in broke down nearby, actually," I say. "So I stayed the night."

"With…?"

I lift a brow.

Earl says, "Oh come on, now. Everyone is talking about how you came to the inn with a young lady. Who is she?"

"Oh, Kayla? She's…" I blink. Who is she? "She's my friend," I say. "Kinda."

He laughs. "Sure she is." Then his whole face changes and goes pale. For a moment, I think he's having a heart attack because his eyes bulge and his limbs go rigid. But then he whispers, "Well, I'll be…"

I follow his gaze and relax a tinge when I realize why his mouth is hanging open the way it is. Kayla has just entered the dining room. And now that she's all cleaned up, she's stunning.

She always looks incredible, but in the morning light coming through the dining room from the dramatic floor-to-ceiling windows she is completely breathtaking. Her hair is tied back in a mess, she's not wearing makeup, and she's dressed in a ratty tank top, torn up jeans, and dirty sneakers. But she's absolutely beautiful.

Which just reminds me of what an asshole I am.

Earl clucks his tongue. "That might be the prettiest girl I've ever seen."

I pull my eyes away from her. "Tell me about it."

"Is that your lady?" he asks with a dirty wink.

I smile tightly. "I wish."

"What happened? Did you screw it up?"

"Yep." I nod. "I sure did."

He sighs. "Stupid boy. I tell ya. Youth is wasted on the young. If I were your age, I'd find a way to keep that girl happy and by my side forever."

"Why?" I say defensively. "Because she's pretty? Because she's more than just her good looks, you know."

"Well, sure—"

"She's smart. And she sews. And she wants to be a nurse. And even though life has been shitty to her she has a kind spirit. And she cares about people even when they don't deserve it—"

I stop talking because now Earl's staring at me like I'm crazy, and maybe I am. In fact, I know I am.

I'm crazy for thinking I was ever good enough to touch or kiss Kayla. And I'm crazy for saying mean things to her and making her cry. And most of all, I'm crazy because I just now realized that I love Kayla Turner.

It just hit me. A lightning bolt in the middle of this dining room. A warm sensation rolls over me, overwhelming me with deep affection as I stare at Kayla across the room. Oh my God. I actually love Kayla. I love who she is and what she wants and how she feels.

And it scares the shit out of me.

Guys like me don't get to have girls like Kayla Turner. Guys like me end up as alcoholics in jail. Guys like me can only dream of girls like Kayla Turner.

So go ahead, Earl Whethers. Look at me like I'm crazy.

Because I AM completely, utterly, irrevocably crazy.

"What?" I snap, staring down at my coffee mug.

Fortunately, Mable comes up to our table just then, saving Earl from my intense eyes, and sets breakfast down in front of us.

On the other side of the room, I watch as Kayla sits down at a table by herself. Mable moves to Kayla's table, and Kayla smiles as Mable introduces herself and starts chatting her ear off.

"This bacon is amazing, isn't it?" Earl says.

I stare at Kayla and distractedly say, "It's really good."

"You know," says Earl as he butters a piece of toast, "I remember when I first fell in love with Vivian." He laughs. "It scared the hell out of me. I never felt worthy of her." He says. "I still don't." He looks at me and smiles. "But you know what? I never regretted going after her." He takes a bite of toast. "And you won't either."

I look at Earl and frown. "You want me to go after Vivian?"

"No, dumbass. You know exactly what I mean."

My eyes catch on Kayla's eyes across the room and my whole body goes rigid as we lock gazes. I know exactly what Earl means.

33

KAYLA

*D*aren's eyes.

They're killers. And if I keep staring into them I'll be a goner for sure.

I drag my eyes from his and focus on the tablecloth, suddenly on the verge of tears again. Never in my life have I been so emotionally desperate for someone else.

I was supposed to come down here, sign my dad's estate papers, then start a new life. It was going to be a crappy, poor life, but it was going to be mine—all mine—without anyone else being a wild card that could bail on me or die at any given moment.

But now...now my plan is blown to hell and all I can think about is how I don't want to leave the crappy little town of Copper Springs because I don't want to leave Daren Ackwood.

I AM A SAPPY, SAPPY GIRL.

My eyes snag on him again. It's simply not fair how gorgeous he is. It's cruel to everyone in the room. He outshines them all. And then add to it that he's actually a good guy and not some arrogant spoiled frat boy and, well, everyone else may as well just give up on life completely.

I inwardly sigh. Why didn't I realize what a gem he was when we were younger and I still had a shot? And why was I so unspeakably cruel to him yesterday? My God. I pushed every vulnerable button he had and watched him just fall to pieces. But the worst part? I love him. I watch as he cuts into his pancakes and my stomach does a summersault.

I love Daren. I love his soul. I love that he wants to do the right thing. I even love all his brokenness and misplaced self-worth. He's crazy and insecure and terrified of getting attached to people and I absolutely love him. If only I'd known this about myself yesterday before I destroyed him with my words.

It's hard to see love when you have it, but when it's gone you're blind to anything else.

He looks up and our eyes meet again. Mine sting with the threat of more tears but I can't seem to look away from him. He tilts his head ever so slightly, like his big heart doesn't want to see me sad, and the stinging grows hotter.

Why? Why in the HELL do I suddenly want to cry all the time?

"Good morning," says a smooth voice. I look up to see Ellen smiling down at me.

"Good morning." I smile back.

"Do you mind if I sit with you?" she says.

"Of course not." I gesture to the seat, and she takes it.

"So. What are you doing today?" she asks.

"Nothing. I have no plan for today or any day after today," I say wistfully.

She nods. "Okay. Well, do you feel like making a little bit of money?"

I raise a brow. "I'm listening..."

She smiles. "I'm short on staff. My prep cook just moved to Phoenix and I desperately need to hire a waitress, so I was hoping maybe you could jump in today and serve tables for a few hours. I'll totally pay you."

My eyes widen a smidge. I could really use the money but I don't know...

"It would really mean a lot to me," Ellen adds.

I bite my lip. "Okay."

"Yeah?"

I smile. "Yeah."

"Excellent!" she says. Then looks across the room. "Oh, some guests are here to check in. I'll be right back."

As she heads to the front desk, I grab my purse and search for my lip gloss. The folder of trust fund papers catches my eye and I pull it out. I go through the statements, eyeing all the withdrawals made in Chicago. I tally up all the withdrawals and feel a little sick to my stomach. Not just because of the insane amount she essentially stole from me, but because all that money went to drugs. Her selfishness had no bounds at the end.

I start stacking the papers back into the folder when a page that looks different than the rest catches my eye. I pull it from the group. It's a printed-out chain of e-mails between my mom and dad when I was nineteen.

Gia,

   I just checked Kayla's trust fund account and it's nearly empty. What happened? I thought we agreed not to let Kayla use it until she was twenty-five.

James

James,

   Some unplanned expenses came up so I dipped into her savings. Don't worry. It's nothing to be concerned with.

Gia

Gia,

If unplanned expenses come up, you're supposed to call me, not use Kayla's money. That was supposed to be for her future. Are you using again? I know Kayla is an adult now, but she still needs you.

James

James,

How dare you accuse me of using. I'm clean. I told you that before. If you're so concerned about the trust account, why don't you just replenish it?

Gia

Gia,

You told me you were clean and then you banished me from seeing Kayla. I will replenish the trust fund if you let me speak with Kayla. You can't continue to keep her from me just because you're scared I'll tell her about the trust fund money. It's been three years, Gia. This has gone on for long enough.

James

James,

It's not me. It's Kayla. She doesn't want to see you and she doesn't want you to come out here or be in her life at all. And I do NOT have a drug problem. If you won't put money back in the trust that's fine. We don't need your money anyway.

Gia

Gia,

I can't help you if you don't want help, but please think about what you're doing. Kayla needs you sober. You don't have to love me or the life we used to have, but I need you to love Kayla. More than yourself. More than drugs. I will help you in any way. Just say the word. And please tell Kayla I love her and miss her deeply.

James

The chain of e-mails ends there and I slouch in my chair, stunned. My mother kept me from my father. All these years I thought he just wrote me off, but really my mom hid me away and told me lies. She told my dad lies too. *Kayla doesn't want to see you and she doesn't want you to come out here or be in her life at all.* Did he believe her? Did my father die thinking I didn't love him?

My hands start to shake and my heart begins to pound.

My addict mom used every penny of my trust account to support her habit, and then blamed our poverty and my *needing to drop out of college* on my father. Such wickedness. Such dark, black evil.

And all because of her addiction.

She took everything from me, including my father. She made me resent him for no reason. She let me cry myself to sleep at night. She watched my little heart break and she didn't even bat an eye.

My pounding heart slams against my chest and I can hardly breathe.

"Sorry about that," Ellen says, plopping down in the seat across from me with a big smile, but her face instantly falls when she sees me. "Kayla, what's wrong?"

I try to fill her in on what I just read, but my words don't come out right so I just hand her the printed e-mails. She reads in silence for a moment, covering her mouth as she reaches the end of the chain, then looks up at me with profound sympathy in her eyes.

"Oh, Kayla." She reaches out and places her hand over mine on the table. "I'm so sorry. This is... this is awful."

I stare at the tablecloth, feeling tears burn behind my eyes but not yet crying. "Do you think my dad died believing I didn't want him in my life?"

"Oh, no. Not at all." She shakes her head. "I knew your father well and he loved you, and felt your love for him, very much."

I blink. "You knew my dad?"

She nods. "He used to stay here at the inn sometimes, when he wanted to get his thoughts clear. He was here a lot this past year."

"Because of the cancer," I say, nodding. "I didn't know he had cancer. No one told me he was sick."

She frowns. "Are you sure? Because I know your father wrote you letters... and called... several times, actually. I was here when he did it. Your mother didn't want him to speak with you. But he asked her to pass messages on to you about how sick he was."

My jaw drops. "My mom knew he was dying and didn't tell me? Why would she do that? Why would she keep so many things from me?"

Lying about my trust fund was one thing, but keeping my dad's terminal illness from me? That's so extreme. And refusing to let a dying man get in touch with his daughter is even worse. My God. The drugs must have really made her a monster.

Sympathy fills Ellen's eyes. "I'm so sorry, Kayla. I didn't mean to upset you."

I shake my head. "No. It's not you. Clearly, it's my mom." I gesture to the e-mail page. "We had all sorts of money from my dad, but my mom squandered every penny and forced us to live in poverty. And forced *me* to drop out of college." My voice cracks. "And she kept my father from seeing me. I just—I just can't believe she would be so vindictive." I swallow. "And she made me vindictive too. She filled me with so much bitterness and hurt that I refused to answer when my dad would call me." I look at Ellen hopelessly. "I didn't say good-bye before he died. And I didn't let him say good-bye."

Oh my God. I didn't let my daddy say good-bye to me.

Ellen squeezes my hand and leans close. "Your father loved you very much, Kayla. And when your mother wouldn't let him see you anymore, he was devastated. He wanted to make things right with you before he died, but he was too sick to fly."

"So he called," I say in a near whisper. "And I didn't return his calls."

I shake my head in silence, my jaw going slack. My father didn't reject me or ignore me. He just couldn't get ahold of me.

Ellen reaches out and puts her hand on mine. "On behalf of James, I want you to know that your dad loved you very much. He spoke about you like you were an angel and he was extremely proud to be your father."

A tear falls down my cheek and onto the tablecloth. "I didn't know…" I look at Ellen. "I was a horrible daughter."

She smiles. "No, baby. You were the best part of his life."

I didn't know *any* of this. And now he's dead and I can't say sorry for being so hateful toward him for all these years. And my mother is dead so I can't even confront her about all the pain she's caused.

My throat closes in, a slow choke wrapping around my neck with icy fingers of betrayal and regret as I blink.

"Please excuse me," I say with a cracking voice. "I have to…" I scoot my chair back abruptly and hurry from the dining room.

I don't know where I'm going, I just go. Through halls and rooms and out doors. I put one foot in front of the other until I find myself in a field of lavender under the morning sky. And there I crumple to the ground and sob against the pretty purple flowers.

I sob for my mother and the way she broke my family. How she let my father shower her with love and affection, only to break his heart. How she hauled me away from our sweet hometown and raised me in a big city where I competed with her unending string of boyfriends for her attention. How she took advantage of my love and used me to fulfill her selfish needs. And finally, how she took her own life, the most selfish act of all, and left me all alone in this world.

I sob for my father, who loved my mother despite her flaws and never gave up on her. How he made me sweet scavenger hunts and left me little notes for my locket. How he kept pictures of me and my mother up in the house. How he tried to call me, without an answer. How he made a scavenger hunt for me after his death as a sign of love, even though I hadn't answered those calls. How he was proud of the baby girl he didn't get to see all grown up.

And I sob for myself and all the things I didn't know. I sob for the hurt I blamed on my father and the many years I that believed he'd never sent us money. For the future I let my mother's habits destroy, and the precious past I refused to let myself indulge in because thinking good memories about my father was too painful.

And I sob for all the chances that I will never have to make any of these things right.

I weep on the pretty purple flowers until there's nothing left to blame or mourn. Then I turn over on my back and stare up at the sky. Lost.

34

DAREN

*S*o?" Ellen leans against the doorframe of my guest room and cocks her head.

"So... what?" I ask as I finished making the bed.

Ellen lifts a brow. "Are you going to tell me about this Kayla girl or what?"

I exhale. "You're really nosey, you know that?"

She smiles. "I do, actually. I think it's one of my more endearing qualities. So what's the deal?"

I shrug. "Old Man Turner left us some money, apparently. But the condition was that we had to be handcuffed together if we wanted to retrieve it."

Ellen laughs. Like full-on throws her head back and laughs at the ceiling. "That's awesome."

"Not the word I'd use."

Her laughter tapers off but she keeps smiling. "Oh come on! James leaves you and Kayla an inheritance but forces you two to be handcuffed together for... how long has it been?"

"Three days."

"Three days!" She laughs again. Then sighs. "I'm going to miss that ol' weirdo."

I smile at the pillowcase as I pull it off the pillow to be washed. "Me too."

Her voice turns sincere. "How are you doing with... you know, everything?"

There's no point in pretending like I don't know what she's talking about because Ellen knows how to magically wiggle her way into my business and make it her own. And if I'm being honest, I kind of like the way she cares.

I let out a long sigh. "I'm doing okay, actually. But Monique got repossessed."

She makes a sympathetic noise. "That's too bad. You weren't able to sell her, then?"

"Nope. My dad was upside down on the loan. I'm trying to save up for a new car since I don't know how I'll get back and forth between all my jobs now."

She straightens in the doorway. "If you need a place to stay, you can always stay here. You can live here for free if you work here, you know. Now that Pixie's moving out, her room will be free. And I have a feeling Levi's room might soon be free as well."

"I told you already. I'm living with friends."

"Yeah, and you're a terrible liar." She smiles. "Listen, I know you haven't taken me up on this offer in the past, but you can always live here, Daren." She looks at me sincerely. "Always."

Warmth flows into my chest as I look at the sincerity in Ellen's eyes. I haven't felt so cared for since Marcella. In a lot of ways, Ellen reminds me of a younger, cooler Marcella. Always in a good mood. Always looking out for me and making me feel wanted and special. Man, I miss Marcella.

I smile at Ellen. "Thanks. But for now, I'm good just working here."

She nods. "Oh! Speaking of which…" She pulls an envelope from her back pocket and hands it to me. "Here's your paycheck."

I take it, puzzled. "Payday isn't until next week."

She shrugs. "I got a little ahead of schedule this month. Oh, and there's some cash in there too from your bar shift last week."

I peer inside and frown at the cluster of bills within. "I only covered for Angelo for a few hours."

"Well it seems the ladies—and their wallets—love the charming Daren Ackwood." She shrugs nonchalantly, but I know it's mostly an act. There's no way I made this much cash last weekend.

"Ellen…" I say, both frustrated and relieved.

"Also, I called a repair guy today and he said he could pick up Kayla's car from the lavender ranch and tow it back to Copper Springs tonight. Where should I tell him to park it?"

I shrug. "Have him drop it off at Latecomers."

"Okay. Be ready to leave this afternoon, okay?" She turns to leave then pauses. "Hey, Daren?"

I look up.

"I'm not sure what's going on with you and Kayla, but she had a rough morning. So maybe you should check on her."

My heart pounds. "Why? What's wrong? Is she okay?"

"Come downstairs when you're done and I'll fill you in," she says, and disappears down the hallway.

My first instinct is to run around the inn looking for Kayla until she's in my arms and I know she's okay. But then I remember how much she probably doesn't want to see me and I stay put.

I look back down at the envelope and count the cash inside and almost want to run after her and hug her. Typical Ellen. Always taking care of me when I don't ask for help.

———

Last year, she found me lying in the middle of Canary Road in the dead of the night. Canary is the back road to get to and from Copper Springs from Willow Inn, and even though Ellen spends every waking minute at her inn, she lives in Copper Springs. She was coming back from buying supplies in town when she saw my wallowing ass and pulled her truck to stop at an angle, blocking the road.

I was drunk and depressed, and didn't give a damn anymore about, well, anything. Charity had just died two weeks prior and I was partly to blame. She and I had just broken up but ended up attending the same party one weekend. We were always breaking up and getting back together, but this particular breakup had been rough. I was hurt and moping around, so when a random girl at the party started kissing me I didn't stop her. But Charity saw us and stormed out of the party, completely drunk, and died in a car crash later that night. So I blamed myself for her leaving that party drunk and setting a series of tragedies in motion.

My life was already a mess. My drunk dad had nearly killed Connor two months prior and sent my life spinning into a never-ending pit of debt and shame, so I'd already been on the brink of a mental breakdown before Charity's death. But after . . .

Like I said, I didn't give a damn.

I'm not sure if I was really trying to kill myself or not, but I certainly didn't care either way, which is just as bad. I remember lying in the road with a pair of headlights shining on me, irritated that someone had found me and dared to interrupt the pity party I was trying to have in the street.

Ellen stood over me, looking down at my pathetic existence

with an arched eyebrow. Her striking good looks caught me off guard for a moment as I gazed up at her. She was wearing a flowy white shirt and had her dark hair loose around her face. She looked like an angel.

I knew she was Pixie's aunt, but Ellen and I had never spoken before.

"Did you fall?" she asked me, glancing around to see where I had come from. Honestly, I didn't even know.

I shook my head, which was heavy with alcohol and heartbreak.

She glanced me over. "Are you sober?"

I shook my swimming head again.

Her long hair slipped over her shoulder as she tilted her head and stared into me with her hazel eyes. Her voice softened. "Do you want some company?"

I started to shake my head again, but it was too heavy and I was too exhausted to lie.

Wordlessly, she lay down beside me in the road and looked up. I remember thinking it odd that this grown woman who barely knew me was willing to sprawl out on the dirty road for my benefit, but I was too hammered to ponder her reasons.

She knew about Charity because Pixie and Charity were best friends. And she knew about my dad because his transgressions had been breaking news around town for the past few months. But she didn't speak a word about either.

We stayed shoulder-to-shoulder for several silent minutes. Just us and the headlights of her truck.

"It's a beautiful night," she said after a while, staring up at the sky. "The stars are lovely."

I stared up at the darkness and all I saw were the things I had lost. My mom. Marcella. Charity. "I don't see them."

She slowly nodded. "You will."

We stayed in that road for who knows how long before I finally pulled myself up with a groan, brushing off the dust and cursing the fog in my head.

"Come on," she said, helping me to my feet. "It looks like you need a ride home."

I snorted. In my head, I said, *What home?* But aloud I think it came out as, "Whamo," as I stumbled into her.

"Okay." She caught me and tossed one of my arms over her shoulder so she could guide me to her truck. "I think I have just the place for you to sober up."

I don't remember much after that. The next morning I woke up in the clean-smelling sheets of one of Willow Inn's guest room beds, still wearing my dirty clothes from the night before. I smelled like hell. I looked like hell. But for the first time in several weeks, I didn't feel like hell.

Later that day, Ellen offered me a job as her stock boy so she wouldn't have to drive back and forth from Copper Springs to Willow Inn as often. At first, I declined. But she got pretty demanding and, honestly, I needed the money. She offered me free room and board as well, but my prideful ass wasn't ready to accept total defeat in my own independence yet. But I took the job. It was one of the best decisions I've ever made. One of the few.

35

KAYLA

After my little breakdown in the lavender field, Ellen told me not to worry about stepping in as a waitress for the inn today, but I insisted because I knew serving food would help take my mind off everything. And I was right.

After serving the lunch rush for a few hours, I feel much better as I enter the kitchen.

"So who's Pixie?" I ask, pointing to the name written on an apron on the wall.

"She's Ellen's niece," Mable says. "Her real name is Sarah, but she also goes by Pixie. She worked with me all summer but she moved out yesterday because she's starting college in a few weeks."

"Oh yeah," I say, nodding as I think back to the Fourth of July party on the lake earlier this month. "I think I met her a few weeks ago. What is she studying?"

"Art." Mable smiles. "What about you?"

"I was hoping to go to nursing school, but things changed and I came out here to take care of some family business."

Her face softens. "Ellen told me about your father. I'm so sorry, sweetie."

I swallow the lump in my throat and nod. "Thank you."

Her eyes fill with sympathy. "I'm so glad you have Daren to help you get through everything."

I inhale slowly, and quietly say, "Me too."

Even though he's only been in my life for three days, Daren really has helped me get through things. But Mable was wrong. I don't have him. At least not anymore.

And...the tears are back. Dammit.

Ellen enters the kitchen and I quickly get my emotions under control.

"Hey, so I've been thinking about how you said you have no plans for, like, ever," Ellen says. "And Mable's been singing your praises all day—"

"I have." Mable smiles.

"And since I need a part-time waitress," Ellen continues, "I thought maybe we could help each other out. You could work here at the inn—just until you figure out what you want to do next, of course—and since I have a resident room opening up you live here for free at the same time."

My mouth falls open. "Are you being serious?"

She nods. "I need the help."

I blink a few times, not sure what to say—or think. Having a new job in a new state away from all my crap back in Chicago would be wonderful. But having a place to live rent-free would be...well, incredible! And it's not just any place. It's a cute little inn, tucked away in a lavender field, free of rodents and cockroaches. And with the money I saved on rent, I would be able to go to college and pursue a career in nursing.

I stare at Ellen, speechless.

"You don't have to answer me right now," she says casually with a wave of her hand. "Think it over and let me know if you have any questions. And Mable?" Mable looks up from a pie dish. "That apple cobbler smells divine. I love you the most, you know that right?"

Mable snorts. "You only love me the most when I have cobbler in my hands."

"And your point is…?"

Mable smiles. "I will save some for you, as always."

"See?" Ellen smiles broadly. "Total love." She turns and heads out of the kitchen. As I watch her walk away, my mind races with all the possibilities working at Willow Inn would give me. I could live in Arizona and start fresh. And I would be so close to Copper Springs…

I'm not sure if that thrills me or stresses me out.

Daren swings into the kitchen from the dining room with a rack of glassware in his hands. Our eyes meet and he stops walking. He opens his mouth, but doesn't say anything.

What do I want him to say? Sorry? I know he's sorry. If anyone should be apologizing for being a giant brat it should be me. But when I try to speak, nothing comes out.

Mable makes herself scarce, coming up with some excuse about piecrusts, leaving Daren and I alone.

"Hey," he says, breaking our silence.

"Hey," I say back.

He clears his throat. "Ellen told me about the e-mails from your mom…and everything." His eyes fill with sympathy, searching my face with his lips parted like he wants to say something. But instead, he slowly wraps his arms around me and pulls me against his chest. I hesitate only a moment before letting myself fall into his embrace with my cheek against his shoulder.

It's just a hug. But the gesture is so sincere I could almost cry. Here in Daren's arms, I feel significant. Safe. Visible.

Loved.

He exhales slowly and rests his cheek on my head, like he has no intention of releasing me anytime soon. I haven't felt this cared for since the last time I saw my dad.

It was the summer I was fifteen and he took me pretend fishing. I thought it was dumb at the time, because I was too old to go pretend fishing, but I played along because he seemed so excited about it. We sat by the river and talked about my mom that day. My parents had been divorced for nearly a decade at that point, but I'd never asked him about it.

He told me that he loved her very much, and missed her every day, but she had made a decision to be without him and he wanted to respect that. He seemed heartbroken when he spoke so I asked him if he regretted marrying her.

He smiled and said that if he'd never married my mother he would've never had me, and I was the best thing that had ever happened to him. He told me that being my father was the highest honor he could imagine and he'd go through heartbreak a thousand times over if it meant having me.

I bite my lip. That was the last real conversation I ever had with my father. He tried to call a few times after mom died, but I was too grief-ridden and heartbroken to return his calls. Now I'll never hear his voice again.

A single tear rolls down my dirty cheek and lands on Daren's shirt. I swallow and pull myself together, lifting my head with a sniffle. "I was wrong about my dad. He didn't abandon me. He didn't stop loving me." My voice cracks. "I was wrong."

He looks at me sympathetically. "You were lied to."

I nod, scoffing as I stare at the floor. "You know the worst part?" I look back up at him. "I can't fix it. I can't apologize to my dad or yell at my mom. I'm all alone. I have no family. I'm just completely alone."

He slowly releases me and presses his lips together. "You're not alone. You have me."

I look at him hesitantly. "I do?"

"Absolutely." He nods sincerely. "I'm so sorry about your mom, though. That's awful."

I nod and try to break up the tension. "I'm sorry about your Porsche."

He softly laughs. "Monique."

I wrinkle my nose. "What?"

"That was my car's name." He nods. "Monique."

"You named your car?"

"Yep."

I sniff. "You're weird."

"I am." He nods once. "Have you eaten yet?"

I shake my head.

"Can I make something for you?" He pulls back to look at me. "I want to feed you."

I nod. "Sure."

Turning away, he starts grabbing ingredients from the fridge and knives from the butcher block. I'm not sure if we're exactly on full speaking terms yet, so I don't ask any questions. But he looks so happy, moving around a kitchen. It's kind of adorable.

For the next half hour, Daren skitters about the kitchen and whips up a gourmet lunch of prime rib sandwiches and a strawberry fields salad. Mable scolds him a few times for getting in her way or using too much salt, but I see the amusement in her eyes. She likes that Daren enjoys cooking.

When he's finished, Daren makes plates for Ellen, Mable, and me, then insists on watching as we take our first bites. It's so delicious that I make an orgasmic noise. Daren's eyebrows raise in appreciation. "You like it that much?"

I nod. "Oh yeah."

"Good." He smiles at me, but then looks unsure. We're not totally broken anymore but we're not yet healed either.

"This is incredible. I had no idea you were skilled in the kitchen, Daren," Ellen says, swallowing a bite. "Now that Pixie's gone, I'm looking for a prep cook, you know. It might be time to change your job title." She smiles.

If I didn't know better, I'd say Daren was blushing. "I don't know. I'm not that great. Cooking is just something I do for fun."

Mable makes a noise of approval. "This sandwich is pretty great."

"We'll talk," Ellen says to Daren. "When you come in for your shift on Monday, we'll talk."

He nods. "Okay."

She adds, "And hey, maybe you can bring Kayla back with you on Monday to help serve lunch."

It's suddenly awkward, since neither of us knows what's going to happen between us later today, let alone on Monday.

"Yeah, maybe," he says, glancing at me. Then he makes an excuse to leave the kitchen and quickly darts away. I stare at my food for a minute, confused and wishing we could just fix things between us, then decide to go for a walk to clear my head.

Leaving the kitchen, I head for the lobby, hoping I don't bump into Daren. Just as I reach the front desk, where Ellen is staring at something on a computer, the inn's front door bursts open.

"Frankly, I'm impressed we made it this far without me killing you," says a pretty girl with long black hair and tattoos covering her arms as she carries in a duffle bag that looks too big and masculine to be her own. She looks vaguely familiar.

The guy behind her grins. "What's with all the death threats? Is that how you handle all of life's problems? By committing murder?" He's handsome and looks like downright trouble.

His dark hair is almost as black as the girl's, but where her eyes are golden and sharp, his eyes are gray and playful. I know I've seen the girl before, somewhere.

Dropping the duffle bag, she spins around and sneers, looking up and down his tall body. "Just the really big ones."

Oh man. She's clearly attracted to this guy. His smile goes crooked. And wow. He knows it.

"First of all, there's no need to take your frustration out on my luggage." He points to the bag on the floor then leans down so their faces are close together. "Second, is that your way of telling me I'm big?"

They lock gazes and the air between them sizzles. Good God, there's a lot of sexual tension in the room.

Ellen, who's been silently watching from behind the front desk, clears her throat.

"Jenna." She smiles. "Welcome to the inn. I didn't know you were stopping by. Pixie's not here, though."

Jenna! That's right. I met her at the Fourth of July Bash at the lake a few weeks ago too.

Jenna whips her eyes to Ellen. "Oh, I'm not here for Pixie," she says. "I'm here to drop off this bozo"—she points to the handsome guy beside her—"so I can be on my way to New Orleans."

"Jenna's not big on road trip buddies," he explains. "And she has a hard time being enclosed in small spaces with me. I'm Jack, by the way." He holds out his hand and Ellen slowly shakes it.

Jenna throws her hands up and growls. "You infuriating man."

He keeps smiling at her. "You're adorable. I'll just take my bag *back* to the car and wait for you until you're done throwing your temper tantrum." He nods at Ellen. "It was so nice meeting you."

Glaring over her shoulder as he leaves, Jenna marches through the lobby and plows right into me.

"Oh! Sorry," she says, taking a step back. Her face softens when she's sees me. "Hey, I know you...Kayla right?" She smiles and all the anger and frustration surrounding her instantly disappears.

I smile. "Yeah. I met you and Sarah—Pixie—Sarah?—at the lake."

"That's right. You stopped to ask for directions to Copper Springs." She adds, "You can call her Pixie, by the way. I do. So what are you doing here?"

"At the moment?" I exhale. "Hiding from a guy."

She scoffs. "I feel ya. I wish I could hide from that guy." She tips her chin at the front door and sighs. "But I can't."

I nod understandingly. "Because he's always around?"

"No." She looks at the door longingly. "Because I don't want to. Don't get me wrong, the guy pisses me off and makes me want to pluck my leg hairs out one by one, but..." She shrugs and a hint of a smile pulls at her lips. "He makes things interesting. Honestly, I'd be bored without him."

Jack pops his head back in the front door and calls out, "I'm ready when you are, Diva!"

Her puppy dog smile is immediately replaced with a look of complete agitation as she whips her head around and yells, "Don't. Call. Me. DIVA!"

He grins at her. "It never gets old."

"God!"

He disappears back out the door and she turns back to me, all smiles and goodness again.

"So this boy you're hiding from," she says. "Does he make things interesting?"

I think for a moment. We jumped out of a train car, fell down a mudslide, slept in an abandoned house, and showered with handcuffs on—and all in the last seventy-two hours.

"Yes," I say. "He's the most interesting thing that's ever happened to me."

She smiles. "Then what are you hiding from?"

36

DAREN

*W*ith carefully planned routes through the inn, I manage to avoid Kayla for most of the day. It's not that I don't like to see her—I very much enjoy looking at her. But I just don't know what to say to her. I loved feeding her, but she was so sad about everything she'd learned about her mom that I felt like drudging up any issue she and I have would have been petty.

I need to say sorry but sorry has never come easy for me, especially when it comes to girls. I've never really put much effort into making up with members of the opposite sex. Once they burn me, I typically back off so I can't get burned again. It's a rule of mine and, up until three days ago, it worked flawlessly.

But for some reason my chest just won't seem to loosen up with all this guilt and gloom. I can walk away from any girl anywhere, but not Kayla.

The sound of jingling keys meets my ears and I turn to see Ellen approaching the front desk, where I've been restacking printing paper for the past ten minutes.

She smiles. "The repair guy towed Kayla's car to Latecomers and gave it a jump, so it should be working now. I'm going to grab Kayla and we'll meet you outside. You ready to go?"

I nod. "Yep. I'll be out in fifteen minutes. I'm sure Kayla wants to get away from me as soon as possible."

Ellen narrows her eyes. "Why?"

"Because," I sigh, angry with myself, "I basically slaughtered her to pieces with my words the other day."

"Ah," she says softly with a short nod. "That explains your guilt."

I frown. I wasn't aware my guilt was noticeable. Shit.

"But what about hers?" she says.

"Hers?" I wrinkle my brow.

"Yeah," Ellen says. "Kayla's been darting her eyes away from you and looking at the floor every time I try to speak with her about you... just like you're doing now."

I snap my eyes from the floor and meet her gaze. "That doesn't mean she feels guilty."

"Well it certainly doesn't mean she's angry. You should talk to her." She smiles. "Girls are big on communication."

"Why, so she can tell me what a jackass I am?"

"Maybe." Ellen shrugs. "But if it meant you'd get her back, wouldn't it be worth it?"

"Get her back?" I shake my head. "I never had her."

Ellen smiles with a twinkle in her eye. "Oh, Daren. There is so much you don't know about women."

37

KAYLA

*F*rom how sexy and beautiful Ellen is and how put together she looks, I expected her to drive something sleek and flashy. Something sporty and wild, or maybe sophisticated and expensive. But instead, she walks me outside to an old beat-up bright yellow truck.

She laughs at the look on my face. "What were you expecting? A Porsche like Daren's?"

I laugh. "No. Yes. Maybe. I think I pictured you driving something fancy."

She nods with a smile. "I get that a lot. I think it's because of the high heels I wear, or maybe just my overall appearance. Whatever the reason, I like to surprise people now and then by doing something that seems 'out of character' for the way I look."

"Oh!" I immediately feel bad. "I'm so sorry. I wasn't trying to stereotype you by your appearance, I swear."

She laughs. "It's no big deal. It's just the way it is. The way I look makes life easier in a lot of ways, but it sometimes leads to people making assumptions about me." She tilts her head at me. "But I'm sure you know all about unfair assumptions based on beauty."

I open my mouth but don't know what to say.

Ellen steps closer. "It's okay to be aware of your beauty, Kayla.

In fact, it's important. It's okay to know you're pretty and to know that the world treats you differently because of it. It's only a problem if you use your beauty to manipulate others, or make others feel bad. Which, after getting to know you a little bit, I'm confident you would never do. So it's okay. Be beautiful." She grins. "Hey and maybe someday you can surprise someone by driving a giant yellow truck."

She gets into the truck and I walk around to the other side. As I slide into my seat I almost feel like crying. In just a few sentences, this woman who was a stranger until just yesterday showed me more understanding than any other woman has in my whole life. And she gave me permission to look the way I do without feeling guilty or ashamed.

Without thinking, I lean over and wrap my arms around Ellen. "Thank you."

She hugs me back, embracing me tightly. When we pull away she looks at me.

"You know what, Kayla Turner?" She smiles softly. "You're amazing. And the world is just going to have to be okay with that."

I laugh and wipe away the single tear dripping down my cheek just as the back door opens. I seriously have a crying problem lately.

"Hey, sorry I'm late," Daren hurriedly says as he climbs inside the truck and shuts the door.

"No problem." Ellen turns the engine on and pulls away from Willow Inn. Then she glances at me with a sympathetic face. "I talked to the tow truck guy and he was able to jump your car and give it a little juice, but he said it's on its last legs and probably won't last much longer."

I sigh and nod. "Yeah. I knew it was coming. It's just a matter of time before it'll just die altogether. But at least it's working for me now and I have a way to get around." I glance back at Daren, knowing he's completely car-less and wondering what his plan is, or if he even has one.

I think about Jenna's words all afternoon. She seemed so frustrated with that Jack guy, but at the same time so sure she wanted him around. Because he was interesting.

Daren has been nonstop interesting—and absolute trouble, just like I thought. But it was the kind of trouble I needed to feel alive. It shook me up. It *woke* me up. It was the perfect kind of trouble.

I glance in the mirror at the beautiful boy in the backseat.

And I want to be in it all over again.

38

DAREN

$\mathcal{T}$he drive from Willow Inn to Copper Springs is just over an hour, but so far it's felt like it's taking us days. Most of the trip has been filled with light conversation—mostly initiated by Ellen—about nothing of real substance. We've stayed away from all the big topics. But during our drive, I learned some new things about Kayla. Like how she's never had any pets and how she dated a jerk named Jeremy for a year, who treated her like a trophy he took out into public and showed off but never bothered to get to know who she really was. And she graduated at the top of her class in high school.

And thanks to Ellen's extensive knowledge of my personal life, Kayla's learned a few things about me. Like how Marcella died of a brain aneurism three years ago and I cried for two days.

But even though the entire ride has been us talking about, well, *us*, Kayla and I haven't spoken—or looked at each other—once. Which is fine with me. But the closer we get to Copper Springs, the sweatier my palms get.

Because both Kayla and I know that she has no place to sleep tonight. And if she spends the money Ellen gave her on another hotel room, she'll be broke by tomorrow. I know Amber can probably give me a ride home from Latecomers, but what's Kayla's plan? Driving to the Quickie Stop?

The idea of Kayla sleeping by herself again at that disgusting motel makes me want to punch something really hard.

If only we'd been able to find the inheritance money none of this would be an issue. Maybe we shouldn't have given up so quickly. We were both frustrated and angry yesterday, neither of us thinking clearly. If we could just work things out between us then maybe we could figure out the last clue and Kayla would never again have to subject herself to a place like the Quickie Stop.

"Can I buy you guys dinner?" Ellen asks as we turn into the Latecomers parking lot. We start to protest, but she dismisses us as she pulls the truck into a parking space by the courtyard. "I insist. Now get out so I can feed you."

The three of us walk into Latecomers and Amber lights up when she sees us. "Ellen!" She comes out from behind the bar and gives Ellen a big hug.

Ellen is good friends with Amber's mom and has always treated Amber like a niece. And Amber thinks the world of Ellen.

"Hi, beautiful." Ellen smiles.

Pulling back from the hug, Amber smiles at us. "Hi guys." She waves us over to the counter. "Come sit at the bar."

We each find a barstool. Ellen sits in between Kayla and me, a human buffer between the tension we've brought to the bar, and Amber takes our drink order. As Ellen and Kayla fall into a deep conversation about her father, Amber sets my drink down in front of me and leans in.

She lowers her voice. "So what's going on?"

I lower my voice to match hers. "What do you mean?"

"I've been hearing all sorts of stories about you and Kayla Turner running around town in handcuffs," she says, lifting a brow. "What's that about?"

I shake my head and quickly fill her in on Turner's will.

"No. Way." She stares at me. "That's insane." She looks back and forth between Kayla and me. "So where are the handcuffs now?"

I scratch the back of my neck. "In Kayla's suitcase, I think. Angelo picked the lock for us and I saw her toss them in there."

"So you forfeited the money?" she squawks.

"We couldn't *find* the money," I say. "So we decided to give up on the scavenger hunt."

"Just like that?" She looks upset. "Why? Why would you give up so easily?"

I shake my head. "It's a long story."

She narrows her gaze at me. "Daren Ackwood. Did you sleep with her?"

"Wha—no!" I say sternly. "No, I did not sleep with her." I pause. "Well, actually I *did* sleep with her—but I didn't have sex with her."

She pins me with her eyes. "What did you do?"

"What do you mean?"

"I mean," she says, jutting her chin, "how did you fuck things up with Kayla?" She nods at Kayla, who's still in deep conversation with Ellen. "You keep looking at her like she's your long-lost puppy, and she keeps glancing at you like she's afraid you're going to take off at any moment. So what happened?"

I play with my glass. "Nothing. She just…She can do better than me."

Amber swats me with her bar towel. Hard.

"Ow—dammit. *What?*"

She points at me and lowers her voice. "I let you throw a pity party for yourself for seven years, but you're a man now. You're a good man who's worthy of a good woman. So suck up your insecurities and go fix things with Kayla."

I glare at her, but I know she's right.

"You like her, don't you?" Amber says.

I stare at the bruise on my wrist and nod. "I like her. A lot."

Amber scans my face for a moment and a smile tugs at her lips. "Oh my. Has Daren Ackwood fallen in love?" She sucks in a breath when I don't respond. "I knew it. I knew the moment I saw your face when she wouldn't shake your hand the other night. You're totally smitten with her." She giggles. "God, this makes me so happy."

"Okay, enough with the mushiness."

Her face turns serious. "You need to make things right with her. Tonight. And then you need to keep her by your side. Forever. Understand?"

Our food comes and saves me from replying to that, but as the three of us eat I can't help but flick my eyes to Kayla. It's easy to keep someone by your side when you're handcuffed to them, but asking someone to be with you—hoping without any guarantee—that sounds hard as hell.

Awkward conversation carries us through the meal and when we're through, we say good-bye to Amber and head back to the parking lot where Ellen parked. My eyes catch on the painted wall of the courtyard, taking me back to the feeling of Kayla in my arms as I pressed her up against that wall and kissed her hungrily. That painted wall was the last thing I saw before Kayla Turner changed me completely.

I walked into Latecomers that night with all my baggage and blues, and walked out with a racing heart and a chest filled with hope.

"Thanks for walking me out, guys. Are you guys sure I can't drop you off anywhere else?" Ellen asks, pulling her keys from her purse. "I know Amber said she can give you ride, Daren, but it's really no problem for me to take you."

"No, you go," I say with a smile. "I'm good. Thanks, though."

Kayla smiles. "Thank you so much for dinner. And for the ride."

"Of course." Ellen smiles and says to Kayla, "And I'm serious about my offer. The job and room are yours if you want them. You have my number, right?"

"I do." Kayla nods.

Ellen inhales. "I really hope you say yes and I get to spend more time with you." She wraps her arms around Kayla in a hug.

I watch them as my mind spins. Ellen offered Kayla a job and a place to stay? That would mean Kayla would stay in Arizona and live at the inn, where I work, and I would see her all the time.

"And you." Ellen turns to me. "I'll see you at eight a.m. sharp on Monday. Bring your kitchen face. I'm going to try my hardest to talk you into being my new cook."

I grin. "Yes, ma'am." The idea of working as a cook at the inn makes me feel alive. And if I could live there for free too...well, I can't imagine a better scenario for my life. I glance at Kayla.

Well, maybe one better scenario.

With a quick wave, Ellen gets in her truck and drives off, leaving Kayla and me standing in the parking lot. Alone.

Awkward silence.

More silence.

Now *super* awkward silence.

"So..." I say, swallowing.

"Yeah..." She looks around. "Okay, well. I need to get going.

Later." She turns and starts to walk to where the tow truck left her car. My chest grows tight.

"Kayla," I say.

She stops and turns around.

"Will you..." I clear my throat. "Would you maybe like to stay at my place tonight? You know, so you don't have to pay for a room?"

She takes a breath. "Oh. Uh...nah. I'm okay. Thanks."

The rejection is expected and I almost let her get away with it. But then I think about Kayla sleeping in the porn bedroom alone and I easily swallow my pride.

I take a step toward her and blurt out, "What I meant to say, was that I really hate the idea of you sleeping in that shithole for even one minute and I'd feel much better if you stayed at my place with me even though it's sort of its own kind of shithole because at least then I'll know you're safe and I realize I have no right to care about where you sleep but I can't help myself and I know you probably hate my guts right now but I swear I'll sleep outside in the dirt or something if it will make you feel better and you'll agree to sleep at my place." I suck in a breath at the end of my crazy rambling and then hold that breath as I wait for her response.

Kayla searches my face and her features soften. I don't know what she sees in my eyes, but I sure as hell hope it's the regret I feel about the other day and the desperation I feel about her now. My stomach knots together with every beat that passes until a slow smile lifts the corners of her mouth.

"Well, how can I say no to another chance to sleep on your virgin mattress?" Her eyes dance and my heart leaps—it fucking *leaps.*

Because I need this girl. Tonight. Tomorrow. Always. And I

have no idea how to make that happen, but her not hating my guts is a good place to start.

"It *is* rather cozy," I say with an embarrassing amount of glee.

"It really is." She nods.

I take a deep breath. "I'm sorry about yesterday. I shouldn't have said those things to you. I didn't mean a single word. I'm an asshole and you are more than welcome to smack me."

She shakes her head. "No, I'm sorry. I was mean. I don't know what my deal was. I just freaked out and thought you just wanted to get away from me—"

"What?"

She looks up at me from under her long eyelashes and lifts a shoulder. "You were stuck with me."

I pull her close and tip her chin up so I can see more fully into her big blue eyes. "Being stuck with you was the best thing that's ever happened to me. And the moment we took those handcuffs off I felt like I was missing something." I cup her face and quietly say, "I *want* to be stuck with you."

She leans in and brings her mouth close to mine, softly saying, "I want to be stuck with you too."

I smile against her lips. "I'm going to kiss you now."

She smiles back. "You better."

Tilting her face in my hands, I press my lips against hers and hold her mouth to mine as she parts her lips and lets my tongue inside the sweet flesh of her mouth. Her tongue dances with mine, sliding into my mouth. I trail my hands over her shoulders and down her back, clutching her hips to mine. She runs her hand to the back of my head, tugging at my hair as her mouth asks for more. As I deepen our kiss, my erection rubs against her belly and she arches her back, pushing her large soft breasts into my chest.

In between kisses, Kayla breathlessly says, "Maybe we should go...back to your place..."

"You mean...you don't want me...to take you against the wall...right here in public?"

She smiles against my mouth again. "Nope...I want you to take me...to your bed..."

My body lights with excitement. "As you wish...milady." I reluctantly pull away from her as we head to her car.

I open the passenger door and climb inside as she gets in.

"Wow," I say. "That was *so* much easier without handcuffs on." She laughs as I look around. "No center console to climb over. No accidental honking. No banging my limbs into the dashboard... I'm not going to lie. I kind of feel like a badass right now."

She puts her seatbelt on. "You're a nerd."

I hold up my unchained hands. "Yes, but I'm a free nerd."

As we drive off and make our way through town, I'm feeling elated. Never better. I might not have any scavenger hunt money, but I have something better. Something worth far more than any inheritance. Kayla.

With a grin I can't control, I glance over at her. She adjusts the rearview mirror a few times and my nerves immediately stand on end.

"What?" I say.

She frowns. "I thought I saw that black car again."

I look out the back window but there are no cars behind us. "Are you sure?"

"No. It was just a glimpse. It could have been a different car." She checks the mirror again.

I inhale, feeling unsettled as hell. "There's no one behind us now, though. So relax. You're safe," I say. "You have me, remember?"

She smiles at me. "You're right."

I smile back but every nerve in my body stands on end the entire drive home. When we get there, Kayla parks in the dark and I try to keep her distracted with trivial conversation as we climb through the window. But my mind is spinning and I can't keep my eyes from darting around the dark house as I hold Kayla's hand and keep her as near to me as possible without alarming her.

We head to the stairs and just as I prop my foot on the first step, a deep, unfamiliar voice says, "Hello, Kayla."

We turn around and I instantly tuck Kayla behind my back as I face off with a tall burly man with greased back hair, a skinny mustache, and a large potbelly.

"Who the fuck are you?" I demand, lifting my chin so he and I are almost at eye level.

He presses his fingers together in a steeple. "My name is Big Joe and I am the private lender of a personal loan Gia Turner secured with me. In her passing, Kayla is now the responsible party and I'm here to collect." He looks at Kayla, thrumming his fingers.

"Get the hell out of my house," I say in a commanding voice that sounds more confident than I feel.

"I'm afraid that won't be happening until I get my money," he says.

"Get out or I will call the cops."

He inhales through his nostrils. "I'm pretty sure that won't be happening either, since you obviously don't own this house and therefore have no right to kick me out of it."

"I already told you, Joe," Kayla says, half-hidden behind me. "I don't have any money."

"Well, you see, that's a problem. Twenty thousand dollars is a lot of money. It's the kind of money that doesn't get forgiven just because someone eats too many pills. So you *will* pay off your mother's debt. And if you don't have the cash, then I'll settle for our alternate arrangement of you working for me without pay." He steps closer to Kayla and smiles lewdly.

My voice is low and menacing. "Back the fuck up. *Now.*" He's got a few inches and a few dozen pounds on me, but I will fucking tear him apart if he even breathes in Kayla's direction.

He steps back, but only an inch. "You need to come back to Chicago with me, Kayla."

"No," she says.

"No?" He rubs his steepled fingertips together. "No is not an option. You can say no all you want, but that won't keep me from getting my money. I'll drag you back by the hair if need be."

I flex my jaw and step right up to him. "You'll be in a shallow grave before you get anywhere near Kayla's hair."

He eyes me. "Big words. I'm not a fan of shallow graves, you see, so unfortunately for you, I brought some insurance."

He tips his head at something, and suddenly four figures creep out from the shadows of the house and surround the base of the stairs where Kayla and I stand. One guy I could handle. Two would be hard, but doable. But five on one? I can't win with odds like that, and a fight would only rile this guy up. Who knows what he'd do to Kayla if he was angry?

"Say good-bye to your boyfriend, Kayla, before someone gets hurt," Big Joe says. "We need to get on the road."

One of the goons reaches for Kayla's arms and I knock his hand away, stepping in front of her more fully.

I look at Big Joe. "Let's talk this out. You need twenty thousand dollars, right?"

He nods.

"Will you accept payment in diamonds?"

"Of course."

"And if you get your money's worth, you'll leave Kayla alone—forever?"

He shrugs. "I have no business with Kayla other than her mother's debt. If she pays up then I'm gone for good."

I nod. "Kayla," I say quietly, without turning to look at her. "Go get my mom's necklace."

I hear her suck in a breath. "But Daren—"

"Nothing in this world is more important than you—especially not a piece of jewelry," I say in a serious tone. "Go get it. Please."

A beat passes then she hurries up the stairs. I hear her shuffle down the hall and through my room, my eyes on Big Joe the whole time. She comes back downstairs with the familiar box and hands it to me.

Our eyes meet when I take it and, right here, in this crazy moment, I know what real love looks like. What it tastes like, smells like. I know what real love feels like, and it feels like home. It feels like Kayla Turner, believing in me. It feels like everything I've ever done right in a pair of bright blue eyes. There is nothing I wouldn't do for her. No necklace, no amount of money, not even the very last breath pulled from my chest is more important than the girl standing beside me.

I hand the box over to Big Joe. He opens it and examines the string of diamonds with small noises of approval.

He slants his eyes to me. "This is a hefty piece of bling. You might be ripping yourself off here."

I glance at Kayla. "Not even a little."

I have the most priceless thing in the world.

Big Joe inhales through his nose again. "Tell you what. Me and my associates here will leave the two of you unharmed tonight, and I will arrange for these diamonds to be authenticated by someone I trust. If these are, in fact, real then the two of you will never see me again. However, if these diamonds are fake, and you've wasted my time, you *will* see me again and there will be much…" He eyes Kayla then me. "Harm. Understood?"

I nod, wishing I had the power to rip his limbs from his body. "Understood."

"Very well." He motions to his goons to leave then stretches a smile over his face. "Have a good evening."

They exit the house and I immediately turn around to face Kayla. "Are you okay?" I touch her head, her arms. I know she wasn't hurt but I just need to touch her. I lead her up the stairs and away from what just happened.

"I'm fine," she says, looking at me in concern. "But you just gave away your mother's necklace—your favorite memory."

I shake my head as we reach my bedroom. "It was a token of a happy time with my parents, nothing more. There's no amount of diamonds I wouldn't give up for you."

"Daren…"

"I'm being serious." I step closer and hold her face, swallowing. "I know this sounds crazy, but I love you, Kayla Turner. And I've never loved anything more."

39

KAYLA

*M*y lips part as I stare up into his deep brown eyes in the moonlight streaming into his bedroom doorway through the upstairs hallway window. Is Daren Ackwood really confessing his love for me? My heart flutters as I search for the right words to convey everything I'm feeling.

"I love you too" is all I come up with. There really aren't any better words. "So I guess we're both crazy."

He smiles. "I guess so."

I smile back and then his lips are on mine, kissing me desperately, again and again until I'm out of breath and grasping at his shirt collar. Tugging and pulling, I manage to pull his shirt off so I can feel my body up against his. I like how strong and big he is when we're standing together, how he can look down on me but not make me feel powerless. He walks us inside his room, shuts the door, and presses me up against it in the now total blackness of his room, kissing my neck and throat as I exhale in bliss and savor the feel of his mouth on my skin.

I go for his pants but he traps my hands at his zipper, moving us over to fall onto the mattress as he starts kissing me all over again. His touch conveys unspoken things, filling me with hope for the future and peace for the present. And his lips pour into me beauty that's unseen and worthiness that's unearned.

"Wait, wait," I say breathlessly and Daren pulls back. I climb on my knees and tug the piece of cardboard from his bedroom window, letting the moonlight fill his room so we are no longer in complete darkness. "I want you to see me."

A wide smile stretches across his face in the soft blue light of the moon. Returning to the mattress, I stretch out on my back as he crawls over me and looks into my eyes. And oh my God, he is the most beautiful thing I've ever seen.

Not because he's handsome and symmetrical, with a broad chest and rippling ab muscles. But because he has a loving heart. And that heart loves me.

40

DAREN

I take her face in my hands, stroking my thumbs over her cheeks as I tilt her head to the side and kiss her. My tongue slides into her mouth and roams over the tender flesh inside, loving how soft and warm she is.

Her body melts against mine instantly, and she relaxes in my arms, running her own up the sides of my body so she can bury her hands in my hair. Gripping the hair at the base of my neck, she tugs on it and I groan into her mouth.

Her soft hands, running over my skin and moving around my body, wrap me in a comfort I've never experienced before.

She arches her back and lifts up, her body trying to get closer to mine, and I run my hands down her rib cage and to the hem of her shirt. Pulling it up, I expose the pale skin of her belly before lifting it higher and taking it off completely, leaving her in only her bra. Slipping my hands around her back, I remove that too, exposing the most beautiful breasts I've ever seen. Large and full and perfectly round, they lie in my hands as I squeeze them gently.

"God. You're beautiful," I say.

Lowering my mouth to one of her nipples, I cover it with my lips—but I don't suck on it, not yet. Instead I watch her squirm beneath me, wanting my wet mouth to pull her nipple into its hot depths, but not being able to control it.

With my mouth set against one nipple, my fingers play with the other, gently grazing over it before softly plucking at it over and over. She arches her back even more, and now her hips are shoved against mine.

"Daren..." she breathes out. "Please."

I pull her nipple into my mouth fully and she moans in pleasure. God, that's a hot sound. I press my body between her legs, keeping her from arching any more than she already is as I move to her other nipple and do the same until both nipples are wet and beautifully erect in the moonlight from the window.

She wiggles and moans as I suck her tight nubs into my mouth and squeeze her breasts. Then, moving back up to her mouth, I kiss along her jaw and over to her ear before running my lips down her throat. She thrusts her head back, carefree and trusting with my mouth against such a fragile place. As I gently lick a trail up and down her windpipe, I run my hand down the center of her chest, lightly touching each of her nipples before moving to her stomach and then into her pants.

I slowly slide my hand inside her panties and between her legs, where she's already warm and wet, and cup her softly as I move my mouth back to hers and kiss her deeply.

She wriggles against my hand, but I refuse to make more than light contact with her most sensitive area. Instead I tease her, lightly brushing a fingertip over her clit. Then I pull my hand back completely before running a finger along the crease of her thigh. Then up to every tender spot on her flesh—except the one she wants me to touch.

She starts to pant and I smile against her throat, lightly tapping her center with my finger.

She jerks then whimpers. I kneel above her and slide her pants off, tossing them to the floor before tucking my fingers into the sides of her panties and dragging them down her legs and over to the floor by her pants.

With nothing on but her desire for me, I run my fingertips up her legs and over her knees. A quiet gasp escapes her mouth as the pads of my fingers trail up her inner thighs, skipping her neediest spot, and brushing up her hips and stomach.

I watch her eyes light up and her body writhe in want as I touch her lightly, and smile to myself. Kayla, who was always so modest, is lying open and waiting for me with passion and love in her eyes. Love for me.

41

KAYLA

*I*t's a foreign thing, this meshing of love and lust deep inside my chest, but it's beautiful nonetheless. I want to both please him with my body and comfort him with my soul, and the odd—yet satisfying—sensation tugs at my heart in a way I've never experienced. Sex and love are two completely different species, but when put together they're a beautiful force.

I run my hands down the hard muscles of Daren's chest and stomach then unbutton his pants so he can spring free. He helps me take his pants off completely, then his underwear, until we're both naked on his virgin mattress in the moonlight.

My skin feels cool all of a sudden, but when he hovers over me, his body heat instantly warms me. He leans down and kisses me while I spread my legs apart and pull his hard body against mine. Moving from my mouth, he starts to kiss a trail down my body, his hot mouth lighting me on fire everywhere he goes. He kisses beneath my jaw, soft and quiet. Then he places a kiss upon my collarbone, sliding his mouth along its length, branding me as his. His lips press above my heart, sure and steady like the rhythm inside my chest, then move to the spot just above my belly button, teasing and wanting. The trail drifts down to my lower hip and he places a gentle kiss on the inside, causing my muscles to flex with the touch, so sensitive and intimate. His kisses are little pieces of him, laid upon my body.

He kisses lower still and my legs start to shake out of pure anticipation. I see him smile against my stomach as his hands glide up the inside of my thighs and open them all the way.

I arch my back so he can see me completely and tip my head back as I feel his hand travel to my core and lightly touch every part of my swollen wetness, except my neediest nub.

I swear he's trying to kill me.

His hot mouth moves to my leg then licks a trail along the crease of my thigh before placing featherlight kisses against my folds. As his soft lips graze my wanting center, he moves his hands to my hips and holds me gently. Then he slips his fingers across my ticklish belly and back down to my thighs.

With my legs shaking and my heart pounding I whimper, "Please, Daren." I can feel my wetness dripping from my body as he licks one long streak around me in a circle, but still not touching the cluster of nerves I need him to.

The tip of his heavenly tongue trails over more of me, wetting my folds on either side of my clit and making my core tighten with need. My legs shake. My belly tightens.

"Daren. Daren. Come *on*," I say, completely out of breath.

He gently kisses my clit, just a peck, his lips brushing the place I need him to but not quite satisfying my hunger. His tongue slips out of his mouth as he exhales hotly against me. Then he licks me once, a long, slow stroke of his soft wet tongue as it rolls over my clit and I whimper, tossing my head back because I want *more*.

I grip his hair, trying to push his mouth lower to my aching body, and feel him smile against my needy flesh.

I'm just about to beg and moan, when he thrusts my thighs

even farther apart and licks at my core, rolling his tongue over my clit again and gain. I cry out and clutch his hair, holding his mouth against me as my body splays out on the bed and my legs begin to tremble more violently.

He starts to lap at my folds, driving me wild and making me blind with desire until I feel myself about to fall to pieces. Gasping, begging, whimpering, I pant as his sweet tongue sucks and licks at my tiny clit relentlessly.

Unlike anything I've experienced before, I'm not afraid to want this, not afraid to enjoy it. For the first time in my life, I'm able to embrace pleasure and let it move through me, setting wild pieces of my soul free.

He groans against my sensitive flesh and licks at me more ferociously until a blinding orgasm rips through me and my entire body begins to quiver and jerk. Gripping two fistfuls of the sheets in my hands I cry out with his head still between my legs.

Now a wet quivering mess, I can't do anything other than beg him to push himself inside me. Which is exactly what I'm doing. Begging in short, clipped sentences.

"Daren. Now. Please. Oh God."

I hear the smile in his voice. "Hold on."

"No. Now. Come on." I look down to see him putting a condom on and, once it's in place, I try to pull him into me.

He waits. With his thick penis set between my legs but not yet inside me, he waits.

"Are you trying to kill me?" I whine.

"No," he says with a smile. "I'm trying to savor this." Then he slowly eases into me and my aching body tightens around him. I hold on to his shoulders and feel him deep inside of me, but just briefly before he eases back out.

I pull at his body again and this time he gives in, sliding into me and filling me completely. I cry out again.

This is the best thing I've ever felt. Pure ecstasy. Not just the sensation of his hard body, stretching out my soft, tight one, but the feeling of Daren inside me, connected to me.

He starts to pump in and out of me, my aching core gripping at his hard length as hot skin rubs against the greedy nerves inside me, and I sink my nails into his back, holding on for dear life.

I was wrong. *This* is the best thing I've ever felt. The hot friction of his thick body rubbing against my soft wet core and easing the pulsing ache inside is almost more than I can stand.

I watch him in the pale moonlight, his square jaw tightened, the corded muscles of his neck pulling taught, and my desire to please him ignites even more. I grab his hips and hold him inside me so we're locked together and he can't withdraw, then I say, "I want to be on top."

He blinks down at me and grins. "Yeah?"

I nod. "I've never been on top before."

"Really?" His grin widens. "Holy hell. This is going to be fun. You're going to like it. Trust me."

In one swift movement, he rolls us over so I'm straddling his hips while his erection still fills my core, and in this new position, he feels deeper. Fuller.

"Oh wow," I whisper, shifting over him slightly. The movement sends a dart of pleasure up my spine and my eyes flutter back. "Oh God."

He smiles up at me. "Told you." His smile melts into a look of hunger as he watches me move, however, and a low, appreciative curse word leaves his mouth.

I rock against him, slowly at first then gain momentum as I get used to the feel of our entwined bodies, until suddenly I'm on fire. I'm sexy and beautiful. I'm powerful and strong. The moonlight shines down on my nude body as I ride Daren and his eyes watch my bouncing breasts, swollen with passion, with great appreciation. I love that he can see me, my nakedness, my desire for him.

I rub against him more fervently and another orgasm tears through me, lighting every inch of my skin on fire as I fall apart on top of him. Daren pulls me down to meet his mouth and kisses me as he rolls us over once again.

With my body a wet, spent mess of quivers and spasms, I'm not sure if I can handle more of Daren inside me. But as he, once again, pumps into me I only feel more bliss run through me. Who knew sex could bring so much pleasure? So much love? So much … everything?

I give my body over to Daren completely, arching my hips and tossing my head back as I claw at his large shoulders, taking him into me, begging for more. We rock against each other in the soft glow of the moon, me whimpering for more and him groaning in pleasure, until our bodies both climax and every muscle in his body grows rigid. We collide with each other, breathless, sweating.

There are no handcuffs binding us, but we're connected just the same. Not by steel but by love. Visible love. Valuable love. A love that sees me just as much as I see him. And I've never felt so beautiful.

42

DAREN

J've never woken up with a girl by my side before—at least not one I've had sex with. I've had a crazy night filled with sex before, sure. But I never stayed afterward and cuddled. Or woke up the next day to chitchat.

But this morning, when I opened my eyes and saw Kayla's small face and naked shoulder nuzzled against my chest, I couldn't imagine waking up any other way. The smell of coconut wraps around me and I can't help but smile.

I trail my eyes along the soft lines of her face and wonder just what the hell I'm going to do now.

Kayla isn't like any girl I've ever known. And sleeping with her isn't the same as having sex with anyone else. She's the real deal. And it doesn't even freak me out that I'm thinking these things.

She knows me, the ugly parts and the hard parts, the shameful pieces and the broken ones, she knows all of me and she still cares for me. I'm dirt-poor and homeless, for God's sake, and the girl still told me she loves me.

Now the only question is, how can I convince her to stay in my life?

She stirs beside me and her lashes flutter before opening. Her blues eyes stare up at me in the hazy light coming in from my window. They widen and I tense, waiting for her to remember last night, and worried that maybe she'll think it was a huge mistake.

But her features melt into a soft smile and she settles closer to me, burying her face into my neck.

"Good morning," she says against my skin.

Happiness fills my chest. I run my fingers down her bare arms and grin when tiny goose bumps rise. "Good morning, beautiful."

Under the sheets, she moves her silky body over mine and snuggles even closer. "You're so warm."

God, I love this. I want to wake up with this girl in my arms every single day—is that crazy?

I wrap my arms around her and tuck her into me. "And you're so soft. I could get used to this."

I hear the smile in her voice. "Me too."

"I'm serious," I say. "I want this. I want *you*. No one else."

She props her chin on my chest and looks at me with big blue morning eyes. "I'm right here."

I swallow. "Yeah, but I don't want you to leave. I don't want to go back to being who I was before the handcuffs. Kayla, I was unhappy before you. And now I'm ... I'm perfect."

She shifts closer and looks directly into to my eyes. "I'm not going anywhere. Before you, I was lost. And now I'm ... home." She kisses my chin. "So I'm staying right by your side, with or without handcuffs."

I trace the shell of her ear. "Promise?"

She slowly nods. "Promise."

Pulling her close, I draw her up to my mouth and kiss her deeply, softly. When we break the kiss, she leans back and smiles.

"So what now, pretty boy?"

I give her a crooked grin. "Well I was thinking we could do a repeat of last night."

She laughs. "Well, naturally. But what about after that?"

I exhale loudly. "Well I'm homeless."

She exhales as well. "And I'm penniless."

"And I don't have a car anymore," I say simply.

She nods. "And my car is falling apart."

"So just to sum up. We're broke, homeless, and nearly car-less?"

"Yep." She smiles.

I smile back. "Then I think the only thing we can do is have some chocolate for breakfast and spend the day in bed."

She kisses my chest. "I like the way you think, handsome."

"And I like the way you taste." I pull her lips up to mine, flip us over so I'm stretched out on top of her, and start kissing my way all over her body.

43

KAYLA

*D*aren. Ackwood.

Never in my wildest dreams would I have guessed that someday I'd be head over heels for Daren Ackwood. But I am completely and utterly in love with the crazy brown-eyed boy standing beside me in the bathroom. And after last night, I completely understand what the big fuss was about Daren in bed. My God. Woman Whisperer, indeed. He kept me up most of the night, pleasing me in ways I didn't know were possible. In his bed. On the floor. Even in the shower, though I now agree that shower sex isn't nearly as hot as, say, sex against his bedroom wall.

"Are you using my toothbrush?" he asks, his eyes bulging in horror.

I laugh through the toothpaste in my mouth. "I couldn't find mine."

"That's disgusting."

I rinse my mouth and scoff. "We shared bodily fluids last night and you're grossed out that our teeth have touched the same brush?"

"Ew. Don't say 'bodily fluids.' That's so nasty."

I laugh. "What about 'pee'? Can I say 'pee'?"

"You know, for such a pretty mouth you say some disgusting words." He leans in and kisses me. "But I still really love your mouth."

"Mmm. My mouth loves *you*." I kiss him on the nose then pad out to his room. I look at his bed with a smile. "I guess your mattress isn't a virgin anymore."

He cheerily scoffs from the counter. "Nothing in this room is a virgin anymore."

Still smiling, I walk to my suitcase and sigh. "Man. I can't believe I lost my toothbrush. It has to be here somewhere." I start yanking things out of my luggage and tossing them aside.

"What's happening here?" Daren walks out of the bathroom and starts picking up my clothes. "Bra...bra...jeans...scarf... gloves..." He looks at me. "You do know you're in Arizona. We don't really get blizzards here."

I laugh. "I know. But we *do* get blizzards in Chicago. And I didn't want to leave my clothes behind."

He picks up more stuff. "Well that explains the trench coat."

A beat passes and we snap our eyes to each other.

"Trench coat," I say.

"There were a bunch of trench coats in the closet at Milly Manor," Daren says with wide eyes.

"'Through the trenches,'" I say, citing the clue. "Did we look behind the coats? Do you think there could be a safe in the closet too?"

"'A safe place through the trenches,'" Daren recites with a smile. "I think we just figured out the clue."

"I think so too! But wait," I say. "What about the handcuffs? We took them off." I bite my lip in distress. "We forfeited all the money."

He twitches his lips in thought. "No. Not yet. We only forfeited

the money if someone told on us. Let me call Eddie and find out."
He grabs his phone, dials a number, and puts the call on speaker-
phone as it rings.

Eddie's voice mail picks up after the third ring and says, *"Hello.
You've reached Eddie Perkins. If this is one of my legal clients, please
leave a message and I will get back to you as soon as possible. If this is
Daren or Kayla, I have* not *gotten* any *reports about the two of you
being at Latecomers without handcuffs on last night. None whatsoever.
So the inheritance is still yours if you can find it. Thank you for calling."*

A long beep follows and Daren hangs up. We stare at each
other.

"So Eddie is going to let us get away with it?" I smile.

"I guess so," Daren says, shaking his head with a grin. "Man, I
love that guy. I'm going to buy him a new bow tie. You know, if we
find the money. Do you still have the handcuffs?"

I rustle through my suitcase and pull them out with a wink.
"Let's slap these babies on, go back to Milly Manor, and dig through
some trenches."

He freezes. "Wait a minute..." Rummaging through his room,
he starts going through the pockets of his jeans.

I watch him. "What are you doing?"

"You know those notes in the blue suitcase, the ones that were
addressed to each of our names? Well I'm pretty sure mine had the
word 'trenches' on it... Aha." He finds the note and quickly unfolds
it. "Yep. See?"

I look. In the bottom left corner it says THE TRENCHES in black
marker with the number twenty-two underneath.

Daren says, "I thought it was just a mistake or that maybe your
dad was reusing a piece of paper, but that can't be a coincidence.
Right?"

I shake my head. "It's *not* a coincidence. My note has a random word and number on it too." Digging through my purse, I hold up the note addressed to my name from the suitcase closet. "See? My note says 'through fourteen.'"

We hold our notes up, side by side, and together they read THROUGH THE TRENCHES 1422.

"We had the clue to the hiding place all along," I say, stunned. "Crap. And my note 'encouraged' me to show it to you too. Dammit. Why didn't I listen?"

"So did mine." He nods. "But it was kind of personal so I didn't show you."

I say, "Yeah, well I chose not to let you read mine because I didn't want you to get a big head."

"Why?" Daren grins. "What did Turner say about me in your note? Can I read it?"

I eye him. "Only if I can I read yours."

We swiftly swap notes and I read the letter my father wrote to Daren.

Daren,

I'm sorry that I'm gone. But more importantly, I'm sorry that I'll be missing out on the rest of your life. Your circumstances have taught you to underestimate yourself and hide behind your reputation. I want to teach you the opposite.

I know you, Daren. All your strengths, all your hopes, all your hesitations. I know the bare bones of who you are, and there isn't a doubt in my mind that you will be very successful and much loved in life. But it's not my doubts, or lack thereof, that matter.

You are about to embark on a journey that will hopefully encourage you, if not completely change you. And I've designated Kayla as your travel partner.

My daughter is just as stubborn and resilient as you, which is why I used handcuffs to keep you together. Had I not, the two of you would still be searching for the inheritance, independent of each other, of course, and with no intention of ever sharing the money. Not because you're selfish people, but because you're impossibly guarded. One of the many things that make you and Kayla so similar.

You're both inverted diamonds in the rough; polished on the outside, cracked and raw within. But priceless just the same.

Yet you both doubt love—despite all I've tried to teach you. But alas, there are some lessons in life that cannot be taught. Some lessons, especially those on finding love, are only learned through time and trust.

And I gave you both the moment you were handcuffed to Kayla.

Happy hunting, Daren. Take care of my little girl.

I finish reading my dad's careful handwriting and look up. He knew. Even though he wasn't really in my life these past five years, my dad knew me and my heart well enough to know that Daren Ackwood was exactly what I needed.

And he didn't hesitate to handcuff us together to prove it.

Daren and I lock eyes.

He eyes me. "Why are you smiling so big?"

The smile I hadn't realized I was wearing stretches even wider. "Because I really love my dad."

44

DAREN

I've never been so happy to see Golf Cart Gus. I flag him down as Kayla and I run toward the town square, and when he stops for us we jump inside.

"Hi," Kayla says with her best smile. "I'm Kayla."

Gus is immediately smitten. "Why, hello darling." He kisses her hand and she giggles.

After throwing clothes on and chaining ourselves back together, Kayla and I went out to her car, only to find it with another dead battery. With no other options, we ran, handcuffed, to the town square and, thankfully, came across Gus.

"So listen," I say. "Kayla and I need to get to Milly Manor, but we don't have any money to tip you with."

"Yet," Kayla corrects. She smiles at Gus. "We don't have any money *yet*. But as soon as we do we'll totally pay you back if you wouldn't mind giving us a ride right now."

He looks her over with a grin. "Anything for you, sugar." He turns to me and says, "You lucky dog."

I glance at Kayla and smile. "I know."

Two minutes later, Gus drops us off at Milly Manor and we fumble around the front yard, tripping over our own feet as we struggle to get into the backyard and dig through the garden to grab the spare key.

Once we let ourselves inside the house, we waste no time running for the same hall closet where we found the blue suitcase. We open the door and shove aside all the coats within.

There, just like we guessed, is a giant safe.

Kayla giggles. "I can't believe it."

I smile. "We should have known. We should have *known*!" I look at her. "You open it. It's your home. Your father. You should open it."

She tries the door. "It's locked. But there's a keypad for a number combination."

I nod. "Try fourteen twenty-two."

"Ooh. Yeah. 'Through the trenches fourteen twenty-two.' You're brilliant." She punches in 1422 and a clicking sound fills the closet. Kayla bites her lip, then slowly swings the safe door open.

For a moment, we stare in silence.

"I don't believe it," she says quietly.

I blink. "Me neither."

Inside the safe are stacks and stacks of money, all hundred-dollar bills, all banded together, and on top of the bills is one final envelope.

Kayla carefully reaches for the envelope and pulls out the paper inside.

My dear Kayla and Daren,

This is my last letter to you, and I hope you find it with different hearts than you had when you set out. I always had money during my life, but I did not always have happiness, and I think that was the lesson I wanted you to learn most of all. People are where our happiness is found.

Daren. You are not my son, but I cared for you as such. There were many days I wished that I could be part of your life in a more significant way. I cannot begin to tell you how proud I always was of you, and how much I believe in you. I hope you learn that your value is not in what others make of you, but in what you find in yourself and what your loved ones see in you.

And my sweet Kayla. Fatherhood did not go as planned for me. I wanted to be more involved in your life than I was, but life is not always fair. All the money in the world could not buy back the years I missed as your father. But I always loved you, never doubt that for a moment. Being your father was the best thing that ever happened to me. I have no doubt you will find greatness in life. No matter what dreams you follow or paths you take, I know that you will shine, my little diamond. I will love you always.

As for the two of you, I don't know if you are still hand-cuffed together, but regardless, I hope you do not resent me for asking you to do it. I knew, from the moment you were young children, that the two of you knew how to love more than anyone else I've ever known. And hopefully, you will use that love to the advantage of your relationship, whether it be for friendship or for something more.

Because money without love is complete poverty. And poverty with love, well that's pure wealth. I love you both so much.

We turn to stare at each other in the hallway as joy fills our faces. We reach into the safe to pull out the bills and, behind them ...

"The box!" I smile broadly and pull out the green box, still wound with ribbon, that Marcella wrapped for me all those years ago. I take the box in my hands.

Kayla gasps. "My locket!" She carefully lifts a small gold necklace from the safe and kisses the heart-shaped locket hanging from its chain. She smiles at the box in my hands. "You got your baseball cards back, I see."

"I *did*, but it was never about the baseball cards. It was about the green box the cards were in." I open the box. Inside are my baseball cards from so long ago, but beside those cards still sits the paperback copy of *Holes* that Marcella gave me for Christmas all those years ago. "Marcella gave me this when I was a kid." I open the first few pages to the inscription. "This was what I wanted to get back."

Kayla leans over and reads Marcella's handwritten inscription out loud, "'To my favorite boy. I will love you forever, *mijo*. Love, Marcella.'"

"It's the only thing she ever wrote to me," I explain. "And after she died, I didn't have anything left of her. But this book was here all along." I look at Kayla's necklace. "I'm guessing that's pretty special?"

She nods. "My father gave it to me and—" She opens the heart locket and gasps. Inside is a note from her father—a new note, probably written just before he died. "'My Kayla,'" she reads out loud. "'It was an honor to be your father. I will love you forever.'"

She chokes up and I pull her against my chest.

As we look down at our precious lost items and the loving words left for us by Marcella and James Turner, Kayla inhales deeply and says, "Wow. That was the best scavenger hunt ever."

Nodding, I look at Kayla, in my arms and in my heart, and smile.

Jackpot.

Epilogue

KAYLA

J dust off my hands as we move the last box of stuff into my new room at Willow Inn. It's been three weeks since Daren and I found my father's hidden money, and in that time I accepted Ellen's job offer as a waitress at Willow Inn, while Daren accepted her offer as her new cook.

He was able to quit his other jobs so he now works full-time in the kitchen with Mable, and I swear he smiles all day long. He can't stop talking about how he wants to open his own restaurant someday.

The girl who was the prep cook before me, Pixie, now lives in Tempe where she's going to Arizona State University. And because Pixie knows a lot of people at ASU, she's going to introduce me to some friends of hers that are currently in the nursing program. Which will be great since I start classes at ASU this spring.

Ellen let me stay at the inn as a guest while she had Pixie's room repainted. The guy who lived next to Pixie, Levi, moved down to Phoenix as well, so Ellen had both rooms painted yellow.

I also bought a working car so I could travel back and forth from Willow Inn to Copper Springs to visit Daren, whom I've decided I completely and forever love.

Daren put his share of the money to fast use, paying off all the medical bills he wanted to take care of and buying a new car for himself as well. As much as he missed Monique, he thought it would be silly to spend so much money on a car. So he bought a truck instead. Overall, things have just fallen into place for us and I couldn't be happier.

Daren enters my room with a giant box in one hand and a bag of cookies in the other.

"Ooh, I love you, I love you, I love you." I smile at the cookies.

"Easy, tiger." He sets down the box and pulls two cookies from the bag.

I look him over with a smile. "You know, I read the book *Holes* last week."

He lifts a brow. "You did?"

I nod and eye him closely. "And at the end, the boy who had to dig all those holes finds a lost treasure and all his bad luck goes away. Pretty fitting, don't you think?"

A slow grin pulls up his face. "I knew I liked that book for a reason." He looks around my room. "So what do you think of your new home?"

I grin at the bright yellow walls and the new blue bedding I bought for my bed. "I love it."

He hands me a cookie. "And you know the best part about your room?"

I eye him. "What's that?"

He grins. "That it's right next door to an empty room that will soon be mine."

"Are you being serious?" I smile so widely my face hurts.

He nods. "We're going to be neighbors—if that's okay with you."

"That is more than okay," I say. "That's incredible!"

"Then here's to being neighbors." He holds up his cookie and grins. "And to handcuffs."

I tap my cookie to his with a smile. "Here's to handcuffs."

Jenna Lacombe needs control—whether it's in the streets, or between the sheets. But the infuriatingly sexy Jack Oliver is starting to strip away her defenses. When Jack's secrets put them both in harm's way, Jenna must figure out how far she's willing to let love in…and how much she already has.

Please turn the page for a preview of the next book in the Finding Fate series,

Right Kind of Wrong.

I

JENNA

*L*ook at you. Being all in love like a grown-up. I'm so proud," I say, smiling at my best friend, Pixie, as we carry boxes into our joint dorm room. "And Levi," I add, turning to address Pixie's hot new piece of arm candy, "you're welcome."

He sets a box down. "Am I now?"

I nod. "If it weren't for me telling Pixie to suck up her fears and just let herself love you, you'd still be a miserable handyman."

"I am still a handyman."

"Ah, but you're no longer a *miserable* one." I grin. "Thanks to me."

He pulls Pixie into his arms and kisses her temple. "Then I guess I should thank you."

As they start kissing, my phone rings and I'm relieved for an excuse to leave them to all their lovebirding.

I slip out into the hall and close the door before answering my cell.

"Hello?"

"Hi, Jenna." The sound of my mom's voice makes me smile. "How's my baby?"

"I'm good," I say. "Pixie and I are almost all moved in. She came down here with her boyfriend tonight so we were able to get mostly unpacked. I just have a few more boxes left at the apartment, but I'm going to pick those up later. How are you?"

She pauses. "Well *I'm* okay."

It's the way she emphasizes the "I'm" that tells me exactly what this phone call is about.

"Grandma?" I sigh in exasperation. "Again?"

"I'm afraid so. She says she can feel the end coming close."

I sigh. "Mom. She's been saying she's dying for ten years and she's never even had a cough."

"I know, but she seems serious this time," Mom says.

Every few years or so, my grandmother announces to the family that she's going to kick the bucket at any given moment. The first two times it happened, I immediately flew back to New Orleans—where she lives with my mother and younger sisters in the house I grew up in—to be by her side, only to find Granny alive and well without so much as a sniffle. The last time it happened, I took a few days to get organized before flying back to New Orleans, where I found my "dying" grandmother singing karaoke at a local bar.

So as you can imagine, I'm not falling for her silly shenanigans this time.

"No way," I say. "I'm not spending my hard-earned money to fly out there again just so Grandma can get on my case about love and fate while belting out a verse of 'Black Velvet.' Tell her that I'll come visit when she has a doctor's note stating that she's at death's door."

"Oh, Jenna. Don't be so dramatic. I swear you're just as bad as your grandmother."

"I know," I say, in mock frustration. "And it's getting hard to compete for the title of Family Drama Queen with Granny declaring her impending death every two years. Could you tell her to just give it up already and let me be the shining star?"

I can hear the disapproval in my mother's voice. "That's not funny, Jenna."

"Sure it is." I smile. "And Grandma would agree."

"Please be serious about this," she says.

"I'll be serious about Grandma's death when she gets serious about dying," I quip.

A weary sigh feathers through the line. "Jenna, please."

"Why do we keep pandering to her, anyway? The only reason she keeps crying death is because she knows we'll all come running to her karaoke-singing side to hold her hand as she passes—which she never does. Why do we keep playing her game?"

"Because she's very superstitious and believes dying without the blessing of her family members is bad luck for the afterlife. You know that."

Now it's my turn to sigh.

I do know that. All too well. Since I was a child, the deep roots of Grandma's superstitions have wrapped their gnarled fingers around my family's every move. If her voodoo notions weren't so eerily accurate and, well, creepy, maybe we'd be able to ignore the old woman's ways.

But unfortunately, Grams has a tendency to correctly predict future events and know exactly what someone's intentions or motivations are just by shaking their hand. It's downright spooky. And I swear the old woman uses our fear of her psychic powers as a tool of manipulation.

Case in point? Her recurring death threats.

"Yeah, yeah," I murmur. "She deserves a pleasant send-off. I know."

I hear my mother inhale through her nose. "She does. But even if that weren't the case, your grandmother isn't feeling well and she'd like to see you. Again." When I don't say anything she adds, "And wouldn't you feel horrible if she was right this time and you missed your chance to say good-bye?"

The guilt card. A nasty tool all mothers use on their children.

"Fine," I say. "But I'm not shelling out the cash to fly there. I'll drive this time."

"All the way from Tempe to New Orleans?"

"Yes. And I will save big money doing it," I say. "I'll get my shifts covered at work and leave in the morning."

"Excellent. Your grandmother will be so happy."

I scoff. "Happy enough for karaoke, no doubt."

She clears her throat. "I'll see you here in a few days then. Love you."

"Love you too." I hang up the phone and head back into the dorm room to find Levi and Pixie making out against the wall.

"God. Seriously, you two?" I make a face. "I know you just got together in the middle of the road a few hours ago, but come on! There are other people here."

Levi doesn't seem to notice me as he continues kissing Pixie's face off, and Pixie takes her sweet time pulling back from her lover-boy before acknowledging my presence.

She shoots me a hazy smile and nods at my phone. "Who was that?"

"My mom." I exhale. "Grandma claims she's dying."

"Again?" She bites her lip.

I nod. "So I'm going to drive out there this week and try to be home before school starts."

She pulls away from Levi, just slightly, but it's enough for him to stop smelling her hair—which I swear he was just doing. They're so in love it's almost gross.

"By yourself?" Pixie's green eyes widen.

Pixie and I met last year, at the start of our freshman year at Arizona State University when we were assigned the same dorm and became roommates. When school let out for the summer and Pixie and I could no longer live in the dorms, we split up. She moved to her aunt's inn up north—where she fell in love with Levi—while I moved into a local apartment with three of my cousins. It was a good setup, for the summer, but I'm happy to be moving back in with my bestie.

She and I are both art students—she's a painter and I'm a sculptor—so we have a ton in common and get along perfectly. She's the closest friend I've ever had, so I try my hardest to take the concern on her face seriously.

"Yep." I put my phone away. "By myself."

Levi reluctantly steps away from his girlfriend and busies himself by unpacking some of Pixie's things.

She frowns. "That doesn't sound like fun. Or very safe."

Levi glances at me. It's one of those big-brother protective glances and I have to bite back a smile. Aw...look at this guy. He barely knows me, but he's still worried about my safety. For the hundredth time, I silently rejoice that he and Pixie got together. She deserves a good guy who looks out for both her and her friends. A guy like that would drive me crazy. But he's perfect for Pixie.

"I'll be fine," I say to both Pixie's big eyes and Levi's concerned glance as I wave them off and grab my purse. "After I stop by work,

I'm heading back to my cousins' apartment for the last of my boxes. I'll probably crash there for the night, so you two can get back to smooching against the wall or whatever." I wink at Pixie. "See ya."

"See ya," she says with a concerned smile as I exit the room.

Jumping in my car, I quickly head to the Thirsty Coyote, where I work as a bartender. It's a decent job for a college student. Good hours. Good money. And it suits me. Pouring drinks isn't my dream job or anything, but it gets me one step closer to finishing school and opening my own art gallery—which *is* my dream job.

I let myself inside and head to the back. It's just past dinnertime so the place is packed and I have to squeeze through the crowd just to reach the bar. When I get there, I lean in and call out to my coworker.

"Cody!"

He turns around and smiles at me. "What's happening, Jenna? Thought you had the night off."

"I do. But I need to get some shifts covered this week so I thought I'd come in and sweet-talk my favorite bartender..." I bat my lashes, knowing full well Cody isn't attracted to me at all. But he's still a sucker for making money, and more bar shifts means more money.

He grins. "I'm listening..."

I whip out my schedule and show him all the days I'd need him to cover. He agrees like the superhero that he is and heads to the back to make it official in the schedule log.

I wait at the counter, thinking about how long my drive to New Orleans will take if I leave tomorrow. Probably at least twenty hours. Ugh. Pixie was right. It really isn't going to be any fun.

My eyes drift over the crowd and fall on a tall figure in the corner. Gunmetal-gray eyes. Tousled black hair. Tattooed arms and broad shoulders. My body immediately goes on alert.

Jack Oliver.

It's not surprising he's here. He comes to the bar all the time, but usually he's with his friends and in a good mood. Right now, though, he's talking on the phone and seems very upset. His gray eyes are narrow slits and his jaw is clenched. But I'm not going to lie. Angry looks good on him.

At over six feet tall, with his broad shoulders and endless tattoos, Jack looks intimidating. But really he's a big softie. I hardly ever see him in a mood other than happy. So this angry version of Jack is a new experience for me. A very hot experience.

He catches me looking at him and tips his chin. His anger dissipates for a brief second as a lopsided smile hitches up the corner of his mouth, but then he turns his attention back to his phone and clenches his fist before ending the call.

In-ter-est-ing.

He shoves his phone into his back pocket and heads my way.

"What's up?" I say. "You seem upset."

He shrugs. "Nothing. Just family shit."

I snort. "God. Yes. I have plenty of that."

He nods and our eyes lock and hold.

One beat.

Two.

I hate this part of our friendship; the part that reminds me of what happened between us last year when we got drunk and carried away one very steamy night. The memory shouldn't still turn me on like it does. But Jack and those gray eyes of his—eyes rimmed with pale green and flecked with dark flints, looking almost silver at times—are hard not to respond to.

We never talk about it, which is better, but in moments like this, when his eyes are on mine with such command, I can almost feel his hands back on my body. Fingertips running the length of my skin. Palms brushing my curves—

"Here you go." Cody returns with the schedule book for me to sign and I silently bless the interruption.

No good comes from me reminiscing about Jack's hands. Or any of his other body parts.

"I switched our shifts and marked you down as *on vacation*," Cody says.

"Thanks," I say, taking the book and initialing by my traded shifts.

"Hey, Jack." Cody nods at him. "What can I get you to drink?"

"Just a beer," Jack says, sitting on the barstool next to me. He's so close I can smell his shampoo. It's a wooded scent, like sawdust and pine, and it plays at my memories in a way that makes my heart pound.

He looks at me. "So where are you going on vacation?" His warm breath skitters over my shoulder and sends a jolt of hot want through my veins.

Damn him.

On second thought, damn *me* for being such a swooner.

I'm not usually like this. I swear it. Guys are the last thing I give priority to in my life. It goes: chocolate, tattoos, a hundred other things...and then men. Because a woman doesn't need a man to have a full life. And I'm living proof of that.

I keep my eyes on the book. "New Orleans to visit my grandma."

He nods. "Is she dying again?"

Even my friends know how ridiculous my grandmother's yearly death threats are.

"Yep." I pop the *p*. "The drama queen just won't hand the spotlight over gracefully."

He smirks. "Like you'd wait to be handed anything."

Jack and I met two years ago, when I first started working at the Thirsty Coyote and Jack was my trainer, but we became friends almost immediately and now he knows me well enough to know that I'm not very patient, and if I want something I usually just take it.

Cody sets Jack's beer down and asks me, "Are you flying out tonight?"

"Nah." I finish signing the book and hand it back to him. "I'm driving there so I'll leave in the morning."

Jack swings his head to me and a slight wrinkle forms between his eyes. "You're driving all the way to Louisiana?"

Jack and I are both from Louisiana. I'm from New Orleans and he's from a small town just north of there, called Little Vail. The fact that we grew up so close to one another, yet met on the other side of the country at this bar in Arizona, was one of the first things we bonded over. That, and tequila.

"Yeah. Pfft. I'm not spending hundreds of dollars on a last-minute plane ticket. Grandma needs to give me at least a month's warning next time she decides to keel over."

Jack takes a swig of his beer, but continues looking straight at me, displeased.

"What?" I snap.

He shrugs. "That's just a long trip to make on your own."

"Yeah, well. Good thing I don't mind driving." I look at Cody. "Thanks for covering for me. I owe you. Later, Jack." I turn to leave just as a drunk guy stumbles into me, knocking me back into Jack's chest.

Jack's hands instantly go to my hips, and my hips instantly want to yank his hands down my pants. My hips can't be trusted.

"Watch it," I say to the drunk guy, giving him a little shove forward so I have room to pull away from Jack.

Jack's fingers slowly slide off my hips, trailing down just before ending contact with my body, and my eyelids lower in want.

Clearly, I need to have sex. Not with Jack—that would be a disaster. But with someone. Soon. So I can sex Jack out of my system. Again.

I've been trying to sex away Jack a lot lately.

I blink up and find Jack's eyes watching mine. He saw my moment of weakness; that split second of desire. Dammit.

"Be careful, Jenn," he says in a low voice, and his words trickle down my skin.

Jack's the only person I've ever let call me "Jenn." Why? I have no idea. I blame his voice, all sexy and deep and brushing along the sensitive places of my ears.

Damn him, damn him, damn him.

"Right." I step back and act casual. "So I'm going to go. I'll see you when I get back. Later."

I spin around and weave through the crowd with a huff, feeling Jack's eyes on me the whole time.

2

JACK

*T*here are only two things I don't ever speak of. My crazy family and my history with Jenna. And both just fell in my lap.

I watch Jenna work her way to the front door and can't help the unease slipping through my veins. I don't like the idea of her going on such a long road trip by herself. She's independent and smart and I know she can take care of herself, but that doesn't lessen my concern any.

Her long dark hair is pulled back into a high ponytail revealing her golden eyes and high cheekbones. Her half-Creole heritage has kissed her skin with a permanent bronze, which only adds to her unique beauty as her shoulders, bare in the strapless shirt she's wearing, show off the numerous tattoos running the length of her arms. The intricate designs disappear beneath her clothes, where I know they continue to travel across other parts of her curvy body. She's beautiful and wild, and drives me absolutely crazy.

Her hips swing as she moves out the door and my gut tightens. If anything were to ever happen to her, if someone ever tried to hurt her, I … well I can't even think about it. Which is why I can't think about Jenna all alone in a car on a series of desolate freeways for three days.

I don't like it. I don't like it at all.

My friend Ethan plops down on the barstool next to me, reeking of cologne. "Hey, man."

"Hey," I say.

I've gone through a series of roommates this past year, but Ethan has been my favorite, so far, or at least the easiest to tolerate. He and I have been friends since I first moved to Arizona and, as very opposite as the two of us are, we get along pretty well.

"Was that Jenna I just saw leaving?" He nods at the door.

"Yep."

Ethan smirks. "What did you do to piss her off this time?"

I grin. I do have a way of getting under Jenna's skin. I can't help it. If she would just be a grown-up and address what happened between us last year then maybe I'd back down. But instead she acts like nothing ever went down and dammit, that's just insulting. Because she's not just some girl I hooked up with a while back. She's Jenna, for God's sake.

But she wants to pretend like we're nothing more than friends, so I go along with it. And occasionally I piss her off—because it's *something*. It's some sign that I matter more than she lets on.

"Surprisingly enough," I say, "I didn't do anything. This time."

Ethan shakes his head. "I don't know why you poke at her the way you do."

"Because it's funny." I shrug. "And it's not like she doesn't piss me off just as much, like when she goes off and sleeps with dickhead guys." I shift my beer mug around in a slow circle, one inch at a time. "When she knows she can do better."

"Yeeeah." Ethan purses his lips. "You care way too much about who Jenna sleeps with. That's not healthy, man."

I stifle a groan. "I know."

Ethan orders a drink from Cody while I stare into my beer. I really shouldn't care who Jenna sleeps with, especially since I'm no angel myself. But damn. I can't help it. I don't like her sharing her body with anyone else.

My phone rings again. I look at the caller ID and groan.

I've been fielding phone calls from my family members for a week now and it's grating on my nerves. Earlier, I was on the phone with my frantic mother, who was babbling about how concerned she is for my youngest brother, Drew. He's twenty and should be able to take care of himself by now, but apparently he's been acting shady lately and his behavior has my family on edge. Now Mom's flipping out and I'm running out of reassuring words.

I thought our last phone call would tide her over for a while, but now my other brother, Samson, is calling. Again.

Not a good sign.

I grudgingly take the call and snap, "What?"

"Easy, bro," says Samson. "I'm just the messenger."

"Yeah, well I'm getting sick of all your *messages*."

"What would you rather I do? Not call you? Let Drew go down on his own?"

I let out a frustrated sigh. "No."

"That's what I thought. Drew's in deep trouble this time, I can feel it. And Mom's losing her shit. I need you out here."

A year older than Drew and a year younger than me, Samson is the middle child, and the most laid-back. It takes a lot to stress him out, so the fact that he's been at my ear these past few days is a red flag in and of itself.

But as the oldest brother—and the only real male authority in my family—it's my job to keep everyone calm, cool, and collected. A task that's growing more difficult by the phone call.

"Not happening." I shake my head even though he can't see me. "I left for a reason, Samson. I'm not coming back."

His voice is strained like he's gritting his teeth. "And just what the hell am I supposed to do without you? You know I don't have the pull or the power that you do."

I run a hand through my hair. "Have Drew give me a call. I'll straighten him out."

"That's just the thing, man. Drew's missing."

My heart stops for a moment. "Mom didn't mention that."

"That's because she's in denial and refuses to accept that her baby boy is caught up in a mess. She thinks he's out roaming, but you and I know better."

Fuck.

I rub a hand over my mouth, trying not to panic. Or growl. This is exactly the shit I was trying to stay away from when I moved away from Little Vail, Louisiana, and toward Tempe, Arizona. And now here I am, getting dragged right back into it.

"Fine," I say, my decision made. "I'll come out there this week. Tell Mom to calm down, would you? Her freaking out will only make things worse."

"Got it. I'll see you later then."

"Yeah." I hang up and run a finger over my cold mug.

Drew is missing.

I knew something like this would happen, eventually. You can't play around with drug dealers and not get jacked down the road.

"You all right, dude?" Ethan asks as Cody sets his drink down.

"What? Yeah." I rub my mouth again. "I'm fine. Just family shit."

He takes a drink. "How come you never talk about your family?"

I stretch my neck. "Because there's nothing to say."

Actually there's a ton to say, but no one would want to hear it. And frankly, I like the life I've made for myself out here in Arizona. No baggage to weigh me down. No expectations lingering around me.

I pull up airfares on my phone and scroll through the prices with a grimace. Damn, it's expensive to fly. My eyes snap up as a thought hits me. Jenna's heading to New Orleans and I need to go to Little Vail, which is only two hours north and right on her way.

A slow smile spreads across my face.

I might just have to tag along on Jenna's road trip.

Pixie Marshall hopes that working with her aunt at the Willow Inn will help her forget her past. Except there's a problem: the resident handyman is none other than Levi Andrews. Now he's right down the hall and stirring up feelings Pixie thought she'd long buried...

Please turn the page for an excerpt from the first book in the Finding Fate series,

Best Kind of Broken.

I

PIXIE

*I*f my bastard neighbor uses all the hot water again, I will suffocate him in his sleep.

I listen as the shower finally goes off and huff my way around my room, gathering my shower supplies. I don't politely wait for him to leave the bathroom, oh no. I stand outside the bathroom door—which has steam escaping from the crack at the bottom—with a carefully applied scowl and wait.

Still waiting.

The door swings open to a perfect male body emerging from a billow of hot fog. His dark hair is loose and wet and frames his face in a haphazard way that manages to look sexy despite the fact that he probably shook it out like a dog before opening the door, and of course he's wearing nothing but a towel.

Kill me now.

I peek into the bathroom, totally pissed, and block his exit with my body. "A thirty-minute shower, Levi? What the hell?"

A smile pulls at the corners of his mouth. "I was dirty."

Oh, I bet.

"I swear to God," I say, "if I have to take another cold shower—"

"You shouldn't swear to God, Pix." He brings his face close to mine and the steam from his skin dampens my nose and cheeks. "It's not nice."

This close up, I can see the tiny silver flecks in his otherwise bright blue eyes and almost feel the three-day scruff that shadows his jaw. Not that I want to feel his scruff. Ever.

I curl my lip. "I want a hot shower."

"Then shower at night."

"I'm not kidding, Levi."

"Neither am I." His eyes slide to my mouth for a moment—a split second—and there it is. The electricity. The humming vibration that never used to exist between us.

He snaps his eyes away and pulls back. The damp heat from his body pulls away as well, and some stupid, primal part of me whines in protest.

"Now, if you'll excuse me…" He waits for me to move out of his way. I don't.

I jab my finger at his chest. "I haven't had a hot shower for three days—"

Cupping my upper arms, he lifts me off the floor and moves me out of his way like I'm light as a feather. Then he walks the ten paces down the hall to his room and disappears inside without a look back.

Jackass.

With a muttered curse, I stomp into the small bathroom and try not to enjoy the smell of spearmint wafting into my nose and settling on my skin. Damn Levi and his hot-smelling soap.

My freshman year of college ended two weeks ago, and since Arizona State dorms don't allow students to stay during the summer, I had to find a new place to live and, consequently, a job. So I started working for my aunt Ellen at Willow Inn because one of the job perks—and I use that term loosely—is free room and board.

And my free room shares a hallway and a bathroom with the only person I was hoping to avoid for the rest of my life.

Levi Andrews.

Hot guy. Handyman. My long-lost...something.

Ellen conveniently forgot to tell me that Levi lived at the inn, so the day I moved in was chock-full of surprises.

Surprise! Levi lives here too.

Surprise! You'll be sleeping next door to him.

Surprise! You'll be sharing a sink, a shower, and a daily dose of weird sexual tension with him.

Ellen is lucky I love her.

Had I known that Levi lived and worked here, I never would have taken the job, let alone moved in. But Aunt Ellen is one conniving innkeeper and, honestly, my only other option was far less appealing. So here I am, living and working right alongside a walking piece of my past.

Since we're the only two resident employees, Levi and I are the only people who sleep in the east wing—a setup that might be ideal were it not for the giant elephant we keep sidestepping during these epic encounters of ours.

Memories start creeping up the back of my neck, and a hot prickle forms behind my eyes. I quickly blink it back and turn on the shower, scanning the bathroom for safer things to focus on.

Little blue dots on the wallpaper.

Purple flowers on my bottle of shampoo.

Dots. Flowers. Shampoo.

With the threat of tears now under control, I thrust my hand into the shower and relax a tinge when hot water hits my fingers. Stripping off my pajamas, I step into the spray with high hopes, but water has just hit the right side of my neck when it goes from warm to ice-cold.

Sonofabitch.

There will be suffocation tonight. There will be misery and pain and a big fat pillow over Levi's big fat scruffy face.

Biting back a howl of frustration, I turn off the water and wrap a towel around my half-wet body. No way am I taking another cold shower. I'll just have to be unclean today. I hastily grab my stuff and yank the bathroom door open just as Levi leans into the hallway.

He's traded in his towel for a pair of low-slung jeans but hasn't gotten around to throwing on a shirt, so I have to watch his chest muscles flex as he grips his bedroom doorframe.

He looks me over with a smirk. "Done so soon?"

I flip him off and enter my room, slamming the door behind me like a fourth grader.

I throw on some clothes, pull my hair into a messy ponytail, and step into my paint-stained sneakers before looking myself over in the mirror. Ugh.

I tug at the V-neck collar of my shirt for a good twenty seconds before giving up and changing into a crew-neck shirt instead. Much better.

My phone chirps on the dresser, and I knock over a jar of paint-brushes as I reach for it. As I pick up my phone, paintbrushes go rolling off the dresser and onto the floor, where they join piles of discarded clothing and crumpled college applications. I glance at the text message and frown.

Miss you.

It's from Matt.

Miss you too, I text back. I do miss him. Sort of.

Call me. I have news.

I start to call Matt but pause when I hear Levi's footsteps in the hallway, making their way back to the bathroom. I hear him plug something in, and the sound of his electric razor meets my ears. I set my phone back on the dresser as a wicked smile spreads across my face.

Levi should know better by now. He really should.

Casually moving around my room, I plug in every electric item I own and wait until he's halfway through shaving. Then I turn everything on at once. The electricity immediately goes out and I hear the buzz of his razor die.

"Dammit, Pixie!"

Ah, the sweet sound of male irritation.

Plastering on an innocent look, I open my door and peer across the hall to the bathroom. Levi looks ridiculous standing in the doorway in just his jeans—still no shirt—glowering at me with half of his face shaved.

He stiffens his jaw. "Seriously?"

I mock a look of sympathy. "You really should charge your razor every once in a while." I exit my room and move down the hall, singing out, "Have fun rocking a half-beard all day."

As I head down the stairs, the wet side of my ponytail slaps against my neck with each step. Another smile pulls at my lips.

If Levi wants to play, it's on.

2

LEVI

*T*welve days.

Pixie's been living here for only twelve days and I already want to stab myself with a spoon. Not because she keeps blowing the fuse, though that reoccurring shenanigan of hers is certainly stab-worthy, but because I can't do normal around Pixie.

But fighting? That I can do.

After pulling a shirt on, I march downstairs and out the back door. The large lavender field behind the inn sways in the morning breeze, and thousands of purple flowers throw their scent into the wind, reminding me of things better left forgotten. Things I used to have locked down. So much for all that.

I blame Ellen. Maybe if she'd given me a heads-up about Pixie moving in, I could have prepared better.

Another breeze blows by and shoves more lavender up my nose. Or maybe not.

The sky hangs above me, bright blue and free of clouds, and the early sun slants across the earth, casting a long shadow behind me as I walk the length of the building. I squint up at the white siding and notice one of the panels is cracked, which is nothing new.

Willow Inn is nearly one hundred years old, and parts of it are just as broken as they are picturesque. It's a quaint place, with white cladding and a wraparound porch beneath a blue-shingled roof, and it sits on ten acres of lavender fields and swaying willow trees. It has two wings of upstairs rooms and a main floor with the usual lobby, kitchen, and dining space.

The newly remodeled west wing has seven bedrooms, each with its own bathroom. That's where all the guests stay.

The east wing has yet to be remodeled, which is why Ellen allows Pixie and me to stay there and why I'm a live-in employee. Along with my other handyman duties, I'm also helping Ellen gut the old east wing so she can have the area remodeled to accommodate private bathrooms in every room.

I reach the fuse box at the edge of the inn and, flipping a breaker I'm far too familiar with, restore electricity to the east wing.

Fortunately, all the gutting and redesigning requires the east wing to run on its own electricity and water supply, so guests are never affected by my hot water usage or Pixie's electricity tantrums, but damn. We really need to find a less immature way to be around each other.

I turn and follow my shadow back to the door, holding my breath as I pass the purple field. The wooden floors of the lobby are extra shiny as I walk inside, which means Eva, the girl who cleans the main house, probably came in early and left before anyone saw her. She's tends to work stealthily like that, finishing her work before anyone wakes. Sometimes I envy Eva that. The solitude. The invisibility.

Back inside, I see a figure up ahead, and a string of curse words line themselves up on my tongue.

Daren Ackwood.

I hate this douche bag and he's headed right for me.

"What's happening, Andrews?" He gives me the chin nod like

we go way back. We went to the same high school and I think we had a class together senior year, but we're not pals. He looks over my partially shaved face. "What the hell happened to you?"

"Pixie," I say.

He nods and looks around. "Is Sarah here?"

Sarah is Pixie's real name. The only people who've ever called her Pixie are me and Ellen and...

"Why?" I cross my arms and eye the case of water he's carrying. "Did she order water?"

Daren is the inn gofer, delivering groceries and linens and anything else the place needs, so unfortunately he's here twice a week with his preppy-boy jeans and nine coats of cologne. And he's always looking for Pixie.

"No, but you never know." He lifts a cocky brow. "She might be thirsty."

"She's not thirsty."

He looks over my facial hair again. "Oh, I think she's thirsty."

And I think Daren's throat needs to be stepped on.

"Morning, Levi." Ellen walks up with a smile and hands me my To Do list for the day. Her long dark hair slips over her shoulder as she turns and throws a courteous smile to the gofer. "Hey, Daren."

"Hey, Miss Marshall."

As Ellen starts talking to me about the fire alarm, I watch Daren's eyes cruise down her body and linger in places they have no business lingering in.

More than his throat needs to be stepped on.

Ellen Marshall is a very attractive forty-year-old who's used to guys checking her out. Not me, of course—Ellen's like family to me and I respect her—but pretty much any other guy who sees her instantly fantasizes about her, which pisses me off.

"...because the system is outdated," Ellen says.

"Routine check on the fire alarms," I say, my eyes fixed on Daren, who is still ogling her. "Got it."

"Can I help you with something?" Ellen smiles sharply at him. "Looks like your eyes are lost."

He readjusts his gaze. "Uh, no, ma'am. I was just wondering where Sarah was."

"Sarah is working. And so are you." Her hazel eyes drop to the case of water. "Why don't you take that to the dining room? I think Angelo is stocking the bar this morning."

He gives a single nod and walks off.

Ellen turns back to me and looks over my face. "Nice beard," she says. "Pixie?"

I rub a hand down the smooth side of my jaw. "Yeah."

She lets out an exasperated sigh. "Levi—"

"I'll check out the fire alarms after I finish shaving," I say, quickly cutting her off. Because I don't have the time, or the balls, to undergo the conversation she wants to have with me. "Later." I don't give her a chance to respond as I turn and head for the stairs.

Back in the bathroom, I stare at my reflection in the mirror and shake my head. Pixie timed it perfectly, I'll give her that. My facial hair is literally half-gone. I look like a before and after razor ad.

I think back to the irritated expression on her face and a small smile tugs at my lips. She was so frustrated, waiting outside the bathroom door with her flushed cheeks and full lips and indignant green eyes...

Why does she have to be so goddamn pretty?

I turn on the razor and run the blades down my jaw, thinking back to the first time I saw those indignant eyes cut into mine. My smile fades.

Pixie was six. I was seven. And my Transformers were missing.

I remember running around the house, completely panicked that I had lost my favorite toys, until I came upon Pixie sitting cross-legged in the front room with my very manly robots set up alongside her very dumb dolls.

I immediately called in the authorities—"Mom! Pixie took my Transformers!"—and wasted no time rescuing my toys from the clutches of the pink vomit that was Barbie.

"Hey!" She tried to pry them from my hands. "Those are the protectors. They kill all the bad guys. My dolls need them!"

"Your dolls are stupid. Stop taking my things. Mom! *Mom*!"

Haunted eyes stare back at me in the mirror as I slowly finish shaving.

I wish I would have known back then how significant Pixie was going to be.

I wish I would have known a lot of things.